THE ROAD TO MONTANA

Up the Bloody Bozeman

Book 7
Home on the Range Series

THE ROAD TO MONTANA

Up the Bloody Bozeman

Rosie Bosse

Cover illustrated by Cynthia Martin

POST ROCK PUBLISHING

The Road to Montana
Copyright © 2022 by Rosie Bosse

ISBN: Soft Cover – 978-1-958227-00-8
ISBN: eBook – 978-1-958227-01-5

**POST ROCK
PUBLISHING**

Post Rock Publishing
17055 Day Rd.
Onaga, KS 66521

www.rosiebosse.com

RIDE AN OL' PAINT

I ride an ol' Paint, I lead an ol' Dan,
I'm goin' to Montana for to throw the hoolihan.
They feed in the coulees, they water in the draw,
Their tails are all matted, their backs are all raw.
Ride around, little dogies, ride around them slow,
For they're fiery an' snuffy an' a rarin' to go.

My feet are in the stirrups, my hand is on the horn,
I'm the best ol' cowboy that ever was born.
But a cowboy rides single, like it or not
So I guess that ol' Paint is the best friend I got.
Ride around, little dogies, ride around them slow,
For they're fiery an' snuffy an' a rarin' to go.

Oh when I die, take my saddle from the wall,
Put them up on my pony an' lead him out of his stall.
Tie my bones to his back, turn our faces to the west
An' we'll ride the prairie that we loved the best.
Ride around, little dogies, ride around them slow,
For they're fiery an' snuffy an' a rarin' to go.

–Traditional Cowboy Song

"Ride an' Ol' Paint" was first sung in cow camps and on cattle drives. There is no written documentation, but it is believed to have first appeared between 1868 and 1874. It might have been even earlier since the cattle drives began in earnest after the Civil War ended in 1865. Regardless, it was well-known before the turn of the century.

Author/composer: Unknown cowboy or cowboys. Words were changed and verses were added by bored riders and creative musicians.

Paint: An abbreviation for the American Paint Horse. This breed of horse typically has bold white markings on its hair coat. Paints are sometimes called "the world's most colorful breed." The flashy white horses are also said to be good stock horses.

Ol' Dan: Cowboy jargon for a mule or pack horse.

Hoolihan/Houlihan/hooley-ann: A word that describes a backwards loop used to rope a horse. The loop is carried in the roper's hand. When the timing is right, it is swung once and thrown backward instead of forward. The special throw causes the rope to roll over and flatten out before it reaches the horse's head. With just one swing, the rope can be thrown as far as thirty feet and can be released with minimum movement. The size of the loop is determined by the distance to the horse to be roped as well as its size.

Coulee: A deep ravine or a gully. It is usually dry and is often created by rushing water during a flood.

Draw: This is the low ground between two parallel ridges. It may be deep or shallow. It may also be called a ditch.

Dogies: This word was originally used to describe rough-haired calves that were thin and in poor condition. Typically, this was caused by a lack of food. The calf might have been an orphan, or its poor health could have been the result of a harsh winter. The word was eventually used by many cowboys to describe all cattle in general.

Fiery and snuffy: This could have several meanings. However, in the context it was used here, I believe it was a description of the temperament of the cattle being handled. Cattle that were jumpy and prone to run were problems on a cattle drive. They were likely to agitate and frighten the other cattle. Stampedes were often deadly, not only to the cattle, but to the cowboys and their horses too.

This book is dedicated to all those who traveled this country in its early years – those brave men and women who hunted, explored, mapped, and rode the trails that became the roads and highways we drive today.

PROLOGUE

The Ames House and Its Talking Bird

The Ames was a boarding hotel in Cheyenne, in the mid 1800s. It was popular with the cowboys fresh off the trail because of its $7 per week rates. The proprietor was a devout Mormon who knelt in prayer every evening in the lobby. He prayed near his pet parrot which was kept in a cage.

Of course, the cowboys made it their goal to teach the parrot words that were not so appropriate. A cowboy who rode for the Searight Cattle Company shared a story about an evening when those prayers were disrupted. The bird joined his owner, talking during the man's holy hour. However, the string of obscenities the bird spewed quickly ended his owner's prayer time…No details on what happened to the parrot.

The area around the Wall was isolated, offering three hundred sixty-degree views. It was surrounded only by far-flung ranches and was at least a day's ride by horseback to any civilization.

Jesse James was said to have visited there.

Etta Place

Etta Place was a woman from history who associated with the Wild Bunch. Robert LeRoy Parker, known as Butch Cassidy, was the leader. The Wild Bunch operated from 1886 to 1901.

Many of the women who frequented Hole-in-the-Wall had formerly worked as prostitutes. They often came from Fannie Porter's Boarding House in San Antonio, Texas where the gang liked to party. "Boarding house" was the proper name at that time for brothels.

The most famous of the Wild Bunch women was Etta Place. While her real name is not known, it is believed to be either Ethel Thayne or Ethel Ingerfield. She was a beautiful woman, a crack shot, and an excellent rider. Those were all beneficial skills for an outlaw's girlfriend.

Etta is thought to have come to the hideout as Butch's mistress. She later changed her affections to the Sundance Kid. While she obviously knew the type of men she kept company with, there is no record of her participating in any of the Wild Bunch's crimes. However, there is now mounting evidence that she could be Ann Bassett. Ann was the so-called Queen of the Cattle Rustlers and a friend of the Wild Bunch. If true, she fooled many people.

I did not include the Wild Bunch in this novel since their timeline was later. Etta Place would have been too young as well. However, I decided to make the elusive outlaw queen a character in this story. I created a personality for her and gave her a place in the James-Younger gang.

Cattle Kate

Ellen Liddy Watson was born on July 2, 1861, around Ontario, Canada. She was the daughter of Thomas Lewis Watson and Frances Close Watson. Ellen was the oldest of ten children. The family moved to Lebanon, Kansas in 1877. She was soon employed as a cook and housekeeper for H.R. Stone in Smith Center. There she met William A. Pickell, a farm worker. They married on November 24, 1879. Her wedding portrait shows her to be a tall woman for her time, around five feet eight inches tall. She had a square face and weighed around one hundred sixty-five pounds. She had blue eyes, brown hair, and spoke with a Scottish accent.

Pickell proved to be abusive. He drank heavily and often beat Ellen with a horsewhip. She left him and returned home in January of 1883. She soon moved to Red Cloud, Nebraska which was about twelve miles north of her family's homestead. She worked at the Royal Hotel there for a year. When her residency was established, she filed for divorce.

That same year, Ellen moved to Denver, Colorado to join one of her brothers. From there she moved by herself to Cheyenne in the Wyoming Territory and then on to Rawlins, about one hundred fifty miles away. She worked as a cook and as domestic help at a restaurant there.

She met James Averell in 1886. He hired Watson to cook at his road ranch which he had just opened on his homestead. Road ranch became another word for trading post during that time because of the number of cattle often traded there. In May of that year, Ellen and James applied for a marriage license in Lander, over one hundred miles from Averell's homestead.

A small cabin and corral were constructed on Ellen's property which joined Averell's. She bought cattle from the emigrants on the trails and fenced about sixty acres of her land with barbed wire. While that was not enough land to graze her livestock, between Averell's and her connecting farms, the couple controlled one mile of water along Horse Creek.

says the underground tunnels allowed a man to enter under the business block, visit the tenderloin area, and return to his business unseen.

By 1900, Madam Grace McGinnis ran the Dumas. Little is known about her or the early history of the Dumas. Through the records of several male boarders, it is known that she employed a servant, a Chinese cook, and four prostitutes. The cost for one tryst at the turn of the century was fifty cents to one dollar. The working girls received around forty percent of that amount plus tips consisting of jewelry and other gifts.

Parlor houses like the Dumas of the late 1800s were a stark contrast to the alley cribs behind the elegant buildings or even those in the basements. The Dumas was welcoming and beautiful as you entered, and the original rooms upstairs reflected that elegance.

Prostitution as a business in Butte was unique from other cities of its time because it catered to the local clientele. Because of that, the business was less clandestine and was more visible to the public. It also had the support of many of the local businessmen and women since the money spent in the redlight district was spent once again in their stores.

The Dumas was finally closed in 1982 after the last madam, Ruby Garrett, was convicted of federal tax evasion. It had become the longest-operating brothel, not just in the West, but in the entire United States. The Dumas was in operation for ninety-two years, long after prostitution was outlawed.

Madam Grace's appearance and personality in this story are completely fictional. I could find few records of her or when she moved on from the Dumas. The historic brothel was not yet built in 1879. However, I decided to include it in this novel.

The Historical Grant-Kohrs Ranch

John Francis "Johnny" Grant was a French-Canadian rancher and entrepreneur in early Montana history. He was probably the first permanent settler in what became Powell County, Montana. Grant had multiple wives, over twenty children, and adopted even more who had been abused or abandoned. He convinced others, mostly traders and their families, to settle near him. Together, they founded the town of Deer Lodge.

Grant was born at Fort Edmonton, Canada. He and his brother, Richard, joined their father at Fort Hall north of present-day Pocatello, Idaho in 1847 when Johnny was in his teens. However, trapping and trading furs as his father did was a dying business, and young Grant turned his business skills to another area.

Westbound emigrants began to arrive in what would become Idaho and Montana in the 1840s. After many miles of travel, their livestock were worn down and exhausted. Road ranches swapped the emigrants' worn-out livestock for healthy animals. Many times, the new animals had been purchased the year before and nursed back to health. They were then sold or traded, one healthy animal for two sick or weak ones, to another emigrant.

Johnny Grant was extremely successful in this venture. By 1863, over four thousand head of cattle and three thousand horses grazed on his ranch. His net worth was an astounding $150,000.

However, the character of the territory was changing. Much business was conducted in English, and the French-speaking Grant was at a disadvantage. Rising taxes and crime created a less hospitable environment for the Métis trader. In 1867, he accepted Conrad Kohrs' offer to buy his ranch along with three hundred fifty head of cattle for $19,200. Two months later, he moved his family and remaining livestock to Manitoba, Canada.

Johnny Grant is recognized for his part in establishing the livestock industry in Montana. The house he built in 1862 still stands today on the historic Grant-Kohrs Ranch.

Conrad Kohrs was a German immigrant who left home in 1850 at the age of fifteen. He worked many seafaring jobs and finally migrated to the United States, first to New York City and then to Davenport,

Iowa. In Iowa, two of the jobs he worked were as butcher and sausage salesman. He also became a United States citizen during his time there.

Gold fever drew him west and by 1862, he was working in a butcher shop in Bannack in the Montana Territory. His wages of $25 per month plus room and board grew quickly since he was a knowledgeable and hardworking employee. He was soon earning $100 per month.

His boss and owner of the butcher shop, Jack Crawford, ran for sheriff. Crawford won the election, defeating Henry Plummer—a man who later became a well-known Montana outlaw. The two fought and even though Crawford wounded Plummer, he feared for his life. He left town with the money in his till. Plummer once again became sheriff, and Kohrs became the owner of the butcher shop where he had been employed.

Kohrs knew money was to be made selling meat to the miners. He soon opened butcher shops in other mining boomtowns where he bought or traded for his beef. When the supplies ran thin, he brought in cattle, first from the northeast and then from Texas. In this way, he supplied his butcher shops but also began to build a cowherd. He sold cattle wholesale to his competitors as well.

Everything from the butchered animals was used, including the beef fat. That tallow was used to make candles. In addition to wasting little, Kohrs had a reputation of selling at reasonable prices instead of capitalizing on a captive mining market as many others did.

After Kohrs bought out Johnny Grant, he took on two different partners and began to diversify his holdings, including investments in mining. However, Kohrs' first love was always the cattle business. Kohrs and his half-brother partner, John Bielenberg, shipped their first cattle—four hundred head—to the stockyards in Chicago in 1874. Soon, they were shipping eight thousand to ten thousand head annually.

Getting cattle to market in the early years of the Montana cattle industry was a challenge. There were no railroads in the Montana Territory, so cattle had to be driven to railheads in Cheyenne or Pine

Bluffs in the Wyoming Territory. Those locations were nearly seven hundred miles away depending on the location of the cattle. Finally in 1881, the Northern Pacific reached Miles City in the Montana Territory. A railhead was then near Kohrs' eastern cattle range.

At the peak of operations in 1880, Kohrs grazed his cattle on ten million acres both on open range and on ranches he owned. His holdings encompassed the largest cattle operation in North America, and he soon bore the title of "Cattle King of Montana." It was a name he would carry for many years.

The Sisters of Saint Joseph

I mention three nuns in this story. Sister Casimir and Sister Rudolph were my great-aunts, and their personalities are accurately portrayed here. Sister Casimir often tied up her long, black habit and played ball with us. My, how she could smack that ball and run!

Sister Edwina was a teacher I had as a feisty seventh grader in Catholic school in Beloit, Kansas. She became one of my favorite teachers. Her personality was much like Spur's Sister Eddie.

All three of these nuns belonged to the Congregation of the Sisters of Saint Joseph. That order was instrumental in building hospitals, orphanages, and schools all over the world. The Sisters of Saint Joseph are specifically mentioned in Helena, Montana's history.

While all three of "my sisters" were born in the 1900s, I made them part of this novel. May you enjoy their stories as much as I enjoyed creating them.

One of the things I find fascinating as I research the history for my novels is how small the West was to those who traveled and lived there. Distance and travel difficulties were something they took for granted.

They adapted or moved on. Because of this, the same names often popped up in many different parts of our great country.

Enjoy this journey with some old friends in the seventh novel of my Home on the Range series, *The Road to Montana, Up the Bloody Bozeman.*

Thank you for choosing to read my books.

Rosie Bosse

Living and Writing in the Middle of Nowhere

postrockpublishing.com

Diamond H Ranch
Cheyenne, Wyoming Territory
Sunday, July 13, 1879

CHAPTER 1

A New Beginning

GABE WALKED ACROSS THE KITCHEN OF HIS HOUSE and leaned against the doorjamb as he drank his coffee. The sun was just rising, and the colors spilled over the horizon. This was his favorite time of day, and if he hurried, he just might catch Merina in time to ride to church with her.

The thought of her made his heart tingle and he grinned to himself. "She finally agreed to marry me. Now I just need to talk her into making it soon."

Nate wandered into the kitchen and Gabe looked around at his younger brother. At fifteen years old, Nate was nearly as tall as Gabe. Both had dark curly hair and their deep blue eyes could sparkle with humor or turn nearly black when angry. Nate's smile lingered close to the surface while Gabe's face was usually more serious.

"Let's get things done here this morning so we can go into Mass today. I want to talk to that priest about marrying Merina. Besides, we need to take advantage of these nice days since it is a twenty-mile ride to Cheyenne."

Nate stared at his older brother a moment and then sat down at the table as he muttered. "We haven't been to church since Ma died. Why is it so all-fired important to go now?"

Gabe grinned at his brother as he walked back into the kitchen. He was finished eating and he set his cup in the wash basin.

"Well, maybe it's time we make a change. Merina's faith is important to her and being connected to a church will be good for both of us." Gabe tousled his younger brother's hair. "Bacon and eggs are on the stove. Eat up and let's get the cattle checked in the south pasture. I heard a wolf last night, and I want to make sure those cows didn't run through the fence if it spooked them. Take your rifle and get a move on. We need to leave here by 8:00 a.m. to catch Merina.

"You take the south pasture, and I will ride along our west boundary next to Lance. There are quite a few herds stacked up around us just waiting to get to the rails. I don't want a bunch of hungry herds breaking through our fence. We need all the graze we have to get us through the rest of the year."

Nate muttered to himself a little more and barely looked up as Angel tapped on the door.

"Good morning, my compadres. I see that Nate is excited to be working so early on this fine Sunday. Perhaps he stayed out too late with young Sam Rankin. I think there are few fish left in that creek as often as they fish it."

Nate looked up. He grinned at Angel and the ornery vaquero winked at him. "I wish my sister would hurry up and marry your grumpy brother so we can have some real food around here. Gabe's cooking skills are limited to three things, and I am ready for a change."

Gabe snorted as he looked at his smiling friend. "And maybe when Merina does marry me, she will not cook for all the hands. You just might be on your own."

Angel shrugged and then winked at the two brothers as he drawled, "Oh, my sister loves me. She would never be able to stand my pitiful crying if she didn't feed me." He added more seriously, "I will ride out with Nate. I want to go to church this morning as well. Perhaps I can hurry him along. I heard that wolf too and I am thinking there might be more than one." He paused as he looked at Gabe and softly added, "There were some Texas horses in town last night."

Gabe looked up in surprise and then frowned as he studied his friend's face. "Most of the herds come up from Texas. Texas brands are common this time of year around Cheyenne."

"Sí, this is true. I did not see who rode them but I recognized the brands. They were from a ranch down by Buffalo Gap." He paused as he looked hard at Gabe. "They carried the brand of the Millett Brothers.

"I will ride out with Nate. We will check the west fence, señor. I think you should ride with Merina. She should not be riding alone while the men who ride those horses are in town."

Gabe could feel a chill rise up in his chest at Angel's words. He nodded as he whistled for Buck. He had his horse saddled and was riding out of the yard within five minutes.

Angel watched him go and then slapped Nate's back. "Perhaps you will be as fine of a man as your brother someday." He smiled at Nate as he added, "But I think you will smile more often." Nate grinned at him as he shoveled his food in. Angel had their horses saddled and they were riding towards the west fence line by 6:30 a.m.

CHAPTER 2

A Sunday Morning Ride

GABE PUSHED BUCK INTO AN EASY LOPE. MOLLY WAS feeding the chickens as he rode by and she waved to him as she called, "If you are looking for Merina, she already left for church. She rode out about ten minutes ago. She said something about going to confession before her service started."

Gabe nodded and waved. He wheeled his horse and rode north toward Cheyenne. Buck wanted to run, and Gabe let him for the first half mile. Then he slowed him down to a mile-eating lope. He caught up with Merina about eight miles later.

Merina heard the horse behind her, and she pulled up to wait when Emilia called out to Gabe. Merina's heart jumped in her chest as she watched Gabe riding toward them with a smile on his face. She put her hand across her chest to slow her heart down as she waited.

Gabe was grinning as he pulled Buck to a stop beside them. "Well good morning to two of the prettiest gals I know. How are you, Emilia?"

The small girl beamed at Gabe. She had just told Merina when she grew up, she wanted Gabe to be her fellow. Merina had laughed and shook her head.

"That is not going to work, Emilia. I am going to marry Gabe, so he will be my fellow. But he will be your Papá. Won't that be nice?" She smiled at her little sister. Emilia had liked Gabe from the first time she met him.

She certainly liked him before I did. I thought he was a brazen gringo. Once I knew Gabe, I realized there was nothing arrogant about him at all. He is brutally honest but he never brags. As Merina thought about Gabe's hard line on honesty, she grew pale. *I must tell Gabe the truth, and it is not going to be easy.*

"I decided to ride to church with my two favorite gals. Then, Merina, we can talk to that priest afterwards about a wedding date."

Merina's face lost a little color as she looked at him and Gabe squeezed her arm. "Now don't you get cold feet on me, Merina. You already said yes, and I am not going to let you change your mind."

Emilia piped up, "Nina won't change her mind, señor Gabe. She said this morning she wished she was already married to you."

Merina turned a dark red and Gabe's face broke into a wide grin. "She did, did she? What else did she say?"

Emilia started to speak, and Merina cut her off. "Emilia, you don't need to tell your señor Gabe everything I say."

Emilia stared at her sister and then pushed her lip out. "Well, you said secrets were a bad thing, so I was going to tell señor Gabe all of yours."

Gabe chuckled as he looked from one sister to the other. Both had dark, black hair. Merina kept hers wound around the back of her head or in a long braid down her back. Emilia wore hers loose and it was pulled into a ponytail. Ringlets hung around her face and the ponytail was full of curls.

Merina was a small woman, but she was strong. Gabe knew the knife she carried was strapped to her leg under her split riding skirt. Her shirt buttoned in the front. It was fitted and did little to hide the curves it covered. Her dark eyes were large, and she looked directly at people when she met them. Merina was a beautiful woman. She carried herself proudly and Emilia was a miniature of her older sister.

As they turned their horses back up the trail, Gabe commented softly, "Angel said there were some Texas horses in town last night. He thought it would be best if you didn't ride out by yourself until they left."

Merina's face went pale, and she gripped the saddle horn with her left hand. She took a deep breath and tried to smile at Gabe. He was watching her carefully with a frown on his face.

Gabe's frown grew deeper, and he looked away for a moment before he spoke. "Merina, I can't keep you safe if you hide things from me. I have to know who your enemies are if I am to protect you."

"I think when Mass is over, perhaps we should speak of something. There are some things I haven't told you." Merina's dark eyes were wide as she looked at him.

Gabe lifted Emilia from Merina's horse and put her in front of him. He studied Merina's face without speaking.

Merina's lips trembled as she whispered, "I will tell you everything after church. I promise there will be no more secrets."

Emilia looked from her sister to Gabe and frowned. "Secrets are bad. You can't keep secrets if they are bad."

Gabe grinned down at the little girl. "Emilia, how would you like to eat dinner in town today after church. I know I will be hungry, and I am guessing Merina will be hungry. Angel and Nate will be in after a while, and Nate is *always* hungry."

Emilia's eyes sparkled as she smiled up at Gabe. "Can I have pie? Nina says it is too much money when she can make it for me at home. Will you buy pie for me, señor Gabe?"

Merina frowned at her little sister and Gabe laughed, "I will buy you pie, but only if you are quiet in church and do what Nina tells you to do." He paused and then grinned at Merina. "It's been a long time since I have been to church so Nina might have to tell me what to do too."

Emilia started to mutter, and Gabe looked over at Merina. "How about we race these horses today? You think Bonita might beat Buck, and I say you are wrong!"

Merina leaned forward and spurred Bonita. The little filly broke into a run, and Buck leaped to keep up with her. He passed her easily and then eased up to keep pace. All three riders were laughing when they slowed the horses down. Gabe reached over and took Merina's hand.

"It's a mighty fine day for a ride with my two favorite ladies. Now what shall we talk about the rest of the way to Cheyenne? Do you want to tell me a story, Emilia? Maybe you can tell me what trouble you and Livvy have gotten into lately."

CHAPTER 3

FATHER CUMMISKEY

GABE HAD NEVER ATTENDED CATHOLIC MASS. HE WAS a little confused with all of the standing and kneeling, so he just did whatever Merina did. She was delighted to have him beside her and Emilia smiled at him constantly. The little girl fell asleep during the priest's sermon. Gabe thought about taking a nap himself. However, Nate was watching him closely, and he didn't want his younger brother to take his bad example to heart.

The service was over an hour long. When it was completed, people began to file out. Father Cummiskey greeted the congregation as they left before coming back inside to talk to Merina and Gabe.

Gabe studied the young priest closely. Father Cummiskey was a large man with a boisterous laugh. He was the new priest in Laramie and was filling in between priests in Cheyenne. Angel had told Gabe the night before that the priest had slugged it out with some rowdies who had attempted to break into his house one night shortly after he arrived. The rough men announced that a priest wasn't needed in Laramie and as the welcoming committee, they would be the ones who would show him his way out. The priest was not only bigger than the men who attacked him—he was also sober. His assailants took a beating and the new priest let it be known that in the future, he would provide himself with stronger self-defense.

Angel laughed when Gabe stared at him and then added, "Sí, he is a tough man. Just last winter, the priest, he traveled with one of the Younger brothers as an escort on a six-day trip in very cold weather."

Gabe looked at his friend in surprise and asked, "Did he know the Youngers are all outlaws and have robbed trains with Jesse James?"

"Sí, he knew the man was a bandito but the priest, he needed a guide and the weather was very cold. Besides, he said two men with guns could fight off the grizzly bears easier."

Angel had laughed when Gabe eyed him suspiciously. "I think perhaps he is just the kind of priest that Laramie needs. That town is maybe not so civilized as Cheyenne." Angel's dark eyes were twinkling, and Gabe had to laugh. Still, he was just a little leery of the smiling priest.

Father Cummiskey shook hands with Miguel and Angel. He winked at the two brothers. "Now think on what we discussed in confession."

Angel grinned at the priest. He grabbed Emilia as he looked back at Gabe. "We'll meet you at the Ames House. They have the cheapest food in town and some of the best as well." He winked and sauntered out of the church while Emilia held both of her brothers' hands and talked constantly.

Father Cummiskey's eyes were twinkling as he put out his hand. "So you are the groom. I have had many conversations with Miss Montero, and I was hoping to see you at Mass. Please, sit down and let's talk about this marriage.

"Have you been baptized, Mr. Hawkins? That is a requirement to be married in the church."

Gabe nodded, "I was when I was small. We attended services in several different churches, and I am not sure where I was baptized. I know it wasn't in the Catholic church though."

The priest studied Gabe's face and then nodded. "Yes, it is not so easy to attend services of any kind. We are working on that here, but we are extremely short on priests." He nodded his head toward the back of the church. "Perhaps your brother Nate might be interested in the priesthood. I have spoken to Miguel about it as well."

Gabe choked and turned red. When he realized the priest was joking, he laughed. "I'm not sure Nate has even been baptized. Our mother was sickly after he was born. She died when he was young. I guess we can work on the baptizing part, but I can tell you that he wasn't overly excited about coming today." He grinned at the priest, "And Miguel as a priest would add a whole new dimension on your calling, Padre!"

Father Cummiskey chuckled and winked at Merina as he agreed. "Now let's talk about this wedding. When would the two of you like to tie the knot? No need in dragging it out since we are all here today."

Gabe looked over at Merina and grinned. "How about this Saturday? That will be July 19. I am tired of eating my own cooking, and Merina won't stay long enough to cook a meal."

The priest's eyes twinkled as he looked at Merina. Her face slowly turned pink, and she muttered in Spanish under her breath. Father Cummiskey's eyes crinkled at the corners as he laughed.

"Miss Merina, I do speak Spanish. Please be careful what you say in God's house. Maybe wait until you are married to call your husband those names."

Merina's eyes opened wide in surprise and the ornery priest laughed. He smiled at both of them again. "Saturday will be fine. How about 1:00 in the afternoon? That will give folks plenty of time to get morning chores done and still be home before dark. Plan to be here around 12:30, and I'll tell you where I want you to stand at the beginning of Mass."

Merina's heart was racing but Gabe laughed as he squeezed her hand. "Will that work for you, Sweetheart? It sounds like a good plan to me. The sooner it is, the less time I have to worry about you changing your mind."

He stood and shook hands with the priest. "We'll see you on Saturday, Padre. Do you need anything else from us? If not, we are going to join our brothers and Emilia for dinner." He paused and then added, "You are welcome to come along if you want."

The priest shook his head. "No, I have commitments this afternoon, but I will hold you to that offer. Maybe after the two of you are married, you can invite me out for a home-cooked meal. Those are the best anyway and as a priest, I don't get many of them unless my parishioners feed me."

Merina nodded her head in agreement and Gabe hugged her as they left the church. "Let's go eat. We can have that talk on the way home. If it's as serious as you think it is, we'll have more privacy riding alone. Just to make sure, we'll ride out to Levi's and have Sadie measure me for that new shirt and vest. That will put the rest of our family on the road before us."

Merina's face paled but she nodded. *Lord, please don't let Gabe be angry with me. He is going to be so shocked.*

CHAPTER 4

A Talking Bird

THE AMES HOUSE WAS LOUD AND NOISY. LOTS OF cowboys ate and stayed there when they ended their drives north. Mr. Ames, the proprietor, was a Mormon. He had the reputation of being a fair and devout man. Most of the cowboys who stayed there once came back to stay again as the food was good and the rooms were clean. Even his pet parrot usually talked politely even though some of the cowboys tried to teach it words that weren't so appropriate.

Gabe glanced at the brands of the horses tied in front and was relieved to see none from the Millett brother's ranch. He laughed down at Merina as he commented, "Take my arm. I want these fellows to all know you are a staked claim."

Merina smiled up at him and they entered the busy room. Nate was watching for them and he waved his hat. Emilia immediately climbed up on her chair and waved as well. Angel and Miguel stood as they laughed.

"I think our sister likes that cowboy. That is fine. They are good for each other," Angel muttered in Spanish to his brother as he grinned at the couple walking toward them.

The full room became quiet as Gabe guided Merina between the chairs. Some of the cowboys stood to give her more room and were rewarded with a smile. The parrot's cage was close to where they were seated, and it let out a loud whistle as it bounced from foot to foot.

"She's a looker, Boys! She's a looker!" It whistled again, and Merina blushed as Gabe laughed. He looked around the room as he nodded his head. "She sure is, and we are marrying in a week. Treat her like the lady she is, Boys." Quite a few of the men recognized Gabe and greetings were hollered from several of the tables.

The talk slowly picked up with men nodding towards Gabe's table. "Didn't ever figure the Preacher there would get married. She's a looker too."

"I heard he settled just south of town somewhere. He told Waggoner he wasn't going to do any more drives."

"How many herds did he take north anyway? Had to be a lot. He's been driving cows since he was just a sprout. Tough fellow too. Word is that nobody ever cut his herd. That was one of the reasons all the big boys wanted him as their trail boss."

Merina listened quietly but Gabe pretended not to hear. When he ordered their food, he added on pie for everyone.

"What kind of pie do you want, Emilia? What's your favorite?"

The smiling woman who took his order pointed toward the board. "We only have apple and cherry left although there might be one piece of chocolate in the back."

Gabe nodded. "Just bring us six pieces of whatever you have, and we will figure it out when it gets here."

The pie arrived with Merina and Gabe's meals. Emilia tasted both the apple and the cherry before deciding to take the only piece of chocolate.

"You need to make this pie, Nina. It is yummy," she declared as she spooned the thick piece of chocolate pie and meringue into her mouth.

Merina smiled at her little sister. She pointed at the clean, folded cloth under Emilia's plate. She leaned toward her little sister and whispered, "Wipe your face, Emilia. You have chocolate all over your chin."

Nate, Angel, and Miguel were soon finished and ready to leave. "You want us to wait on you? Otherwise, we'll take Emilia on home with us."

Gabe nodded. "That will be fine. I want to have Sadie measure me for a shirt and a vest for the wedding. I might do that before we leave if she has time."

Angel nodded and scooped up his little sister. Emilia wanted to stop and talk to the bird on the way out, but it covered its head with its wing. Gabe could hear her complaining as Angel carried her away. He laughed as he sat down.

He looked over at Merina. "Now it is just you and me. I have a couple of hours before I have to get home, so let's enjoy our time."

Merina frowned and then whispered, "Gabe, I want to tell you now. I don't want to wait. I won't be able to enjoy the rest of the day with you."

Gabe studied her face and slowly nodded as he looked around. "That will be fine, but I don't know where we will find a quiet place here in town."

"The cemetery will be quiet. We can ride our horses there."

Gabe looked in the direction of the cemetery and slowly nodded.

"I reckon it will at that. Well, let's go. No point in dragging this out any longer." He dropped some money on the table and took Merina's hand as he led her out of the eating house.

The bird began to whistle again. As they walked past, it hollered, "Hey, pretty lady! Let's dance!" It jumped from foot to foot as it squawked, and Merina blushed as she rushed out.

Gabe laughed as he helped her up on her horse. He squeezed her leg and whispered, "Merina, there is not a thing you can tell me that will make me love you less." He smiled up at her and squeezed her leg again before he mounted his horse and led the way to the cemetery.

CHAPTER 5

MERINA'S SECRET

CITY CEMETERY WAS QUIET ALTHOUGH THE EVIDENCE of new graves was everywhere. As they made their way to the only tree, Gabe read some of the stones. *Most of the folks buried here are young men, and some don't even have a name on their marker. Lots of mamas out there who are wondering when their boys are coming home. Of course, they could be like Merina and me. They might not have much for folks.*

He looked over at an open field. No markers were posted there but the evidence of graves was scattered over it. A small wooden sign labeled it as "Potter's Field." *The folks who are buried there didn't even have anyone around to claim their bodies, let alone pay to put them in the ground.* Gabe stared at the open field a moment and then shook his head.

When they reached the tree, he took off his jacket and spread it on the ground. "How's that for comfort?" he asked with a grin.

Merina let Gabe help her to sit. He dropped down beside her and took her hand. "Now tell me what is eating you up."

There were tears in Merina's eyes when she looked up at him. "It seemed like the right thing to do at the time, but now I feel like such a—a—la mentiroso—I think you say liar."

She took a deep breath. "Emilia is my daughter, not my little sister. Only my mother knew the truth. Angel might have figured it out because he always knows things he shouldn't, but Miguel has no idea."

Gabe stared at Merina for a moment and then he squeezed her hand. "I guessed that shortly after I met you. I was surprised she was your sister. The two of you are so similar. But then, as sisters you could be as well. I didn't give it much thought." He kissed her fingers. "So tell me what is so terrible that you can hardly breathe."

Merina's eyes were wide as she stared up at him. "You aren't angry I didn't tell you the truth?"

Gabe's eyes were dark as he looked at her. "Merina, you are a fine woman and an honest one. If you passed your child off as your sister, it was to protect someone. Now why would that make me angry with you? It does make we want to hurt the person who frightened you enough to make you lie though."

Tears slid from Merina's eyes before she turned her head to face forward. She spoke softly. "Mamá conceived a child shortly before Papá was killed. They were surprised but so excited. Papá was forty-five and Mamá was forty. She had much trouble in the beginning but she didn't care. She couldn't wait to have another little one. It had been many years since she had conceived. I was fifteen at the time, Miguel was sixteen, and Angel was eighteen.

"One day shortly after Mamá became pregnant, Digger Thume came by." Gabe frowned, and Merina whispered, "He is the father to Rance and Jack. Everyone was gone but me. Papá was supposed to help Digger move some cattle across the Brazos River, so I didn't think anything of it." Merina was twisting her hands and Gabe wrapped them up in his large one.

"He was friendly at first, but he stayed too long. I finally realized that his intentions were no good. I tried to run but he caught me. He beat me and then he—he." Tears ran out of Merina's eyes as she faced

Gabe. "He stole from me, Gabe. He took what I wanted to give to my husband on my wedding day and made it a dirty thing. And he hurt me."

Gabe wrapped Merina up in his arms as she sobbed. His face was hard as he tried not to let his anger show. He kissed Merina's hair and whispered to her. "Merina, please don't cry. I told you before there was nothing you could tell me that would make me love you less. That is still true."

Slowly, Merina's sobs subsided. Her voice was brittle as she continued. "Papá was killed that day. The men who were helping thought it was an accident but Angel was there. He told me Digger ran those cattle over Papá on purpose."

Merina looked up at Gabe and whispered, "Digger is a very cruel man but he pretends to be kind. I know he killed Papá to remind me that he had power. He was warning to me not to talk." Merina was quiet for a moment. She looked over the tombstones before she began again.

"When Mamá came home, I was huddled on my bed crying. My dress was torn but the bruises were all in places no one could see. Mamá cried with me. She packed our few things. She said when Papá came home that we would leave." Merina stared over at Gabe as the sadness she felt filled her eyes.

"But Papá never came home and Mamá's heart never healed. Angel took a riding job with the Hash Knife Ranch and was rarely home. Miguel left for Kansas. He wanted to see more country.

"Mamá and I told no one what had happened. When I became pregnant, I was terrified. I wanted nothing to do with the baby inside me, but Mamá said we would love it. She said my baby would be part of our family."

Merina's voice was almost a whisper when she continued. "Mamá lost her baby. My little brother came at night and was born dead. We had no time to get help, so Mamá told me what to do. She was so sad, but even then she had a plan. She said, 'Merina, when your baby is born, we will pretend it is the child I have lost. We will raise it as your little sister or brother, and no one will know differently.'"

Gabe wiped Merina's cheeks with his thumbs. He wrapped her tightly in his arms and rested his chin on her head.

"I went into labor the next day. Emilia was born early but she was healthy. Mamá nursed her. I laid on the floor in my room and cried. I thought my life was over." Merina wiped her eyes. Her voice was quiet but it was hard.

"No one knew. Everyone thought Emilia was my little sister and we let them believe it.

"Digger came by shortly after Emilia was born. I know he thought she was mine, but I looked as I did the day he took me. I didn't grow large with Emilia, and no one could tell I had just had a child.

"Mamá answered the door. I had Papá's rifle and if Mamá hadn't been in the way, I would have killed him then. Mamá was carrying Emilia. She acted as if nothing had happened when she showed Digger her beautiful daughter. Everyone knew that Mamá had been pregnant and so it started."

Merina smiled sadly at Gabe. "Not long after that, Spur started to come over. He knew the Thumes and he despised them. He gave me his big knife. Angel made me the holder to strap to my leg and after that, I wore it always. I felt safer when I had it on.

"The night Jack Thume pushed his way into Cole's house, I attacked him. He shoved the door open. Then he stood there and laughed. He didn't know I carried a knife. He thought I would run. When I came toward him, he let me get close. He called me bad names. He was sure I was going to give him what he had come for. Instead, he received my knife.

"I knew we had to run away. The Thume family was important, and I had no one to defend me. I packed our few things along with señor Cole's important papers. I woke Emilia and we left that night. We took Diablo and his ten best mares.

52

"Mostly, we traveled by night. We followed the stars. The few towns along the way were avoided, and we ate the canned foods I had packed. The horses moved quickly, so quickly that Emilia and I arrived in Dallas four days later." Her dark eyes were unreadable as she looked up at Gabe.

"It was a difficult journey."

Gabe lifted Merina onto his lap and held her tightly. "Merina, nothing good can come from telling Emilia any of this. She will soon be my daughter, and no one will ever know anything different."

Merina tried to smile up at Gabe as she cried, and her heart finally broke free. She whispered, "Mi Amor. I will keep no more secrets from you."

Gabe nodded as he kissed her gently. "No more secrets between us."

Slash B Ranch
Bitter Root Valley
Montana Territory
Monday, July 14, 1879

CHAPTER 6

OLD MEMORIES

STUB SAT UP IN BED, BREATHING HEAVILY, AS THE sweat ran down his neck. The memory that had haunted his sleep for the last fifteen years came again last night and was vividly clear in his dreams.

He wiped his face and slowly dropped his feet to the floor. Daylight was just breaking in the east and he shakily stood up.

Tuff opened the bedroom door. The big smile on his face slowly faded as he studied his older brother.

"I have breakfast ready. Thought I would try griddle cakes today. Clare showed me how to make them. I hope you're hungry because I got just a little carried away with the amount of flour I used."

Stub smiled slowly at his younger brother and nodded. "That sounds fine, Tuff. Shoot, another couple of years and you'll make some gal a fine wife with all your cooking skills."

Tuff grinned at him and pulled the door shut. He looked younger than his thirteen years and his face usually showed a smile. He frowned as he returned to the kitchen. "Stub needs to talk to someone. He won't talk to me but I know those nightmares are because of that War Between the States. He said those Rebs were tough. Some of them were even old friends he knew from the past."

Stub slowly dressed and thought again about the dream. It always started the same way with bodies everywhere and men moaning. He could see himself ride through them. He didn't help anyone even though the wounded men begged for water and tried to grab at his horse. Stub shook his head. He hated to relive the Battle of Peachtree Creek.

That battle was fought in northern Georgia, close to the growing town of Atlanta. The Rebs had snipers who were deadly with their big guns. They always tried to take out the officers first to throw the troops into confusion. That had happened at Peachtree Creek. The Union captain had been shot down. The men were confused until the little drummer boy put on the captain's coat, mounted the captain's horse, and finished the charge. The young drummer was only ten years old at the time and was shot down by a Reb sniper. Instead of shaking the men though, it rallied the Union forces as the young man had been a favorite. They had even trimmed down a musket to make it closer to his size.

Still, it shocked them all, especially Stub, who had treated the young man like a little brother. His name had been Johnny Walker, but he wanted to be called Sam. "Johnny is a Reb name," Sam always said with a scowl.

Sam was an orphan and had run away from the streets he was living on at the age of ten to join the war. He tried to enlist with several units but wasn't accepted because he was too young. Finally, the First Battalion of the Georgia Infantry accepted him as a drummer, and he became their mascot. Stub shook his head as he muttered, "During the first few years of the war, boys of any age could join as a musician. Heck of thing for a kid that young to be in a war like that."

Stub laughed as he thought about how Sam could play his little wooden flute and dance a jig at the same time. Then his face became solemn, and he shook his head. "You shouldn't have even been there,

Sam. You were too young to see the things you saw. Heck, *I* was too young to see the things I saw."

When the Peachtree Creek battle was over, the creek banks and fields around it were covered with the dead and the dying. Over four thousand men lost their lives that day. Stub shook his head again.

By that time, Stub was a sergeant, and his boys were supposed to sweep the battlefield to pick up any Union wounded. They were also to take prisoner those Rebs who could walk who had been left behind in the retreat. Rebs with life-threatening wounds were left there and men were moaning everywhere. The loss of life and limbs still made him nauseous, and Stub began to sweat again as he dressed.

"We just left them. Some of my men wanted to shoot the Reb survivors but I wouldn't let them. I said, 'Their friends will be back to pick them up. Fill your canteens and let's get out of here.'

"I led my horse into the creek and bent down to fill my canteen. The water was streaked with blood." Stub swallowed hard to push the memory down.

"I looked to my left and saw a streak of red water seeping from under an over-hanging root of a big tree. As I stared, I looked right into the eyes of a teenage boy just a little older than Tuff is now. There were three of those young Rebs under that overhang. The two young men on the outside were holding up the young man in the middle. Their eyes were terrified and for a moment we stared at each other. Then I turned away from them and pointed downstream. 'Let's fill up our canteens downstream a ways. This water isn't even fit for a horse.' As I turned to lead my horse out of the creek, I saw a rifle barrel pull slowly back into the brush behind me."

Stub shook his head. "I guess that sniper was watching out for those boys in the creek. Sure am glad he didn't take a shot at me or I wouldn't be here today." His eyes went to small metal box sitting on the shelf across the room. *That's when I ran into that young Reb soldier laying half in the water. He was dying and grabbed my pants as bent down to fill my canteen.*

"Please. Just a drink of water. I can't move and I am so thirsty."

Stub's eyes watered and he roughly wiped them as he walked over to the little box. He lifted a tattered letter along with a tintype out of the box and studied them. "I gave him a drink. His name was Zeb and he gave me this box to give to his kid sister. I never opened the letter and now it's been fifteen years. I should read it or just throw it away. I have no idea who he was or how to get hold of his sister.

"How many times have I thought about opening this envelope? Then I tell myself I would be invading a dead man's private thoughts." Stub grimaced and stared at the letter. "After fifteen years, I don't reckon it matters much either way." He dropped the letter back into the box.

"Sorry, Zeb. I failed you. Your sister will never know what happened to you because I have no idea how to contact her. You died before you could tell me your last name, and there were no last names in any of your sister's letters."

Stub took a ragged breath and opened the door. He forced himself to smile as he looked at his younger brother.

"So what did Rock tell you he wanted us to do today, or did you spend all afternoon in the house with Clare?" Stub grinned at his brother as he quizzed him.

Stub was the same height as his little brother. When Stub was younger, he had hated being short. Now he didn't mind it so much. Still, he was reminded of it today as he looked at Tuff.

"I swear, Tuff. We need to get you some new britches the next time we go to town. Those pants are halfway up your legs."

Tuff grinned at him. "That's 'cause they are yours. Clare said she'd fix mine for me, so I left both pairs with her. You had an extra pair and I borrowed them."

Stub laughed as he studied his younger brother. "Well, you'd better tuck them into your boots. You'll look like a durn hillbilly if someone sees you today.

"And don't be bothering Clare with our mending. I can show you how to fix your own britches."

"Clare likes me and she offered to do it. Why should I learn if a woman offers to do it for me? Besides, I fixed her chicken coop while I was there. Nora helped me. She sure is a sweet little girl."

Stub studied his younger brother and then looked away. Clare was a good woman. Rock had married her just a year ago and they were a good team. She softened up his hard edges just a little. They had both been married before and their spouses had died. They each had a four-year-old child. After they were married, they had adopted Nora, Clare's niece.

"Well, just don't take advantage of her. Clare has a kind heart and sometimes, she is just too generous."

"Like when she hired you and took care of me after I was shot? I think you have benefitted from her kindness too, big brother."

Stub roughed up Tuff's hair and then sat down. "That's enough talk. Let's try these griddlecakes and then I will tell you what the boss wants us to do today."

CHAPTER 7

ROCK'S SURPRISE

CLARE WAS HUMMING AS SHE STRAINED THE MILK. Her smile faded as she thought of Dally and how he had loved the little Jersey milk cow. "I hope you are happy, Dally. You and Pete and your little Grace too." She quickly wiped her eyes and dabbed her face with her apron. "You were all three so young to die."

She turned to the window and smiled as she watched Rock walk across the yard. Zeke was on his shoulders while Annie and Nora each were hanging on an arm. They were all laughing as he staggered and stumbled.

She put her hand over her heart and then looked down at her stomach where a new life was growing. "Everyone I love is right there—and here. We'll tell your Daddy today, little one. I am sure he will be as excited as I am."

Rock stopped in the doorway and proceeded to drop all three children. They ran giggling across the floor and headed for the table. Clare shook her head and pointed at the wash basin. "No breakfast until you wash up. And no arguing about who goes first."

Rock grinned at her. "Good morning, Beautiful. Have something tasty cooked up for me this morning? Let's eat quick and then I have a surprise for you."

Clare put her arms around Rock's neck and let him pull her close. "How about biscuits and gravy with sausage and wild strawberries? Think that will fill you up this morning?"

"That will start and maybe a little dessert later."

Clare blushed as she pulled away. She pointed her finger at him, and Rock laughed as he sat down. The kitchen was bright and airy. Clare's red curtains fluttered at the windows and the room was neat and tidy. She had given all the children baths the night before, and they were still clean since they had just awakened. Rock smiled contentedly and relaxed in his chair until she pointed at the wash basin. He grinned at her as he scrubbed his arms and hands.

"We all have to be nice and clean for your mother. No slackers allowed in this house." Gomer brayed and pushed through the door to stand beside Clare. "Except Gomer," Rock added with a chuckle. "I sure never saw the day that darn donkey would be sleeping in my house."

Clare kissed the donkey's nose and gave him an apple. "Go outside now, Gomer. Keep an eye out for trouble."

Gomer backed out the door. He brayed as he kicked and bucked across the yard towards the trees.

Rock shook his head. "I swear, Clare. That donkey seems to understand what you tell him." He grinned at the kids. "I sure hope I never make your mother mad enough for her to sic Gomer on me!"

The discussion was soon loud at the table as the three children discussed just what would happen if their mother did get that mad.

Clare clapped her hands. "That's enough chatter for now. Fold your hands while your father leads us in grace."

The kids bowed their heads and Rock winked at Clare before he started. "Lord, we thank you for this food and for this family. Keep us all safe as we go about our work today. Thank you for all these hands who work and live here. Thanks especially for sending that new hand, Tom, since he likes to milk cows. Amen."

Clare tried not to smile but it bubbled out of her. "Well, for a man who hates to milk, you sure seem to enjoy all the tasty things that milk allows us to make!"

Rock laughed and leaned back in his chair. "Sure do. And I am darn glad I married a woman who knows how to cook."

The kids ate quickly. When they were finished, Rock looked around the table with a smile. "Kids, I am leaving for a trip to Cheyenne in the Wyoming Territory today. I am going to buy some cattle while I'm there as well as pick up some horses in Salmon down in the Idaho Territory. Now you need to be good and help your mother." The children all stared at Rock with big eyes. He rarely was gone from the ranch overnight, and they were all trying to figure how many nights away a trip to Cheyenne would be.

Rock handed Clare a large envelope. "A surprise for you, Sweetheart." As Clare stared at it, the three children jumped from their seats to gather around her. "Open it! Open it, Mama!"

Clare looked from the envelope to her smiling husband and slowly opened it. Inside were train tickets. As she stared at them, the kids began to clamor, "What are they? Are we taking a trip?"

Rock's grin showed his pleasure and excitement, but Clare's face became pale. "I don't want to take a trip without you. I won't know anyone."

The kids were running around the table screaming and Rock pointed at the door. "Out! Go play outside while your mother and I talk."

As they raced outside, Rock pointed at the train tickets. "There are seven train tickets. You will ride with an army patrol south to Chief Joseph's Pass and then head southeast to catch the Utah and Northern Train.

"Stub, Tuff, Sandy, and Wiley will ride down with me to Salmon. Sandy and Wiley will bring the horses back up here while Stub, Tuff, and I ride on down to Blackfoot to meet you." He studied Clare's face and commented softly, "I guess I expected a little more excitement from you. What's wrong, Sweetheart?"

"We can't all go. Who will do the work around here? My garden needs to be tended and there are the chickens and the cow—"

"Now you told me you had all of the green beans put up, and the fall tomatoes shouldn't be ready for another month at least. And I know you washed every piece of cloth in the house on Saturday. What else is there to get ready?

"Maggie and Ike will be here while we are gone. Plus, the hands will be here. Wiley and Sandy will be gone two weeks before they get back to the ranch with the horses. Shorty, our new camp cook, is going to handle all the meals. He told me that Ike and Maggie can even eat with the men if Maggie doesn't want to cook."

He tapped the envelope and then turned it over so Clare could see the map on the back. "I figure it will take the army around seven days to make connections with that train headed south. There is lots of troop movement right now and they are moving fast. That trip would usually take around ten days, but Captain Baker said the brass wants him in Eagle Rock as soon as possible. He is going to push to make thirty miles per day if he can. The tracks stop at the southern border of the Montana Territory. I was hoping they would be up to Butte City by now but they're not. I'm not sure if the railroad ran out of money or what.

"Anyway, you will take the train south from there to Blackfoot in the Idaho Territory. That leg will take about three or four hours. The boys and I will meet you there and we'll all take the train on south to Ogden. That will take another five or six hours. Then it will be about another day from Ogden into Cheyenne. You will be gone about three weeks, maybe four if you decide to stay longer." He smiled as he squeezed her hand. "Word is that in another five or six years, we will be able to take a train all the way across the Montana Territory."

The kitchen was quiet for a moment and then three little faces disappeared from the doorway and went screaming across the yard.

Rock cleared his throat before he added, "I won't come back with you. I am going to help trail those black cattle up here. I don't want to leave that long of a drive up to my hands. If I can't arrange an escort from the army at the rails end, some of the hands will be there to pick you up." He sat back in his chair with a pleased look on his face. "So you see, it is all planned out."

Clare stared at Rock and he took her hand to pull her toward him. When she was on his lap, he smiled. "Now that's better. What do you think, Sweetheart? Ready to take a trip south?"

Clare studied his face and then smiled as her blue eyes sparkled. "I think a trip to Cheyenne would be wonderful. This is good timing as well. Not only is it summertime but in another six months, we would have to take a baby with us."

Rock stared at her for a moment in confusion and then his eyes lit up as they dropped to her stomach. "A baby? Why a baby will be a fine addition to this house!"

Clare wrapped her arms around his neck. "Just in time for Christmas. I am about three months along if I figured correctly. I think it's a good thing you were already planning to add onto the house."

Rock smiled as he nodded. "Ike is going to oversee that addition while they stay here. He'll keep the boys on track and make sure they have all the supplies they need."

Rock studied his wife's face as he grinned. "Now I know you have more questions. Let me have them so I can get outside."

Clare laughed and then her face became more serious. "I know you have been in contact with a rancher down by Cheyenne about buying some purebred cattle. William Sturgis, I believe. Now tell me just how you are going to get them up here."

Rock laughed as he shook his head. "Well, that has been a little tricky. Stub and I looked at several options, but we finally decided to follow the old Bozeman Trail. Most folks around here call that trail the Road to Montana and I reckon it is. I am familiar with that route although it's been some time since I was over the full length.

"We'll pick up the cattle at Sturgis' ranch north of Cheyenne about forty miles. We'll head out from there, trailing northeast for a time. We'll pass the bones of Fort Reno and Fort Phil Kearny in the Wyoming Territory. The trail swings out around the Big Horn Mountains between what's left of those old forts. We have to pass through the Crow reservation once we cross into the Montana Territory.

"We'll follow the trail on up to Butte City. There's a nice valley north and west of that town. I hope to graze there a few days in that valley. The actual trail drops down to Virginia City, but we'll go on up to Missoula. We'll bring the cattle in the north end of our valley. Virginia City is almost straight across from us here, but we can't bring the cattle over the Sapphire Mountains. They are way too rugged. In fact, I don't know how those teamsters get their wagons through Skalkaho Pass.

"I wrote Badger down in Cheyenne last year. You have heard me talk about him before. I asked if he knew any cattlemen in his area who raised Angus/Hereford cross or purebred Angus breeding stock, men who would be willing to sell. Badger gave me Sturgis' name. I have been writing back and forth with him for almost nine months now." He frowned as he looked toward the barn.

"Stub is kind of quiet when I talk about buying cattle from Sturgis. I think maybe he knew some of Sturgis' family, but he just clams up when I ask him anything." Rock's frown turned to a scowl and he shrugged his shoulders. "Hope there's not a problem there.

"Originally, I thought about driving the cattle straight north of Cheyenne and then cut west toward Big Hole, but I think that route is too rough. That pass is just too high to take a herd through. I think our best route will be to take them up the Bozeman Trail and through the north end of the Bitter Root Valley. We'll drop south to Stevensville. From there, we will almost be home."

Clare was quiet as she listened and Rock continued, "I'd like to get those cattle back up here before the cold sets in if I can. I figure it will take us pertineer three months to trail them north. Maybe less if we make more than ten miles a day. That will still put us toward the end of September, so I want to get down there right away.

"Badger knows a fellow he thought might be willing to hire on as trail boss. I want to take Stub and Tuff along, but we'll need to hire some more hands as well.

"There are a couple of fellows down there by the name of Rankin, and one of them deals in horses. I want to look at his Morgans and range stock. If I buy them, and I'm guessing I will, we can use them as the remuda." He paused and frowned for a moment. "I am hoping the Rankins might be able to suggest some hands for me to trail north. We'll need eight to ten men, and I only have three right now. Of course, there are lots of herds still coming into Cheyenne, and some of those cowboys will be looking for work."

Rock chuckled as he added, "Badger told me the fellow I am hoping to hire as trail boss even has a range cook who is just finishing a drive up this way. The man was going to retire to fulltime ranch cook, but he hasn't sold his chuck wagon yet. Badger didn't think it would take much talking to get him to agree to go along." He shifted his legs as he kissed Clare. "It will be a busy few days in Cheyenne before I head out with the cattle. We can stay in a hotel in there or if you'd rather, it sounds like Badger might have a house we can stay in while we are there." He paused as he smiled at her. "Of course, if we stay in a hotel, you won't have to cook while we're gone."

He looked seriously at Clare. "I could go alone but I would prefer to take you and the kids with me. We never took a honeymoon so maybe this trip can make up for it."

As Clare started to make a list in her head of all the things she needed to do, Rock whispered, "Visiting, riding out with me to look over cattle and horses, meeting some other women, a little shopping in Cheyenne—now what woman wouldn't want to take off and do that?"

Clare eyed him carefully. "You still haven't told me what day the children and I meet the army. Knowing you, I am guessing it is soon."

Rock's eyes glinted with humor as he laughed. "The boys and I are leaving at noon today. We will meet a fellow by the name of Tall Eagle in Salmon. I've done business with him before and he knows his horseflesh.

"I'll look them over. Once they are paid for, Wiley and Sandy will start them back up here. Like I said, they will probably be gone about a week or so."

Clare stared at her husband and slowly shook her head. "I can't believe you planned all of this without me being suspicious—but you still haven't told me when I am leaving."

Rock grinned and squeezed her. "We did most of the planning while we were working, so not much was discussed in the house.

He kissed her cheek and stated nonchalantly, "The army will be going through Stevensville tomorrow afternoon, so you need to be in town by noon tomorrow."

Clare slid off Rock's lap and stared down at him. "I can never be ready that fast! Why I—"

Rock interrupted her as he stood. "You just get us packed. Everything else is taken care of. Tuff found out today, but Stub has been in on the planning. He has stayed away from here for the last several weeks. He knew if you asked the right question, he would spill the beans." He kissed Clare's cheek again as he smiled down at her. "Tuff thinks you are just the nicest lady in the entire country, and I'm certain Stub feels the same way.

"Maggie and Ike will be out this afternoon. You will take their wagon to Stevensville tomorrow. You can leave it at the livery and then bring it back when you get home. I knew you'd fuss for as long as you had to plan. Now you can't worry too long."

Clare's panic slowly subsided and she could feel her excitement grow. She pushed Rock toward the door. "I am going to need to bathe everyone tonight if you wouldn't mind bringing some water in before you leave."

As Rock sauntered toward the well with four buckets, Clare patted her chest. "My goodness, my heart is beating so fast. A trip to Cheyenne! I have never ridden on a train before, and I have certainly never been out of the Montana Territory!" She rushed into the bedrooms and studied their small selection of clothes. "I am so thankful I did all the wash on Saturday. I need to pack and...I guess that is all that really has to be done before I leave other than weed the garden."

CHAPTER 8

THE METAL BOX

STUB LOOKED AT TUFF WITH SURPRISE AS HE TOOK A bite of his griddlecake. "Why, Tuff, these are downright tasty. I believe they are every bit as good as the ones Clare makes."

Tuff grinned at Stub. It made him proud to receive a compliment from this brother he admired. The griddlecakes *were* good though.

"Well, Clare is a good teacher. Tomorrow, she is going to show me how to make stew. I can get the meat tender but hers has way better flavor. I just can't figure out what she does to make it taste that way. Clare said to come over after supper tomorrow and she would teach me."

Stub was quiet for moment. His eyes were twinkling as he studied Tuff's face and then he shook his head. "Tomorrow is not going to work. We have big plans and they don't include you riding off for a visit."

Tuff started to protest but when Stub grinned, he leaned forward with excitement. "We going somewhere? Maybe to Stevensville? I've been saving my money and I almost have enough to buy my own rifle now!"

Stub laughed as he leaned back in his chair. "What would you think of going to Cheyenne and then working your way back up here behind a herd of cattle?"

The surprise and excitement registered on Tuff's face. "Camp out all night on a cattle drive? Say, I'd like that a lot!"

Stub pulled a paper and a short pencil out of his pocket. He explained the trip to Tuff. The young man studied the route and then looked up with wide eyes. "That will take some time. We might be gone for a month or more."

Stub nodded. "Nearly three months plus the trip down there. An Indian by the name of Tall Eagle will meet us at Salmon in the Idaho Territory. He trades horses with the Nez Perce and trains them. Rock is buying some horses from him. Wiley and Sandy will ride down with us. They will bring the horses back here, and the rest of us will head on south toward Cheyenne. Tall Eagle may help us on the drive—I'm not sure about that." He paused and added, "He's a good man. I met him once before when I was working on a spread over toward Lewiston in the Idaho Territory.

"We are leaving at noon and I laid your bedroll out. You need to get your pants from Clare. Pack a needle and thread. I'll show you how to mend. We can't ask Clare to fix your britches with all the other work she has to get her family ready to leave." He studied his younger brother's face and then added, "Roll up a heavy blanket. We'll be sleeping on the ground most of the time we are gone." He laughed at Tuff's excited face, "And you'll be looking forward to a bed by the time we get back home. Sleeping outside isn't so much fun when it rains or snows."

Tuff jumped up from the table, nearly knocking his chair over and pulled on his hat. Stub grabbed his arm and pointed at the table. "Not until this mess is cleaned up and you do your chores. Pack your bedroll using this list." Stub laid a list on the table. "We will both ride over to the main ranch as soon as you are done. Rock wants to head out by noon today." He slapped his younger brother on the back and laughed as he strolled out the door.

The little valley they lived in was beautiful. The sun was just peeking through the hills and the grass sparkled with the fresh dew of the morning. Stub took a deep breath and shook his head. "I sure am glad Clare talked me into changing my ways, and that they hired both of us. I like this life way better than the life of an outlaw." Stub walked back inside to grab his bedroll.

His smile faded away as he thought again of the war and all the men on both sides whom he had watched die. "Yep, when I was caught rustling cattle, I was offered a rope necktie or the 'opportunity to serve my country.' I chose the army. I figgered I'd be fighting Indians right here, but the Union needed men and I was available. Those army bosses promptly shipped me back east to fight in a war I knew nothing about." Stub's mind went again to the little metal box on the shelf in his bedroom. "I take that box with me anytime I might meet people. I want to be ready just in case I run into someone who might know that soldier or his little sister."

The young girl's name was Addie. She had talked about their home in Texas and how their father was planning to move as a result of the war. "Papa says we are poor now. We are going to move someplace where he can make a living. He wants to go west but Mother said our family is in Georgia. That's where she wants to go. I don't think that is a good idea since that war tore Georgia all up. Besides, our Georgia relatives are poor too." Addie didn't say how old she was but from her letters, Stub guessed she was ten or eleven. She told her brother often how she missed him.

Stub scowled and muttered, "I guess Addie could have been younger. Girls seem to use more words than boys do, and that never changes." The letters were in cursive, but it was the handwriting of a new learner.

"I wonder if any of those cowboys who work for the Rankins might know someone I could give that box to. I haven't done a thing with it in fifteen years. Just maybe if it was gone, I would stop having these darn nightmares."

Stub shook his head again. He picked up the metal box and headed to the barn. He dropped it into his saddle bag and saddled both of their horses. Rock wanted them at the main ranch by 8:00 a.m., and they needed to hustle if they were to be on time.

CHAPTER 9

LAST-MINUTE PLANS

ROCK WATCHED THE TWO BROTHERS RIDE UP THE lane and he smiled. Stub had been his best friend growing up. When Stub had rustled his first cattle, they had parted ways. Rock wanted nothing to do with stealing.

In the ensuing argument, Stub had stubbornly insisted it wasn't stealing. He believed they were owed. They both said some angry words that day nearly ten years ago. Rock never expected to see his old friend again. In fact, he wasn't happy when Clare took Tuff in while he was gone. He didn't mind helping a wounded boy, but he didn't believe in accommodating outlaws, even if they were kids.

He grinned as he watched the brothers talk. Stub had called himself Black when they rode together. He had grown a beard early and had thick, black, curly hair. His face showed little emotion but his eyes were alive. Stub's light blue eyes showed everything he was thinking. He was strong as a bull and even though Rock was nearly six inches taller than Stub's five foot, ten inches, he was quite sure Stub could whip him in a fight. Stub was a hard worker, loyal to the bone, and calm under pressure.

Rock was happy to have his old friend back and pleased they had been able to mend their friendship. He stepped away from the barn and called to the riders, "Taking the day off, are you? It's not like we have any work to do or anything."

Tuff grinned and waved his hat as the two brothers rode toward their boss and friend. The young man's eyes were excited as he blurted out, "Stub told me we are taking a trip, and that we will be trailing cattle back up here. He said we would be riding the train down to Cheyenne!"

Rock laughed as he looked at Stub. His friend shrugged and chuckled. "Tuff is a little excited. I told him at breakfast this morning. Clare doesn't need to be mending his britches either. We'll pick those up while we are here."

Clare waved at them from the kitchen window and then came to the door. She called, "Tuff, I have your pants mended. Be sure to pick them up before you leave today."

Rock grinned as Tuff rode toward the house. "Clare thinks the world of Tuff."

"Yeah, well Clare is going to make his courting a little harder when he gets older. She has set a pretty high marker for him."

Rock's eyes were serious as he looked at his friend. "She's a good woman. I should have married her sooner."

"Sure should have but as I recall, you have this problem with forgiving and forgetting," Stub replied dryly.

Rock laughed as Stub dismounted and the two of them walked toward the house. "I want to go over this trip with you one last time to make sure I haven't missed anything." He frowned as he added, "I hope this drive is a good idea."

Stub slowly nodded. "Well, you know the Montana Territory and the country around the route we'll take better than most folks do. I am familiar west and south of here down to Salmon, but I was only down in southern Wyoming Territory this past summer when you sent me to Cheyenne to look at livestock. That was only a few months ago though, so it is fresh in my mind.

"This fellow you are thinking of hiring as trail boss…has he moved many herds?"

Rock shrugged. "I haven't met him but Badger is confident of his skill as a trail boss. He said the fellow was experienced. Said he was the best he knew." Rock paused and frowned.

"He is originally from down in Texas, so I don't know if he has ever trailed this far north—or even if he is interested. Of course, his cook just returned from a drive in this country. If that cook is worth his salt, he may be of some help."

He slapped Stub on the back. "I've never moved cows this far, so it will be a new venture for me. I'm glad you'll be with me. I'll have at least one experienced rider."

CHAPTER 10

HEADED SOUTH

THE MEN ATE AN EARLY DINNER AND WERE HEADED south before noon. Clare watched them go with a touch of apprehension. "What if something happens and they are not at Blackfoot when they are supposed to be?" She pushed down her anxiety and hurried back inside. She was thankful she had canned last week. "Now if the tomatoes hold off like they are supposed to, they will be ready when I get home."

It wasn't long before Gomer brayed. Clare wiped her hands on her apron and walked out to meet her friends.

Ike's blue eyes were snapping with orneriness and Maggie was breathless. "I have had a terrible time keeping this all a secret. And even I wouldn't have known a thing if Ike hadn't spilled the beans to me!

"Now you tell me what you need help with and let's get you to bed early tonight."

Clare patted her chest. "I am so excited and nervous too. Do you think there will be other women traveling with the soldiers?"

Maggie nodded. "I know of at least three other women. Several of the officers are being transferred, and their wives are moving with them. The third woman is a young lady who is joining her fiancé. He is mustering out of another unit and she will be meeting him farther south. And don't worry about taking lots of blankets. You will be in a tent every night so just take one each plus an extra or two. They will probably have extra horses if you want to ride part of the way as well." She hugged Clare.

"You are all going to have so much fun. I traveled all over with my Paddy. I am perfectly contented to stay put now, but oh my, how I loved it when I was newly married. Every move was a new adventure."

Clare and Maggie bathed the children and put them to bed early. Clare had to scold them three times before their little bedroom finally became quiet. Ike dumped the bath water on the garden and then hauled in more so Clare could bathe.

"Ya should have time to clean up in Blackfoot. Rock told me that ya might even be there a day ahead a him. If ya are, he wants ya to stay in a hotel fer the night. Yur tickets south are fer July 22, but Captain Baker is a goin' to try to be there by the evenin' of July 21." Ike nodded at the women.

"It were a hard thing to keep from a talkin' 'bout this here deal."

Maggie and Ike fussed over Clare until the water was heated and poured into her tub. "Now you just call for Ike when you are done, and he will haul it out for you." Maggie paused and then whispered, "We don't want you lifting too much now that you are carrying a baby!"

Clare looked up in surprise and Maggie laughed. "Rock told us before he rode out. He is so excited."

Clare laughed and her blue eyes sparkled. "I am too. We should have our little one by Christmas."

Ike winked at her. "Well, Ike's a fine name in case ya need a little help there. An' Maggie Mae is too fer that matter.

"I'll be in the bunkhouse if ya need me," he commented as he sauntered out of the house, whistling as he looked around.

Clare slipped into her bedroom to take a long bath. "I am going down to Stevensville first thing tomorrow morning. Rock said they wouldn't be leaving until afternoon, but I don't want to keep those soldiers waiting in case they want to leave earlier."

She enjoyed her bath but it didn't relax her. She finally went to bed. Her trunk was mentally repacked three times before she finally dozed off.

CHAPTER 11

PRIVATE ZIMMER

THE STREETS OF STEVENSVILLE WERE BUSY AND teeming with soldiers. Clare hurried her team to the livery. The young hostler took the lines as she jumped down.

"Come, children. Grab your bags and your blankets. We need to hurry." The young man lifted Clare's heavy trunk out of the back of the wagon and she struggled to drag it up the rough street.

She herded her little family toward the soldier who was barking orders.

"Excuse me, sir. I am Clare Beckler. Can you tell me where you want me to go? My husband arranged a ride for us with you and your men."

The sergeant paused a moment as he looked at her and then his face broke into a grin. "Mrs. Beckler! I am Sergeant Berg. Right this way. We have an ambulance for you over here. Bring your personal items up to the wagon, and the private here will help you in. This will be your ride for the next seven days, and Private Zimmer there will be your driver.

"Here, let me have that trunk."

As the young private saluted him, the sergeant barked, "Private, Mrs. Beckler and her children are in your care. I expect you to do all you can to make sure they have a safe and comfortable ride."

The private saluted him again. He jumped down to help Clare load her bags and the large trunk the sergeant had set in front of the ambulance.

"Mrs. Beckler, it is my privilege to drive you and your family. Captain Baker was hoping you would be early. He wants to leave as soon as final preparations are done." He offered to lift the children up, but all three climbed in by themselves.

"If you brought something to eat, go ahead and feed the kids. We will be eating our rations as we ride. There are three other women traveling with us. The captain said to apologize for not introducing you. We are in a hurry to leave, but you will meet them this evening."

The small party of soldiers and civilians was soon on their way. Clare sat back in her seat. She tried to calm her pounding heart before she smiled back at the children. "Zeke, you pass out the food and, Annie, don't spill your water. You each have a canteen and it needs to last until we stop."

"Sarge is going to push us these first sixty-five miles or so," Private Zimmer stated. "We'll take Chief Joseph Pass down at the bottom of the valley. It will drop us out on the east side. That will probably be the most rugged part of the trip. Still, we will be following trails more than roads. That means it will all be rough."

The mules moved out smartly and the young private looked over at Clare with a smile. "I can talk the entire trip or be quiet. You just let me know which way you would like it."

Clare laughed as she looked over at him. "You just go ahead and talk. I always enjoy a good conversation."

Private Zimmer liked to talk and Clare was easy to talk to. They visited long after the children had gone to sleep.

"Are you married, Private Zimmer?"

The private shook his head. "No, but I hope to be someday. I muster out right before Christmas, and I want to spend it with my Ma. I haven't seen her for over three years."

"Do you have brothers and sisters?"

"Naw, just me. Ma married late in life and Pop died when he rolled our wagon. I was just a little tyke when it happened, so it's only been Ma and me for nearly as long as I can remember. I send my wages home to her each payday, and she is saving them for me. I don't need much here so I'm able to save most of what I make."

"Why that is wonderful, Private. What do you want to do when you get out of the army?"

"I'd like to get a little ranch of my own. There's an old fellow outside of our little town who told me he'd wait for me to come back. He offered to sell his place to me over time. He has a small spread and does a little farming too.

"Ma has worked in the dry goods store in our town most of her life. I think she'd enjoy being out in the country too."

Clare smiled at the sincere young man. "I think that is wonderful, Private. I'm sure you will be a success at whatever you do."

Private Zimmer smiled shyly at Clare. His eyes were brown and his face was boyish. A shock of light brown hair hung over his forehead. "Call me Johnny. We are going to be riding together for some time, and I'd like you to call me by my given name."

Clare laughed as she agreed. "But only if you call me Clare." Johnny smiled and Clare thought about his mother. *How difficult it would be to send your only child away and not see him for over three years.*

Salmon, Idaho Territory
July 17

CHAPTER 12

SOME FINE HORSES

ROCK WAS UP EARLY ON THURSDAY MORNING. THEY had made the one hundred thirty-four-mile ride from Stevensville to Salmon in three days. He smiled to himself. *And a darn pleasant ride at that. Nice weather, good company, and an easy riding horse.*

He looked over at his riders with a grin. "I hope you all enjoyed this roof over your heads because you will be sleeping under the stars for some time. Now let's go eat some breakfast, so we can look at those horses first thing."

The eating house was nearly full at 6:00 a.m., but the men found an empty table. Plates were promptly set in front of them.

Rock grinned as he looked around at the surprised riders. "Now this is efficient. Just eat what they give you and ask for more if you are hungry."

The men ate quickly and moved outside to give their table to the next hungry patrons. A band of horses was being driven down the street followed by a man in buckskin. He was riding a beautiful Appaloosa stud.

Rock stepped into the street and watched the horses go by. He reached his hand up to the rider with a smile. "Right on time, Tall Eagle.

It is good to see you. I'll follow you down to the pens to look them over. They sure look good from here though."

Tall Eagle shook Rock's hand and nodded before he moved his horses toward the pens on the south end of the busy town. Rock and his riders followed. They climbed up on the corrals and stared at the herd of Appaloosa horses.

Wiley let out a low whistle. "Now, that is what I call fancy horseflesh. How many are we taking back with us?"

Tall Eagle rode his horse over to them with a smile. He nodded toward the horses as he looked at Rock.

"You ordered twenty head of mares. You also mentioned studs. How many do you want? We'll pull those off and then the rest are going to Cheyenne. Rowdy Rankin down there put in an order. He'll take the other forty head of mares and that last stud."

Rock was quiet as he studied the horses. He climbed over the fence and walked through them. The animals were tame. They snorted a little at the smell of a strange man but hardly shied at all when he petted them.

"I am thinking that I want a couple of studs along with those mares. I am mostly looking for breeding stock, but I'd like to use them too."

Tall Eagle nodded. "If you are going to take two studs, I would recommend the two on the end. They are two different blood lines. In addition, they don't fight each other as much as the flashy one up front does."

Rock studied the two studs. One was mostly black with white spots and the other almost looked speckled. It was white with brown markings.

Tall Eagle pointed at the speckled one. "When the spots are all over the body, it is called a leopard appaloosa. That horse has the heart of a lion. He will give you all you ask and more if he learns to trust you. The black one will make up to people slower and is selective on who rides him." He grinned at Rock. "Not a horse for a tin horn."

Rock laughed. "Well, I don't have any of them around and with my low tolerance for foolishness, I doubt I ever will.

"I like the looks of both of them. How about mares? Those two fellows have girlfriends they will fuss about leaving?"

Tall Eagle laughed as he opened a gate and let the two stallions into a second pen. Six mares followed closely behind and two more pushed to get through the gate before it was closed. "Those eight mares stick close. The rest will be up to you."

He pointed to various horses as he talked about them. He knew most of their dams and quite a few of their sires. "There are a few fillies in there, but most are three- and four-year-old mares." He pointed toward a quiet horse standing by itself. "That palomino is probably the calmest horse in the bunch, but she is a cutting fool. She can work cattle all day. She is the only five-year-old in the pen."

Rock studied the horses a while longer and then pointed to the ones he wanted. He chose the palomino appaloosa first. The rest were a mixture of base colors. Some were snowcaps. They almost looked like they were wearing a white, speckled blanket.

Tuff was quiet until Rock finished picking his horses. He looked over at Stub and commented softly. "I don't think I have ever seen a nicer pen of horses. I almost want to go back home so I can start riding them!"

Tall Eagle cut out the horses Rock was buying. As soon as they were sorted, Sandy and Wiley started them north. They moved out easily and their bright colors were a beautiful contrast to the summer grasses. The two men waved and Wiley called, "See you in a few months, Boss."

Rock lifted his hat as he watched his horses start up the trail. "Let's get you paid, Tall Eagle. I need to get down to Blackfoot to meet up with my family." He paused a moment and then added, "Will you be trailing the rest of the horses to Cheyenne or catching the train partway?"

Tall Eagle grinned. "I don't like trains. I prefer to ride under a blue sky, but I might see you before you head home from Cheyenne.

"I hear you are pushing a herd of black cattle north." He studied Rock a moment and then added, "If Gabe Hawkins hires on as trail boss,

I will sign on too. I only ride with him though." His dark eyes glinted as he added, "That way, you will pay me to ride back home."

Rock looked startled and then he laughed. "I reckon that would be fine. Let's go have a piece of pie and we can both be on our way."

Rock knew about what the horses were going to run in price, and he didn't try to negotiate Tall Eagle down. The man only worked with the best horses, and he broke everything he sold.

As they shook hands, Rock nodded his head. "I'll see you in Cheyenne, and I sure hope you are on that drive with me. I know you're a top hand, and I'd be pleased to have you along."

Rock had the waitress pack them some food, and the men were riding southeast by 7:30. Rock looked over at Stub and Tuff. "It's about two hundred miles to Blackfoot, and we need to make it in five days. Let's get a move on. Stub, you know this area so you lead out."

Stub pointed south. "Our next town will be Challis, and it is about sixty miles south. Root Hog Station is a stage stop. It is about eighty miles southeast past Challis. They will offer meals there, but the food is usually cold, greasy, and bad. From there to Blackfoot is another sixty miles."

The three men loped their horses on the flat ground and took the climbs slower.

Rock smiled as they rode. He always enjoyed seeing new areas and this was a part of the country he hadn't ridden in before. Stub pointed out different ranches as they rode and told stories.

"Yeah, Root Hog Station earned its name all right. It was so rough around there that even the emigrants passing through on the Oregon Trail didn't stop. Some folks called that trail 'The Longest Graveyard' and I reckon it was. Even at that, those folks just kept on moving when they reached Root Hog.

"It was a rough place. I've heard it hasn't changed much since I was last through there either. Time to time, someone will say, 'Root Hog or die.' I reckon they died 'cause they sure didn't settle in Root Hog."

Cheyenne, Wyoming Territory
July 19

CHAPTER 13

A NERVOUS BRIDE

SATURDAY, JULY 19, FINALLY CAME. MERINA PUT HER hand on her chest. She could feel her heart pounding through the lace of her wedding dress and sweat droplets were forming on her forehead. "I think I am going to faint!" she whispered to herself as she slowly sat down on the bed.

A soft knock sounded on the bedroom door. "Are you ready to go, Merina? It is time to leave for the church. Badger has the surrey pulled up in front." When Merina didn't answer, Martha opened the door to peek in. She hurried to the young woman sitting on the side of the bed.

"I don't think I can do this, Martha," Merina gasped. "I—I hate to be stared at, and there will be so many people there. I don't think I want to go. I think I should wait and maybe marry another day."

Martha sat down on the bed and put her big arms around Merina. "Now, now, Merina. There is only one person you need to look at, and I am guessing he is just as nervous as you are. Lots of brides get anxious on their wedding day. I know I was."

Merina looked at Martha in surprise. "You were nervous? Why you and Badger act like you have been married for years!"

"We might act that way, but we only married eleven years ago. I had actually met Badger less than a month before we married. I knew him less than twenty-four hours when he asked me to marry."

When Merina looked at her in shock, Martha laughed softly. "Badger rattled my comfortable world. I had been married to my first husband for over thirty years and it was a loveless marriage. He needed a wife and after my father died, I could not run our family's dry goods store as a single woman.

"Walden and I eventually moved to Manhattan, Kansas. He died there about ten years after that move." Martha smiled as she looked out the window. "I didn't really miss him. We were more like roommates who rarely talked than like a husband and wife. When he passed, my life barely changed. I was used to being alone and I was quite contented." She laughed softly as she added, "And then Badger stepped on my toes in church.

"He was so full of life. His ornery eyes just snapped with vitality, and I knew then that I was tired of my placid life. I was ready for a change.

"He bought my meal at the box supper after church." Martha's eyes became misty. "My box brought more than any box there even though it was made by a middle-aged widow. I listened to Badger as he talked all through that meal, and I knew I wanted to know him better. I invited him over for supper. He was busy but he said he'd be by for breakfast."

Martha beamed at the young woman beside her. "Badger did come for breakfast and after we ate, he asked me to marry him. I said yes and I haven't had a boring day since.

"Oh, but I was nervous when that train pulled into Julesburg. What was I thinking, giving up my settled life for a man I barely knew! What if he wasn't there? What if he had changed his mind?"

Martha hugged Merina as she kissed her cheek. "He was there, all right. He had arranged for a band to play as he led me off the train, and he introduced me as his bride to everyone we met on the street." She smiled at the pale young woman beside her.

"Now didn't you tell me you knew you loved Gabe not long after you met him? Well, love only has two ways to go. It can grow and burst into this beautiful flower or it will fade and die.

"I think you and Gabe have that special kind of love—the kind that allows you to laugh and be silly with each other. A love that allows you to share your heart and know the other one will accept your gift of honesty with tenderness." Martha's eyes were misty as she hugged Merina again.

"That kind of love doesn't come along every day, and even though it's scary to step into the unknown, love is worth it.

"Now I want you to smile at me. When we get to that church, you keep your eyes on Gabe's face. His eyes and his smile will let you know that this new life is going to be all you have ever hoped for."

Merina stared up at Martha and slowly smiled. "I do love him," she whispered. "I fell in love with him in Dodge City, but he loved a woman who had died. It was her letter to him as she was dying that made me see him for the man he is. He asked me to read it aloud, and he was so broken-hearted. Then when he started to play his harmonica again, I knew his heart was healing."

She smiled at Martha as her eyes filled with tears. "I love him so much, Martha. I don't even understand why I am so emotional today."

Martha pulled Merina up and led her to the wash basin. "Of course you are emotional. You are wearing the wedding dress your grandmother made for your mother and a veil made by your great-grandmother. Those are wonderful gifts. Still, they make you sad because the loving hands who made them, and the beautiful women who wore them are gone."

She kissed Merina again as she whispered, "But they will be here in spirit. Besides, you have a new family now, and we all love both of you very much. You are going to be a beautiful bride in your Spanish lace, but even more than that, you are going to be a wonderful mate for Gabe.

"Now you wash that pretty face, and let's get over to the church. If you are late, that big man you are marrying may faint himself out of nervousness!"

Merina nodded as she smiled, and Martha hurried toward the door, closing it behind her.

Badger was standing in the kitchen when Martha rushed out of Merina's bedroom. His blue eyes were sparkling, and he grabbed his wife to swing her around.

"Oh, my Martha. You is my purty flower a love. Ol' Mule an' me knowed what we was doin' the day we was wed," he whispered in her ear. "I was so durn nervous that day, I plumb couldn't eat—an' ya know I never turn down food. I jumped up in that there train car, jist a prayin' that you was on it. When I saw yur purty face, my ol' heart jist about busted wide open." He kissed Martha's happy face and swung her around a few more turns as they both laughed.

When Merina stepped out of the bedroom, Badger whistled as he offered his arm. "I reckon ol' Gabe won't be able ta breathe when he sees you'ins a walkin' up that aisle. You'ins is the picture a purty, that's what ya is." He winked at Merina. Then he offered each woman an arm and danced them out the door.

Merina was laughing when Badger lifted her up on the seat. Her heart was still racing but now it was pounding with excitement and anticipation. She leaned toward Martha and whispered, "Thank you, Martha. No wonder you are so loved. You are like a mother to all of us."

Martha beamed at her and Badger hurried around the surrey to jump up on the front seat.

CHAPTER 14

DIGGER THUME

DIGGER THUME UNLOADED HIS HORSE FROM THE train when it stopped to refuel outside of Cheyenne. The train ride from Texas had been a long one, and the rage that filled him was even stronger.

"I'll make that little gal pay for the death of my sons if it's the last thing I do," he muttered to himself as he rode his horse into Cheyenne. "I'd like to take her for another romp in the hay before I kill her, but either way, she'll be dead before I leave."

The hostler wasn't around when he arrived at the livery, so he watered his horse and put him in an empty stall. He looked around and found a small stash of grain which he dumped in a tin pan.

"You rest up, boy. This job shouldn't take too long, and then we are going to hightail it out of here. We'll follow the rails south toward Denver. When that train catches up with us, we'll jump on. We can ride it on into Denver, and then catch another one south to Texas."

He grabbed his rifle off the saddle and walked to the open door of the livery. He stopped there to stare up and down the street. There seemed to be quite few people around, and the town hummed with activity.

Digger Thume was a tall man. His eyes were gray and looked like flat pieces of slate in his face. They showed little emotion. They did reflect the arrogance with which he viewed the world, as well as those around him. His hair was just starting to gray, and his body didn't reflect his fifty years. Digger might have been considered a handsome man in passing, but if one looked closely, his face was cruel. He rarely smiled. Money was Digger's god and people were only worth what they could do for him.

A short man with a rooster feather in his top hat was hurrying toward the livery. He slowed and wiped the sweat from his bald head when he saw the stranger standing in the doorway.

"Howdy. Rooster Smith is the name. Did ya find a stall fer yore hoss? She's a busy day today. Weddin's, funerals, an' dances bring all the fellers to town, an' we's a havin' us a weddin' today."

Digger was only half listening as he stared up the street. When Rooster stopped talking, he turned to him. His hard eyes bored into the smaller man.

"I'm lookin' for a Mexican gal, pretty but trampy. Heard she was in Cheyenne an' I'm hopin' to find her. Know where she might be? I'm guessin' she might work in one of the saloons. She traveled up the trail from Kansas with a bunch a cowboys."

Rooster studied the man in front of him with his bright eyes. The man talked like a Texan. *The word 'round town is that little Merina killed a feller down to Texas what was botherin' 'er. I don't know much 'bout that deal or her, but I think a lot a Gabe. Since she's a gonna' marry that tall cowboy today, I reckon it's my business ta find out more 'bout this here snoopy feller.*

"Cain't say as I do. 'Course folks come through here all the time. Most of 'em don't stay long. We ain't a friendly town—to outsiders, that is—at least not till we knows 'em better." Rooster paused as he stared at the man.

"What ya want 'er fer? I know lots a folks an' cin pass the word along—if yore reason be a good one." Rooster's bright blue eyes were bland as he watched the man in front of him. The stranger hadn't introduced himself and that alone was enough for Rooster to be wary.

The man's hard eyes narrowed down as he studied the hostler. "My reasons are my business." He turned out of the doorway and strode down the street.

Rooster watched him go for a moment and then called after him, "I see ya give yore hoss a bait a grain. I'll go ahead an' unsaddle 'im. Looks like he could use a rubdown too."

The man swung around abruptly to face the hostler. "You just make sure he has some hay. I'll handle the rest of my horse's care." He turned around and continued down the street, his orders given.

Rooster's eyes narrowed down and he muttered, "Shore now, that feller is up to no good. I believe I'll loosen that girth a bit. Make that hoss more comfortable. It might slow that ol' boy down, jist in case he ain't on the up an' up." Rooster loosened the girth strap that circled the horse's stomach slightly. If someone tried to mount, the saddle would slip sideways. His blue eyes were gleaming when he left the stall.

"Mebbie I should have me a little confab with Badger. He might want to send ol' Mule to keep an eye on this here feller."

Badger's house wasn't far from the livery. Rooster turned Mule loose and then followed him towards Badger's house as he whistled. Once he was off the main street, he picked up his pace. "The weddin' 'ill be startin' shortly, an' I shore want to pass this news on to Badger 'fore then."

CHAPTER 15

AN OLD SCALLYWAG

BADGER HAD JUST TURNED HIS TEAM TOWARD THE church when Mule charged toward the surrey. The old man stared at his mule before he turned in his seat to see Rooster hurrying toward him. He studied Rooster's face a moment before he pulled his team to a stop. He handed the lines to Martha.

He jumped out of the surrey and called over his shoulder, "I'll jist be a minute, Sweetheart. Ol' Rooster looks like he has somethin' he needs ta tell me. I don't reckon it'll take no time a'tall."

Rooster nodded toward the livery. His face was serious as he spoke softly.

"Strange feller in town. Ain't real friendly. Wanted to know where to find little Merina. I don't know what he has planned but he don't want his hoss unsaddled. That means he's a plannin' to leave town in a hurry an' he only jist got here."

Rooster's eyes were hard as he shared his suspicions with Badger. He had turned his back to the women as he talked, and Badger's neck hairs raised as he listened to his friend. When Rooster finished, Badger waved to Martha.

"Jist go ahead an' take Merina on over ta the church. I'm a gonna hep Rooster here a bit. I be there soon as I cin."

Martha picked up the lines and scooted to the outside of the seat. She knew something was going on, but she didn't want Merina to worry.

"That Rooster is an old scallywag. He has his finger on the pulse of this town though. What Badger doesn't know, Rooster does. Between them, there is not too much they miss.

"I'm sure whatever it is, they will take care of it quickly. Now let's get you to that church and to your groom!"

Martha urged the team to a trot, and they were soon pulling up in front of the church.

Gabe was waiting outside. He strolled over to the surrey to help the women down. "Martha, thank you for driving my bride to the church. I reckon my ol' heart is about to beat right out of my chest just waiting on her." As he looked at Merina he added softly, "And looking at you here, why I can't hardly get my air at all."

Merina blushed as she smiled at him. Angel good-naturedly pushed Gabe aside. "My friend, I have not yet given my sister to you. Go into the church and wait for her as the priest told you to do. You know I take my duties very seriously where women are involved…and even more since this one is my sister."

Gabe grinned at his friend and winked at Merina. "I'll be waiting for you inside. Now if I stutter, just go on with the service. You know I'm going to say, 'I do,' so don't hold things up if I can't get it out!"

Angel lifted the laughing Merina down and led her toward the church. Martha paused in the doorway and looked back for Badger. He was nowhere to be seen and she frowned a moment. However, she was smiling again when she turned around.

A nervous Gabe was standing in front of the altar with Rusty and Nate. Larry, Molly, and Sadie were standing on the other side, and all three women were smiling. Beth was kneeling on the floor as she talked to Emilia. The little girl was excited to throw the flowers she was carrying.

"No, Emilia—you don't throw them—you *drop* them," Beth whispered. "You need to walk very slowly and just drop them on the floor when we tell you."

Emilia nodded excitedly and Beth giggled. *I don't know what she is going to do but I am quite sure it won't be what we tell her.* She kissed Emilia's cheek. "Now be a quiet girl and watch for our signal."

Beth was ready to get in her seat when she realized that Badger wasn't with Martha. "Where is Badger? We are almost ready to start!" she whispered.

Martha smiled and bobbed her head toward the back of the church. "He'll be coming. We won't wait in case he is held up."

CHAPTER 16

Up to No Good

AFTER MARTHA DROVE AWAY, BADGER HURRIED BACK
to his house. As he saddled Mule, he muttered, "I think ol' Mule an'
me 'ill try ta find that there feller. Sounds like he's up ta no good fer sure."

Rooster waved and called over his shoulder, "I'll jist go on back
to the livery an' watch fer 'im. If I see 'im, I'll bang on a wagon wheel
three times an' ya cin come a runnin'." He headed back toward the livery
walking as fast as his bowed legs could carry him.

Badger took Mule's head in his hands as he talked to him. "Mule,
a feller come in town lookin' fer Merina. Now I know that little gal is
special ta you'ins, an' I think we need ta track that there feller down.
We cin be neighborly like an' see if'n he needs some help whilst he's in
town." Mule snorted and Badger mounted quickly.

They rode slowly toward the church. Mule was sniffing the ground
and picking his way carefully while Badger was looking around for the
man Rooster had described. The animal stopped abruptly and snorted
as he looked to the left.

Badger slid off and talked softly to the mule as he gestured and
pointed. He cautiously walked toward the shack that Mule was staring
toward.

A rifle was protruding from the window, pointed toward the church. Badger's face drew down into a scowl and his eyes became hard. He waved his hand at Mule and the animal walked quietly toward the front of the shack.

An old cistern was close to the shack. A rusty pump sat on top of it, the metal covering bent and broken. Badger squatted down on the ground behind the cistern. He commented softly in a conversational voice, "Mighty unfriendly thing ta do ta come ta our town an' try ta bushwhack a body right off the bat."

The man inside the shack remained silent but Badger could hear him moving around. He squatted closer to the ground and leveled his gun at the shack.

"Ol' Betsy an' me," Badger added as he held his buffalo gun, "we been together a long time. Now me, I'm a cautious sort a feller. Ol' Betsy though, she's jist sudden. I reckon ya better drop that there gun an' high tail it out a there 'fore she loses what patience she has."

The rifle fired from inside the shack. It ricocheted off the cistern and twanged off to the right.

Badger whistled and Mule charged. The man inside the shack screamed once and Badger whistled again. He stood and slowly walked to the entrance of the shed. The man lay on his back on the floor. He had been stomped and was having trouble breathing. Badger stared at him for a moment and then kicked the rifle farther away.

"I reckon ya should a listened ta me when I said ta drop that there gun. Now I'm a gonna ask ya this question jist once. Who was ya plannin' ta bushwhack with yur gun pointed toward the church like that?"

The man didn't answer, and the mule moved closer. Mule's head was almost in the injured man's lap as the man moaned and held his arm.

Badger added softly, "Better speak up, Mister, lest I turn my mule loost again—an' this time, I won't make 'im stop."

The man spat his words out. "I'm Digger Thume. That Mex gal killed my boys. She killed Jack in Texas and Rance up here. I'm going to kill her. She's nothing but trash and no one will even miss her."

Badger was silent a moment and then he answered softly, "You'ins boy down Texas way attacked Miss Merina when 'er menfolk was gone. Tried ta have his way with 'er an' she poked 'im with that pig sticker she carries. You'ins other boy busted into 'er house here an' was gonna cut 'er ta get revenge. My mule here done stopped 'im." He paused and then ground out, "She didn't kill that second boy a yurs—my mule did."

Digger's breath caught in his throat and then he tried to breath evenly. The mule's mouth was close to his face, and it was all he could do to keep from trying to roll away.

Badger stared from Digger to the man's rifle. He backed up a step.

"Why don't ya jist go ahead an' try fer that there rifle. I'll back out a here ta make it more even. Or you'ins cin stand up an' I'll walk ya down ta the sheriff's office. You'ins cin tell 'im yur story. Mebbie you'ins 'ill convince 'im that ya been ree-formed an' jist want ta go on home." Badger whistled softly and Mule backed up to the open doorway of the shack.

Digger was an angry man. In addition, he was a man who was used to being listened to. Money opened a lot of doors, and it also padded lots of pockets. He had no intention of being intimidated by a small man who looked too old to shoot, and a cantankerous mule who supposedly took orders from the same old man. He made a grab for his rifle.

Mule charged and Badger walked away. When the noise stopped inside the shack, Badger mounted Mule and rode him down to the livery. He pulled the saddle and bridle off and put Mule in a stall.

He looked over at Rooster. "Tell the sheriff they is a dead bushwhacker in that ol' shack down by the church. He cin see where the feller tried ta shoot me, an' he fer sure were plannin' ta shoot someone in that thar church. Mule kilt him an' I'm a guessin' there ain't much left. I didn't care 'nough ta look.

111

"An' don't tell 'im till after the weddin'. I don't want nothin' ta ruin those kids' day."

Rooster grinned and nodded. "I reckon I cin do that. I'm gonna ride out ta the party at the Rankins'. I cin tell 'im when I git back." He paused as he studied Badger's face and then softly added, "Wanted ta hurt that little gal, didn't he? That whole durn family were mean."

Badger didn't answer. He was already hurrying back toward the church. If he could pick up the pace just a little, he would only be a little late to the ceremony.

CHAPTER 17

A Weak-Kneed Groom

SOME OF THE PEOPLE IN THE CHURCH LOOKED UP when they heard the shot. They listened for a second shot. When none came, they relaxed.

Lance looked toward the back of the church for Badger. His eyes narrowed when he didn't see the little man. He thought he heard a scream but the sound was muffled. The church was a little noisy with all the restless little ones. Martha smiled at him and he slowly relaxed.

Merina was just walking up the aisle when Badger entered the back of the church. He couldn't see Merina's face, but he saw Gabe's—right before Gabe passed out and hit the floor with a crash. Merina never missed a beat. She kept right on walking although the blush on her neck moved up to her face.

Angel, Miguel, and Rusty began to laugh. Nate stared down at his older brother in shock. Slowly the guests began to chuckle, and before long, nearly everyone in the church was laughing. When Larry bent over Gabe and shook him, Martha hurried to the front. She handed Larry her smelling salts.

As Gabe slowly came around, the laughter became louder. Father Cummiskey tried to get everyone under control while doing his best not to chuckle himself. He barked at the altar server next to him and the young man rushed to the side of the church. He was back quickly with a dipper of water.

Gabe took a long drink of water and his mind began to clear.

Rusty and Nate lifted Gabe to his feet and when the priest asked, "Who gives this woman?" Angel scratched his head. "I'm not sure we should do this, Padre. Perhaps señor Hawkins has been drinking."

Merina jabbed Angel with her elbow. He grinned as he grunted, "Her brothers, Miguel and Angel Montero, give our sister to this man."

Gabe stepped forward carefully to take Merina's arm. He whispered to her, "See? I said you'd be so beautiful that I wouldn't be able to breathe. You sure are."

Merina held tightly to Gabe's arm, and the rest of the ceremony went off without a hitch—at least until it was over and was time for Emilia to scatter the flowers.

She handed the basket to her little friend Livvy. "You throw the flowers. I am going to walk with my new papa!"

Livvy bounced out of her seat before Lance could stop her and tossed flowers everywhere as she sang her own version of "Buffalo Gals, Won't You Come Out Tonight?" Molly's face was red as she followed Merina down the aisle, and Lance was laughing.

Gabe grinned down at Emilia. He lifted up the happy little girl and carried her in one arm while he held Merina with his other one. Badger rang the church bells, and everyone thought it was a fine wedding.

"My beautiful Merina," Gabe whispered, "I don't have a ring yet, but one is coming—one beautiful enough for my bride."

Merina smiled up at him and Gabe stopped in the middle of the aisle to kiss her. Emilia commented, "Nina, you said grownups were only supposed to kiss in the dark." Merina drug Gabe the rest of the way out of church while he laughed.

CHAPTER 18

PLAY ME A PRETTY SONG

BADGER HAD ARRANGED FOR A BUGGY TO CARRY THE newlyweds to the Rankins' Rocking R Ranch for their reception. Emilia wanted to ride with Livvy in the Rankins' wagon. Pauline, the three-year-old daughter of Rowdy and Beth, decided to join her two friends. Merina and Gabe were finally alone.

A big sign on the back of the buggy read *Just Married!* Tin cans on strings were tied to the back axle. As the new couple started to drive away, the cans rattled and bounced over the ground. Horses and mule teams began to spook. Gabe stopped and cut the strings before they proceeded south out of town.

Gabe smiled down at his new wife. "Did your mother wear that dress when she married?"

Merina nodded as she touched the hand-tatted lace. "She did. My grandmamá made it and Great-grandmamá made the veil." She lifted the veil off her head and carefully folded it. She touched the old veil and smiled up at Gabe. "I am the fourth generation of women in our family to wear the veil."

Gabe looked at her hair and then looked again. "What is all over in your hair? It looks like beads and little flowers."

Merina laughed softly. "Josie came over this morning and did that. It will probably take me an hour to get all of the pins out, but she wanted to prepare it for me. She said since my mamá and grandmamá weren't here to do it, she would do it for me."

Merina paused and added quietly, "Everyone here is so friendly. I have never had many friends before, but these women are so welcoming."

Gabe nodded. "I have seen that too. I met lots of folks as I followed herds, but not many I saw on a regular basis. Most folks I met one time and never saw again. I guess I was too busy trying to make a living to enjoy things most of the time. I sure do enjoy having Rusty and Angel around though." He grinned at Merina and nudged her with his elbow. "Guess your ranch and mine are joined now. Rusty is my business partner and Angel is my ranching partner."

Merina stared at him for a moment and then asked softly, "And what am I? Am I not a partner in your ranch?"

Gabe laughed and hugged her. "You are an owner. You own half of all I have, so you had better plan to stick around. And we need to keep growing. With Angel and Nate, the cattle might have three families to support someday. And who knows about Miguel!"

He pointed toward Margaret Endicott's ranch in the distance. "I think Margaret will be selling her place this year now that Cappy and she are married. I believe we ought to try to buy that. Might be a nice place for Angel and Miguel." He studied the ranch in the distance. "I haven't been down to the ranch headquarters. I actually don't even know how much land they have. Margaret hasn't stocked it herself since her husband died so someone is renting it. Cappy said he and Margaret were staying out there tonight since it's closer than riding back to Cheyenne." Gabe was quiet a moment and then commented, "I think maybe we should pay them a visit next week."

He laughed as he nodded his head toward the trail in front of them. "You know Lance is land-hungry, and the fellow who is renting may have already talked to them about buying."

Merina studied Gabe's face from the side, "I think you are land-hungry too, Gabe. I think maybe you would like to own much more land than you do right now."

Gabe nodded absently. "I would. It takes quite a few acres per cow/calf pair up here, and like I said, we need to support three families."

Merina laughed up at him. "I think I would rather listen to your harmonica than talk about cattle right now. Play me a pretty song and make my heart sing."

Gabe looked at his wife in surprise and then pulled out his harmonica. Soon the soft melody was trailing back to the rest of the travelers on the road behind their buggy. Merina scooted closer to Gabe and smiled as he played.

CHAPTER 19

THE WEDDING PARTY

MOLLY AND BETH HAD TAKEN OVER PLANNING THE reception. Gabe and Merina had no idea what food would be served. All they knew was that Lance's camp cook, Gus, was going to make a cake.

As they drove into the yard, the smell of pork filled the air. Six cowboys were in the process of lifting a whole pig out of a pit. Gus was directing them, and they set it down on a long picnic table.

Gabe helped Merina down and they walked over to look at the pig closer.

Gus' wrinkled black face smiled up at them. "You must be the newlyweds. I'm Gus. Let me get this pig lined out, and I will show your bride her cake."

Once he had the pig situated like he wanted, he wiped his hands on the white apron he wore before he put out a hand to Gabe.

"Since you are the groom, you must be Gabe." His old black face was a sea of wrinkles when he smiled. "This pretty lady must be Merina." He touched Merina's arm and pointed inside his kitchen.

Merina gasped when she saw the cake.

"My Auntie Maria used to make cakes like that! She promised she would make a tall cake for my wedding. I guess since she couldn't do it, she made arrangements with our Dios." Tears filled Merina's eyes. "Thank you, Gus!"

Gus grinned at both of them and shooed the little kids out. "Now I don't want any finger trails in that cake, so you all stay out of it." As the children rushed outside, he laughed. "And there will be trails all over the bottom. Make sure your piece is from the front—there will be fewer finger tracks there since they can't sneak bites so easily."

Gabe laughed and Merina was smiling. They walked back to the buggy and Gabe lifted Merina's veil off of the buggy seat.

"I need to get these mules unhitched. Why don't you go on in the house? Have Molly stash your veil someplace safe. I'll be in to get you as soon as I finish."

Merina hesitated a moment and then walked slowly toward the house. Beth saw her coming and gave a happy squeal.

"Come inside, Merina! I want you to taste the tortillas. Josie showed us how to make them. We are going to wrap the pork in them.

"Josie even knew how to make sopapillas, and Molly had us fill them with apples like Gabe likes." Merina paused as she looked around the busy kitchen.

She stared at all the food and then looked at the women in amazement. "This is what my family would have prepared for a wedding meal! How did you know?"

Josie laughed as she hugged Merina. "I was raised in south Texas, so I went to many parties and weddings down there. I thought you might enjoy food today that would remind you of home. Gabe said he didn't care what he ate, so we took him at his word."

When Gabe finally made it inside to collect his bride, she was in happy conversation with the other women in the kitchen as she tasted all the food they had made. He spied the sopapillas and took two of them.

"You ladies know the way to a fellow's heart. I just love these little apple pillows." He smiled at the women and the put out his hand to Merina. "Come with me. There are some people you need to meet." He tipped his hat as he backed out the door. "Thanks again, Ladies. This spread makes a man's mouth water."

Lance and Molly had invited all the neighbors as well as Chet and Nancy Reith. Gabe had purchased Reith's ranch from them shortly after he moved to Cheyenne. That was where Larry and Rusty were living with their twins.

Nancy's father didn't come. "He doesn't like crowds or traveling very far," Nancy explained.

All of Rowdy and Lance's hands were there. Tiny and Annie came out from town along with Levi and Sadie. Doc was holding Charlene as he watched the children.

Martha and Badger seemed to be grandparents to *all* the children, and Martha was having a ball. Father Cummiskey even came out. He was sitting with the men and laughed as he drank a root beer.

Mule showed up part way through the meal. He wandered over to where Merina was sitting and rubbed his head on her. She gave him a sopapilla and he chewed it contentedly before he wandered back across the yard. He let himself into the corral and pulled the gate closed behind him.

Most of the men stopped talking to watch the mule. Anyone who was near backed up to give him a wide berth. They stared as Mule rubbed his nose on Merina, and they didn't talk again until he was back in the corral.

"Looks like ol' Gabe acquired himself a mule, don't it?" Rusty's blue eyes were twinkling as he laughed.

One of the men muttered, "I wouldn't have that animal on my place. He's dangerous. You never know when an animal like that will turn on you."

Gabe shook his head, "Not when he protects your family. Nope, I reckon that mule has a home here as long as he wants to stay."

CHAPTER 20

SCHEMING FRIENDS

THE GUESTS SLOWLY PEELED OFF. SOME NEEDED TO be home in time for chores while others had made plans to stay longer. By 10:00 p.m., the dance was in full swing. Merina refused to do the Mexican hat dance with Angel, so he talked Josie into dancing with him. Gabe played it on his harmonica. The dance was fast and wild. Even though Angel was a smooth dancer, Josie was out of breath by the time they were done. Gabe grinned at Merina as he tapped out his harmonica.

"Your brother is a smooth one. He would make me look bad if I danced that with you."

Merina laughed as she agreed. "Yes, he is smooth and very fast. I was afraid he would tear my dress, so I told him no."

Gabe's eyes were intense as he looked down at her and then he chuckled. "Well, maybe we should ditch this party and head on home. Then you can take that dress off. It would be a shame to damage it."

Merina's face began to turn red, and Gabe squeezed her as he laughed. "And don't go calling me bad names in Spanish because I will understand every one of them!"

Beth rushed over and held out a package. "I am going to put this in your buggy, Gabe. It is the leftover pork and a few tortillas. There isn't much but it might be enough for a meal."

Gabe stood and took the package. "I'll put it in the buggy. We surely do thank you ladies again for the nice party." He reached his hand down to Merina. "Ready to go? I want to tell the rest of the women thank you and settle up with Lance for the hog."

Lance waved his arm. "We can settle up this next week. We'll have you down for supper. I want to talk to you about a business proposition anyway. How about Tuesday night?"

Gabe was surprised but he nodded. "That should work."

The women were done cleaning up and Merina hugged each one as she thanked them. Gus had saved Gabe and Merina each a piece of cake, and Molly handed that to them.

The kids had gotten into the cake early, and the back half of the cake was gone before the meal started. Little hands had pulled chunks of cake out. By the time the adults noticed, the cake was tipped at a dangerous angle. Sadie quickly cut it and placed it on plates. There was still enough for every guest, and the kids wiped up the tray.

Molly was angry. She had wanted the new couple to cut it themselves and taste the first piece. Gabe just laughed. "We saw it when it was whole and pretty. Let them enjoy it. I'm sure it tasted even better since no one saw them sneaking bites!"

Molly frowned for a moment and then pointed toward the little girls. "Why don't you let Emilia spend the night? I will make sure she is up early so Merina can take her to church if she wants. Nate can spend the night as well." She smiled softly as she looked toward the two young men. "Sam has never had a friend his age, and the two of them have become as thick as thieves. Their next plan is to figure out how to go on a cattle drive together."

Gabe looked over at Lance and grinned. "Well, I do have John Kirkham's address. Besides, I'd like to see Tobe and the other fellows.

Shoot, maybe one of them will marry old John's daughter. Those boys took that job because of Miss Ann. Maybe we'll all go to a wedding in Nebraska before long!"

Angel glided by with a smiling Rachel on his arm. "Don't wait up for us, señor. Miguel is going to take Miss Rachel home—when she is ready, of course. Rusty and Larry invited us to spend the night with them." He smiled down at Rachel, "Perhaps not much of the night will be left. We are young vaqueros who do not sleep so much, unlike my patron who must go to bed early." His dark eyes were dancing and Gabe looked sideways at Merina. She blushed, and both Angel and Gabe began to laugh.

Rusty and Larry paused as they danced by. "Looks like yore ranch will be quiet tonight, Boss. I reckon I'll be listenin' fer that harmonica to start and then stop." He grinned and Larry tried not to giggle as Merina once again blushed.

Gabe looked around at all the smiling faces and he laughed. "I think I'll go ahead and take my bride home. Thanks for the party and for all the scheming you have done this evening."

He lifted Merina up in the buggy and they headed on south toward their ranch. They rode quietly the first few miles, and then Gabe pulled the buggy to a stop.

"I reckon I can't go any further without a little spooning with my bride. I have always enjoyed the moonlight, but I have never seen it look so beautiful."

Merina laughed softly and the buggy stayed where it was for a time as the mules stamped impatiently.

CHAPTER 21

OLD FRIENDS AND GOOD NEWS

WHEN GABE AWOKE THE NEXT MORNING, IT WAS TO the smell of bacon and biscuits cooking. Merina's hair was down and it was every bit as curly as Emilia's. He watched her from the bedroom door for a moment. She was humming softly, and he moved up behind her quietly as he put his arms around her. "Good morning, Beautiful. And if this is how every morning is going to go, I think I am going to like this marriage business."

Merina jumped as his lips touched her neck. She turned around with a smile. The sound of horses in the yard stopped both of them. Gabe pulled his shirt on and grabbed his rifle as he opened the door. His frown changed to a grin when he recognized the three smiling riders.

"Well, good morning, Boys! I guess you didn't get married after all. Good to see you. Come on in here and my new bride will fix you some breakfast."

Merina appeared in the door behind him, and the three riders pulled off their hats as they grinned at her.

"Good morning, Miss Merina. I see you finally showed old Gabe who was really the boss." Tobe winked at Gabe as he climbed down off his horse.

Gabe's smile became bigger as he looked at each of them. "Tobe, Bart, Rufe. I hope you are looking for riding jobs. I am ready to hire some hands, and I could sure use you." He looked back down the road behind them. "What did you do with Tab? Didn't he stay in Ogallala with you fellows?"

Bart snorted disgustedly. "Shore, Kirkham hired him. Then Miss Ann took a fancy to him. Now he's a runnin' the whole durn ranch. They'll be gettin' married sometime soon I reckon. An' I sure ain't a gonna work fer Tab!"

Merina laughed out loud and Gabe chuckled. "I guess you just can't figure love out now, can you? Well, put those horses up and let's have some breakfast."

As the three men dismounted, Gabe asked, "Did you trail some cows up here or just ride up on your own?"

Tobe nodded over his shoulder toward Cheyenne. "We brought a herd up for Kirkham. He said he'd wire us our pay once he heard from the buyer. I think the government bought 'em. Not sure if they are for the military or for one of the reservations. Yore two old girlfriends led us all the way up here."

Gabe looked at the man in surprise, and Tobe pointed toward the corrals. The two cows who had led Gabe's herd all the way from Texas were standing at the gate, waiting to get into the pasture.

Bart laughed as he pointed at them. "Kirkham said to leave 'em here with y'all. Nobody can keep 'em in.

"The feller you sold 'em to in Ogallala was tired of fixin' fence. He sent them with us to lead this drive. Kirkham said mebbie y'all can plan a drive north, an' they can march right on up to Canada!"

Gabe laughed. "Well, I don't intend to go on any more drives. I guess we'll see if they stay. I kind of missed them anyhow.

"One of you open that gate and let them into the pasture. Those fences are pretty tight. You can put your horses in the corral. Throw your packs in the bunkhouse and then come on in."

He shook hands with each of them. "It sure is good to see you fellows. Welcome to the Diamond H."

Gabe went on into the house and put his arms around Merina. "Now where were we when we were interrupted?"

She pulled away and pointed toward the door as she muttered at him. Gabe grinned and grabbed the water bucket. "Those words sound so much nicer in Spanish. I reckon I can't get mad at you even if you are calling me bad names."

Merina's face slowly blushed and then she laughed. "I am going into Mass this morning. I will pick up Emilia on the way. Do you want to come with me?"

Gabe nodded. "That will work. I'm guessing you'll want to leave here before long." He paused and then added softly, "You sure look pretty in the morning, Merina, and you make this house a home."

Gabe's heart was light as he sauntered toward the well. He spotted a horse coming down the road toward him and he muttered under his breath. "Now what is Sheriff Boswell doing out here so early? No one that I know was in town last night.

"Morning, Sheriff. Lost this morning or just out for an early ride?"

Sheriff Boswell studied the tall man in front of him. Three riders walked slowly toward Gabe and scattered out around him facing the sheriff.

"A man died in town yesterday by the name of Digger Thume. You know him?"

Surprise registered on Gabe's face and then his eyes narrowed down. "I know him. I didn't help kill him, but I sure am grateful to whoever did. And I know I didn't do it because yesterday was my wedding. That means that none of my friends did either because they were at the wedding and party after."

"What about these fellows? They look like strangers to me."

Bart started to curse, and Gabe took a step toward the sheriff as he ground out, "These men are my riders. You can see their horses in the corral. Mrs. Rankin had our wedding party at her house last night and every one of my hands was there."

Sheriff Boswell pushed his hat back and muttered under his breath. "Yeah, that's the same story Badger gave me. Said his mule was the one who did it. He told me that Thume had a rifle pointed at the church about 12:30 yesterday afternoon. He said they exchanged words. Things got loud and Thume started to shoot. Somehow Mule got in that shack and stomped him to death. Reckon he was defending old Badger." He studied Gabe's face.

"So what would Digger Thume have against you?"

"Digger was a cow thief and a loudmouth who thought money could buy him everything. We've had plenty of words over the years. I never liked the way he treated women, and he didn't like the beating I gave him and his sons. I reckon he was looking for revenge." Gabe spit on the ground. "And good riddance. Both the Wyoming Territory and Texas are better without the three of them."

Gabe could see Merina's pale face in the doorway of their home from the side of his eye, and the rage he felt inside boiled over. "Anything else, Sheriff? Otherwise, I have breakfast that is getting cold and talking about Thume puts a bitterness in my mouth."

Sheriff Boswell shook his head. "No, I guess that takes care of it." He started to turn his horse and then pulled it to a stop.

"I don't want that mule in town. He's dangerous and I just might have to shoot him the next time I see him."

Gabe took a slow step toward the sheriff and stated softly, "That mule never hurts anyone who doesn't need killing. You shoot him and I just might have to shoot me a sheriff."

Sheriff Boswell looked at the big man in front of him in surprise and then he shook his head. "Well, at least try to keep him out of Cheyenne. It's my job to protect the folks there."

Gabe's face broke into a grin. "Maybe you should make Mule a deputy. Then everyone's problems would be solved."

The sheriff chuckled and waved his hand. "Maybe I should do that. You and your new missus have a good day." He studied Gabe and then added seriously, "Try not to be so sudden, Gabe. It's never good to threaten a peace officer."

Gabe stared at the sheriff and slowly nodded. "I reckon that is sound advice. You leave that mule alone and I will keep my kind of peace out of Cheyenne."

Sheriff Boswell sat quietly on his horse and stared at the four men. Finally, he swung his horse around and headed north. He shook his head as he rode back toward Cheyenne. "That is one hard man and those three Texans behind him looked just as tough. Well, I am guessing Gabe is a man of his word. He will probably keep his riders under control." Then he glared and cursed under his breath. "I'll only have trouble with that darn mule."

Gabe watched the sheriff go with a scowl on his face and then turned to face his men. "Give me just a minute with Merina and then we'll have that breakfast.

Merina had slid down inside the door and was sobbing quietly. Gabe lifted her up and held her tightly as he pushed the door shut with his foot.

"It's over, Merina. Digger is gone. He can't hurt you anymore." He kissed the top of her head and whispered, "Don't cry, Sweetheart. My heart hurts when you cry."

Merina's sobs were silent, and the shaking of her body slowly eased. Finally, she pulled back and smiled up at Gabe as she wiped her eyes.

"I am glad he is gone. I was so afraid that someone might tell Emilia who he was someday. Now I will think of him no more."

Gabe hugged her tightly and shook his head. "She will never know. Now throw on some extra bacon. Let's get those men fed, so you and I can head into church."

He cupped her face and kissed her as he smiled. "I'm so glad you stole a ride on that train into Dodge to meet your brothers."

Merina laughed as she wiped her eyes, and Gabe called the riders in.

Boundary of Montana and Idaho Territories
Monday, July 21

CHAPTER 22

PRIVATE JOHNNY ZIMMER

CLARE PUSHED HER HAIR BACK INTO THE BONNET ON top of her head and looked back at the children. They were tired but they seemed to be handling the long trip well. All three were currently asleep, and she was thankful for the lack of arguing.

Private Zimmer pointed his whip in front of them where a few houses were huddled together. "There's Allerdice, ma'am. That means we aren't far from the end of the track. I don't think the captain wants to stop here for long, but you can get down and stretch your legs."

He looked at her shyly and blushed a little as he added, "Once we get to the tracks, I wouldn't venture too far from the train if I were you. I know you'd like a bath, but these end-of-track towns are usually rough. Not a good place for a lady to be alone. Maybe just wash up at the horse tank and wait to take a bath once you get to Blackfoot.

"The captain said the train usually pulls in around noon, so we'll be there in plenty of time." He looked at his pocket watch. "It's just now 9:00 a.m. The captain told me to have you at the train station by 11:00. I think he is going to have me take you and Miss Hendrix down. Both of you are catching the train."

Clare smiled at him and nodded. "Thank you for all your help these last seven days, Johnny. I think you probably did more than was required of you. I do appreciate it."

Private Zimmer blushed as he smiled. "I was glad to help, ma'am. My old ma always made me behave around women. I didn't always see the need when I was a young squirt but I am thankful now."

"I think your mother would be proud of you, Johnny. I know I would. It is hard as a mother to guide children. There are no rule books that tell you how much is too much or too little. In addition, every child is different." She paused as she looked back at her little ones sleeping quietly. "Our little Nora is crushed if you scold her but scolding rarely bothers Annie at all." Clare sighed. "Annie is precious and precocious at the same time."

Private Zimmer laughed and he agreed. "Yes, Captain Baker wasn't very impressed when she climbed up on his horse and tried to take a ride."

Clare's neck turned red and she shook her head, but Johnny laughed. "I wouldn't worry too much, ma'am. We all thought it was funny. The captain isn't a bad guy, but he takes life too seriously sometimes. We all stopped to watch when the captain hollered for her to get off. She put her little hands on her hips and cocked her head at him. When she said, 'My, aren't we cranky today,' I about busted a gut laughing!"

Clare's face turned a darker red and Johnny laughed a second time. "I hope I see her again in ten years or so. I am guessing that spunky little girl will be a spunky young woman."

Mary Hendrix rushed up to the wagon. "There you are! Johnny, can you bring your wagon over to mine, so we can load my personal effects? Captain Baker wants you to leave in ten minutes. At least that is what I think he said. He is always giving orders as he speaks." She turned to Clare and whispered, "We women are going to form a circle to relieve ourselves if you would like to join us."

Clare nodded gratefully. "Yes, that would be nice. I'd like to take the girls as well." She turned around and called to the children.

"Wake up! We are ready to load and leave for the train. Annie and Nora, come with me to Mrs. Hendrix's ambulance. Zeke, you stay here until we get back. I don't want you to wander off."

"I don't need to pee with the women, Mama. I can just squat here." Annie dropped to the ground before Clare could stop her. She finished quickly and shook out her skirts. She slapped her leg and then pulled her skirt up to look for whatever bit her leg.

"I don't like dresses much, Mama. Too many bugs can crawl up my legs." She hiked her skirts up above her knees and stared down at her legs.

"Annie, put your skirt down now."

The little girl's face squinted as she frowned. "I don't want to wear this dress anymore. I want my britches back."

Clare sighed and held out her hand. "Your britches are dirty. Now come with me. You too, Nora. Let's go with the rest of the women over by those bushes. And once we wash our hands, I will have a snack for each of you."

"Me too!" called Zeke as Clare led the girls away. Clare smiled over her shoulder.

"Yes, you too, Zeke."

When they were done, Clare called Zeke to join them at the water tank. She scrubbed each of their faces with one of Rock's bandanas.

Captain Baker came over to say goodbye. Clare stood with a smile and offered him her hand. "Thank you so much, Captain. I know it is not easy to take families along when you move your troops, but we do appreciate you helping us."

Captain Baker smiled and then laughed as he looked down at Annie. "Now Annie, you have fun in Cheyenne. And don't be trying to steal any horses while you are there!"

Annie glared up at him but before she could speak, Clare grabbed her arm. "Thanks again," she called over her shoulder as she quickly pulled Annie away and back towards the ambulance.

"I wasn't going to steal his old horse. I was just tired of riding in the wagon. If he was a nice man, he would have let me ride with him." Annie stomped beside Clare and pushed out her lip as she complained.

Clare dropped down in front of Annie and took her by the shoulders as she spoke. "Annie, soldiers have many responsibilities, and one of those responsibilities is keeping us safe. Now does your papa let you ride with him when he is sorting cattle?"

Annie slowly shook her head.

"That's right, because he needs both of his hands and all of his attention on his job. That is why Captain Baker was angry with you. Now you and I are going back there, and you are going to apologize to him. And you will thank him for letting you ride in his wagon.

"Nora and Zeke—you get in the wagon and stay there until we get back. Annie, you come with me."

CHAPTER 23

YOUR PAPA IS MY FRIEND

CAPTAIN BAKER TURNED AROUND AS CLARE approached. He stepped toward her with a questioning look on his face.

"Captain Baker, Annie has something she would like to say to you." Clare pulled Annie around from her side until the little girl was facing the captain. Annie glared at him before she spoke.

"Mama says I have to say I'm sorry and to thank you for riding in your wagon. And I wasn't going to steal your horse. My bottom hurt from sitting in your old wagon, and I wanted to ride a horse." Tears sparkled in the corners of Annie's eyes as she looked up at Captain Baker.

The surprised officer dropped down to squat in front of the little girl as he smiled. "Why thank you, Annie. Apologizing is a hard thing to do, and I am sure your papa would be proud of you." He smiled at her and then softly added, "Your papa is my friend. Did you know that?"

Annie's eyes grew large and she shook her head.

"Your papa saved my life one time. He shot a buffalo bull that was charging me. He took that big buffalo down in one shot. If he had missed, I wouldn't be here today." He pulled a small piece of brown hair that was braided tightly together from his pocket and held it out to her.

"This is some hair from that buffalo's tail. You can have it if you want since it was your papa who shot it."

Annie took the hair almost reverently. She stared at it for a moment and then peered up at the captain in surprise. "I can keep it?"

Captain Baker closed her hands over it. "It is yours, Annie. It can be a reminder of what a brave man your papa is."

Annie gave him a glorious smile and squeezed the hair. "I will keep it forever! Thanks, Mr. Soldier!"

She raced back to toward the wagon shouting, "Zeke! Nora! Look what that cranky soldier gave me!"

Clare's face colored slightly and she shook her head. "It is time to get her out where she can run. Annie isn't used to being cooped up."

Captain Baker laughed as he watched Annie show her brother and sister the small piece of hair. He turned his eyes back to Clare and his face became serious.

"That was a true story I told her. What I didn't tell her is that I was on the ground. I was a private and as green as the grass.

"We had decided to chase some buffalo one day on patrol. My horse stepped in a hole and broke his leg. A big buffalo bull swung around and charged me. Rock was from up that way or working up there. I'm not sure which. Anyway, he heard the shooting. He raced up just as that buffalo charged and shot it. Then he gave all of us a tongue-lashing for wasting meat.

"He made us skin and butcher all of the buffalo we had shot. I think that was one of the hardest jobs I have ever done. There was a little Indian village not far from there. We packed all the meat we could carry on our horses. There were ten of us and five dead buffalo. We had to walk and lead our mounts because there was so much meat. He led us into that camp, talked to their old chief, and made each of us apologize for taking their food. We gave all that meat to those Indians. Rock didn't even let us keep a tongue or a hump."

The captain's face drew tight as he shook his head. "That camp was full of women, children, and old men, but shortly after we arrived, a large band of young braves showed up. They surrounded us. If Rock hadn't been able to speak their language, I don't think any of us would have made it out of there alive.

"I didn't know much about Indians back then. I was a new recruit from Indiana. Looking back, I am guessing they were Crow. Rock seemed to know them. He talked to them in their language and several of them laughed.

"We left there a subdued group of soldiers. Before we had traveled much more than a quarter of a mile, those Indian squaws were headed out to collect the hides and the rest of the meat." The captain looked down and shook his head.

"I haven't shot a buffalo in fun since. It was a good lesson to me on how important food is wherever you are. I'll let the men shoot a buffalo if we need meat but only if we can use all of it.

"Of course, I've seen places where the buffalo lay in piles on the ground with only their tongues or the hump cut off. Sometimes hunters just take the hide." He paused and frowned before he continued. "Some folks even believe if we kill off all the buffalo, the Indians will be easier to control." He blushed slightly. "That's enough military talk. You have a safe trip the rest of the way to Cheyenne."

Captain Baker gave Clare his arm as he walked her to the ambulance. "Your husband is a good man, Mrs. Beckler. He saved me twice that day. Little Annie has a lot of him in her. Don't be too hard on her." He touched his hat and turned back toward his men, barking orders as he organized them to move out.

His troops had been ordered to make a fast march from Stevensville to the Colorado Territory. They were to assist in an Indian outbreak, and they would be moving out quickly.

As Clare climbed into the ambulance, she could hear some of the soldiers talking. Private Matter nodded his head toward the east. "We won't be in Colorado long. They will send the captain north. Utes up on the Milk River are giving an Indian agent by the name of Meeker some trouble. 'Course Meeker thinks all Indians should be farmers. He wants to break those Utes down until they beg him for food and a place to live. Durn fool if you ask me, but he's friends with some big dog officer back east. He's a bad agent and they still let him stay.

"Private Zimmer over there speaks the Ute language. No one knows where he's from because he never talks about home. He can sure talk Ute though. Those Utes respect the captain too. He can usually negotiate when no one else can."

Clare listened to the soldiers talk as she arranged their items in the back of the ambulance. She said a quick prayer for all of them and smiled at the three little ones sitting in the ambulance bed among all the bags and parcels. They were all staring at the braid of hair and talking excitedly. Annie let each of them hold it for just a moment. She looked up at Clare and smiled as her eyes shined. "I am going to keep this forever, Mama."

CHAPTER 24

RIDE THE TRAIN SOUTH

PRIVATE ZIMMER WAS CORRECT. HIS AMBULANCE arrived at the tracks at 11:00 a.m. sharp. The southbound train was already there. The private quickly unloaded all their bags while Clare and Mary Hendrix rushed into the train station.

"You are just in time, Ladies," the agent stated as he took their tickets. "This train is supposed to leave at noon but sometimes we leave at 11:30." He handed Mary's ticket to her quickly and addressed Clare. "I see you will be connecting with the next train south to Blackfoot and then on down to Ogden in the Utah Territory. Will you be continuing on from Blackfoot today or tomorrow?"

"I plan to leave Blackfoot tomorrow. Do you know if there is a hotel there? I have three small children, and I would like to get them bathed and rested before we continue on." She pointed at her tickets. "I have seven tickets total. My husband and two of our riders will be joining us tomorrow."

The ticket agent stamped her tickets and nodded. "Blackfoot has one hotel. There will be some boys hanging around the train waiting to carry bags. I suggest you ask one of them to run down the street and secure you a room. Rooms usually sell out if the train is full and she is today."

Clare nodded and then looked behind her at the three little faces. "I assume they will have a fee. What is the going rate?"

The ticket agent's eyes twinkled as he smiled at her. "They are good boys. Several of them don't have any folks, so that is their eating money. Two bits or less will make them run. Offer one an extra two bits to carry your bags when he's done, and he will be back in a flash!"

Clare smiled and picked up her tickets. "Thank you, sir, and you have a wonderful day." When she turned around, she saw Private Zimmer hurrying her children toward the train. He drug her trunk with one hand and was loaded down with her other bags.

"Hurry, Miss Clare. The whistle is blowing and the train will be leaving soon. This car has some empty seats so I'll put your bags in here." He lifted the children in and gave her a hand up. They all waved and called to him, and the young private backed away with a smile on his face. As he hurried back to his team, he thought again of his own mother. "I'd better write Ma a letter. Miss Clare was right. I think Ma would be proud of me, and I know she'd like to receive a letter."

Private Zimmer did write his mother. He wrote her that evening and told her all about the seven-day trip he had just completed, as well as the young family he had escorted. He thanked his mother for teaching him to be a gentleman. He told her he would be home by Christmas as his stint in the army would be up by then.

Mrs. Harry Zimmer never received that letter. Private Johnny Zimmer was killed on September 26 of that year. He died in a battle with the Ute Indians on the Milk River in the northern Montana Territory. The letter in his pocket was lost on the battlefield along with his identification papers. His mutilated body was transported to the nearest post where he was buried. Mrs. Zimmer never heard from her only son again.

BLACKFOOT, IDAHO TERRITORY

CHAPTER 25

A Friendly Stranger

CLARE SANK INTO HER TRAIN SEAT. "I AM SO TIRED," she whispered as she looked toward the open door of the train car. The children were clamoring for something to eat and she smiled at them. She pointed to the pack Captain Baker had sent with her.

"Thanks to Captain Baker, we have food to eat today. Now bow your heads and let's say a prayer of thanksgiving for all the nice people who have helped us on this trip."

The prayer was quick, and Clare passed out the food. Captain Baker had sent beef jerky, two cans of peaches, three apples, some prunes, and three pieces of hard candy.

The children began to eat eagerly and talked excitedly to one another.

A tall cowboy with a mustache dropped into the open seat beside Clare just as they were closing the doors. He smiled down at her.

"Howdy, ma'am. Hope ya don't mind if I sit here. This train is completely full."

Clare shook her head and laughed. "Feel free to sit but we are all dirty, and my children will probably be loud. We have been in a wagon for seven days." She smiled as she put out her hand. "I am Clare Beckler. These are my children, Annie, Zeke, and Nora. Say hello, Children."

The cowboy stared at her a moment before he took her hand. "George Spurlach but my friends call me Spur. Pleased to meet you, Mrs. Beckler." He studied the children and then asked, "Is your husband Rock?"

Clare nodded, just a little surprised. "Yes, he is meeting us south of here at Blackfoot. We are going on down to Cheyenne from there. He is buying some cattle north of Cheyenne and will trail them back up here." She paused a moment and then looked at the man carefully. "You know my husband?"

"I bought a horse from him about five years ago." Spur grinned at her as he added, "But I don't remember seeing you around then. I think I would have remembered a face as pretty as yours."

Clare laughed, "Well, I have only been around for a little over a year. Rock lost his first wife when Annie was born. My husband died and things just worked out. Nora is my niece. We took her in when my brother was killed. Yes, Rock's family grew quite rapidly."

"I am headed to Cheyenne too. I work for Rowdy Rankin down there. He runs the R4 and he sent me up here to buy some horses. He likes Appaloosas and the Nez Perce know their horseflesh. Some Nez Perce wranglers met me in Missoula." He stretched out his legs and nodded toward the door.

"I almost didn't make it in time. This train left thirty minutes early, and I barely had time to load them. The boss told me to try to catch this train if I could. Otherwise, I would trail them on south until I caught the train east to Cheyenne.

"A fellow named Tall Eagle is delivering some horses to us as well, but he refuses to ride the train. He says it is too noisy and wastes too much time." Spur laughed and settled back in his seat. "It may not be fast but at least I can sleep. And don't worry about keeping those kids quiet. They won't bother me a bit."

Clare dozed off and on. Spur watered the horses at one stop, but he slept the rest of the way. She sighed. *I wish I could sleep like that. I am almost afraid to sleep with these little ones. Who knows where Annie might go if no one stops her?*

Finally, the kids fell asleep and Clare slept as well. It wasn't long before the whistle blew, and the train car became loud as passengers gathered their possessions.

Spur stretched and then stood. "Is your husband meeting you here? If not, I can give you a hand with your trunk."

Clare looked at him in surprise. "Are you staying in Blackfoot?"

He shook his head, "No, but they will make a longer stop here since we left early. They probably have extra freight to load." He nodded at the eager boys gathered around the train station as they pulled in. "Of course, if I help you, those young men won't get their tip," he added with a grin.

Clare laughed and Spur took her arm to help her down. A small boy with holes in his britches and a torn shirt rushed up to her. "Help ya carry yur bags, ma'am?"

An older boy shoved him out of the way. "You're too small, Rabbit. Get out of the way."

Clare looked at the small boy and smiled. "Rabbit, I am guessing they call you that because you are quick. Would you like to run down to the hotel and secure us a room? I'll give you two bits if you can be the first one there."

The little boy stared at her and then turned around to race down the street. He passed the boy in front of him and reached the hotel first. He paused at the door to wave with a grin on his face before he disappeared inside.

Spur chuckled. "That was one way to make sure you get a room. They sell out fast here and there is only one hotel."

Clare laughed. "Yes, the ticket agent at Allerdice where we boarded suggested I do that. And I will take you up on your offer to help with my trunk. I'm not sure how well its small wheels will roll on this rough street.

"Come children. Let's get our room and then we are all going to take a bath."

Rabbit was back quickly and Clare handed him his money with a smile. "Rabbit, you certainly do live up to your name. Now if you would like to help the children carry the rest of the bags, I will buy you some supper. You can eat with us. I assume there is an eating house here?"

Rabbit studied her face and Clare added, "Or I can give you another two bits. Of course if you eat a meal with us, you will be money ahead." She smiled at him again before turning to her children.

Spur ducked his head and tried not to grin. *Rabbit has been mostly on his own for as long as I have come through Blackfoot. Count on a mother to see that he's hungry and try to fix it.*

Rabbit grabbed the heaviest bag and hurried up to walk beside Clare. He jerked his head over his shoulder and asked, "Those all yur kids?"

Clare looked startled and then laughed. "They sure are."

"They all have different pas?"

Clare missed a step and looked at him in surprise before she nodded slowly. "Well yes, they do. My husband and I were both married and lost our spouses. Zeke is my son and Annie is my husband's daughter. Nora is my niece but now we are all one family."

Rabbit watched Clare for a moment and then he looked away. He was quiet for a few steps before he asked, "Ya like yur kids?"

Clare's face paled a little as she looked down at the earnest little boy. "I love all of them very much. How about you, Rabbit? Do you have a family?"

"Naw, I ain't got one here. Ma took sick an' died a while back. We lived in a shack on the edge of town. Big Nell lets me sleep on her porch but it is sure cold." He paused and then added, "I have a letter that my pa sent to my ma. She threw it away, but I dug it out an' kept it. I cain't read but I know he was from Texas. Ma was real mad when she read it but I kept it anyhow. When I get enough money saved, I'm gonna go on south an' see if I can find 'im."

Clare's face turned white and she was quiet as she walked. She finally stopped and looked down at the little boy. "Rabbit, I have an idea. Why don't you come with me? We are going south as far as Cheyenne. Maybe we will run into some Texas riders who know your pa. If we do, you will be that much closer to Texas."

Spur spoke up quietly. "I know a fellow down there who just brought a herd of cattle all the way north from Texas. He owns a little ranch south of Cheyenne. We have been friends for a long time, and he would be a good one to talk to. He knows fellows all over Texas, and he just might be able to help you out."

Rabbit looked hard at the faces of the two adults and then shook his head. "I reckon I cain't do that. I don't have no money yet for a ticket."

Clare leaned down and whispered, "You don't need a ticket. I'll just tell them you are my son. We bought seven tickets, and now any kids over that amount ride for free."

Spur choked and almost tripped but Clare didn't miss a beat. "Of course you will need to help me with baths. I need to bathe the girls, and Zeke is too young to leave by himself. Maybe you could take a bath when he takes his, so you can keep an eye on him."

Rabbit studied her face before he slowly nodded. "I reckon I could do that, but it'll cost ya."

Clare nodded just as seriously. "Probably another two bits but you have to take a bath too. It won't work if you just wander around."

Excitement flickered through Rabbit's eyes before he answered. "I ain't had a bath since Ma died. I reckon I can do that."

Clare nodded. "We will bathe and then we will eat." She patted Rabbit's shoulder as she smiled at him. "I sure am glad you offered to carry our bags, Rabbit. It is nice to know such a helpful young man."

Spur set the large trunk down inside the hotel and then put his hand out to Clare as his eyes twinkled.

"Mrs. Beckler, it was my pleasure to meet you. I will look forward to seeing you when you get to Cheyenne." He tousled Rabbit's hair.

"And you too, young man." He tipped his hat to Clare and winked at the little faces smiling up at him.

"You kids have fun now. The eating house makes ice cream every Tuesday evening. You make sure your mother buys you some." Excited little voices followed him, and Spur headed back up the street with a smile on his face.

"I reckon that little fellow is going to have a home one way or the other," he commented to himself as he grinned. "That's a good deal. He's too little to be running loose on the streets, and Big Nell's sure isn't a place for him to hang out—even if his ma did work there before she died." Spur was whistling when he reached the train. He watered the horses and arranged for some hay. By the time the train left, he was once again asleep in his seat.

CHAPTER 26

AN ANGRY MOTHER

AS SOON AS THEY WERE CHECKED INTO THEIR ROOM, Clare called for the children and they headed across the street to the dry goods store.

"I am going to buy each of you some new britches and a shirt. You can come in for just a moment to pick out an apple. Then I want you to wait outside for me."

Rabbit hung back and Clare pointed toward the apples. "You pick one too, Rabbit. Supper is going to be late tonight. In fact, I might get a few extra. If you are as hungry as I am, you might be able to eat two."

Each child picked an apple and wandered back outside. They were standing by the door when a large man walked by. He grabbed Rabbit by the collar of his jacket and shook him. Annie began to yell and call the man names. Soon she and Zeke were kicking him while Nora pulled on Rabbit.

Clare dropped the clothes she was looking at and rushed outside.

"Children! Stop that now. And you, sir. Unloose that boy."

The burly man turned to face Clare in surprise, and the sun glinted off the star on his chest.

"Now see here. I'm the sheriff in this town. I could have all of you arrested for assaulting an officer."

Annie kicked him again and Clare pulled her back as she stepped closer. Her eyes were dark with anger, and she almost hissed the words she spoke.

"Sheriff, have you ever seen a mother grizzly react when you get between her and her cubs?" As the sheriff stared at her, Clare took Rabbit's arm.

"Now I am asking you nicely just once more to unhand this child, or you are going to find out what an angry mother does when you hurt one of her children."

The sheriff dropped Rabbit and Clare caught him as he stumbled. She patted his arm and pointed south. "You go get your things, Rabbit, and hurry back here while I talk to this man." She pointed at a bench behind her. "Children. Sit."

When she turned back to face the sheriff, he backed up at the fury pouring from her eyes. Her breath was coming quickly, and she took another step toward him.

"How dare you grab that child! Even if he had stolen that apple *which he didn't*, I wouldn't blame him. What kind of a sheriff are you to allow someone so young to try to fend for himself on the streets of *your* town? I am sure you knew he lost his mother. Yet you have allowed him to sleep in a whore house, and on their cold porch at that. You are shameful." She stepped back a step and added softly, "That boy is in my care. If I see anyone attempt to harm him in any way, that person, even if it is you, is going to have an angry mother *and* a pack of children all over him."

The sheriff's mouth fell open in shock. When Clare turned around, she was smiling. "Now children, you sit there quietly and eat your apples. I will only be gone for a moment."

She stepped back up to the counter of the dry goods store and spoke calmly to the gaping owner. "I need those four pairs of britches and these

154

shirts." She gave him a cold smile that did not go to her eyes, and the man felt a chill go through him. *I believe she is capable of attacking the sheriff. That smile almost cut me in two.*

He handed the clothing to Clare and she paid him quickly. She thanked him and turned towards the door. Pausing a moment, she turned back. "And shame on you as well. I believe you could have afforded to feed a starving little boy," she stated in a brittle voice. "You people are shameful." As the man started to argue, Clare leaned across the counter and snapped, "And don't bother to excuse yourself by saying his mother was a whore. I am guessing half the men in this town visited her at one time or another."

Clare spun around and stomped out of the store. "Come, children. We are going to take a bath."

Rabbit slid to a stop with a small bundle tied to a stick. He gave Clare a grin and nodded down the street. "I can show ya where to go."

When they arrived at the bath area, Clare put the girls in one of the tented rooms and the two boys in the other. "Now give me your clothes. I will make a bundle of the laundry, and you may put on your new clothes."

As the boys stripped down, Clare could hear them talking.

"Yur ma have manfriends?"

There was a moment of silence before Zeke answered, "No, Ma never let no fellows come around. After my pa died, lots of fellows wanted to, but Ma wouldn't walk out with any of them. She wouldn't go riding with them either. But when Uncle Rock invited her to go riding, she did and I got to go along. Now they are married and Uncle Rock is my pa.

"You have a ma?"

"She died but I have a pa down in Texas. That's why yur ma is lettin' me go with ya to Cheyenne. I don't know how far Texas is but I reckon I can find it."

Zeke didn't speak for a moment and then he commented softly, "Maybe you could come and live with us. I'd like to have a brother."

Clare couldn't hear the rest of their conversation over the splashing but her eyes filled with tears.

Nora looked up at her seriously. "Are you sad, Mama? Did that mean man make you sad?"

Clare shook her head as she kissed Nora's head. "No, I'm not sad. I just feel very blessed to have three wonderful children." She leaned closer as she whispered, "And I was proud of how you tried to help Rabbit today. Kicking adults is usually wrong but today I don't think it was." She smiled at both girls. "Now hurry and wash. I need to take a bath when you are done."

When she had scrubbed both girls and washed their hair, she called to the boys. "That's long enough. Get out and dry off. You wait outside the tent until I come out…and do not get off of that bench until I say."

CHAPTER 27

An Extra Child

SOON FOUR LITTLE VOICES COULD BE HEARD OUTSIDE and Clare sank into the water. It wasn't as warm as she would have liked but she could feel the grime melting off her.

The laundress poked her head in. "Need more hot water?"

Clare nodded, "Please. We came down from Stevensville and it has been a long seven days."

The woman was back quickly with two buckets of hot water. "Want me to wash those dirty clothes? I can have 'em ready for you by 7:00 tomorrow mornin'. The next train won't be through till 'round 9:00 a.m. so there's time. Still, I'd be at the station by 8:30 to play it safe."

Clare smiled at her. "That would be wonderful. We are meeting my husband here. We will all leave tomorrow." She sank back in the tub. *Just a few minutes. If I can soak just a few minutes.* She shook her head and hurried to bathe.

A man's voice came to her through the tent and she sat up with a smile. *Rock is here!*

She grabbed the towel the woman had left and dried off quickly. She could hear the children laughing as Rock counted.

"One. Two. Three. Four. The last time counted, I only had three kids. Let me do this again. One. Two. Three. Four. Now I know I didn't count wrong twice. Who is this fine-looking young man?"

A chorus of voices shouted, "That is Rabbit. He is coming with us to Cheyenne!"

"Oh he is? Well, I reckon that is all right. Where is your mother?"

"She's taking a bath and she said to stay right here."

Rock's voice sounded ornery as Clare hurried to dress.

"Maybe I should go check on her."

Clare's voice was clear as she called. "You stay where you are, Rock Beckler. I will be out in a moment."

Rock grinned and stood up. As he took a step toward the tent, Nora shook her head.

"I don't think you should go in there. Mama got really mad at a man today, and I think she is still kind of mad."

Rock dropped back down in front of the kids and studied their faces. "And what was Mama so mad about?"

Annie looked at her father seriously. "A mean man was hurting Rabbit, so we kicked him. Then Mama came and she yelled at the mean man too." She leaned forward and whispered loudly, "And we didn't even get in trouble for kicking him!"

Clare pulled the tent flap back and stepped out with a bright smile on her face. Rock grabbed her and gave her a big kiss. "Hello, Beautiful." He smiled down at her as he smacked his lips. "Been terrorizing the men of Blackfoot, have you?"

Clare blushed as she rolled her eyes. She stepped back. "I promised these hungry kids some supper. Do you want to come with us or take a bath first?"

Rock grinned and nodded toward the tent. "I reckon I'll take a bath first. By the time you get all these kids wrangled into their seats, I just might be done anyway."

He looked over at Zeke and winked. "I hear they are running low on ice cream. Your mother should probably order that first."

The kids were screaming in excitement and Rock sauntered toward the tent. "I'll see you in just a little bit."

"Leave your dirty clothes by the tub and ask that nice woman to put them with ours," Clare called after Rock. She looked at Rabbit's raggedy clothes and she felt anger rise up in her again.

"Rabbit, would it be all right if I throw these away? We will keep your coat, but I don't think I can mend the rest of them."

Rabbit touched the new clothes he had on and slowly nodded. "I reckon that will be alright. I only need one set of clothes." He grinned up at Clare. "I can show ya where the eatin' house is. I sneak in there all the time."

Clare called to Rock, "I am going to set the boys' clothes outside your tent. Make sure the laundress gets them too."

Clare could hear the smile in Rock's voice when he answered, "Why don't you just come in and add them to the pile yourself?" She blushed as she muttered under her breath and backed away. She could hear Rock laughing as she gathered the children. "That ornery man!" she whispered to herself as she gathered the children.

"We'll follow you, Rabbit. Now let's get these hungry kids some supper."

Supper was lively. Rock joined them just as the ice cream arrived, and he ate with them.

CHAPTER 28

RABBIT'S LETTER

THREE LITTLE HEADS WERE DROOPING BY THE TIME the meal was over. Rabbit didn't seem to be tired at all though.

Rock and Clare laid the three sleeping children down on the floor of their room on blankets and slipped out. Rock led them outside to a small bench under a large tree. He pulled Clare onto his lap and then grinned at Rabbit.

"Tell me a little about yourself, Rabbit. Did you get that name because no one can catch you?"

Rabbit grinned and nodded. "I'm purty quick." His face clouded a little as he continued. "My ma told me my name was Roland. She said she named me that after my pa but she always called me Rollie." His eyes slid over to Clare as he added softly, "Ma cried a lot. She cried real hard when the letter from my pa came. I asked her if it was 'cause he didn't want me but she said that wasn't true. She said he loved me a lot, an' he wanted me to come to live with him."

He studied the faces of the two adults. "Kids ain't liked much at Big Nell's. Some a those ladies yell all the time. Ma was usually nice unless she drank. She drank a lot more after Pa's letter came. I think it was 'cause he wanted me to come to Texas an' that made her sad."

Clare's heart hurt for the little boy. "Would you like me to read your letter to you, Rabbit?"

The little boy hesitated and then slowly nodded. "I ain't let no one read it. It's like my own special secret, but maybe ya can tell me the name of my pa. That might make it easier to find 'im."

Rabbit pulled out a tattered and worn envelope. It had two letters in it in different handwriting.

Clare looked at the little boy in surprise.

He shrugged. "One is from my pa to Ma but I'm not sure about the other one. Ma threw that one away too. If she wrote it, she never sent it. If it come from someone else, I don't know who it would be. I saved it just in case it was from Ma so I can give it to Pa when I see 'im."

Clare smiled at Rabbit and scanned the letter quickly. Her lips stopped moving as she stared at the wrinkled paper.

Rock watched his wife closely and then took the letter. "Clare, you never have been able to read at night. See all that squinting is making your eyes water. Let me read that letter."

The planes of his face grew hard as he scanned the letter. "I can't make out all that it says, but it looks like your pa has two other sons. He'd be powerful proud to have you come and live with him." Rabbit smiled happily and then Rock scanned the second one. He frowned and folded the letter up. When he looked at Rabbit he was smiling.

"Yep, that second one was from your ma to your pa. She must have loved him a lot to say all the things she said." He tousled Rabbit's hair and held up the letters. "How about you let Clare hang onto these? She has a bag where she puts all of our important papers, and Clare never loses anything. Then you won't have to keep track of them."

Rabbit smiled happily. "I reckon that would be all right." He smiled up at Clare. "Thanks, Miss Clare. I think yur just a real nice lady."

Clare tried to smile but her laugh was more of a sob. She leaned down and hugged Rabbit tightly. "I think you are a special boy, Rabbit, and I am pleased you will be riding with us to Cheyenne. Now let's get you up to the room." She turned to Rock. "Rock, why don't you go get Rabbit's train ticket. I told him we bought so many tickets that he would be able to ride for free if I said he was my son."

Rock looked startled and then he laughed. "Yep, volume discounts. Sure am glad the railroad offers those. I will do that and then I'll be up." He tousled Rabbit's hair again. "You're a fine young man, Rabbit."

Rabbit looked up at the two smiling adults. "I reckon ya can call me Rollie. I don't s'pose my ma would mind none."

Clare was still awake when Rock returned. He could see in the dimly lit room that her face was streaked from crying.

"That poor little boy," she whispered as Rock held her. "And that terrible, hateful man. He doesn't deserve to have a child as sweet as Rollie." She looked up at Rock as tears leaked from her blue eyes. "Let's take him home with us," she begged. "We will love him as our own."

Rock kissed his wife gently. "We will if he doesn't have any other relatives. The letter from his pop mentioned two sons. Maybe Badger will have an idea of who to talk to when we arrive in Cheyenne. He seems to know people everywhere." Rock pulled his wife tighter and smiled down at her. "You have a tender heart and a fierce soul, Clare Beckler. Any child would be lucky to have you as a mother."

Cheyenne, Wyoming Territory
Tuesday, July 22, 1879

CHAPTER 29

A Hint of What's to Come

"ARE YOU READY TO DO A LITTLE VISITING, MERINA?
Lance invited us down for supper tonight. He said all the hands could come too." Gabe frowned a moment and then grinned as he added, "Of course, he doesn't know I just hired three more. I guess we will see if any of the boys want to go along. Let's plan to leave here around 5:00."

Gabe picked up his new wife and swung her around. "I sure am glad you finally agreed to marry me. I just don't know when I have been happier."

Merina wrapped her arms around Gabe's neck as her dark eyes danced. "I think perhaps you are happy because you have someone to cook for you." She cocked her head as she laughed up at him and added, "But Cookie will be here tonight so now maybe I won't."

Gabe looked down in surprise. "Cookie is back? I didn't know that. Now how in tarnation did you find that out?"

"Molly told me yesterday. He didn't sell his wagon or his mules. I'm not sure what his plan is but he was in Cheyenne yesterday. He said he would be out today sometime."

"Well good deal. I'll tell Rusty today. Old Cookie was pretty attached to Larry by the time we made it up here. I'm guessing he would like to see the babies."

"They will be coming with us to the Rankins, won't they? Maybe you should invite Cookie so he can get acquainted too."

Gabe nodded his head. "I think I will have Nate ride over this afternoon and make sure Molly knows how many riders we have. I don't want to run them short on food for their own cowboys."

Gabe turned around as he heard little feet hitting the floor and padding toward the kitchen. He squatted on the floor with a smile and held open his arms.

Emilia rolled into him and smiled when he lifted her up. "Good morning, Papa. We are going to Livvy's house? Can I go now? I can get dressed really fast."

Gabe kissed her before he set her in her chair. "Not now but we will go over there for supper. Now you help Nina. Get all of your work done so you are ready on time."

Nate wandered in followed by the rest of the crew. Merina quickly served the food and then Gabe turned to Nate.

"I want you to ride over to Sam's. Make sure Molly knows how many hands we have now. With the three new riders, we will be bringing ten. Eleven if Cookie comes. I haven't seen Miguel since the wedding so who knows about him."

Gabe looked hard at his brother and added, "And you be back here in two hours. You don't need to be sneaking off with Sam to fish so early in the morning."

Nate grinned and shoveled his food in. His horse was saddled and he was gone before the rest of the crew finished breakfast.

Tobe pointed at the cloud of dust and laughed. "Looks like Nate made him a friend. Just be glad it ain't some little gal who has him so excited."

Gabe stared at the tall cowboy for a moment and then shook his head. "I'm sure that day is coming. So far though, all Sam Rankin and Nate are interested in is fishing, roping, and riding. And going on a trail drive." He laughed with the rest of the men as they moved outside to start their day.

Merina hurried to clean up and was outside about twenty minutes after the men. Gabe had Mascota saddled and he grinned at her.

"I thought you might want to help today. I sure am glad that I married a woman who likes to ride!"

The Rocking R ranch yard was full of horses and rigs when Gabe's crew arrived a little before 5:00 p.m. Gabe looked around in surprise. "I didn't know they were having a party tonight."

Merina laughed. "I guessed they were when Nate told me to make sopapillas. I am going to take these inside."

Lance strolled over with a grin. "So, are you ready to lead a drive up into the Montana Territory? I hear you're the best trail boss around."

Gabe stared at him for a moment and then slowly shook his head. "Not planning on any more drives. I'm comfortable with my little ranch. Besides, I like my wife."

Lance laughed as he walked away and Gabe stared after him with a frown on his face. "Now what was that all about?"

Tobe watched the exchange between the two men and then nudged Gabe. "Well, the good news is that your two old girlfriends are ready to go whenever you are—if you decide to make a drive."

Gabe frowned. "I'm done crossing boggy rivers. I promised myself that our drive to Ogallala would be my last, and I don't intend to change my mind."

The women carried the food out and placed it on boards that had been laid on top of barrels. Everyone mingled and the new hands were introduced. Gabe's newest riders even recognized several hands who rode for Rowdy and Lance.

Rowdy commented, "You Texas boys sure put on a lot of miles... and there are lots of you."

Gabe laughed. "There wasn't much for work in Texas after the war, so lots of fellows who followed herds kept right on going north. Those boys tend to run into each other over the years." He added quietly, "It's always good to see a face from home though."

Rowdy nodded. "Think you'll take any more herds north? I hear a fellow from up in the Montana Territory is looking for a trail boss."

Gabe's face showed his surprise. "He's coming here for cattle? Don't they usually bring their livestock in from the east or west?"

"Purebred Angus. Hard to find just yet since they are a newer breed. There's a fellow up north of me who has some for sale, and that Montana rancher is coming down to look at them. I'm guessing he will buy. When he does, he'll have to trail them home. No rails go that far north yet."

Gabe studied Rowdy's face but before the man could say anything else, some cowboys called his name. Rowdy waved and followed them toward the house.

Merina was carrying her sopapillas on a tray when Gabe caught her. "The women talking any about a trail drive? Rowdy and Lance have both mentioned one."

She looked up in surprise as she shook her head. "No one has said anything to me."

Just then, Badger drove a spanking new buggy into the yard. As everyone gathered around to look at it, he jumped down with a big smile. He winked at Gabe.

"Hello there, boy. How's things at the ranch?" He looked around as he spoke. "Where's my mule?" Just then, Mule came racing up, scattering men as he charged through the crowd. He nuzzled Badger and rubbed his head on Martha. Merina dropped her arm over his neck and Mule leaned against her as he wobbled his lips.

Badger laughed wickedly. "Shore now, Mule likes yur feisty little wife, an' he don't like jist any folks.

"So you'ins ready ta trail a herd a black cows up north? Feller up there is lookin' ta put riders together, an' I give 'im yur name. Said you'ins was the best." When Gabe frowned, Badger added, "Yur cook done signed on yesterday." He slapped Gabe on the back and sauntered over to help Martha down.

He tossed the lines to Paul. "Put them thar mules in yur barn, Paul. An' dig out that hard candy. Give it out ta the little ones."

CHAPTER 30

No More Rivers

MERINA WATCHED BADGER GO AND THEN TURNED TO Gabe. Her face showed her surprise. "You are taking a herd to Montana?"

Gabe shook his head and frowned. "This is the first I've heard of anything. It looks like some plans are already in the works but they don't involve me. I'm happily married now." He grinned as he pulled Merina closer to him and the two walked toward the house. "Have anything heavy you need carried? Or anything I should taste?"

The meal was relaxed and the men broke into groups. Gabe wandered over to where Lance and Rowdy were standing by the corral. Both had finished eating. Each had a leg up on the bottom board with their elbows leaning over the top rail.

Gabe grinned at them. "You fellows almost look the same from the back."

Rowdy laughed, "Yep, that's what Lance's Indian brother calls me. 'Same.'"

"So about this drive. Both of you mentioned it, but tonight is the first I have heard of it. What makes you think I would be part of it?"

The two men turned to face Gabe, and Lance was serious as he answered. "Fellow by the name of Rock Beckler will be in Cheyenne by tomorrow night. Badger is going to invite you over to meet him.

"Beckler is going to buy a herd of black cows and trail them back up to the Bitter Root Valley in the Montana Territory. He plans to follow the Road to Montana."

When Gabe looked at the men in confusion, Lance added, "That's what most of us around here call the old Bozeman Trail.

"Beckler's lived and worked all over that area. Of course now with all the reservations, it is going to be a little touchy to pass through their lands. Tall Eagle said he would go if you were trail boss." Lance laughed and added, "I think he has family in most of the Indian tribes in the Montana Territory. He'd for sure be an asset."

Lance elbowed Gabe. "Talk to Badger. He's known this fellow for some time. In fact, Beckler is ranching on Badger's brother's place. They worked out some kind of deal before old Darby died.

"Beckler sounds like a nice fellow. Real cowman. His wife and kids are coming down here with him."

Gabe stared from one brother to the other and slowly shook his head. "I'm not familiar with that land at all, and I have crossed all the rivers I want to cross. No more quicksand and mud for me." He looked out over the corral and then back at the two men.

"What would that be, a two-month drive? When do you start getting snow up here? Kind of late to start, isn't it?"

Lance shrugged. "You could get snow. You are more likely to run into it on the way home if you move too slow. It shouldn't take you longer than two and a half to three months to get up there plus another two or three weeks to get back home. You sure won't want to mess around either way though."

Gabe frowned. "What about fall roundup? If I'm gone, I'll leave my men short-handed. Tobe and his boys would probably go with me, and Nate will want to go. That won't leave many to help. Angel and Rusty are top hands, and Merina will want to help but that's not enough." His frown turned to a scowl as he added, "And I don't count on Miguel for anything."

Lance laughed. "Shoot, we have been covering for Badger for years! One more year won't matter that much. Sam is chomping at the bit to go on a trail drive, and I'd sure rather he go with you than some greenhorn."

He added seriously, "Wait until Thursday to make up your mind. You will have a chance to meet the owner then. He wants to pull out as soon as he can though, so I look for him to be gone by Saturday."

Gabe stared at Lance for a moment and then his eyes moved across the yard to where Merina was talking with Molly. "I'm not excited to leave Merina alone, and I sure don't want her to come with me...which is exactly what she will want to do," he commented softly. "I had better talk this over with her before I meet with anyone."

Rowdy listened quietly and then commented. "Spur should be home tomorrow. I will send him along if you decide to take the job. Either way, he will be headed back up that way to deliver some horses to the military at Fort Ellis. That is just little ways east of Bozeman. He can travel that far with you since that is the route you will follow. Coming home, he can cut through the south end of the Bitter Root Valley. Spur is familiar with that area up there, so he would be handy to have along."

Lance nodded and added, "You can make Sam wrangler since he will be low man on the totem pole. Whatever you decide, Spur will give you another hand on the drive. That way, there will be two of them on the horses. Nate might even want to take Spur's place so he can ride with Sam."

Gabe stared at the two brothers and shook his head. "It looks like lots of folks have done all sorts of planning on this deal. Funny thing to make all these plans for me and not talk to me first."

Lance laughed and slapped Gabe's back. "You have been kind of busy. First, you got yourself gored by a bull and almost died. Then you had to win your girl back. Finally, when you got all that done, you went and got married.

"We decided to just wait and talk to you tonight. This way you have two days to think on it before you meet with Beckler on Thursday.

"Badger has been the go-between on this deal. You will meet with Beckler at Badger's Thursday night for supper."

Gabe stared from one to the other and then scowled. "We'll see." Just then, Merina waved at Gabe from across the yard and he walked over to her.

She started to speak and then looked closely at his face. "You are angry?"

Gabe shook his head, "No, more like confused. Apparently, this cattle drive has been planned for some time. I was recommended by Badger as trail boss, but no one told me anything until tonight. And they will probably want to leave on Saturday!"

Merina stared at him and then started to speak. Gabe shook his head, "And no, you cannot come along. It will be nearly a three-month drive, maybe even longer. Besides, we could be caught in snow. I don't want to take a chance with either you or Emilia." He waited for Merina to argue, but she was quiet as she watched him.

"If I do this, I need for you and Angel to be here to help Rusty with roundup. I will take Tobe, Bart, and Rufe with me." He cursed softly. "I will certainly miss having Angel and Rusty along although Lance said Tall Eagle will go with us if I am trail boss.

"Cookie already signed on and since he just got back, he knows the trail." He paused and added softly, "And I hate to leave you."

Merina put her hand on Gabe's arm. "Let's go home. It is late enough and Emilia will be tired. Since we must go to Cheyenne on Thursday, we need to make this an early evening." She smiled at him. "Besides, we can talk on the way home, and I will be able to see your face."

Gabe nodded. "That's a good idea. I'll get the horses and you find Emilia."

Badger caught them as they were leaving. "Now you'ins come on in fer supper on Thursday. The Becklers 'ill be there an' ol' Rock 'ill have lots a questions. My Martha 'ill have food ready by 5:30 if'n that works fer you'ins."

CHAPTER 31

MAKING NEW FRIENDS

MERINA PLANNED AND PREPARED THE NEXT TWO DAYS for Gabe to be gone. He claimed he hadn't made up his mind, but she was sure he would go. Nate and Sam were excitedly making plans. Tobe, Rufe, and Bart were willing to go as well. Merina frowned as she thought about her conversation with Angel.

"I think I should go with him, Merina. There are too many aspectos—maybe factors—that are new to him. My compadre needs men around him who know him and know drives." He studied his sister's face. "I think I will go along. I will make sure my new brother comes home safely."

Merina hugged her brother. Her eyes were watery when she looked at him but she was smiling. "Sí, you go with him. Take Miguel too. Bring my husband back to me. And ride with us to Cheyenne. You can be there for the planning as well."

Gabe was surprised when Angel was waiting with horses for the three of them. "You are riding to Cheyenne on a Thursday? Have a new gal in town?"

Angel grinned at his friend. "I think I will go with my old boss on this drive. I think perhaps he needs a vaquero as skilled as I am with a rope to make sure the vacas cross all those rivers safely."

Gabe scowled. He looked over at Merina. Her eyes were sparkling and she was trying not to smile.

"It looks like the two of you have discussed this already, so I am not even going to try to argue with you." He gripped Angel's shoulder. "It will be good to have you with me, my friend," he said softly as he smiled at both of them. "And maybe you can convince that brother of yours to stay home while we are gone. Rusty is going to need some help to keep things together here." He grabbed Emilia as she ran out of the house and swung her up in front of him.

"Well, let's get on up to Cheyenne. Emilia has been talking about going to see Grandma Martha and Pappy Badger all day." He grinned down at the little girl as she launched into a story about all the fun she was going to have.

Merina smiled at her. "You are going to make some new friends today, Emilia. Grandma Martha invited a family from the Montana Territory for supper. They have two little girls and a little boy close to your age."

Emilia's eyes became large. "Can we take Livvy too? She would like to make some new friends."

Gabe laughed and shook his head. "Not tonight, Emilia. But I am guessing Livvy will get to meet them before the week is over. Now you hang on and let's see if Buck can beat Mascota today!"

Merina was already spurring Mascota before Gabe finished talking. Buck gave it his best and was slowly gaining on the younger horse when Merina slowed Mascota down.

Gabe laughed as he pulled up beside her. "You didn't want to get beat, did you? You quit when old Buck was just getting started!"

Merina's eyes were sparkling and she laughed as they walked their horses. "I believe I was in front. That makes me the winner."

Gabe started to answer and then just shook his head. "Your sister is a cheater, Emilia. I sure hope you play fairer when you race Hawk against me."

Emilia was quiet a moment and then she shook her head. "I think Hawk's legs are shorter than Buck's. I think I would give Hawk a head start and we would not slow down." Gabe was laughing when Angel caught up with them.

Angel smiled as he looked from Gabe to his sister. "My friend, when will you learn that Merina always makes sure she has an edge. She leaves nada al azar—nothing to chance as you say."

They arrived at Badger and Martha's home around 5:00. Four children were playing in the yard and Emilia raced out to join them. She was soon swinging with one of the little girls while the second little girl dug in the dirt with two boys of about the same age.

Spur rode up just as they arrived and he grinned at Gabe. "So you are trailing a herd of black cows north, are you? Think I'll tag along to make sure you get there."

Gabe snorted. "You are going to make sure I get there, and Angel here is going to make sure I make it home. I guess I won't have to worry about anything." All three men laughed as they strolled up to the house.

A tall man was standing outside. A shorter man with black hair was talking to him. Sam Rankin and Nate were talking to a young man just a little younger than them.

Spur walked up to the tall man with his hand extended. "Rock, good to see you. Let me introduce you to your new trail boss." He grinned over his shoulder at Gabe.

Gabe put out his hand as he stepped forward. "Gabe Hawkins. This is my wife, Merina, and her brother, Angel."

Rock's eyes were friendly as he nodded at Merina. He reached for Gabe's hand. "So you have decided to trail with me? Tall Eagle and Badger have both told me you were the best. In fact, Tall Eagle said he would ride as a hand if you were trail boss. Otherwise, he won't go."

Gabe grinned and waved as Tall Eagle rode up. "Tall Eagle is a fine rider, but he's a little choosy who he associates with." He bumped Angel and added, "He likes Angel here though. Between those two, we lost very few cattle to boggy rivers." His eyes were serious as he studied Rock's face. "So how are the rivers in your country? I have been looking at maps, and it appears that we will be crossing a fair number of them."

Rock looked at Gabe in surprise and shrugged his shoulders. "Never worried much about rivers. I am more concerned about crossing the reservations we have to go through."

Gabe frowned as the conversation moved in the direction of Indians and reservations.

Tall Eagle had joined them quietly and he commented, "I think we should take extra beef as we have done in the past. I know some of the chiefs whose land we will pass through. The older chiefs just want to feed their people and be left alone. However, many of the young braves are angry about being sent to the reservations. Some may want to cause trouble.."

Gabe listened awhile and then spoke up again. "Tell me more about these water crossings. I have had my fill of quicksand and boggy rivers."

Angel's dark eyes were laughing as he looked at Gabe. "But, señor, in the north country, their rivers, they are lined with rock. The vacas just go skipping across them with no trouble."

Gabe stared at Angel in surprise and then looked toward Rock. The big man shrugged again and nodded. "Most of our rivers have rock or gravel on the bottom. They are only deep in the spring with the winter melt. The rivers should give us little trouble."

A smile began to build on Gabe's face and his friends laughed.

"Well, I guess that seals the deal. Ol' Gabe will fight Indians and outlaws, but he is done crossing boggy rivers!" Spur elbowed Gabe as the men laughed.

CHAPTER 32

ANOTHER HAWKINS

A TALL, SLENDER WOMAN WITH A WEALTH OF REDDISH-brown hair tied at the back of her neck came to the doorway. She called to the children and five little ones raced up.

Spur grinned as one of the little boys turned and ran towards him. His dark hair was curly and his eyes were a deep blue. His grin was large when he saw Spur.

"Howdy, Spur. Did ya find some Texans for me to talk to about my pa?"

Spur nodded seriously and pointed to Gabe. "This is the fellow I was telling you about, Rabbit. Why I believe he knows nearly every rider in Texas as old as he is." He looked around at Gabe expecting a smile, but the man was staring at Rabbit with a strange look on his face.

Gabe dropped down on one knee in front of the young boy and put his hands on Rabbit's shoulders. "Who are you looking for, Rabbit?"

Rabbit's eyes were intense as he studied the kneeling cowboy in front of him. "I'm lookin' for my pa an' my two brothers. My ma died up north in Blackfoot, an' Miss Clare said I could ride down here to Cheyenne with her family. She said she'd try to help me find 'em." He looked over at Spur as he added, "And Spur said ya might be able to help too."

Gabe was quiet as he listened. "Do you know your pa's name, Rabbit? Or your brothers' names?"

Rabbit nodded excitedly. "My pa's name was Roland an' that's why my ma called me Rollie. I don't know my brothers' names."

Gabe's face was pale as he rocked back on his feet. Merina sucked in her breath sharply as Gabe dug his wallet out of his vest pocket. He pulled out a picture of a small boy and showed it to Rollie. "Recognize that fellow?" he asked.

Rollie studied the picture and then looked hard at Gabe. "I reckon that's me. My ma had a picture feller take that when he come through. She told me she traded 'im for it. But after he give it to her, it disappeared." He cocked his head and studied Gabe. "How'd you come to get 'hold of my picture?"

Gabe's face was still pale but he was smiling at the young boy. "Well, Rollie, it appears you have found your brothers. My name is Gabe and that's Nate over there." He whistled and then waved at the group of young men. Nate looked up and walked toward them when he saw Gabe's signal. He joined the men with a smile on his face. Gabe pointed at the little boy.

"Meet our little brother, Nate. This is Rollie."

Nate's face registered the confusion he felt as he stared from Rollie to Gabe. "We have a brother?" When Gabe nodded, Nate's face turned red. Rollie was looking from brother to brother.

Clare covered her mouth. "Oh, my heart," she whispered as she watched the exchange.

Rollie cocked his head and studied the two brothers. "So yur pa's name is Roland too? He live 'round here?"

Gabe's face drew down even as he tried to smile. Merina leaned down and wrapped her arms around Rollie. "My name is Merina, Rollie. I am married to Gabe and we would love for you to come and live with us." She whispered, "Your pa passed away some time ago, but he gave that picture to Gabe. We were hoping to find you someday, but we had no idea where you were."

Rollie's little face was slowly relaxing and he finally smiled. "You want me to come an' live with ya?" he asked Gabe.

Gabe picked Rollie up and hugged him hard before he set him back down. "We sure do. I have been carrying that picture in my wallet for two years just hoping to see someone who knew you. I didn't tell Nate because I wasn't sure we would ever find you. We are happy we did and we sure hope you will live with us."

Rollie looked back at Clare and frowned. "'Course that means I cain't live with Miss Clare an' her kids."

Clare's eyes were red as she smiled at him. "You have a family, Rollie, and that's what you wanted. Two wonderful big brothers. Merina will be your mother and her brothers will be your uncles. You will even have a little sister."

Emilia rushed up and grabbed Rollie's hand. "You are going to live at our house? Now we can play every day!"

Rollie looked from Emilia to Clare and then at his two brothers. "Will you tell me 'bout my pa? I ain't never had a pa an' I sure wanted to have one."

Gabe's face grew pale again but Merina smiled. "We will tell you all about your pa and all the wonderful things he did."

Rollie's smile became larger. "You knew my pa too?"

Merina hugged him quickly. "I have wonderful stories to tell you. Why there are so many, it will take me a very long time."

Rollie's smile was huge as he looked at Gabe. "I reckon I want to live with ya." He looked back at Clare and stuttered a little as he added, "But can I stay with Miss Clare tonight? I won't see her for some time after she leaves an'...." His voice trailed off as he looked at Clare.

Badger and Martha were listening. Martha stepped up. "I tell you what. We will all go out to the Hawkins' ranch tomorrow. Some of the men are going to look at cattle and the rest of us will just have ourselves a party. Molly can bring over all her kids and Beth too. You children will have so many friends to play with that you just won't know what to do."

Rollie nodded excitedly and then raced off to tell his friends his big news.

The men avoided looking at Gabe. They knew that Rollie was a surprise to him. That meant Gabe's pa had roamed where he shouldn't have.

Spur squeezed Gabe's shoulder and muttered, "Yore pa was just no good, but he sure made some fine boys." Gabe looked at his friend in surprise and Spur grinned. "Can't none of us pick our families. We can pick our friends but families we're stuck with." He grinned at Gabe as he added, "Sure am glad ya picked me to be yore friend."

Gabe laughed dryly and he rubbed his hand over his face. He walked over to where Clare stood. "Mrs. Beckler? I want to thank you for taking Rollie in and bringing him down here. I'd like to talk to you more about him. Now or maybe later if you don't mind."

Clare pulled Gabe's face down to hers and kissed him quickly on the cheek. As he looked at her in surprise, she whispered, "That is for being a wonderful big brother."

She had tears in her eyes as she handed Gabe a battered envelope. "These letters belong to Rollie. He doesn't know what they say. He can't read and we led him to believe that his father wanted him." Her eyes were sparkling with tears as she looked toward Merina. "Your wife handled that just wonderfully.

"It is going to be so hard for me to let him go even though I have known him less than a week." She smiled at Gabe.

"I am so happy he found his family. That precious child was living on the street and I just couldn't bear it. Rock and I were going to keep him if we didn't find someone who knew who he was.

"And what were the chances? I never dreamed we would find his family, let alone right here in Cheyenne."

Gabe's face was drawn as he looked at Clare. He took a deep breath and shook his head. "Our pa never was worth much. Ma found that picture in the fireplace one night, and enough of a letter to know Pa had another son. The envelope was burned though, so she had no idea where it came from. She gave it to me before she died and asked me to find Rollie."

He stared out where the kids were playing and cursed under his breath.

"We assumed Pa did nothing to help provide for Rollie, but we didn't know where the little boy was or how to find him. I jumped Pa about Rollie before he died. He yelled at me and then he cried. He said the boy's mother was a whore. In his words, 'Who knows if that kid is even my boy?'

"He refused to talk about it again. He left and Ma died shortly thereafter. We never saw Pa again. Some riders from up by Dallas told me he died up there. He picked a fight with a gambler who was slick with his knife."

Gabe nodded toward Rollie and spoke softly. "When I saw him here today, I was shocked. Rollie looks just like Nate did when he was that age. I knew he was our little brother before I even heard his story." He smiled at Clare.

"So thank you for finding him and for taking him in. We would never have known where to look. We'll plan to keep him tomorrow when you come out with Badger." His smile became bigger as he added, "We'll even try to come up and visit so you can stay in touch."

Clare laughed and wiped her eyes. "That would be wonderful. I am going to get your address before we leave. I want to stay in touch with your wife. Now introduce me so I know whom I will be talking to when I write."

CHAPTER 33

PLOTTING AND PLANNING

THE EVENING WAS RELAXED. MERINA AND CLARE visited easily while Gabe was impressed with Rock. He liked the man's no-nonsense attitude.

The Becklers were staying in one of Badger's houses in Cheyenne. Martha invited Gabe, Merina, and Angel to spend the night. "That way, you can all get out of here quickly in the morning. I know that Rock wants to look those cattle over as soon as possible."

Gabe muttered, "I never did agree to do this."

Merina laughed. "But you never said no. I will make sure Tobe has his men ready. They will probably need to get some warmer clothing before you head out. How about Nate and you? You should both have a heavy coat of some kind."

Cookie poked his head in the door just then. "I heared there was a party here this evenin' an' thought I'd stop by. I'll be leavin' town fer the north country first thing Saturday mornin'." He paused and winked at Gabe. "Have somebody tell my boss, will ya? I been chargin' all kinda things to his account."

Gabe grabbed Cookie's hand and then pulled him in for a hug. "Good to have you back, you old sidewinder. No drive would be complete without you. You are on your own this time though. No cook's helper!"

Cookie chuckled and then looked around. "Where is my little Larry? I 'spect to see my grandbaby 'fore I take off."

"One of the twins had a cough so they decided to stay home. They should be over tomorrow though since it won't be as long of a ride." Merina smiled as she hugged the old man. "It's good to see you, Cookie."

Cookie grinned and then paused as he stared at her. "Did you say *twins*? Little Larry had *twins*?"

Gabe grinned as he nodded. "A boy and a girl. The boy even has red hair. I think old Rusty is going to have his hands full."

Tall Eagle listened quietly as the men talked. He slipped out the door when the meal was over and Angel followed him.

"You will go with us, yes?"

Tall Eagle nodded. "I will be there. Gabe will want to leave from Sturgis' ranch first thing on Saturday. I will meet you there. Tell him to bring some extra cattle as well. We will cross maybe five places where he will need to pay a toll."

"The extra cattle can be longhorns. I'm sure Mr. Beckler won't want to give up any of his black cows." He thought a moment and then added, "He could also do horses but cattle are cheaper."

"I am pleased you will be riding with us, my friend," Tall Eagle commented quietly as he shook Angel's hand. His eyes twinkled as he added, "Perhaps you will show these men how you dance with cattle."

"Sí, it is a delicate thing, señor. Only a few very special vaqueros can do it," Angel agreed seriously as his dark eyes gleamed. "And I am pleased you will be riding with us as well. I must bring Gabe home undamaged, or Merina will take her anger out on me." He added seriously, "My sister is a difficult woman. I am blessed that señor Gabe has taken her off my hands."

Tall Eagle was laughing as he walked away and Angel called after him, "Until Saturday, my friend."

The tall Indian made no reply. Angel chuckled to himself as he walked back into Badger's crowded home. His smile became larger when he saw Gabe with Emilia on one knee and Rollie on the other. Both children were smiling at whatever Gabe was telling him.

"My sister chose well. Gabe is a good man."

CHAPTER 34

NEW FRIENDS AND OLD ACQUAINTANCES

ROWDY APPEARED IN THE DOORWAY AND SCANNED the noisy room. He recognized the tall cowboy leaning against a doorway from the description Spur had given him. He crossed the room with a grin on his face and stretched out his hand.

"You must be Rock. I'm Rowdy, owner of the R4. Spur rides for me. I just wanted to make sure you were good with Spur trailing along with you. He is delivering some horses to one of the forts along your way, and it will give you one more man." His grin became wider as he added, "Of course, he will be working for me which means you won't need to pay him."

Rock shook Rowdy's hand as he laughed. "One more rider would be fine and even better if he works for nothing. I have a couple of young fellows I might have wrangle though. I hear he is a top hand."

The two men visited a while longer and then Stub strolled up. Rock introduced him and Rowdy studied the stocky rider. He frowned slightly and then put out his hand.

"I believe I owe you a thank you for helping take down Curly Joe Sturgis. Without you fellows, I might have lost all those horses." Rowdy's frown grew deeper and he shook his head. "Curly's pa is a darn nice fellow and honest to deal with. That boy was in trouble before they came west though, and he just never did learn to ride straight."

Stub was quiet as he listened to Rowdy and then nodded slowly. "I knew Curly from some years ago. He was wild and getting in more trouble all the time even then." Stub shrugged. "Maybe he could have been turned around. Who knows? He almost did once. He just couldn't resist easy money or being a big man."

He looked over at Rock. "You want me to meet you in the morning to look at cattle? If so, what time and where? I think I am going to take Tuff on out to Lance's ranch. Sam told us we could bunk with their hands."

Rock had listened quietly as Stub talked and he shook his head. "Naw, it won't take me long to look them over. Meet me at the Tin House around noon tomorrow and we'll line out the drive. I want to leave as early on Saturday as we can." He nodded his head at Tuff and grinned. "Besides, Tuff found a rifle he thinks he should have. You make sure he's outfitted and ready to go."

Stub chuckled. He nodded at Rowdy as he put out his hand. "It was nice to meet you, Rowdy." He moved across the room to where Tuff was talking to Sam and Nate. Tuff listened as Stub talked. He said something to the other two young men and the three of them followed Stub out of the house.

Rock studied Rowdy's face. "Think Curly Joe's shooting will affect my dealings with Sturgis? Stub never told me anything so this is the first I've heard of it."

Rowdy shook his head. "I don't think so. Gabe is the one who shot Curly, and he talked to William Sturgis that night. As a pa, Sturgis was pretty torn up about it. As a man though, he knew Curly was in the wrong." Rowdy added seriously, "Gabe is a good man and is known as one of the best trail bosses out there. He's as honest as the day is long and he knows his business. Take him with you tomorrow. You are going to need some extra cattle to use as barter for crossing the reservations. Gabe will know what to buy and how many you will need." He laughed as he nodded his head toward Gabe.

"His newest boys just brought up a herd from Nebraska. They even trailed the two old lead cows that led Gabe's herd all the way from Texas. Shoot, this drive will be a cakewalk. Experienced drovers, strong lead cows, *and* a trail to follow!"

Rock grinned. "I hope you're right. I am anxious to see those Angus cattle. We have a few in our country but not enough that anyone is willing to sell breeding stock yet. I sure like the way they cross with the Herefords. I want to phase out my longhorns and go with all Angus and Herefords. Some I'll cross and others I'll breed to my Angus bulls."

Rock leaned forward and his face showed excitement. "George Grant down in Kansas brought in the first Angus bulls. The newspaper up in Helena had an article about them back in '73. I studied that paper and then I wrote Grant a letter asking some questions. Grant wrote me back. He told me what he liked and how he brought them in. I wrote him again last year. I was hoping to maybe get some Angus cows from him.

"His niece wrote me back. She said Grant had passed away. Then she told me a fellow here in Cheyenne was creating a herd. By then, I had already brought some bulls of my own in from the coast. Cows are harder to come by though." He paused and nodded outside where Badger's voice could be heard.

"Badger helped me to set this deal up. I live on the place his brother Darby settled. I met Badger after Darby died." Rock grinned and added, "Him and Mule."

Both men laughed. Rowdy nodded his head.

"He's a heck of a man. Martha and Badger are the heart and soul of our little community. They have both done a lot, not only for us, but for other folks as well." Rowdy chuckled as he added, "And Badger seems to know everyone.

"See that picture of a mule over there on the wall? He brought that back with him when he went up to visit his brother six or seven years ago. That's probably when he met you. Some priest up there painted it for him."

Rock stared at the picture and laughed. "I bet I know that priest. He paints, doctors, welds, carves wood…he can fix or heal just about anything. Father Ravalli. Badger mentioned that picture the day he left. A man would have to think a lot of a mule to have a picture done of him."

Rowdy agreed. He waved his arm around the room and commented, "I think you'll have a good drive. Gabe has a hard bunch of riders to trail north with you."

Rock was quiet as he listened. His eyes moved around the room as Rowdy talked about the different riders.

"Angel there is one of the best vaqueros I have ever met. He can snake a rope on a cow in the most impossible situations. Miguel too. Both of those men carry knives, and they know how to use them although Miguel prefers his guns.

"Gabe was going to leave them here to help with roundup but Merina insisted they both go." He chuckled as he added, "I think they are to make sure her new husband makes it back home."

Rock grinned and nodded.

"Tall Eagle and Angel are quite the team. Of course, Tall Eagle won't trail with just anyone. He is selective about what jobs he takes. He will be an asset too. He knows his horseflesh and he's savvy around cows."

Rowdy nodded across the room where Spur was talking to Lance.

"Spur is my best hand. I consider him my foreman even though I run him all over the country buying and delivering horses for me. They don't come much better than him.

"Nate there is Gabe's little brother. He's young but he's a worker. Sam Rankin and he are tight as ticks, and they are both growing into fine young men. Sam is Lance's son. He has never been on a drive, but

196

he grew up on a ranch. He lives and breathes cattle, and he cut his teeth roping.

"The three drovers Gabe just hired on are trail-hard and gun-tough. They were all on several drives with Gabe before he moved here. They came up from Texas with him on his last drive to Dodge, and then on north to Ogallala, Nebraska. They worked on a ranch there for a time and just showed up here on Sunday. They had trailed a herd up here for their boss and then drew their time. They would rather work for Gabe."

Rowdy grinned and slapped Rock on the back. "So tell your wife to relax. You are in good hands."

Rock nodded and smiled as Clare glanced his way. His heart caught for a moment. He turned back to Rowdy and shook his hand.

"I appreciate you letting me use Spur, and for giving me a rundown on all of the hands. I think I will collect my wife and take our wild kids back to where we are staying. Tomorrow is going to be a full day."

Rowdy laughed and Rock crossed the room with a smile on his face. He put his arm around Clare.

"Ready to call it a night? I want to get an early start tomorrow." He pulled her closer as he whispered. "Want to ride out with me and look those cattle over tomorrow morning? I remember the last time you did that."

Martha smiled as she watched them. "You kids just go on home and leave your little ones here. We'll let them play until they drop and then we'll put them to bed. You go on out and look those cattle over together." She smiled broadly at Gabe as she added, "Gabe can help me with baths since two of them belong to him."

Gabe laughed and nodded, "I reckon that's true. You want to watch all of them tomorrow? If you do, I'll take my bride with me as well."

Martha beamed at them and nodded. "That will be fine. In fact, why don't you just spend the night with Rock and Clare since they will have an extra bedroom now. That way the four of you will get some sleep. Now shoo, get out of here."

Gabe was surprised. He looked over at Merina and she frowned. "I don't think we should take advantage…"

Badger bounced up and looked from one couple to the other. "Now you'ins go on an' git on back ta the house. Don't no one want ta git twixt Martha an' her little ones." He squeezed Merina and winked at her.

"'Sides, newlyweds like you'ins need a little time together 'fore yur man takes off a gallivantin' 'round the country." He looked over at Rock as his grin became bigger. "An' you'ins too. Now git."

Both women blushed and the men began laughing.

Gabe grinned down at Merina. "Let's do that. The earlier we leave in the morning, the sooner we can be back. I have lots to do to get ready for this drive."

CHAPTER 35

A Busy Day

COOKIE HAD TAKEN THEIR HORSES TO THE LIVERY with him when he stopped, so the two couples walked the short distance to where Rock and Clare were staying. The men visited about the next day while Merina and Clare dropped back to walk together.

Clare looked over at Merina and smiled. "Badger said you and Gabe are newlyweds. When did you marry?"

"We were married on Saturday. I met Gabe on the drive from Texas, but he didn't court me until we were settled here. Angel is my brother. He joined Gabe's crew in Oklahoma and Miguel, our other brother, met them in Dodge City. There was nothing left for me in Texas, so Emilia and I met them in Dodge."

Her eyes were sparkling with humor as she added, "Gabe wasn't pleased at the prospect of another woman on the drive but he had no choice." Merina's chin jutted out a little as she stated, "Besides, I can ride and rope as well as my brothers."

Clare's eyes opened wide and then she laughed. "Well good for you. Sometimes these men just think they know so much." She giggled as she whispered, "Rock didn't like me much when we first met either."

Rock looked back with a grin and then shook his head. "We probably shouldn't let them spend too much time together, Gabe. It sounds like we both married women with a little wild girl in them."

Gabe grinned at Merina and laughed. "Wild girl? I reckon that's right."

The men slowed down and Rock looked from one woman to the other. "So what time do you want to get rolling in the morning? Gabe said the Tin House starts serving breakfast at 5:00. We could eat a quick bite and then head out from there. He said Sturgis' place is over an hour north and west of here. I'd like to be there before 8:00.

"Gabe and I can pick up the horses and then come back here for the two of you. That work?"

Both women agreed. As the men turned around, Merina whispered, "Let's be ready to leave at 5:00. We can save some time if they don't have to come back for us. Besides, Cheyenne mornings are beautiful. There is nothing like a morning ride." She smiled over at Clare. "Do you like to ride?"

Clare nodded happily. "I do." Her face clouded a little as she looked at Rock's profile. "I am so afraid for him to do this though." Her voice caught as she whispered, "I worry that something will happen and he won't come back."

Merina was quiet for a moment and then she nodded. "Sí, it is a dangerous thing to trail vacas, or cattle as you say. Gabe lost men on the trip to Dodge City in Kansas. Stampedes, rivers, and bandits are always a problem." She looked directly at Clare as she added softly, "But I think our Dios is in charge. I will pray for all of them to return safely.

"I would like to go with them but I must help with roundup. We will be shorthanded with so many riders gone. Besides, we have two little ones who must be watched."

She smiled at Clare and took her arm. "I am sure our men have taken many chances. Still, both are here today. We will pray that our Dios will let them continue in this life for a while longer."

200

Clare studied Merina's face and then she nodded as she faced forward. "Your faith is a wonderful thing, Merina. Mine is not as strong but I am working on that. We have a wonderful priest at the Mission, and he is teaching me to trust in God.

"I just don't know what I would do if something happened to Rock." Her breath caught and she whispered, "I grew up afraid of everything, and sometimes that fear just consumes me."

Merina's heart grew tight as she listened to Clare but she smiled. "Faith is not always so easy, but it lifts you up when you are afraid. Now come, let us talk of happier things.

"Martha is planning a party tomorrow so you can meet more people. Let me tell you about the rest of our friends."

CHAPTER 36

LET'S GET THIS SHOW ON THE ROAD

THE MEN WERE SURPRISED BUT PLEASED WHEN BOTH Clare and Merina were ready to leave with them. Breakfast was full of planning as the men talked about the trip ahead.

Merina finally looked at both of them and asked dryly, "And why did you ask us to come along? Certainly, it wasn't to include us in this planning."

Rock looked startled and Gabe grinned ruefully as he squeezed Merina's hand. "You're right. Slide over here and we'll go over this map with both of you."

Rock pointed at the map. "I haven't been on the southern part of this route through the Wyoming Territory for some time, but we have several riders with us who have ridden it recently. Both Tall Eagle and Spur are familiar with the entire trail. Once we get through the Big Horn Mountains, I will recognize the landmarks.

"I think our biggest problem on this drive will be navigating the reservations and roving bands of Indians. Most of them want to hunt off their reservations and then they run into other bands." He frowned and added, "There are always a few young men who want to pick a fight just for the fun of it.

"Outlaws could be a problem too."

Merina stared at the map quietly and then commented, "You will be crossing many rivers."

Gabe squeezed her hand as he laughed. "They don't worry about rivers up there, Merina. Most of them have rock on the bottom!"

Rock nodded absently and then tapped the map as he frowned. "We will cross through the Crow and the Northern Cheyenne reservations. I lived with the Crow for about four years when I was young. They have always been family to me.

"I killed one of their renegade braves last year though." He shook his head. "I'm not sure how they will accept me. I haven't seen my brothers since then." He pointed at another section on his map that read *Common Hunting Ground*.

"Some of the tribes consider this area their hunting ground. In fact, it was given to them in a treaty in '55. We will be passing through that as well. With all of the horses we'll be trailing, we'll have to keep our eyes open."

He pointed toward the center of the map. "We will be just south of the homeland of the Blackfeet and they may want a toll. Of course, they could have hunting parties out as well, and they don't like the Crow.

"Tall Eagle is our hole card. I have been told he's related to someone in nearly every tribe. He is Shoshone but has family everywhere." He tapped the map.

"Our first three hundred miles will be the easiest. We'll angle northwest across the Wyoming Territory. The trail will keep us east of the Big Horn Mountains. That's good because they are rugged."

Gabe pointed at a cluster of bluffs and asked, "What about Hole-in-the-Wall? Will those boys give us any trouble when we pass?"

Rock studied the map and then shrugged. "Depends on who is there. Some of those outlaws just want to rob banks while others like to rustle cattle. They are not just one gang of outlaws though. It is more like any outlaw who wants to hole up will try to get in there. They are selective though.

"Word is that no lawman has ever wormed his way in pretending to be an outlaw....or at least he didn't tell if he did.

"Stub used to run with some fellows who hung out there from time to time. He's straight as an arrow now, but he will know them if they try to cut the herd."

Gabe's face was hard as he muttered, "No one cuts my herds. Never have and I don't plan to start now."

Rock grinned and slapped Gabe on the back. "You and I are going to get along just fine."

A cowboy turned around to look at them and then walked toward their table with a grin on his face. His grin became wider when Merina looked up at him.

"Howdy, Miss Merina. Looks like you and the boss finally worked some things out."

Gabe looked up in surprise and then his face creased into a wide smile.

"Dink! What are you doing up here? It's good to see you!" Gabe stood as he grabbed Dink's hand. He turned to Rock.

"This is another of the fellows who trailed north with me. Dink Deaver—Clare and Rock Beckler." He turned back to Dink.

"I am trailing a herd north to the Montana Territory for them." He paused and looked closer at Dink. "You looking for a riding job?"

Dink's face turned pale and he shook his head. "I'm not trailing any more cattle. If you need a hand on your ranch though, I'd sure take a riding job."

"We do need a hand, Dink. Gabe is taking most of the riders with him, and we are going to need help during round-up." Merina smiled at him and then at Gabe as her dark eyes sparkled. "You don't get to take all of the good hands north, Gabe."

Gabe studied his wife's face and then laughed. "Well, that takes care of it. Meet us at the Tin House at noon and we can all ride out to the ranch." He added more seriously, "And Merina's right. We do need more help during roundup. Do you want to start right away?"

Dink nodded. He was smiling once again. He tipped his hat to Merina as he backed away. "I'll get me some warmer clothes and see you at noon."

Gabe's eyes followed Dink as he walked back to a table of riders. Several of them had their arms in slings and one favored his leg as he stretched it out in front of him. Gabe said nothing as he sat back down. *Looks like Dink had a hard drive. I guess I won't bring that up in front of the women.*

Neither woman commented and Rock grabbed the map they had been studying. He rolled it up and stood as he reached his hand out to Clare.

"Well, let's get this show on the road. I think we have studied this route as much as we can for now. We'd better get a move on if we are going to be back in Cheyenne by noon."

The two couples hurried toward the door. They were mounted and riding north out of Cheyenne by 6:00 a.m.

CHAPTER 37

OF CATTLE AND WOMEN

THE MORNING WAS COOL. BOTH MERINA AND CLARE wore jackets while Rock and Gabe just wore vests over their long-sleeved shirts. Gabe talked about the land and pointed out ranches as they rode.

Clare was quiet. Her horse was following a little behind Rock's as the two men talked. Merina finally slowed her horse and dropped back to ride beside the other woman.

"Do you worry about Gabe when he leaves like this?" Clare asked softly.

Merina thought a moment and then shrugged her shoulders. "We have only been married a week, so this is the first time he will leave me.

"I met Gabe shortly after Emilia and I arrived in Dodge City." She smiled a moment before she continued. "It is true that drives can be dangerous, but our men can be hurt every day. Gabe was gored by a bull shortly after we settled here. I was afraid then he would die.

"Life can be mucho…very difficult but our Dios is always beside us." She smiled at Clare as she added, "I think no one of us will leave this world alive. It is the moments that make us happy."

Clare stared at her and then gave her a small smile. "I admire you, Merina. I struggle with worrying. I was just getting used to being alone when Rock and I married.

"When my first husband died, I was terrified about providing for Zeke. I managed though.

"Then Rock came along. We had known each other for seven years. In fact, I was his wife's best friend. She died when Annie was born. Annie and Zeke are nearly the same age." She looked away and added softly, "I think I have loved Rock most of my life. Maybe that is why I am afraid. I am happier now than I have ever been. Maybe I am too happy."

Merina looked at Clare in surprise and then shook her head. She touched her arm. "Happiness is a wonderful thing. One can never be too happy. We will pray that our Dios brings our men home to us." Her dark eyes sparkled as she added, "And that the little one inside you will be a happy child."

Clare's hand touched her stomach as she looked at the young woman beside her in surprise. She pulled her jacket tighter as she murmured, "I didn't think it was that noticeable."

Merina laughed as she shook her head. "Not to men but to a woman who knows, yes. You protect the little one inside you with your hands." She smiled and touched Clare's hand. "I think you have much love for your family."

Tears sparkled in the corners of Clare's eyes. "I wish we were closer, Merina. I believe you would be a wonderful friend."

Merina laughed. "I think señor Rock needs to give Stub more time off so he can find a wife. Then you will have another young woman to talk to."

Gabe and Rock turned around at the sound of hoofbeats behind them. They slowed their horses and Gabe grinned.

"Well, look who decided to join us.

"Spur. Stub. I wondered if you boys would show up this morning."

Spur looked at the two couples and drawled, "Well, durn. We saw two purty gals out for a ride and thought we'd join them. Shoot, if we'd known their men were along, we'd have stayed back in Cheyenne and taken the morning off." His dark eyes were twinkling and Gabe laughed.

"Spur, I don't know that any women are safe around you. It's probably a good thing Rowdy keeps you in the saddle as much as he does."

They crested the hill and looked down at the valley below them. The Laramie mountains were in the distance and black cattle covered the valley floor. They pulled up their horses and Rock whistled.

"Now isn't that about the prettiest thing you ever did see?"

Spur grinned and looked over at the two women. "Second prettiest, I'd say. You fellows had better shy away from calling cows prettier than your wives."

Rock looked startled and Gabe laughed. "I'll agree with you on that, Spur. Let's get down there and talk to Sturgis. We have a lot of ends to tie up before tomorrow morning."

CHAPTER 38

BLACK COWS

WILLIAM STURGIS WAS RIDING THROUGH HIS CATTLE. He stopped to wait for them. He reached to shake hands with the men and then waved toward the herd of black cattle in front of him.

"Well, Rock, those are your cattle. A few heifers but mostly young cows. I do have a couple of bulls if you want to look at them. Fifteen hundred head. I figured we'd go ahead and move them up here, so you can pick them up first thing tomorrow. I know you are following the Road to Montana most of the way. This will put you a day or two farther north on your drive.

"You'll have some steep passes when you reach the north country, but these girls are used to being moved around. I think you'll be fine. One of them will probably work her way into a lead cow if you don't have one of those."

"We have a couple of cantankerous cows that led us all the way up from Texas." Gabe grinned and jabbed his thumb south. "A couple of my boys brought a herd up from Ogallala last week. Their boss sent them along as lead cows. He said to leave them with me. I think they have visited every ranch in the Sandhills since we sold them this past summer.

"The first fellow sold them within a month. The next rancher pulled their calves off and sent those two troublemakers north. He said he was tired of trying to keep them from wandering."

He looked over at Rock and grinned as he added, "And I might leave them with you. They are a couple of traveling girls, and they don't think fences were made for them. They calve every year but you won't see those calves until they are about a year old if you don't look for them.

"They are good lead cows though. I told Tobe to turn them loose this afternoon and head them on up here."

Stub chuckled. "They went through town right behind us. Shoot, the way they were moving, they might be here by noon!"

Rock and Gabe followed Sturgis as he rode quietly though the cattle. He talked about the mothering instincts of the black cows.

"They aren't as hardy as longhorns but they have wintered well here. I think their condition is even better than the longhorns after a long winter.

"All of them should be bred. They should calve sometime in the next three to five months. Of course, that's hard to track." He grinned at Rock. "If you don't have any trouble, you might even make it all the way home before any calves drop."

Rock and Sturgis talked a little more and then they shook hands. "I'll leave a bank draft at the First National Bank of Cheyenne. Robert Baker will have it for you." Rock studied the bulls.

"I think I'll pass on the bulls. Maybe we'll do this again and I can add bulls on that drive.

"I am going to cross this bunch with my Hereford bulls. I have thirty-five coming next week from a ranch a little closer to me. With those and what I have already, I should be in good shape for bulls." He grinned at Sturgis and then nodded toward the herd.

"Herefords I can find in my area. It is the Angus cattle we have to bring in."

They met Tobe and Rufe as they headed back toward Cheyenne. The two lead cows were marching up the road as fast as they could walk.

Merina watched them for a moment and then commented seriously, "I think we will call them Mija and Mona." Her dark eyes were sparkling and Gabe snorted.

"Honey and Cute. Well, it sounds better in Spanish. Mija and Mona they are." He visited with Tobe and Rufe for a bit. He waved his arms behind him as he talked about where to put the cows when they arrived.

Rock laughed as the two cows kept right on moving with no riders behind them. "I am seeing now why you want to take them with us."

He called back to Tobe and Rufe, "We'll take it easy on the way back. You boys might even be able to catch us in time for dinner."

Tobe nodded and the two men cantered to catch up with the fast-moving cows. Tobe laughed as they rode. "Those two cows don't know where they're going, but they sure are in a hurry to head on north."

Rock looked behind them. When he didn't see the other two riders, he asked Gabe, "Where are Spur and Stub? Are they going to wait and ride back with your other two boys?"

Gabe frowned and shrugged his shoulders. "I'm not sure. Stub wanted to talk to Sturgis about something. He didn't say what though."

CHAPTER 39

I KNEW YOUR SON

WILLIAM STURGIS WATCHED SPUR AND THE MAN with him curiously. They had hung back when Gabe and Rock rode out so he knew they wanted to talk to him.

"You boys need something?"

Stub cleared his throat. "Mr. Sturgis, I knew Joe and I just wanted to tell you I am sorry for the loss of your son.

"We rode together for a time. Curly Joe wasn't all bad. He was wild and reckless but he had a good streak too. I just wanted you to know that."

Sturgis studied Stub's face and slowly nodded. He waited for Stub to continue.

"We hung out at Hole-in-the-Wall for a time. There was an old man who had a cabin not far from there. He wasn't an outlaw and we were supposed to leave him alone. 'Course some of those boys just couldn't do that. Curly caught them harassin' him and tryin' to run his livestock off. He put a stop to it and made those boys apologize. Then he made them chop and split enough wood to last that old man a couple of winters. When they got it done, he went back and worked there for most of two days, patchin' the barn roof and mendin' things around there." He paused and added quietly, "I know 'cause I followed him when he rode out. No trust among outlaws, you know.

"The third day he went over there, I rode with him. He shot a couple of grouse and a rabbit. He told me that old man reminded him of his pop. He said your pa was real special to him. We sat on that old man's porch and drank tea like a couple of fussy fellows." Stub grinned and added, "'Course, we were bored in the hideout. Not much fun to sit around and do nothin' for days on end."

Stub's face tightened as he added, "Curly was my friend. I just wanted you to know that, even though I was one of the men who helped catch him the night he died."

William Sturgis drew a shaky hand across his face. He looked away before he turned his head to stare at Stub. "You're Black, aren't you? You used to have a big, black beard. I remember you now."

"Curly thought a lot of you too. He said you had a level head and that you tried to make sure the jobs you were on didn't end with someone dying." He took a deep breath and added, "I sure wish you had taken him with you when you decided to leave that life." He waved his hand over the cattle as he continued in a bitter voice, "He was my only child. I have no one to leave this to. Kind of hard to build something and know there will be no heirs to take it over when you're gone."

He was quiet a moment and then chuckled softly. "Did you know he named his horse Andy after a little gal he was sweet on? She told me that when I let her know he died. I just went ahead and gave her that horse.

"She married one of my cowboys several months ago and doesn't live far from here." He shifted in his saddle and added, "I think a lot of her. Sure wish she could have made him stay. She's the kind of little gal a man would like to have as a daughter."

Stub nodded. "Andy almost had Curly talked into goin' straight. When he left that last time, he sure meant to go back. Things just didn't work out like he planned." Stub watched Sturgis quietly for a moment. He added, "Maybe you should make that young cowboy your foreman and groom him to take over. Just 'cause they ain't blood don't mean you can't still be a grandpa to those kids when they come."

William Sturgis looked surprised and then he laughed. "I'll have to think on that." He reached out his hand to Stub. "It's good to see you again, Black. Good luck with that drive now and stay safe.

"And you too, Spur. You probably know that country as much as Rowdy runs you all over."

Spur grinned as he shook Sturgis' hand. He was chuckling as they rode off. When Stub looked over at him in question, Spur grinned at him.

"That young fellow Sturgis was talking about used to work for Lance. In fact, he was Lance's foreman for quite a few years. He quit that job shortly after you were down here and went to work for Sturgis as a regular cowboy—just so he could be closer to Andy."

"I think he fell in love with Andy the first time he saw her. 'Course, he was too shy to talk to her. He bid on her box at a church social about six months ago, and that was the start of it." Spur's dark eyes danced as he laughed.

"Lance lost one of his best men over a little bit of a blue-eyed girl."

Stub studied the man next to him and then chuckled. "I don't suppose you had anything to do with that fellow knowing which box to bid on?"

Spur's grin became bigger. "Well, maybe I did and maybe I didn't. I do make it a point to know what all the pretty girls bring when there's a box supper involved. Then Lance and Rowdy's hands all chipped in money to make sure Joe got her box. Brought nearly $25."

His face became bleak and he shook his head. "Joe was in the war. They were just kids—him, his brother, and his cousin. They didn't know anything about the war or even what the fighting was over. They were just hungry kids from Kansas. The Reb who recruited them promised them a paycheck and steady food. The next thing they knew, they were fighting a man's war. Of course, the pay was short and food was shorter.

"Smiley, Joe's cousin, was shot during a battle in Georgia. I think they called it the Peach Creek Battle or something. Joe told me how the three of them hid under the root of a big tree that hung over that river.

"The Union boys won that battle. Joe said those Yanks were going through the field picking up their wounded and taking prisoners.

"He told me it was a bloody battle. Over four thousand men were killed, and more wounded that day. Smiley was bleeding bad and his blood ran right down the river toward a Blue Belly officer who had stopped to water his horse. That officer looked right at those three boys. Joe said time just stood still as they stared at each other. Then that officer turned away and led his men down the river away from them. Joe heard him tell his men the water was better further downstream.

"'Course what that officer didn't know was that Rowdy was behind him in the trees with his big gun. He was a sniper and he would have taken out that officer along with some more Union soldiers if they had tried to fire on those boys."

Stub could feel the hair come up on his neck as he thought about Rowdy holding a sniper's gun. "I'm guessing Rowdy was deadly with that gun," he stated quietly.

Spur nodded. "He was. The Union boys called him 'One Shot,' and they had a bounty on him. He finally got hit hard at the Battle of Columbus and was almost left for dead. Doc Williams saved Rowdy's life and now they are brothers-in-law." Spur paused and added softly, "Four Rebs came out of that war alive because one Union soldier was tired of killing and walked away. It's a strange old world."

Stub was quiet. His heart beat heavily as he thought of that day in the river. He forced his hands to relax their grip on the reins as he pondered over what Spur had shared.

Most of the men in his command had heard stories about One Shot. No Union soldier knew what he looked like, but he was deadly with his big gun. And even when they tried to track him, he just seemed to disappear.

One time though, we did catch his horse. We penned it with some of our mounts. It wouldn't let anyone near it so we weren't able to hobble it. Several of the men wanted to shoot it, but I was sergeant and I wouldn't let them. I suggested we use the horse to catch the rider.

"Let's turn it loose in the morning and follow it. This horse has been cared for so its owner is a horseman. His mount will find him and if he's wounded, we might be able to take him." That horse broke loose during the night though. It escaped and took nearly half our stock with it. We had cavalry horses scattered over ten miles of brush and forest.

The captain was furious. There were too many tracks to find the Reb horse. Besides, half of our men were on foot until they captured their own mounts. We never saw that horse again and that was as close as we came to catching One Shot.

Stub thought about the metal box in his saddlebags but said nothing. *I reckon I won't even bring you up on this trip, Zeb. That battle touched a little too close to home for some of us, and on opposite sides of that war too. I think it's best we leave all that in the past.*

When I get back home, I'll bury your letters in our little cemetery. We'll just never know who you were. I'm sorry I failed you.

Stub glanced over at Spur and commented, "Rowdy's a lucky man to have made it out alive. That was a vicious war of friend against friend and neighbor against neighbor. It didn't just kill lots of men. It maimed nearly as many, and some of those boys were hurt on the inside. Those kinds of wounds don't show where folks can see them." Stub spoke quietly and Spur stared at him in surprise.

He started to speak and then changed his mind. The two men rode in silence for nearly ten miles before Stub spoke again.

CHAPTER 40

SISTER EDDIE

THE FAREWELL PARTY AT GABE'S RANCH WAS IN FULL swing when Spur finally rode in. He had the horses gathered and had pushed them up to the north end of Rowdy's land. He didn't intend to stay long. Spur knew Rock wanted to leave before daybreak, and he intended to have his horse herd at Sturgis' ranch when Rock's crew arrived.

He grinned as he looked over the busy scene. Women were hurrying everywhere, carrying pans of food.

"Maybe I'll eat before I head for home. Looks like they are going to have quite a spread of food here. But then, these gatherings always do...and that's why I try to hit all of them."

He loosened the girth on his saddle and turned his horse loose to graze. "You enjoy a little grazing, old fellow. We have some long days in front of us."

Clare was talking to Annie. It looked like she was scolding the little girl and Spur grinned again as he sauntered up to them.

"I wouldn't worry too much about bad behavior here, Clare. There are enough kids running wild that three more misbehaving won't really matter."

Clare looked up in surprise and Annie took Spur's comment as her que to run away. Clare frowned and shook her head.

"Annie is precocious and delightful all at the same time. I just don't know what I am going to do with her." She paused and watched the little girl splash water from the horse tank as she ran by. "Although she is much better behaved when her father is around."

She smiled when Spur laughed and then studied his face. "You never married, Spur? I know your boss keeps you on the move. Do you avoid women on purpose or don't you have time to court?"

Spur grinned and his eyes twinkled as he glanced at her. "Naw, I'm a runner. I head out when things start to get too serious. I guess I'm a little afraid of commitment. That's why my job with Rowdy suits me mighty fine."

"Does your family live around here?" Clare watched Spur as he frowned and kicked at the ground with the toe of his boot.

He looked over to where Rollie was running with Zeke and slowly shook his head. "My start was a lot like Rollie's. My mother was a madam in a fancy whore house down in New Orleans. She didn't like me much as a kid. In fact, as I think on it now, I'm lucky she didn't figure out a way to get rid of me before I was born.

"I was basically on my own like Rollie there by the time I was five or six.

"Shoot, I don't even know exactly when I was born 'cause Madam Bella didn't like to talk about it." He grinned at Clare and added, "Although, being street smart isn't all bad. I learned a lot about human nature." He was quiet for a moment and then chuckled.

"Sister Edwina was a nun who worked with the girls on the line. I called her Sister Eddie. She offered to take me in. Madam Bella didn't want me but neither did she want the nuns anywhere close to her fancy entertainment house. Sister Edwina was persistent though. She wanted the children of Madam Bella's bordello to attend Saint Ann's Boarding School instead of running loose all day on the streets. Of course, we always made it home to Madam Bella's by dark and that wasn't good either.

"Finally, Sister Eddie told Madam Bella she would send in the law every day if I wasn't turned over to her. I think that was after I started a fire in the kitchen trying to make myself something to eat." He chuckled as Clare stared at him. "I know what was said because I was hiding on the big staircase at Madam Bella's listening to their entire conversation.

"Madam Bella must have believed Sister Eddie because the next day, I was enrolled at Saint Ann's. My days of running loose on the streets were over." He winked at Clare and added, "And so were my nights of sneaking around Lady Bella's House of Entertainment and relieving the patrons of their change." Spur looked away.

"I called my mother Madam Bella. She wanted to be called Lady Bella but I refused. She was a madam and that's what I called her. It used to make her mad."

Spur was quiet a moment before he stated softly, "It was hard at the boarding school though. I was used to doing as I pleased. I ran away if anyone tried to discipline me. I certainly wasn't used to anyone showing me any kind of love.

"Sister Eddie wouldn't give up though. She was patient but firm. There was no give in her. She loved me with a kind of tough love. I'm thinking now she might have had a rough start herself.

"It wasn't long before I made my First Communion, and then she started to groom me to be an altar boy.

"I stayed at Saint Ann's until I was fourteen. Sister Eddie died suddenly and I left the day she was buried."

He added softly, "I owe that nun everything. I hate to think what I would have become if she hadn't taken an interest in me. I have skated all over the line between honesty and outlaw. Somehow, I managed to mostly stay on the right side, and I credit that to Sister Eddie."

Clare listened without talking. She could almost visualize a young Spur running wild on the streets of New Orleans, and she shuddered.

"Thank heavens she took you in."

Spur laughed and nodded. "I try to say thanks every day, although I think my start did make me a little skittish when it comes to settling down. I admire family men but I'm not sure I could ever be one."

Clare's eyes wandered over toward Rock as he talked to Annie. Then he scooped up Nora and gave her a kiss. When he caught Clare's eye, he grinned at her and headed across the yard.

She looked over at Spur and whispered, "I'm a lucky woman. The Good Lord has blessed me with a good man and a wonderful father.

"I hope you find contentment someday, Spur. Marriage is a wonderful thing if you are married to someone you love. "

Rock pulled Clare close and hugged her. "Giving Spur here marriage advice? Better listen to her, Spur. She's a wise woman. Of course, she can be an angry one too!"

Clare elbowed Rock and laughed over her shoulder at Spur. "It was nice to visit with you, Spur. Do stop in if you are ever up our way on one of your horse-dealing trips." Her eyes sparkled as she added, "I might even be able to line up a lady friend who would change your way of thinking when it comes to marriage—not that I know many myself who haven't lived on the fringes of lawlessness!"

Rock grinned and nodded in agreement. "My wife didn't have many respectable women friends when I met her." Clare was smiling up at him and Rock was laughing as they walked away.

Spur looked around the yard. For the first time, he realized the men he admired the most, those whom he considered his closest friends, were nearly all happily married.

He chuckled when he saw the laughing Angel. "Well, not all of them." His eyes wandered back over to Gabe and Merina.

"I didn't deserve you, Merina, and you found a good man. I will do my best to see he makes it safely back to you."

Spur wandered through the happy gathering and talked to just about everyone. He tasted every dish there and was ready to head home by

6:00 p.m. He was just mounting his horse to leave when Rollie rushed up to him.

"So long, Spur. I reckon I'll be seein' ya 'round since I'll be livin' down here with my brothers." Rollie looked over at Merina and scowled.

"Merina says I have to go to school. I don't want to go to any ol' school. I been gettin' along mighty fine on my own without no book learnin'."

Spur dropped down in front of the little boy and grinned at him. "Rollie, you know I used to think a lot like you. An old nun got hold of me and made me buckle down. She made me go to school, go to church, say my prayers, and quit stealing." He put his hands on Rollie's shoulders and gave them a shake as he chuckled.

"You go along with what Merina wants you to do. A fellow needs a family, especially one that loves him and wants him." He put out his hand to Rollie. "And when I get back, I will look forward to seeing and hearing all of the things you learned while I was up north."

Rollie frowned at him for a moment and then grinned as he shook Spur's hand. "I reckon I can do that, Spur. See ya 'round."

Spur grinned as the little boy raced away to play with his friends. He mounted his horse and rode towards Rowdy's spread. His single bed in the bunkhouse seemed a little lonesome that night as he wrapped his fingers together over his head.

"It's been a long time since I pined for a family, and I sure have never shared with anyone all that I did tonight with Clare." He frowned as he thought of what he had told her. "I just don't know where all that talk came from." A jolly nun's face filled his head and Spur smiled contentedly as he fell asleep. "Thanks, Sister Eddie. I sure miss you."

CHAPTER 41

LET'S GO, BOYS

MERINA WAS UP BEFORE THE MEN AND PREPARED A large breakfast. She kept herself busy so she couldn't think about Gabe being gone for nearly three months.

Breakfast was quiet. It was early and the men had a lot on their minds. Gabe stayed behind when the men headed out to saddle their horses.

"Merina—"

She shook her head. "Don't worry about us, Gabe. We will be fine."

He pulled her down onto his lap and stared into her face a moment before he kissed her. Then he looked toward the room where Rollie and Emilia were still sleeping.

His face drew down in hard lines and he quietly cursed. "My old man was worthless. It's lucky for all of us that Clare found little Rollie and picked him up."

Merina smiled up at Gabe. Her dark eyes sparkled as she wrapped her arms around his neck.

"I think I don't hate your father so much. He made three fine boys. The oldest is a good man. He is a fine example to his brothers and he is my husband. No, I think I would thank your father if I knew him—but I would not invite him to live with us."

Gabe chuckled and Merina added more seriously, "I am going to write new letters for Rollie. I will copy your father's handwriting. I will write Rollie some letters that will make him happy when he reads them." Her eyes were dark as she looked toward the room where Rollie slept. "And then I will burn the hateful letter your father wrote." She smiled up at Gabe and he pulled her close.

"Merina," he whispered, "I am going to miss you. From now on, where I go, you go."

She laughed and slid off his lap. "Sí, I am like pockets and you miss your pockets when they are not around." She pointed at two sheepskin coats rolled up on the floor inside heavy blankets. "I added a heavy coat and an extra blanket to your bedroll, and to Nate's too." Her dark eyes were serious as she added, "Come back home to me, my husband."

Gabe grabbed the bedrolls off the floor and hugged Merina again. "Once we deliver the cattle, we should be home in three weeks." He was quiet a moment before he spoke again.

"Tell Rollie I will see him in three months or less. I sure hope he can spell his name by then. And hug Emilia for me every night."

Gabe moved quickly toward the group of cowboys gathered in front of the house.

He looked around at the men before he mounted. His eyes settled on Dink.

"Dink, I sure am pleased that you signed on. Lance said he would talk to you and Rusty. He'll make sure you are all lined out on how they handle roundup. Rusty will keep an accounting of numbers, so you don't have to worry about that. Study the cattle though. I want to talk to you both about what we need to cull when I get back. Pay attention to the condition of the grass and water too."

He mounted his horse and leaned down to kiss Merina one last time. He swung his arm toward the lane.

"Let's go, Boys."

CHAPTER 42

THE ROAD TO MONTANA

TALL EAGLE WAS THE FIRST TO ARRIVE AT STURGIS' ranch. He had camped near there the night before and was waiting when Rock's crew arrived. Wind Dancer, his favorite horse, wore a war bridle. The leather-covered rope circled the horse's bottom jaw. For a novice, this would be a harsh bridle as a horse's mouth is sensitive. However, Tall Eagle guided his horse with his legs and the movement of his body.

The traditional saddle he used was simple. It looked more like a blanket with a rawhide rope. The rope circled Wind Dancer's stomach like a loose girth. There were no stirrups. Instead, Tall Eagle's knees were slid under the rope. His moccasined feet hung naturally down the sides of his horse.

His dark eyes sparkled as he watched the cowboys ride towards him.

"Good morning, my friends. I see you are getting a late start this morning."

Rock looked at him in surprise but Gabe chuckled. "Well, some of us wanted to take advantage of a soft bed and a warm wife as long as we could.

229

"And good morning to you, my friend. I see Wind Dancer is ready to dance with more cattle. Perhaps you and Angel will have to show Rock how you do that."

Tall Eagle laughed. He shook hands with Rock and the men quickly began to move the cattle northeast.

Gabe pointed in front of the cattle. "I am going to ride ahead and look this trail over. I hope to make over ten miles per day but I have never moved black cattle." He looked at Rock. "Think they will move slower than longhorns?"

Rock shrugged. His eyes glinted as he nodded toward his herd. "I've never trailed longhorns so I guess we will both find out soon enough.

"I'll ride ahead with you." He nodded to the northeast. "Some folks have started to call the Road to Montana the Bozeman Trail, but it was around long before Bozeman. He just helped widen it out to take wagons over it. The old Road cuts diagonally across the Wyoming Territory as it goes north. It offers good grass and water too besides avoiding the mountains.

"When it came into heavy use as a road to the gold fields, folks started calling it the Bloody Bozeman. That was because of all the Indian hostilities.

"If the old chiefs are in still charge, we should be all right. The young warriors are angry though at their way of life being taken from them. Can't say as I blame them either.

"I hope that renegade I killed last year won't affect my standing with the Crow people." Rock frowned as he added, "Hard to tell."

He waved his hand in front of them. "It's nearly eight hundred miles from here to Missoula and then we'll drop south into the Bitter Root Valley. We should make the trip in two and one-half to three months. I'd like to move right along, so if we can make more than ten miles per day, I'd be fine with that."

Gabe nodded. *If the route is as easy as he says, we should be able to. I'm not going to bank on it though.*

230

Rock pointed slightly northeast. "When we get further up the trail, you will see the North Platte River over there. We'll cross the Laramie River at Fort Laramie just before the confluence of it with the North Platte. The Platte makes a horseshoe bend so we'll cross it near the ruins of Fort Casper." They rode in silence for a while as they both studied the country.

"The maps didn't show much for towns along this route," Gabe commented.

Rock agreed. "The Army built three forts along this trail in '67 and '68. They abandoned them shortly after that as part of a treaty with the Indians. Of course, the Indians looted and burned those forts as soon as they were abandoned. All we'll see on this trip is what's left, and that's not much.

"Spur was talking about a new town in the makings though. They are going to call it Buffalo since it was formed on an old buffalo trail.

"That will bring in more settlers, so I suppose it will be another place for ranchers and farmers to argue with each other." He grinned at Gabe. "We ranchers seem to be able to get along better with the farmers in the Montana Territory than you Wyoming boys do down here."

Gabe laughed and shrugged. "Well, I don't really know since I have only been here for a few months. I can tell you there were lots of problems all the way north from Texas though. Farmers are part of the reason the cattle drives will soon be over—that, and the railroad."

The men followed the trail northeast for a couple of hours and then cut back towards the north. The North Platte River was soon visible. It was close to the trail they were following.

"Water won't be a problem on this part of the drive. However, when we leave the Wyoming Territory, we will be in the land of the Crow and they will want their payment.

"Right now, we are on land that traditionally belonged to the Cheyenne. They are on two reservations now. One is just over the border in the Montana Territory and the other is down south in the

Indian Territory. They aren't happy about being confined to a reservation though. They are used to hunting and not in a small area." Rock glanced over at Gabe.

"Sturgis told me you added fifty head of young longhorns. I think we will need every one of them." The two men rode in silence for a time and then Rock pointed to the northwest.

"You asked about Hole-in-the-Wall before we left." When Gabe nodded, Rock continued. "We'll pass close to that north of the ruins of Fort Casper. We will probably run into some outlaws there and they will want to cut the herd.

"Of course, it depends on the gangs that are present. Those gangs are territorial too. They all kind of keep to themselves when they are holed up in there, but they have a system and they seem to get along."

Gabe stared at Rock for a moment. "You've been inside? I didn't think they let any outsiders in."

Rock shook his head. "No, I haven't but Stub told me. He said that was where he met Jesse James. Shoot, I didn't know those southern boys came this far north."

Gabe nodded slowly. "Angel knows the James brothers too. Met them down in the Territory. I think they were hiding down there after robbing a bank or a train north of there in Kansas." He paused and then added, "If the Jameses are around, the Youngers will probably be there too. They kind of run together.

"I ran into Cole Younger one time. I'm not sure if he'd remember me though. It was a long time ago."

They could now clearly see the North Platte River. Rock pointed toward a little valley. "Let's bed the cows down there tonight. They'll have good grass and water. We should be able to make Fort Laramie in three or four days."

CHAPTER 43

"Big Talker"

DAY THREE DAWNED BRIGHT AND SUNNY. TALL EAGLE looked over the riders. His face never changed expression but his eyes sparkled as he studied them.

"I suggest you southern boys pull out your heavy coats. We are going to ride through snow today."

Nate stared at his departing back and then tossed out his coffee.

"I sure am glad Merina sent along a heavy coat. I believe I will do as Tall Eagle suggested and put it on."

Gabe frowned but even he tied his coat behind his saddle. By 10:00 a.m., they were in a full-blown snowstorm. The cattle were trying to turn around but Tall Eagle signaled to Gabe to keep them moving forward.

Gabe rode back and hollered at his riders, "Keep pushing them. We don't have much more of this." As Fort Laramie came into view, the snow stopped and once again the sun shined.

The herd of black cattle followed the two lead cows to the Laramie River. Mija and Mona never hesitated. They plunged right in and walked across the shallow water. It was barely over their hocks and Gabe smiled. "I reckon I can handle a couple of hours of blowing snow if all of our rivers are this easy to cross. Shoot, their tails barely got wet." Even Cookie was smiling as his mules pulled up the bank on the other side of the river.

Gabe looked back at Nate and Sam. Both were smiling as they pushed the last of the cattle into the water. Tuff was with them and it looked like the three of them had hit it off well.

The horses moved faster than the cattle and Spur was waiting on the far side of the river with the remuda of horses. He usually grazed them further from the herd and then brought them back to use the same crossings as the cattle.

"You boys get caught in a little snow, did you? You need to have a straighter line to the Maker. He told me to move along if I didn't want to ride in snow…and I sure listened!"

Gabe snorted and Spur chuckled as the Texas riders glared at him.

"Don't mind Spur, Boys. He's from Louisiana and they all think they're funny down there. They aren't like us serious Texans." Gabe kept a straight face and it was Spur's turn to snort.

Spur looked more seriously at Rock and then nodded up the trail. "You'd better decide how many cows you are going to give up. Several bands of braves rode around me early this morning. I'm guessing they will be waiting outside of Fort Laramie.

"Little Wolf and Dull Knife fled the reservation in the Indian Territory last year. They led their bands north. Dull Knife surrendered first at the Red Cloud Agency in Nebraska. Little Wolf just surrendered this year to General Miles at Fort Keough in the Montana Territory. They let him stay this time and put him on a little reservation between the Wyoming and Montana Territories. His people are hungry though and the young men sneak off to go hunting. Of course, the buffalo are gone so your cattle are going to look mighty tempting."

Gabe looked over at Rock. "How many are you thinking?"

"Well, the Crow have more tribal members and a larger reservation so they will expect more cattle. The Cheyenne don't really have a right to any as we won't be crossing their lands. Still, it would be good for relations if we give them a few. Besides, if we don't, they will probably try to spook our cattle and take some anyway.

Gabe stared at the cattle. "Let's see what they ask for. We'll start the negotiations at three and go up to five if we have to."

Rock nodded and the men moved the cattle up the trail, past Fort Laramie. A few soldiers came out of the fort to watch them pass but no one spoke.

Indian braves began drifting toward the herd. They were coming in from both sides until ten of them were watching the cattle trail by. Gabe looked them over and then rode his horse toward the brave who held himself most aloof.

Gabe spoke in the tongue of the Southern Cheyenne and the brave looked startled.

"Greetings to my friends, the Northern Cheyenne."

The brave grunted and then pointed at the cattle. "Where do you take the ve'ho'eotoao'o? Some of them have lost their horns."

Gabe kept his face serious but his eyes twinkled as he answered. "Yes, the Great Spirit gave them a large head. He said he would keep their horns for a weaker animal."

The brave stared at Gabe. He made a motion with his knife. "You cut them off?"

Gabe shook his head, "No, the Great Spirit does not give them horns. None of the black cattle have horns, neither males nor females."

The brave stared at Gabe for a moment and then pointed at the cattle. "We take cattle. Braves are hungry."

Gabe frowned. "Braves are strong and they can shoot their own meat. I give a cow to your little ones but not to your braves."

The brave's eyes glinted. "Our children are hungry. One cow will not feed them."

Gabe pointed toward several cows. "I give you three cows. Two are heavy with calves. One is not. You eat the baron cow and save the other two. Soon you will have four head of cattle instead of two."

The brave studied Gabe's face and then he pointed toward the cattle. "I will take those two and one of the black ones."

"The black ones do not belong to me. I can only give you what I have to give."

"Then I will take four. Two to eat and two for the calves in their bellies."

Gabe looked from the cattle to the brave. "And in return, we will have safe passage across your ancestral lands? It will take us nearly thirty moons to cross."

The brave nodded. "You may go. Little Wolf grants you passage."

Gabe turned to Rock. "Write out a bill of sale for four head. I don't want to be responsible for any stealing accusations."

When Rock had finished, Gabe signaled to his riders. "Cut out those four head and push them to the west of the herd. Little Wolf and his braves are taking them." He handed the paper to Little Wolf and then pointed at Rock. "White Eagle gives you his cattle. This paper will allow you to take them to your home." He raised his hand in a greeting. "Go in Peace, my brother."

Little Wolf raised his hand as well. He looked from Rock to Gabe. "Little Wolf thanks White Eagle and Big Talker. Go in Peace."

The braves drove the cattle away and Spur began to laugh. "Big Talker, huh? I think I like that name."

Gabe glared at him and the men began to chuckle.

"All right, you slackers. Move 'em out. We have a drive to finish and we have only just started."

The men fell into position and the cattle were once again following the tracks of the old Road to Montana.

CHAPTER 44

A Hungry River

DAY THIRTEEN ON THE TRAIL PUT THEM AT WHAT USED to be Fort Casper. The wind blew a few pieces of old, charred wood around but the looters had been thorough. There wasn't much left of the old fort. The adobe had deteriorated into piles of crushed rock, and anything that could be used had been carted away.

Rock pointed at the ruins and grinned. "That fort was manned for a time by galvanized Yankees."

When Gabe looked at him in confusion, Rock explained, "They were Reb prisoners of war who won their freedom by swearing allegiance to the Union. The brass sent them out here to fight Indians just in case that allegiance wasn't genuinely strong.

"They enlisted those Rebs in the Union Army and shipped them west. There were close to six thousand of those soldiers who came out here. Some joker in a newspaper started calling them 'Galvanized Yankees' since galvanized metal changes colors when it's coated with zinc.

"But say what you want, those boys could fight. Once the war back east was over, most didn't have anything to go home to. Oh, a few went back to their families. It was hard though because most were looked on as turncoats by the South. A lot of them stayed out here after they mustered out of the army. They made new lives for themselves.

"We even have a few in our valley. Good men. They don't talk about the war though. Most don't want to remember it."

Gabe listened quietly. *That war was tough on lots of folks.* He didn't have time to ponder on it though. He had a herd to cross.

"This is where we cross the North Platte, isn't it? It looks like it will be deeper than the last crossing." Gabe was studying the water as he listened for Rock's answer.

"It will be deeper. There's a ledge out there that just drops off, so the cattle will have to swim for a bit. Then they'll be back on higher ground and they can walk on out."

Gabe walked his horse to the edge of the water. "I'll go ahead and put Buck in. Let me cross first." He looked at the charred ruins of the bridge. "Sure wish that bridge was still here."

He looked up as one of his men called. "We found a raft! It was partly buried under the dirt but it looks solid. Want to try to get Cookie on this?"

Gabe nodded. The cattle were wandering down to the water to drink. The two lead cows were eyeing the other side, and he chuckled as he put Buck into the water.

The horse snorted as it delicately walked out into the river. When they were about thirty feet out, the horse stepped off a ledge and was instantly in deep water. Buck struggled and then swam another forty feet before he was once again on a solid base.

Gabe put Buck in the water in three different places but the ledge was the same.

"Let's put them in easy. I don't want them crowding over each other. I don't know how deep that water is, but it is deep enough that Buck had to swim. It's not at its highest from the looks of the banks, but it is still over a hundred feet wide.

"Get our two old girlfriends out in front. Then ease the rest of them in." He looked around at the men as he added, "And if you can't swim, I want to know that now. I don't want anyone to go down and not be able to swim free."

Rufe slowly turned red and then waved his arm. "I cain't swim, Boss, but I don't never fall off my horse neither."

Gabe stared at him for a moment and then nodded his head toward another rider. "You stick close to Tobe."

He looked back at the three young men. "Can you fellows all swim?" When the boys nodded, Gabe pointed at the far bank. "When those cows come out of the river, you boys push them out onto the flat. We don't need a jam of cattle on the riverbank."

He waved his arm toward the river. "Let's get these cattle in the water."

Some of the cattle panicked when their feet went off the ledge but Angel, Miguel and Tall Eagle were ready with their ropes. One cow went down and the cattle around it tried to mill. Tall Eagle slapped the churning cattle with his rope, and Angel swung his riata as he waited for the cow that went down to surface. When her head surged up and out of the water, he snagged her and headed down stream. Once she was free of the swimming cattle, he plunged his horse into the deep water and headed for the far shore.

His long rope allowed his horse to have its feet on the riverbed before the cow realized she was being pulled. When she did, she fought the rope and pulled back. Angel charged his horse out of the water and up the riverbank, pulling the struggling cow. She bawled and choked as she jerked back. When her feet hit the solid river bottom, she shakily staggered to her feet. Angel snapped the rope and flipped it over her head while the cow climbed up the riverbank on her own.

As the cattle came out of the water, Tuff, Sam, and Nate pushed them away from the river so the rest of the cattle could climb up the bank.

Just as the last group of cattle was stepping off the ridge into the deep water, Rufe's horse reared. It plunged sideways and lost its footing. It fell off the ledge taking both the horse and the rider under water.

Gabe charged Buck toward the churning water. The horse surfaced about ten feet away from where it went down. Gabe lifted his foot to pull off his boot just as Rufe's head came up. He was limp and as his head went under, Gabe forced Buck into the deep water. He grabbed Rufe by the collar of his shirt and pulled the drowning cowboy toward him. Then he dropped down beside Buck.

He slid his right arm under Rufe's and gripped the drooping cowboy while hanging onto the saddle horn with his left hand. "Take us across, old fellow. You'll have to pull both of us, and these boots are going to drag." When Buck staggered up into the shallow water, Tobe rushed toward them. He drug Rufe up the riverbank and dropped him on the ground. Gabe followed him hollering, "Flip him over and beat on his back. If that doesn't work, hit him in the chest."

Tobe pounded Rufe's back and then hit his chest a couple of time. Rufe began to choke and spit out water. Tobe sat back on his haunches and took a shaky breath. Then he looked at Rufe and grinned.

"Dadgummit, Rufe. If ya cain't swim, ya dang well need to ride that horse down an' come up on it when it goes under water!"

Rufe grinned at him as he choked. "Well, I tried but my boot got hung up in the stirrup an' I panicked. My horse must a nicked me with his foot 'cause that's all I remember." He scowled as he looked down at his feet. Water was running from one boot and the other was missing. "Now I'm a goin' to have to finish this here drive with one boot."

Angel rode his horse toward Gabe as he wound his rope. The slim cowboy nodded back at the river. "The Platte, she was hungry today. I think she is not so happy we did not feed her."

CHAPTER 45

A Little Swim in Cool Water

ANGEL LOOKED TOWARDS THE GROUP OF MEN. HE stared at the soggy Rufe for a moment and then started to strip his clothes off.

"One of you gringos tell me where Rufe went down, and I will show you how a fine vaquero can dive in the water."

Gabe was laughing as he rode Buck back into the water and pointed toward the middle of the river.

"Right about there, Angel. Now you make sure you come back up. I don't want to face your sister if you drown."

Angel grinned at him and then dove smoothly into the river. The longer he was under, the more concerned the other riders became. Gabe finally hollered at Miguel.

"Get over here. Keep an eye on that water. If I don't come up, get in there and pull us out." He was stripping his britches off when a smiling Angel surfaced. His arms held four boots. He climbed out of the water and dumped the boots beside Rufe.

"I did not know which one was yours, señor, so I collected all I could find."

The men began to laugh and Rufe stood shakily. He dumped the water out of his boot and pulled it on. He put his hand out to Angel.

"Angel, I thank ya. Y'all are about the handiest feller I ever did meet. I sure am glad ya chose this here outfit."

Bart looked at the dripping boots on the ground and then at the broken-down boots he was wearing.

"Shoot, Boys. Those boots are better than the ones I have on. I think I'll jist take 'em along with me." He climbed off his horse and picked up the soggy boots. "Jist as well take all three. Never know when we might need an extra." He shook the water out of them and whistled as he tied them behind his saddle.

Gabe wiped his forehead with the back of his hand. He could feel his heart hammering in his chest, and he forced his breathing to be normal. "I don't think I will ever get used to crossing rivers," he muttered to himself.

"Rufe, you push those cattle up further onto that flat area. Spur needs to bring those horses across. The rest of you wait until Spur gets the horses over and then go help with that raft."

He waved his arm at Spur and the tall cowboy pushed the horses into the river. They crossed with no problem.

The old pulley system that had been used to tow the raft across the river was long gone, so several of the men went to work to secure the raft. Angel and Gabe threw one end of their ropes toward the men in the water. Those ends were quickly attached to the front corners of the raft, and the other ends were secured to their saddle horns. Miguel and Tobe hooked their ropes onto the back corners to keep the raft from floating down the river. Three riders held the front of the raft still until Cookie drove his mules onto it. Then the horses began to pull.

It was an awkward method but they finally made it across. The mules leapt for the shore when it was close, and the chuckwagon went up the bank in a rush.

Gabe took a deep breath. He had seen the scattered crosses that marked graves along the riverbank when they first rode up. His stomach was still tight. "Rufe could have been another," he muttered softly as he untied his rope. He stared at the water and shook his head. "I think I am starting to dislike water. Rivers for sure."

Angel chuckled and turned his horse to ride beside Gabe. "It was not so bad, my amigo. Just a little swim in cool water. Now I have had my bath, and I will smell sweet for the ladies." His eyes were twinkling and Gabe laughed. He squeezed Angel's shoulder.

"I am glad you came along, brother," he said quietly, and the two men rode side by side toward the cattle.

CHAPTER 46

DON'T FALL OFF AGAIN!

GABE RODE SLOWLY THROUGH THE HERD OF CATTLE. They had already settled down and were beginning to graze. Several of them had scrapes on their legs, and a couple were favoring a foot. Overall, they had come through the crossing fairly sound.

He rode toward Rock and pointed at two of the limping cows. "We need to keep an eye on those two. Might just be a bruise but we need to watch them."

Rock rode slowly into the herd. He rode beside the limping cows for a moment and then rode back to Gabe.

"I don't think they broke anything, but a bruise could slow them down." His eyes were serious as he looked at Gabe.

"That Angel is quite the rider. You are too. I thought Rufe was a goner."

Gabe nodded and watched the slim vaquero as he rode toward the herd. Angel was talking as he rode by Bart. Bart listened to him and then laughed at something he said.

"Miguel and Angel are both good men. Angel was the first to sign on, and Miguel joined the drive in Dodge. Angel has been the head of their family for some time now, and he is the best friend a man could have." He grinned at Rock.

"I think Merina sent him along to be sure I make it home in one piece." He looked away and then added, "Miguel is a little younger than Angel. I was hoping he would stay home and help with roundup, but Miguel kind of does what he pleases. He's a good man to have along though. They are both wizards with their long riatas. Miguel is a little quieter than Angel but he can be deadly. Both are good men to have on our side."

Rock listened closely and then nodded. "Yeah, Clare was worried about this drive. I don't tell her all the things that go wrong almost every day but she is a savvy one." His eyes were more serious as he looked over at Gabe. "Clare said you were only married a week when we left."

Gabe nodded. "Merina rode the cars north from Texas with a stud she broke. She joined her brothers in Dodge City. I wasn't too excited about having a woman on the drive, but she is a hand with both horses and cattle." His eyes twinkled as he added, "She made it clear to me that she was going—either with the herd or following behind. Angel told me Merina was a difficult woman, so I knew I wasn't going to win. Besides, little Emilia liked me a lot and I couldn't tell her no."

Both men laughed and Gabe added, "I liked having her around so much that I just decided to marry her. It took me some time to win her over though. She finally agreed to let me court her. Now we're married and I'm a happy man."

Rock smiled as he listened. He agreed, "Women can be difficult for sure, but they make a house a home. I married Clare four years after my first wife died. I should have married her sooner. She's a fine woman and a wonderful mother. Good thing too since we have three kids." His smile became wider as he added, "Clare told me before I left that she is expecting. We'll have a new little one by Christmas."

Gabe looked at the man in surprise and then laughed. "Well that's fine news. We'd better make sure you get back home in one piece as well."

Rock grinned and then chuckled. "Best do that. Clare has a temper. I wouldn't want her to unleash it on any of you fellows."

He nodded toward the herd. "I can see why you wanted to bring those two lead cows along. They do like to travel."

The two lead cows were back in front of the herd as they grazed north. Gabe chuckled. "Yep, I sure am glad those two old girls decided to come on north."

As Rock rode away, Gabe pushed his horse toward the two cows to get them started. "Let's keep moving. No point in wasting time."

He waved his hand to Cookie, and the chuckwagon led the way up the trail once again.

Rufe's face was even redder than normal when he rode towards Gabe. "Sorry, Boss. I have always been afraid of water so I avoid it as much as possible. An' that fear jist about did me in."

Gabe grinned at Rufe as he turned his horse to face the rider. "Well, I can't fix that but you should learn to swim. I sure don't want to lose a fine Texas hand like you just because of a little water." His grin became bigger as he added, "But then our creeks don't run nearly this deep around Cheyenne, so I reckon you will be all right if you stay in Wyoming. And don't fall off again!" He slapped Rufe on the back and the red-haired cowboy rode away with a grin.

CHAPTER 47

A Few Outlaws

THE TRAIL THEY WERE FOLLOWING WAS MARKED BY wagon ruts. Gabe could easily see where they wound through the prairie in front of him. The trail skirted the mountains and for the most part had been an easy drive so far. "Of course, we have only been trailing north for eighteen days," he muttered to himself. "This drive isn't even out of the Wyoming Territory yet."

They saw very few Indians and those they saw stayed in the distance. Gabe shook his head as he thought about what Tall Eagle had told him in their last conversation. Crooked Indian agents and a government that didn't keep its word were causing problems. To cap it off, two traditional enemies, the Crow and the Cheyenne, were forced onto connecting reservations.

"Your government believes if we kill each other off, they will have fewer problems," Tall Eagle had told him.

Gabe frowned as he looked over the grass. "No buffalo to hunt as well as skimpy and spoiled rations. What are those politicians back east thinking? Proud and idle men will find something to fill their time. I just hope it is for the good of everyone," he growled to himself as he watched Tall Eagle.

Spur had brought his horses in closer. He rode toward where Rock and Gabe were riding point, one on each side of the herd. Gabe crossed in front of the cattle to see what Spur needed.

"We are about forty miles from Hole-in-the-Wall. We won't go right by the hideout but you can bet those outlaws know we are here. When we get a little closer, I think you should ease a couple of fellows away from the herd—two of your best rifle shots. Plant them down low on that mountainside." Spur pointed toward the towering red walls to their west. "You might need some bargaining power."

"Maybe I will put the boys with the horses and bring you up closer to the front of the herd." Gabe grinned at his friend. "You can help me negotiate." He looked back to where Angel was watching them. "Angel is one of our best shots but I want him with me. Miguel's good too, and he's quiet. I'll send him."

He looked out over the men and his eyes studied the young men riding drag. "Let's send Sam, Nate, and Tuff out to relieve you. Have them trail out singly. Send Rufe and Tobe to the back of the herd to take drag. Wait about ten to fifteen minutes. Then you ride back in and take Miguel's place on flank. Have Tuff wait another ten minutes, and then he can ride back in slowly. Have him take Tobe's place on drag and Tobe can move up to flank.

"Sam is a good shot. He can go up on one of those sidehills with Miguel. Tell Nate to stay with the horses. I want those horses in sight of the herd so none of those outlaws get any ideas." He grinned at the two men in front of him.

"That might be enough movement to distract whoever's watching. Maybe they won't realize that two of our riders just disappeared."

Spur grinned and then scratched his head. "Shoot, I'm even confused but I like it." He rode back slowly and visited with the riders on Tobe's side of the cow herd before he turned back toward the remuda of horses. Before long, Sam rode toward the horses. Miguel was about five minutes behind him. After a bit, Nate rode back down the trail they had just followed. He returned following a single horse. He guided the animal into the remuda and then rode over to talk to Spur. Tuff left his drag position and joined them. They were too far away to hear what they were saying but Gabe could hear Spur laugh from time to time.

Before long, Spur was back. He took a flank position on the west side the cattle and relaxed in his saddle. Tuff rode back to the herd and relieved Tobe at drag. Tobe moved up to a flank position on the other side.

Gabe turned to study the cattle behind him. He glanced at the horse herd and almost smiled. Miguel and Sam had disappeared. Nate was riding around the horses, talking softly and singing to them.

Angel rode his horse forward until he was within earshot of Gabe. "Señor, you can direct the riders like music. That was beautiful, my friend."

Gabe didn't look back but he laughed to himself. *Count on Angel to have it all figured out.*

Several hours passed and then six riders rode out from the red hills to the west of the trail. They stopped in front of the herd bringing the two lead cows to a halt. The rest of the cattle began to mill around. Rock, Gabe, Angel, Tobe, and Spur rode around the herd and met the men on the trail. Bart hung back. His rifle was in his hand.

Rock looked at the riders. "You boys are blocking the trail. Move your horses aside so my cattle can pass."

The men in front of them began to laugh. The largest one sneered as he spoke.

"You boys are in our territory now. You have to pay a toll to cross here."

Gabe started to push his horse forward and Spur laughed. "You boys sure picked the wrong herd. The Preacher here, he don't let anybody cut his herd. You boys should know that." Spur jerked his thumb toward the glowering Gabe as he spoke.

One man leaned forward and stared at Gabe. "You the Preacher? I've heard a you." When Gabe didn't answer, Angel laughed.

"Sí, señor. There are many stories of the Preacher and the many men he has killed who have tried to cut his herds." He pointed toward the cattle behind them. "There are not so many black cattle in this country. I think you will do well to leave these cattle alone."

The first man who spoke laughed roughly. "Well maybe we'll just kill the whole passel of ya an' take all your cattle. Then we won't have to worry 'bout being caught." He sneered again as he added, "We have a man up in those red hills an' his gun is pointed on ya right now."

Angel leaned forward on his horse and then pointed to the side. "You mean that man, señor? I think he is not so helpful today."

The outlaws swung their heads to look up toward where their man was supposed to be. He was standing out in the open. His boots were gone and he had his hands in the air. He shouted, "Don't do anything brash, Fellers. These boys are just plumb eager to shoot!"

When the outlaws looked back at the men in front of them, they were surprised a second time. Gabe's gun was pointed at the man in front of him. Rock, Tobe, and Spur also had their guns drawn.

Gabe's voice was dangerously soft. "You boys make one wrong move and we'll mow you down. Now drop those guns." When the guns hit the ground, he pointed his gun to the side of the trail. "Get over there and take your boots off. Then lay down on your faces."

One of the outlaws began to curse. He moved his hand toward his coat and Gabe shot him. The man fell heavily from his horse. One of the other outlaws cursed. "Ya done killed Jesse's best man, an' he wasn't even packin'. Jesse'll come fer ya now."

Gabe's eyes were cold as he pointed his gun toward the man who had spoken. "You want to be next? Keep talking."

The outlaws were quiet as they pulled off their boots and lay down on the ground. Spur gathered the reins to all of their horses. He started up the trail while Angel dismounted.

"I will keep your boots safe with me, señors. Perhaps I will drop some of them though. There are many to carry." He started up the trail behind Spur tossing the boots randomly as he rode away whistling.

Gabe was the last to ride away. "You boys had better think hard before you try to sneak up on us tonight. If we are attacked, I'll kill every one of you if I have to come into your hideout to do it."

One of the outlaws started to answer and his buddy kicked him. "Shut up, Sloan. Let the boss handle this," he hissed.

The cattle once again began to move. Sam and Miguel never came down the hill but Gabe could see a single man gingerly picking his way over the rocks in his socks. He grinned as he rode to the front of the cattle.

He hollered back at his crew. "Bunch them up, Boys. I'd like to get through this narrow area before we stop for the night." He moved back to take Angel's place alongside the cattle.

Rock remained at point. He finally turned around in his saddle to look at Gabe. He commented quietly. "You're sudden, Gabe. Mighty sudden."

CHAPTER 48

HELLO THE CAMP!

THE MEN WERE ON EDGE THAT EVENING, AND GABE put extra men out to watch the cattle. Stub and Sam came in to eat and then went back out to stand guard. Miguel said nothing as he slipped out of camp. He circled the quiet cattle and stared toward the direction of the hills. He continued to move around until he spotted riders in the distance.

He slid down in the brush and watched as five men rode slowly toward the camp. It was nearly 8:00, and the light was fading as the sun sank behind the hills. Miguel's gun followed the men and when they were close, he cocked his rifle.

The four riders stopped and the tallest one called out, "Is that you, Miguel? I saw the tracks of that big black stud horse you are so proud of.

"I asked the boys if they saw you this afternoon and no one had. I figured you were one of the fellows up on that hill.

"What are you doing with this outfit—trying to go straight?"

Miguel chuckled softly.

"We all have our time, yes, señor? I came on this drive to help my brother and my sister's husband. As you know, blood is thicker than water.

"I will keep my rifle on you, señor Jesse, and if your men try anything, you will be the first to fall.

"And you tell those two men who are following you to go back to their hole and wait. They make enough noise to wake a tired man. And if they don't go, you will be short two more men."

Jesse stared toward Miguel's voice and then shrugged. He turned around and waved his hand as he pointed toward the hills. Two men stood and nodded before they faded back.

Jesse looked toward where Miguel had been. "We'll go on in now. We'll keep this a friendly visit."

Miguel's voice came from another direction. "Of course, señor. I would expect nothing less."

Jesse chuckled and rode on. The light from the campfire was nearly a quarter of a mile away and it flickered through the shadows.

When Jesse was closer, he called out, "Hello, the camp! We're coming in friendly."

The riders around the campfire quickly disappeared into the shadows. When the visitors arrived, only Rock and Gabe were there. Even Cookie had disappeared.

The three riders who stepped down looked around the campfire in surprise. Several looked even more startled when Spur spoke from the shadows before he strolled up to the fire.

"Evenin', Fellers. Jesse, Frank, Cole. Didn't expect to see you boys so far north."

The man he called Cole was studying Gabe. "I know you. We met somewhere before."

Gabe grinned recklessly at him. "Sure did. I whaled on one of your men for roughing up a gal. You told me that I had better be wearing a gun the next time I saw you." Gabe turned to face Cole and his voice became hard. "Well here I am and I'm heeled. It's your call, Younger."

The man Spur called Jesse interrupted. "We didn't come here to fight tonight. We are here to collect our fee for letting your cattle pass by Hole-in-the-Wall."

Gabe glared at Jesse. His face was drawn down in hard lines when he answered. "There won't be any toll. You don't own that land. We'll pass these cattle by safely or you will lose some more men. And then I will be back with an army of men just itching to clean you out.

"Right now the law leaves you alone but all that can change. I'll make sure it is hot enough around here that none of the neighbors will want to help you out."

Spur chuckled as he nodded his head toward Gabe. "The Preacher don't like his herd to be cut.

"Now you fellows just ease your guns to the ground and let's have us a little confab. This deal can end peaceful like or it can end with bloodshed. And that would be a shame 'cause there ain't enough money in this entire camp for one cowboy's wages for a month."

A ruckus was heard in the brush and Miguel appeared, dragging an angry woman by her arm. She was twisting to get away from him. She came to a sudden stop when she saw Spur.

"Well hello, Etta. I wondered where you had gone. I looked for you at Madam Bella's the last time I was there, and they said you had gone to Dodge City. I sure didn't expect to see you this far north." Spur was smiling as he studied the small woman in front of him.

Etta Place was smart and pretty. She knew she had what men liked, and she made sure she was noticed.

Her face broke into a smile. "Spur! What are you doing up here? I had no idea you were in the Wyoming Territory." Her voice was soft and she almost purred when she spoke.

"I live in Cheyenne now. I am taking a herd of horses up to Fort Ellis." He looked around at the group of men. "And that's another reason you boys don't want to mess with this drive. Those soldiers about have all the Indian problems under control. They'll be looking for a reason to clean out some outlaws."

Etta shrugged Miguel's hand off her arm and strolled across the camp area toward Spur. She made sure her movements captured the eyes of every man present. She snuggled up next to Spur as she took his right arm.

Spur looked down at her and grinned as he loosened his arm. He put her on his left side and hugged her before he released her. "Now, Etta, we are too old of friends for me to fall for that little act. You sit down over there and we'll catch up—as soon as we get your friends lined out."

Etta's face drew down in a scowl. She looked the men over and then started to walk towards Nate. Gabe stepped in front of her. He pointed to a spot behind Spur.

"Huh uh. You sit down back there. And you stay put or I'll tie you up."

Etta flounced over to the spot that Gabe had pointed to and dropped to the ground. She pulled her skirt up and adjusted her garters. Then she pulled on her corset as she adjusted it as well. Gabe snorted and turned his back on her while Nate and Sam stared. She batted her eyes at the two of them and then pulled her skirt high to reveal even more of one leg. Jesse and Frank were laughing but Cole glared at her. Gabe planted himself between her and the young men. "You have something to say, James? Then say it and let's get this deal over with."

Jesse James scratched his head and then grinned at Gabe. "I was hoping to collect a toll for safe passage, but since you boys are so all-fired ready to fight, I might just offer to trade you for some flour and sugar instead."

Gabe stared at him for a moment and then shook his head. "We don't have any extra. We are barely into this drive, and we have over six hundred miles to go. We can spare you some tobacco though." His face was serious as he added, "For some of those fresh vegetables it is rumored you grow back in those hills." Gabe's eyes were twinkling as he watched Frank's and Jesse's faces.

The outlaws stared at him a moment and then they all began to laugh. Frank dropped down on the ground beside the campfire. "Well, bring out some of that tobacco and let's do a little haggling."

When the evening was over, the outlaws carried away fifty pounds of flour and a sack of sugar. They left a new rifle, a bag of prunes, and a promise to bring some fresh vegetable down the next day. As they rode away, Jesse turned around in his saddle. He looked over the group of cowboys.

"Any of you fellows decide you want to make your money a little easier, you come see me." His eyes moved around the small group of men until they rested on Gabe. "Especially you, Preacher. I like men of action, and because of you, I'm out a lieutenant." His eyes were hard for a moment and then he smiled again.

Etta didn't want to leave but Spur lifted her up onto her horse. "You go on now, Etta. You are my friend but we don't need your kind of trouble on this drive." He paused and then added with a grin. "You can come see me in Cheyenne this winter." Etta's face lit up in a smile and Cole cursed under his breath. Spur's grin became bigger as they rode away.

Gabe looked over at his friend and shook his head. "I may be sudden but I didn't goad Cole Younger about his woman. I wasn't sure how much more poking he was going to take before he cut loose on you."

Spur laughed. "Etta is all talk and Younger knows it." He grinned as he winked at the group of men. "He's jealous though and I do like to poke him. Etta and me are like brother and sister. There never was anything between us. If Etta needed help though, I'd be right there.

"She's not a bad girl. She just grew up rough and now she's surrounded herself with rough men." He shook his head as he watched their horses disappear into the shadows.

"I told her to stay away from Younger though. He's a dark man and he will get her killed." He shrugged his shoulders as he added, "She thinks she loves him, but sometimes, love just isn't enough."

He looked around at the camp. "I think I have had all the excitement I can take for one day. Somebody call me when it's my turn for nightguard." Spur rolled up in his blankets was almost instantly snoring.

Gabe started for his horse but Angel stopped him. "I'll bring Stub and Sam in, señor. An older married man such as yourself should get more sleep." Angel's eyes were twinkling as he rode into the night, singing a Spanish ballad.

CHAPTER 49

THE NEW TOWN OF BUFFALO

T HE LONG LINE OF BLACK CATTLE TRAILED PAST THE
new town of Buffalo on August 16. It was their twenty-second day
on the trail, and the men looked longingly at the makeshift saloon.

Gabe waved in the direction of the little town. "We aren't stopping
so don't even ask. Cookie is going to try to buy more flour, but he is the
only one who is riding in. You can all give him your lists if you want
him to pick up anything."

He looked over at Bart. The cowboy had on two of the boots that
Angel had pulled from the river. Not only did they not match, but they
were also two different sizes. Gabe chuckled as he pointed at them. "You'd
better hope you don't have to walk anywhere, Bart. You'll have blisters
in places you never knew existed."

Bart looked down at the boots and grinned. "Ya jist never know. I
might find the owner of one a these here boots somewhere an' be able
to sell it back to 'im." He lifted up one foot. "This here is the finest boot
I have ever worn even if it is too big."

Several cowhands rode out to meet them on their first day out of
Buffalo. They watched as the cattle slowly moved north, and then rode
forward to talk with the trail boss. Rock rode over to meet with them.

The oldest rider nodded toward the cattle. "The boss says you need to get your cows off his graze. He don't take kindly to outsiders."

Rock's face was bland as he answered. "We are just trailing north. I have a ranch south of Missoula, and that is where we are headed."

The cowboy frowned. He looked over at his companion and then back at Rock. "That's no good. The boss said to run ya off if ya didn't back that herd off. We have twenty tough boys an' the boss, he means what he says.

"'Course, ya can always have a meetin' with 'im if ya want to talk it out."

Rock studied the cowboy a moment. "Take me to your boss and we'll work this out. Gabe, you come with me."

Gabe paused a moment and then waved back to Stub. "You come up here and ride point." He looked over at Angel. "You come with us."

The three men followed the cowboys about six miles west. A line camp was down in a little valley with a shallow stream running close to it. They didn't see any cattle as they rode that way.

"How many head does your boss run? I haven't seen any cattle yet." Rock was studying the grass. "You still have plenty of feed for this late in the season."

The first cowboy was quiet a moment before he looked over at Rock bleakly. "There's been lots a scrappin' 'round here. More since that new town went in. The settlers are tryin' to fence off the water. This here is all free range, but the settlers are filin' on the land 'round the water holes." He pointed toward a small creek in the distance.

"We've set up line camp down there since we'll be doin' our fall gather 'fore long. The ranch headquarters is 'bout ten miles back to the southwest."

He looked hard at Rock. "I hope ya watered good at Buffalo 'cause ya ain't gettin' any water fer the next two days."

Rock didn't answer but his face drew down into a scowl. Gabe cursed under his breath.

As they rode up to a barbwire fence, Gabe looked around in surprise. "I thought this was public land. Why is there a fence here?"

One of the cowboys grinned at him and the other one laughed.

"John Booker is a big man 'round here. He makes the rules an' the Wyomin' Stockgrowers Association backs 'im up." He stepped off his horse to open the gate and pointed toward the creek. "The boss is down there." His voice was quiet as he added, "Ya boys are outsiders. Ya best turn those cows back an' hike it on out a here. This here country is 'bout to blow wide open."

Angel began to sing softly in Spanish—except the words he was singing weren't the words that went with the music. He sang, "señor, I think this could be a trap. I don't think we should go down to that creek. If they kill us, they can take the cattle and no one will know the better."

Gabe turned his horse to the side. He looked over at Rock and then pointed his finger at the man on the ground. "Go ahead and shut that gate.

"You tell your boss we aren't turning around. This is public land.

"Be sure to tell him too that the trail boss of this drive owns a ranch down by Cheyenne. I was just accepted as a member of the Wyoming Stock Growers Association—and I don't think your boss wants to make the Association investigate itself.

He looked hard at the riders as he added, "If we come to a fence across that trail, we are going to cut it." He paused and then ground out, "And it won't be fixed when we're done."

As the two cowboys stared at Gabe in surprise, Rock spoke. "You boys drop your guns. You on the horse—get down. We'll turn your horses loose when we get back to the herd. Maybe you can catch them before they head for home.

"I'm sure your boss will try to stop us, but we aren't going to make it any easier for him than need be."

One of the cowboys edged his hand toward his gun and Angel slid his knife under the man's chin.

"I think, señor, you do not want me to use my small knife. She will make no noise as she takes your life away."

The two men threw their guns down. Angel picked them up. "Your boots too, señors. I think perhaps a small walk on such a pleasant day will do your temperamento—your—your—the way you act—a little good." The slim vaquero was smiling but his dark eyes glittered as he touched the tip of his knife.

"My small knife as not been used so much on this drive. She is anxious to become acquainted with you."

The men dropped down to remove their boots. They sat quietly as Gabe grabbed the reins to their horses. His voice was rough when he addressed them.

"You tell your boss that we have a crew of work-hardened and trigger-happy cowboys who are itching for a fight. If he sends men after our herd, some of you will die. Maybe some of us too, but whoever you don't kill will tear down that fence. These cattle are moving north over open range and he can't stop us. In fact, if he pushes too hard, we might even burn him out." As the cowboys stared at Gabe in shock, he walked Buck close to them. His voice was soft and deadly as he repeated himself. "You tell him that. We'll be ready."

CHAPTER 50

A Time of Reflection

THE TWO COWBOYS ON THE GROUND WATCHED THE three men ride away. Two pairs of boots dangled behind the saddles of their own horses. One lifted up his foot and pulled his sock off in disgust.

"You know what I think? I think we should hightail it out of here. Booker pays top wages but I don't like what he's a doin'. Those fellers were right. He cain't fence public land an' do it legal. Somebody's gonna get killed an' then he'll blame that on his riders. He won't never go to jail but we sure could."

The second rider listened quietly and then agreed. "How do you think they knew we had an ambush set up? They didn't seem to think nothin' was up when we rode this way."

"I don't know but I don't like that Mex. He's a little too anxious to use his knife, an' I don't want to be cut up like no Texas strawberry.

"Let's look around here an' see if we can catch our horses. If we can, let's just ride out of this country an' don't look back."

Before long, their horses appeared. They shied away when the riders tried to catch them. The two men cursed loudly as the horses dodged through the open gate and raced toward the line camp.

"Nearly a mile on bare feet. I won't be able to walk for a month," commented the second rider as he limped along.

The first rider laughed. "Well, brother, if it works out, we won't be walkin'—we'll be ridin' an' ridin' fast at that."

The rest of the cowboys were gathered around the corral when the two men finally limped up.

"What happened? Booker ain't gonna be happy you didn't bring those fellers back here."

Neither man answered. They both grabbed their boots and pushed their sore feet into them. They tied their bedrolls behind their saddles.

As they mounted, the oldest of the two brothers pointed behind him.

"Adios, Boys. That herd is guarded by some tough men. They said if anyone followed them, there'd be a fight. Then they told us that whoever was left alive would be back to burn the boss out. We ain't so fond of our jobs that we want to die. We're ridin' out.

"You can tell the boss to keep our wages. We're cuttin' free of Wyomin'. We're headed back south. We just might be in the Indian Territory 'fore the first snow catches us."

As the two men rode away, the other riders watched them. "Those McCandless brothers are tough. Never thought I'd see the day they'd back off from a fight."

One of the riders who hadn't spoken grabbed his bedroll. "I think those boys have the right idea. This country is goin' to bust wide open, and then who will decide who's in the right? You boys know the big dogs never go down. It's us peons who will swing. So long, Fellers."

He urged his horse to a run as he hollered at the riders in front of him. "You boys wait up! I'm comin' too."

CHAPTER 51

CATTLE KATE

THE REST OF THE DAY WAS QUIET. THE MEN RODE ready for trouble. Gabe put out extra night riders and the rest slept in their boots. Dawn broke gray and chilly.

When breakfast was done, Gabe threw out his coffee grounds and faced the men.

"I'm going to ride up ahead and see what water is available. We might have to trade some stock, but I want to get out of this country as fast as possible. It has all the makings of a cattle war.

"Spur, you come with me. Nate, you are in charge of the horses. Tuff, you help him. The rest of you ride ready. I don't know the man who thinks he is boss in this country, but he seems to ride roughshod over folks. I'm guessing we haven't seen the last of him." He looked over at Rock.

"I think you should stay with your herd. Swing around it and watch for riders."

As he headed for his horse, he stopped beside Angel. "You keep an eye on Rock," he said softly. "He'll be in front of the herd and will be easy to pick off if they attack. You watch his back."

Angel nodded and grabbed the horse Nate led toward him. "Come, señors. Perhaps today will be the day we help clean up this territory."

As they rode away, Gabe looked over at Spur. "Have you ridden through this country? Good grass but it looks understocked to me."

Spur nodded. "I know Booker. He's arrogant and likes to throw his weight around. Down around Cheyenne, the Association works for the cattlemen. Up here, it seems like it is run by a few big ranches. Booker is one of them.

"They think they are above the law, and so far, that has proved true." He was quiet a moment and then added softly, "Angel told me what you said you'd do if they bothered the herd. No one talks to Booker like that. I don't think he will take it lying down."

Gabe nodded. "I figured as much. Men who break the law and expect to get away with it get my ire up. I knew it was brash when I said it but I said it anyway." He grinned over at Spur. "Besides, I think it would do him good to get a thrashing. I just hope we are close enough to the edge of his range that we only have to fight him one time."

Spur chuckled. "You're just sudden, Gabe. Plumb sudden. Little Merina don't know what kind of man she tied herself to."

Gabe laughed out loud. "That coming from you is downright laughable." He pushed Watie to a gallop. "Let's get up this trail and see who it is that has the water all tied up."

They saw the fence before they reached the homestead. The spread was small and a fence connected it to a second small ranch. The two of them together appeared to be less than four hundred acres. A swift-flowing creek ran through both homesteads.

Gabe looked around in surprise. "Can't run many cattle here—not enough land—but they sure have a nice water source all fenced off."

A woman stepped into the door of the cabin and cocked her gun. "Ye boys just keep on movin' now. Not a thing to see here, aye? Ye not be wanted an' ye sure not be invited."

The woman had a square face and looked capable of protecting herself. Her brown hair was pulled up in a loose bun. Her eyes were blue and her accent said she was Scottish or Irish. Her clothes were rough, and the body they covered was sturdy but tall. Spur stared at the woman for a moment and then he began to laugh.

The woman looked up sharply when Spur laughed and then slowly lowered her gun.

"George Spurlach! Well I'll be hornswoggled! What are ye doin' in the Wyoming Territory?"

Spur's grin became bigger. "I could ask you the same thing, Kate. Last time I saw you, you had married up with some farmer down in Kansas. Leave that no-account behind, did you?"

Kate chuckled and then looked over at Gabe. "Who is your friend? Don't say much, does he?"

Gabe chuckled as he tipped his hat. "I try to talk only when I know what I'm talking about, and I am out of my league here."

Spur laughed as he pointed toward Gabe. "Kate, this is Gabe Hawkins. I've known him since I was a pup. He's the trail boss for the herd we are trailing. They are behind us several miles.

"Gabe, meet Ella Watson otherwise known as Cattle Kate."

Kate snorted. "I reckon Booker would tell ye that I be Cowshit Kate, but what he thinks don't be botherin' me none."

Gabe laughed as he shook the hand Kate offered him.

"Nice to meet you, Miss Kate."

Kate waved at the gate in front of them. "Come on in through that gate if ye want to get down. Ye can tie ye horses up by the house." She looked behind at them as she walked and asked, "Coffee?"

Both men agreed and they followed her into the house.

Kate set out some coffee and cut each of them a large piece of pie. She stared at them a moment and then asked, "So what brings ye up this way? Ye takin' sides in this range war, are ye?"

Gabe looked startled but Spur shook his head. "Nope. We are trailing our herd of black cows straight through. We are taking them to the Bitter Root Valley in the Montana Territory. We were hoping you would let us water them here. We have about fifteen hundred head and we want to move them right along." He paused and looked at Kate directly before he continued. "Had a little altercation with some fellows who ride for Booker. Their boss seems to think he can fence and control public land. We didn't agree."

Spur nodded his head over toward Gabe and grinned. "Gabe there informed them that if Booker bothered us, he'd kill every man who tried to stop us. Then he'd burn Booker out." Spur's grin became larger and his dark eyes sparkled as he added, "But then, Gabe has always been a little sudden. Just brash is what he is."

Kate stared from one man to the other. Then she threw back her head and laughed. "Ye boys be all right. Now ye just go ahead an' bring those cows right on down here. Shoot, if I thought it would save ye time, I'd let ye cut through me land. That won't help ye get home though. Besides, if ye keep goin' north, ye will have to cut Booker's fence to get ye cattle through. He fenced off the whole durn trail." She grinned at both of them and her blue eyes snapped. "I might park me horse down there an' watch that party though. It will be a sight to see, I think."

Gabe ate his pie while Kate and Spur caught up and shared stories. They had been there nearly an hour when they finally rose to leave.

"You have another gate you want us to use to get those cows to your water?" Gabe's hat was in his hand and his face was sincere when he looked down at the tough woman.

Kate stared at him a moment and then laughed loudly. "Another gate! That's rich. The only way into this place is right by me house an' ye won't be bringin' a bunch of hungry cows in to tear up me garden. I rarely leave an' no one but my neighbor be around here who is welcome. That means I don't need no other way in here but that gate ye came through. Nope, I reckon ye will just have to cut me wire, and it had better be

270

fixed fine before ye leave. I don't want that scallywag of a Booker tryin' to sneak up on me of a night."

She pointed down her fence line to where they were to cut the wires. "Water them an' get them out. I don't have enough grass for the cows I have so I don't be plannin' to share none with those greedy girls ye be drivin'."

Both men thanked her as they left. Gabe turned and called back as they rode away. "We'll camp down below. We'll move our cattle in and out about two hundred at a time. Why don't you just come on down and eat supper with us? We have a lame cow we can send with you if you want her."

Kate was quiet for a moment and then nodded. "I'll just do that. And a lame cow would be fine. She be fittin' in right fine with the rest of me sorry excuses for beef, she will."

Gabe was smiling as they rode back toward the herd. Finally he laughed out loud. "Spur, I sure am glad you had to trail those horses up this way. Why I think you know half the folks who live in this territory. For sure the ones who skirt the law or just plain defy it."

Spur chuckled and then his face became serious. "I think our trouble will come at Booker's fence. Hard to tell how many men he will put on it."

Gabe nodded. "I've been thinking on that. I think maybe when we are a couple of days out, we should take a few boys and pay them a little night visit. Stampede their horses, destroy their camp, and tear down their fence. We'll see how much fight they have left after that."

Spur looked over at his friend and grinned. "Sudden. That's what you are. Well, make sure I'm part of the welcoming committee. That sounds entertaining."

CHAPTER 52

WE FOUND WATER

THE RELIEF SHOWED ON ROCK'S FACE WHEN SPUR AND Gabe rode up to the herd. Spur's grin was wide and Rock could feel himself relax.

"I take it you found water?"

"Sure did. We'll camp about eight miles up ahead tonight. There's a little ranch there. We can take the cattle in two hundred head at a time. We want to keep them from grazing as much as possible. The gal who is letting us water doesn't have any extra grass. Her name is Kate, and Booker has been giving her plenty of trouble. She can barely leave her place."

Gabe paused a moment and then suggested, "I thought maybe we would leave one of those lame cows with her. The smaller one is walking better but that big one is still limping. I don't think she'll make it all the way to your valley."

Rock looked out over his herd and nodded. He hated to leave even one head of his black cows behind but Gabe was right. The cow had hurt her leg crossing the North Platte, and her limp was getting worse.

"I guess we just as well. Let's put her in the last group to water. Then maybe she won't be so hard to sort off. I'm guessing she won't want to be left behind."

They pushed the cattle into the evening and arrived at Kate's ranch around 7:00 p.m. Angel and Tobe immediately cut the fence and the watering began. Each group of two hundred took nearly forty minutes to sort, water and bring back. It was a long night but the cattle bedded down easily. Kate came out to watch but she didn't stay long.

"We probably ought to water them again in the morning. Kate said there is a water not far after that fence Booker threw up across the trail. There are just small creeks after that. The next good water will be nearly three days." Gabe was staring across the cattle as he talked.

Rock agreed. "Let's give the boys a little break. Then we'll start watering again around 3:00 a.m. As they water, push them up the trail. Make sure your old girlfriends are in the first group."

Gabe laughed. "I don't think we have to worry about that. Those two are bullies. They don't hold with anyone trying to get in front of them."

He was quiet a moment and then he looked over at Rock seriously. "I think tomorrow night we should send out a little greeting party. I am guessing Booker has guards posted at the fence. I'd like to sneak in there and shake things up a bit."

Rock stared at Gabe a moment and then then slowly nodded. "Who do you have in mind?"

"Tall Eagle, Angel, and Spur for sure. Maybe Miguel and Stub. After that, we'll have to see. All of them will want to go, but we need a heavy guard on the cattle too." He looked at Rock. "You need to stay with your herd. If I take those boys, all of your lieutenants will be gone, and the rest of the boys need a leader.

"You can start to move the cattle about 1:00 a.m. We just might be able to get them through the hole we make before Booker has time to recoup and organize his fighters."

Rock studied Gabe's face intently and then looked away with a low curse. "It almost looks like you are trying to protect me, Gabe. They are my cattle. I should be part of the raiding party."

Gabe laughed and shook his head. "I don't care what it looks like. They are your cattle and that's why you need to stay with the herd. Let the boys have some fun. You hold the fort together here. I think we will keep the horses penned in close too. We'll want to be sharp. They may have the same idea we do."

CHAPTER 53

BOOKER'S FENCE

THE NEXT DAY, TUESDAY, AUGUST 19, WAS A LONG ONE. Both the cattle and the riders were tired. Gabe finally called a halt at 5:00 p.m.

He gathered the men before they chose nightguard.

"Tonight, I am going to take some boys and see if we can't shake up Booker's camp a bit." As the men began to volunteer, Gabe shook his head. "I can't take all of you. I need men here too and the rest of you need to be vigilant. I am thinking Booker may try the same thing on us, so we all may get a little fighting in tonight.

"Tall Eagle, Spur, Angel, Miguel, and Stub. You are with me.

"Tobe, I want you to line out nighthawk. If they come, I think it will be between midnight and four. The extra horses need to stay penned but every man needs to sleep in his boots and be ready to fight. Keep your horses and your guns close. I told Cookie to park the chuckwagon away from the camp. He will be on guard too."

Gabe looked his riders over. Every man there was his friend, and he didn't want to lose anyone.

"I think they will try to stampede the cattle through the camp. Leave the fire burning but move your beds away from the fire. Give yourselves enough room so you can get away in case of a wreck.

"Tobe, put the youngest fellows on nighthawk at 10:00 p.m. Then I want them out on that prairie listening for horses moving.

"Tuff, I've heard you mimic a wolf. Give a long call if you see something moving."

He looked at all of them intently and then added, "And any rider coming up on a camp in the night without hallooing is an enemy. Shoot him.

"Cookie will have supper ready in about an hour. Get some sleep when you can. This is going to be a long night for all of us."

Rock listened quietly as Gabe lined out his men. *This is why Gabe is so well liked and highly recommended as a trail boss. He's savvy, prepares for problems, and cares about his men. Why those fellows would ride through fire for him.* Rock rolled out his bedroll. *I think I'd rather sleep than eat just now*, he thought as he dropped off to sleep.

The night was quiet when Rock awoke. He could hear Gabe's men leaving quietly. He checked his pocket watch. It was midnight. He started to roll up his bedroll and then paused. He rolled some rocks into it and then walked away from the camp. The night was quiet. He spotted movement to his right and hissed, "You fellows doing all right?"

Tuff's voice was barely above a whisper. "Doing fine. Had me a nice little nap and I'm ready to go." There was no sound from Nate or Sam.

Rock slipped back into camp. He checked the girth on his horse and then settled down against a rock to wait. A whisper of sound put him on alert and he eased back behind the rock.

A wolf howled out on the prairie and two men stood upright. One whispered loudly, "You hear that, Ned? That old she-wolf is close tonight. Their calls just send shivers up my back."

The other man didn't answer and Rock slowly eased the hammer back on his six shooter.

The two men were quiet for a moment and then the first man whispered again. "The boys should be up to the herd by now. Let's ease back so we don't get trampled when those cows stampede through here."

There was a rustle in the grass behind the two men and then a grunt. Two bodies hit the ground and Rock slipped back further into the darkness. He heard horses running as he crouched low.

The wolf howled again and Rock raced for his horse. Three men rose out of the grass behind the cattle, hollering and waving blankets. The cattle lunged to their feet and chaos broke out.

Rock hollered, "Push those cattle to the west. I don't want them to run through a fence." He charged Red toward the three men who had started the stampede, firing as he rode. Two of them went down and the third ran awkwardly toward his horse. Rock was fighting to turn the cattle away from the fence. When they started to turn, the full force of the herd stampeded toward the running outlaw.

Suddenly, Rufe and Tobe were beside him. He could see Tuff and Sam in the distance but he couldn't see Nate. Bart was racing toward the front of the herd and Rufe followed.

Rock pulled up his horse. He could hear gunfire in the distance and then the sound of men screaming. He looked toward the camp. Nate was nowhere to be seen and neither were the horses. He rode toward the area where they had been penned. The rope and the pens were gone. He laughed and then raced his horse after the stampeded herd. Tobe and Rufe had the cattle slowly turning in a circle. Rock joined them as they pushed the swirling cattle tighter and tighter until they came to a stop.

Rock looked over the men and drew a shaky breath. Everyone but Nate was accounted for. He glanced up when Sam pulled his horse to a stop with a smile on his face.

"Nate move the horses away from the camp?"

Sam nodded. "He sure did. He did it so quiet that no one woke up. I dumped the rope an' the pegs in the chuckwagon." His smile became bigger as he added, "Cookie almost shot me. He told me not to be sneakin' up on him like that." Rock could hear the laughter in Sam's voice and he chuckled.

"Yes, it's best not to scare the cook. Well, let's go ahead and start these cattle moving north. They are up and ready to go so there is no sense in wasting around."

"Tuff, you and Sam break camp. Get the bedrolls loaded in the chuckwagon. Count them so you don't miss any. They will be scattered all over. And tell Cookie we're moving out."

The cattle had moved nearly three miles when Gabe's crew appeared. Stub had a bandana tied around his arm and Gabe's hat had a hole in the crown. They were all smiling though as they moved into position around the cattle.

Rock studied the six riders for a moment and then pointed north. "Lucky for us we have a moon tonight. You boys think you made a big enough hole in that fence for these cattle to get through?"

Gabe laughed. "What fence? We tore it down. Booker has posts and wire strung all over the prairie. Once we knocked down what we could, we pulled up the wire around the trail. Then Stub drug Booker's chuckwagon over the areas where any posts were still standing." Gabe's grin was big as he added nonchalantly, "Not sure which he damaged most—the posts he broke off or the bottom of that fancy Studebaker chuckwagon.

"Stub drove like he was in a chuckwagon race. He lined those posts up between those two mules and after the first couple of post splintered under that wagon, he didn't to have to make those mules run. He bailed off when the chuckwagon started to roll. Those mules were still running south the last we saw them, the tongue of that wagon just a bouncing along behind them."

Rock grinned and the men all began to laugh.

"Booker there?"

Spur spoke up disgustedly. "Heck no. That weasel sent his men out to do his dirty work for him. He stayed home."

Rock was quiet a moment and then asked, "Anyone left alive?"

Angel nodded. "Sí. Two hombres riding one horse raced off toward the south I don't think they will be slowing down for some time." His face was mournful as he added, "Unfortunately, the rest of their vaqueros, they were not so fast with their guns. I think that señor Booker will have many graves to dig in the morning." He frowned and drew his knife. "It happened so quickly that I did not have so much time to use my small knife. I think perhaps señor Gabe tried to shoot all of them by himself."

Gabe snorted. "Don't anyone be fooled. Tall Eagle and Angel sneaked into their camp. They had those boys thinned down by the time the rest of us arrived. And the ones who managed to slip away ran into Miguel.

"The rest were given one chance to surrender." He paused and added quietly, "And most of them chose not to take that opportunity."

He started to walk away and then turned back to the men. "Keep those cows as far east as you can. We pulled up wire for over two hundred yards, but it's a mess the further west you go."

CHAPTER 54

A Night Drive

THEY MOVED THE CATTLE THE REST OF THE NIGHT. AT 7:00 a.m., they stopped. They had moved nearly fifteen miles but Rock was worried.

He watched the trail behind them. "Fifteen miles isn't enough distance. We need to push on. We are still a ways from the border of the Montana Territory. Once we cross that border though, we will be on the Crow reservation. We'll have to worry about entering uninvited, but the law here won't be able to touch us."

They rested the cattle and the men for three hours and then continued north. Gabe stopped them again at 1:00 p.m. He knew they were quite a ways north of the bones of Fort Phil Kearny but they had too far to go to waste time.

"We'll let them graze for a couple of hours and then we are pushing on. Let's stay alert. We don't want to be caught off guard."

At 2:30 p.m., the herd was once again on the move. They crossed some small creeks and the cattle watered well. Gabe kept a worried eye on the trail behind them. So far, it was clear. The grass was thick by the water and the cattle spread out to graze. They were tired and the men were as well.

283

Gabe rode ahead to talk to Cookie. "Let's stop here and feed the men. Then we are going to push all night. Rock thinks we are about thirty miles from the reservation. That is too long of a drive for one night but we are going to go as far as we can."

Cookie had supper ready by 4:00 p.m. Once again, the cattle were pushed north. When the sun went down, they were driven by the light of the moon. By 1:00 a.m., Gabe figured they had made another fifteen miles. He rode ahead and found a little valley with water and grass.

"Take them up that valley, Rock. We'll bed them down there until morning."

He looked around at the men. "You fellows have given your best and you are appreciated. We have one more hard push, and then I hope to slow down. Figure out night guard. Whoever is on, stay awake. We can't afford to get caught this close to the border."

Angel and Tall Eagle took first watch. Angel's voice was soft and soothing. Most of the cattle just bedded down. As the night went on, more were up and grazing.

Gabe was up most of the night. Around midnight, he finally mounted Buck and rode south. All was quiet on the trail behind them. He was just turning back toward camp when he heard the creaking of saddles. He whispered to Buck and laid the horse down quietly. The men's voices carried through the night.

"No way they came this far. No herd could move that fast."

"There are tracks here. Some cattle definitely moved past this area and recently."

"Well, old Bob Smith was going to move his herd to his fall pasture yesterday. He paid the boss to cross here. I think that black herd is holed up and we rode past them. Let's head back south. Shoot, we can't see anything in the dark anyway. Booker is getting the Livestock Association boys together and he'll be out here by noon. We can catch them then."

Gabe waited until the men's voices disappeared. Then he mounted Buck and rode back to camp. It was after 1:00 in the morning. He woke the men up.

"Change in plans, boys. We are moving now. A posse is going to be out here by noon and we need to be across that border."

Camp was quickly broken and the herd was gathered. The night was short but the cattle had fed and watered well. They moved out easily in the cool air.

It was a hazy night. The clouds were flitting over the moon and it was difficult to see. That didn't seem to bother the two lead cows though. They plodded north into the night and barely shied at any noise.

By 6:00 a.m., Gabe estimated that they had covered another ten miles. He rode back along the trail of cattle and talked to each man.

"Let's keep them moving as long as we can. We should be less than twenty miles from the border. If we cross by 10:00 this morning, I will feel a whole lot more comfortable."

CHAPTER 55

THE CROW RESERVATION

BY 8:00 A.M., THE CATTLE WERE DRAGGING. SOME OF them were beginning to limp. Rock shook his head. "If we lame them, this will all be for nothing. I won't be able to drive them the rest of the way period."

Gabe nodded and signaled to the riders to ease up. "Bring those laggers on up here. We'll rest an hour and then move them again."

Rock's eyes lit up as he pointed at a pile of buffalo skulls. He grinned. "We made it! That is the Crow marker for the border of the reservation. Push the tail end of this herd up. We are home free!"

Rock and Gabe rode their horses back to the riders on drag. "Push them up. The border is just ahead and we need to get them across."

Rock's cows were tired and didn't want to hurry. The men swung their ropes and finally got the cattle to trot. The last of the herd crossed onto the reservation just a little before 10:00 a.m.

The men almost fell out of their saddles. Once again, Tall Eagle and Angel offered to take first watch. The rest of the men rolled out their bedrolls and fell asleep without waiting to eat breakfast.

Spur drove his horses in and while they put up the rope pen, he nodded with his head.

"I saw some Crow warriors over that hill as I rode in. Chief Plenty Coups is the principal chief. He won't come down to greet you, but you had better plan to make that trip to meet up with him soon."

Gabe nodded dully. "How is he to work with?"

Spur shrugged. "The Crow are our allies. Still, we are here and we didn't ask permission to come. I think you need to take some cows and head for his camp right away." He looked over where Rock was talking to Tobe and added, "Rock lived with the Crow for a time. He knows their language and these are his cows. This needs to be his deal."

Gabe listened and then stood wearily. He waved at Nate. "Saddle Watie for me and Red for Rock. Sam, you and Tuff cut out fifteen head of the best longhorns. Cookie, make us a pack. I need tobacco, sugar, and coffee."

He walked over to Rock. Both men's eyes were bloodshot. Gabe grinned as he studied the rancher.

"If I look as tough as you do, we are both sorry examples of men to negotiate with." Rock laughed and Gabe continued, "Let's plan to meet with Chief Plenty Coups right away. I'd like to take our time crossing this reservation, and that will depend on this meeting."

"You want to take anyone else?"

"I'd like to take Spur. He knows this area as well as you do, and I swear, he knows just about everyone we meet."

Cookie handed each of them a cup of coffee and thrust a burrito into their hands. He handed Gabe the pack he had asked for. "There are more burritos in there in case you are still hungry." His hard old face grew serious. "Luck, Boy," he stated as he gripped Gabe's shoulder. "I'll have dinner ready around 2:00. I think these boys need sleep more than they need food."

Gabe nodded. He caught Tall Eagle as the man rode toward the cattle. "See if you can graze those cattle northwest. I'd like to get them further inside the reservation if we can."

Tall Eagle dipped his head slightly and then continued on toward the cattle.

CHAPTER 56

CHIEF PLENTY COUPS

CHIEF PLENTY COUPS WAS NOT AT HIS TIPI. WHEN Rock asked the woman who was cooking there where he was, she pointed toward an open area beyond the encampment.

Rock bowed his head to her. "Thank you, Strikes-the-Iron." He handed her the package of sugar. "This is for you. May you have many more seasons."

The woman nodded in appreciation but said nothing as she watched the men leave. They had left the cattle at the edge of the camp. Some young boys were watching them as the cattle grazed.

The chief looked up as the three men approached him. He was sitting on the ground. A group of young men in their teens was listening to him as he talked. He dismissed them with a smile. The young braves answered him respectfully before they rose and left.

Chief Plenty Coups stood and approached Rock with a smile on his face. He extended his hand.

"White Eagle. It has been many moons since we have seen our brother. What are you doing in the land of the Crow?"

Rock's pleasure at seeing the chief was evident on his face.

Gabe didn't understand any of their conversation since he didn't speak Siouan, the language of the Crow. Spur only caught a few words. Spur did understand "brother" though. His smile was wide when the chief reached to shake his hand. Gabe's handshake was friendly as well.

"Come. Sit with me by my fire. Strikes-the-Iron will fix us something to eat." His sharp eyes missed nothing and he quickly spotted the cattle. He stared at them for a moment and then turned his eyes back to Rock.

Rock handed him the package of tobacco and the coffee.

"For you, my friend. For when the days turn cold. For those days when you must sit and think."

Rock looked around. "Little Bear is not here? I was hoping to see my brother."

The chief shook his head. "No, he has been gone for two moons. He searches for a man. He took six braves with him. I think he will not return until the man he seeks is found."

He smiled at Rock. "Little Bear tells me you have taken another wife. It is good. Small ones need a mother to guide them."

Rock laughed and agreed. "Yes, it is good since we have three small ones. We will add another when the snow falls and the bears sleep in their caves."

Plenty Coups nodded approvingly. Strikes-the-Iron arrived with a stew for each of them. She served Plenty Coups first. He in turn passed the stew to each man, beginning with Rock and ending with Gabe. He took the last bowl for himself.

There was little talking while they ate. Once they were finished, Plenty Coups filled his pipe and passed it to the three men who had eaten with him.

They smoked in silence for a time. Plenty Coups finally locked his eyes onto Rock's.

"Life has been hard for Flying Duck since the death of her son, Beaver Tail."

Rock's face slowly turned red. He nodded in agreement. "Beaver Tail was a strong warrior."

Plenty Coups took several more puffs on the pipe before he continued. "His death has put bad blood between her family and yours."

"Not between me and all of the Crow people?"

"In the Crow tradition, murder is between the two families. Since you are Little Bear's brother, it has affected his family as well. It would be good for you to heal your families."

Rock nodded slowly. "How do I do that? If I hadn't killed Beaver Tail, he would have killed my wife." Rock's voice was hard as he continued. "I am not sorry I killed him, but I am sorry his death hurt his mother and my brother's family."

The chief's eyes glinted and he nodded. "Give her some of your fine beef. Her cooking pot is empty and she often goes hungry. She will not accept the help that Little Bear offers her. Perhaps if you talk to her, her heart can forgive you and be happy once again."

Rock's chest tightened at the thought but he nodded. He stood and looked down at the chief. "Tell me where her lodge is and I will talk to her."

The chief pointed toward the end of the encampment. "Flying Duck lives in the last lodge. I will wait for you to return."

CHAPTER 57

FLYING DUCK

ROCK WALKED TO WHERE THE YOUNG MEN WERE watching the cattle. He mounted Red and cut out two of the best cows. Both were heavy with calves. He also took a third cow that had lost her calf on the drive. He slowly drove them to the end of the encampment and turned them loose to graze.

An old woman was sitting in front of her lodge. She ignored him when he walked up to her. Rock sat down, cross-legged, in front of her.

"Old Grandmother. Flying Duck. I am White Eagle."

The old woman didn't move but her eyes burned in her face. She spat on the ground.

Rock's neck turned red but he leaned forward. "I am sorry the death of Beaver Tail has put bad blood between us." He nodded toward the three cows. "I brought you a gift of cattle." He stretched his hand out to her, palm up. "I ask for your forgiveness." Rock's face was sincere and his words were from his heart.

The old woman stared at him. "Beaver Tail was my only son. Cattle will not bring him back to me."

"This is true but two of the cows carry calves. Perhaps you can use the cow with no calf inside to fill your cooking pot. The two cows with calves inside will birth soon. Then you will have four head of cattle."

"My son was a good boy. He took care of his mother."

Rock didn't answer. He doubted that was true but Flying Duck needed to hold happy memories of her son in her heart.

Flying Duck stared at Rock. Her eyes were so intense that he had to resist the urge to squirm and run away. Instead, he returned her gaze. After a moment, she looked away. When she looked back, her eyes had tears in them.

"Why did you kill my son?"

Rock could feel his neck become tight. He didn't want to tell this mother why he had killed her only child. He shook his head.

"It is best to leave the past in the past."

She shook her head furiously. "Tell me," she demanded. "Tell me so I can make peace in my heart. Little Bear would not tell me. You must tell me."

Rock stared at her for a moment and then he looked away. When he looked back at the grieving mother, he said simply, "He tried to kill my wife."

Flying Duck's lips quivered and she gripped her hands tightly.

Rock understood then what this mother had known all along. She knew her son was not the man she had tried to raise him to be.

He leaned forward and touched her hand as he stated softly, "Beaver Tail fought bravely. He was a strong warrior. He did not beg for his life." Rock had fought Beaver Tail and the man *had* fought bravely.

He didn't tell the grieving mother how her son died though. He only told her part of what happened, and that part was true.

Tears slid from Flying Duck's eyes. She looked away from Rock and then looked at the cattle. When she looked back, her face was stoic but her eyes were alive.

"I think you are a fine warrior and a good man, White Eagle. Little Bear told me you were but I did not believe him.

"I will take your gift of cattle. Today, we end the anger between our families." She smiled at him. "It is good you came today."

When the old woman struggled to stand, Rock stood and gave her a hand.

Her old eyes shined as she smiled up at him. "I think your mother would be pleased. I think you are a son to be proud of."

Rock hugged her briefly and then stepped back. His voice was gruff when he spoke. "If you ever need a home, you come to me. I will take care of you in your old age. I owe you that for taking your son."

The old woman chuckled. "I don't think you know what you say but I will not come. My home is here. By the next moon, I will be gone to greet the Great Spirit, and Little Bear will take care of my cattle. Go in peace, White Eagle." She paused and then turned around. "I will see your first wife there I think." Turning slowly, the old woman shuffled into her lodge.

Rock stood for a moment staring at the lodge. Her words hit him hard. *How did she know about Suzanna?* He stared at the lodge a moment longer and then walked slowly toward Red. *Plenty Coups was right. It was good to come here today.* He mounted Red and rode slowly back to the other side of the encampment.

Plenty Coups watched Rock ride toward him. He nodded in approval as he looked at Gabe and Spur sitting silently in front of him.

"White Eagle is a strong warrior and a fine man. You will miss him when he goes to meet the Great Spirit."

Both men stared at him but Plenty Coups said no more. His eyes glinted at the look of surprise on both men's faces. He stood and led the way toward the cattle.

"Come. Let us go see these cattle that White Eagle brings to buy passage across the land of the Crow." He was still chuckling when they reached the cattle.

=== CHAPTER 58 ===

A Crooked Sheriff

THE RIDERS GRAZED THE CATTLE SLOWLY ACROSS THE Crow reservation. Some of the livestock had sore feet, and Rock wanted them to rest well before they continued on.

Around 2:00 p.m., a group of armed men arrived at the reservation border. One man left the group and rode his horse up to the encampment. He demanded that a young brave take him to Chief Plenty Coups.

The chief listened to what the young brave shared with him and then he slowly walked toward the mounted man.

"You are harboring cattle thieves here. We want them. Send them out and you'll have no trouble with us."

Chief Plenty Coups stared at the man. His eyes glinted in anger.

"White men are not welcome here unless they are guests. We did not invite you to come. Go now."

The man sputtered in anger. "I'm Sheriff Beason. I represent the Wyoming Stock Growers Association. You are harboring men who broke our laws. Turn them over to me."

Plenty Coups smiled slightly. "White man, you should study your own laws before making such demands.

"This is the Crow reservation. You have no right to be here. In addition, this reservation is in the Montana Territory. You are from the Wyoming Territory. Even by your own laws, you have no authority here.

"Take your men and go home. There is nothing here for you."

The sheriff grabbed for his gun but stopped when he heard a voice behind him.

"Go ahead and pull that gun. I'll cut you down and we'll wipe out every one of your gunmen as well.

"Plenty Coups is right. You are out of your jurisdiction. Now if you want to file a complaint in Cheyenne, go right ahead. My name is Gabe Hawkins and I am a member of the Association there. On the other hand, I think maybe it's time we clean house with you fellows, so make it easy for us. Pull that hogleg."

The sheriff started to answer and Gabe pushed his horse into the sheriff, forcing the man's horse to back up. His voice was hard as he growled his words at Beason.

"Get out. Get out or we'll mow every one of you down, and the law here will back us up.

"Booker is a corrupt man. If he isn't reined in, you are going to have a cattle war on your hands. I suggest you pay attention to where he is putting his fences instead of looking for trouble up here." He gestured at the mounted cowboys lined up behind Beason.

"You have seven men and we have twelve, so you go ahead and pick a fight for your boss. Plenty Coups has nothing to do with it though, and I'll file a report with the next military post we pass stating just that. Now you back up and go home, or you haul iron."

Beason stared at the hard-eyed man in front of him and then swung his horse around. Eleven riders of varying ages were lined up behind him. All but one had their guns out. Some had six shooters pointed at him while the rest had rifles pointed toward his men. The only man who didn't hold a gun was fingering a large knife.

That man's voice was soft as he spoke. "I think, señor, you should ride back quickly to where you came from. My knife, she is lonely. You have a large belly, and it would be so nice for her to rest in." He smiled at the sheriff and then shrugged. "Oh well. Perhaps tonight, yes?"

The sheriff's face blanched from red to white and he slowly backed his horse away from the mounted men. He rode back to the gunmen who waited outside the border of the reservation. They gathered around as he spoke. They stared as he headed his horse down the trail. Several started to argue as they swung their horses around.

Angel called to them, "Tonight, perhaps, I will come to visit you. Don't sleep so soundly. I will be very quiet, and my small knife, she will be happy."

Gabe's riders started to laugh and Rock shook his head. "You boys are just on the prod all the time, aren't you? You don't even try to walk a situation back."

"Not with men like that. They would have ridden right in here if they could have gotten by with it." Gabe's eyes were angry. He looked over to where Plenty Coups was standing.

"I'm sorry, Plenty Coups. We didn't mean to bring you trouble. I meant what I said about stopping at the next fort."

Plenty Coups' dark eyes gleamed and he laughed. His English was clear when he replied. "I think perhaps someday, I will ride with you. Someday when I am old…when I don't care if I live anymore." He chuckled as he walked away and Gabe slowly grinned.

"Well there you go, boys. You are taking your life in your hands with me. Now let's get those cattle moving northwest. Today is our last day of taking it easy."

CHAPTER 59

HEADED WEST

THE MEN AND THE CATTLE RESTED ANOTHER DAY before they pushed on. They were already on the western side so it wasn't long before they left the Crow reservation. They moved quickly, and were soon back on public land.

Gabe looked at his tally book. "August 24. We've been on the trail for four weeks—a week short of as long as I have been married," he muttered to himself. "I wonder how Merina is doing. I sure miss my little family."

He looked toward the back of the herd where the three young men were riding drag and he laughed. "They don't even seem to mind that position. They are just happy to be here and to have buddies to ride with."

The cattle crossed the Big Horn River with no problem and moved on west. They were traveling on the south side of the Yellowstone River. Rock rode up to join Gabe and he described the next eight to nine days of their route.

"We're about eighty miles or so from Big Timber. It's not much of a town but we should be able to restock supplies.

"Water won't be a problem since we'll follow the Yellowstone River for quite some time. Our next big river crossing will be at the Yellowstone

Ford. We are late in the season though so the water shouldn't be so high. The cattle won't even have to swim. It will have a strong current though. The bottom of the river will be mostly covered with round rock, and those rocks can be slick. We should be all right if we just take it slow. I think we'll want to put ropes on the chuckwagon though to keep it from washing downstream.

"Once we cross the Yellowstone, Bozeman Pass will be just another thirty miles or so on west. Fort Ellis is just west of that pass. Spur will be delivering his horses there.

"He'll continue on with us until we are across from Skalkaho Pass. It is a little north and west on past Deer Lodge. He'll take that pass west through the Sapphire Mountains, and follow the Bitter Root Valley south. He can go right out the south end into the Idaho Territory." Rock paused as he looked over the long line of cattle. "Wish we could take that route. It would cut off a lot of miles. Too rough though. The cattle wouldn't be able to navigate those narrow ledges and steep climbs." Rock looked off in the distance and then frowned as he shook his head.

"I've always been leery of that pass. I sure wouldn't take it in the dark."

Gabe listened quietly and then asked, "So how many miles from here to Missoula?"

Rock thought a moment. "About three hundred fifty I'd say. Could be a few more or a few less. We have some passes to get through though, so some of those miles will be slow ones. Still, we should be in Stevensville in forty days or so." He grinned at Rock.

"Of course you still have to get home, but that won't take so long since you can move faster on horseback. You can even catch the train south in Salmon in the Idaho Territory if you want. That might save you a little time.

"Missing that little wife of yours, are you?" Rock asked with a laugh.

"It's a whole different deal when you have someone waiting on you."
Gabe grinned back at Rock and added, "Which means don't expect me
to do another drive if you buy more black cows.

"So who figured out all these passes? Lewis and Clark's expedition
surely didn't find all of them."

"The Indians used the same trails we are following. They were game
trails before that, and now we are building roads in the same locations.
Old Jim Bridger even guided a mapping expedition over it in '59 and
'60. The army was trying to figure out wagon routes through this area,
and this trail was one they chose."

Rock grinned again. "I sure am glad someone before me mapped all
of this out. I'd hate to be the first one trying to figure out how to wind
my way back home."

CHAPTER 60

PAINTED WAGONS

THEY ARRIVED AT BIG TIMBER ON AUGUST 31. THEY had averaged about ten miles per day the last eighty miles. Gabe gathered the men in.

"Well, we are about two hundred sixty miles from Stevensville now. Cookie is going to restock here in Big Timber so supper will be late tonight.

"We want to put a little extra weight in the wagon. If it's heavier when we cross the Yellowstone, the current won't push it so much.

"We'll need to make twelve miles tomorrow since Yellowstone Ford is about that far. I want to camp one or two miles from there tomorrow night. That way, the cattle will be fresh the next morning when we put them in the water.

"We are crossing the Yellowstone at about its lowest level of the season. It shouldn't be too bad. Whoever found this ford found one of the few places where the banks aren't high and steep. The water will be moving fast though, so we'll want to take it easy. We don't want any horses to go down.

"We'll let the cattle take their time too. The water will be clear and cold so they may want to drink as they cross. We'll let them go as slow as they want."

He grinned at his men as he looked at each of them. "That means you have a little time tonight. You might want to take a bath and wash out your clothes." His grin became bigger as he added, "Or you can take a dip in the water if you fall off your horse. Your call."

Spur had his horses penned and he strolled up to Gabe. His face was serious but his eyes were twinkling.

"Saw a couple of wagons out on the prairie today. Painted up all bright and purty. Couple of men escorting them. They'll probably be crossing the river about the same time as us." He added softly as he tried not to smile, "They looked like right friendly gals."

Gabe looked up at Spur in surprise and then glared. "They aren't camping with us. We sure don't need distractions like that around."

Spur chuckled. "I figured as much. I just thought I would give you a little notice in case they show up tomorrow. Maybe even tonight. That would be handy like since you just sent the boys down to the river to take a bath."

Gabe muttered a curse. "That's all I need. Well, I'll head down there now. If I see those wagons, I'll clear our boys out." He was muttering and cussing under his breath as he grabbed his warbag. "Women and drives are never a good idea. Well, sometimes they are, but not when they are party girls!"

Supper was over and the men were just rolling out their bedrolls when a man called out.

"Hello the camp! Can I come in?"

Gabe stood with a frown on his face. "You can come in but come in alone."

A man of average height with bright blue eyes strolled into the camp. He looked around and his bushy mustache spread wide as he smiled.

"Now I've run mule teams up an' down this trail for nigh on ten years an' this is the first herd of black cows I've seen." He put out his hand to Gabe. "Posey Ryan is the name." His eyes twinkled as he asked, "You boys headed somewhere in particular or just takin' yore cows on a picnic?"

Gabe chuckled as he shook Posey's hand. Spur stepped forward.

"Howdy, Posey. I didn't figure to see you this far north. How have you been? I thought you'd have a passel of kids by now."

Posey grabbed Spur's hand. "Well I should have known a cow outfit with this many horses would have you as part of it. Good to see you, Spur." He chuckled while he looked around the little group. "We have two kids so far but I reckon there will be more."

His eyes were serious as he nodded his head over his shoulder.

"Thought you'd like to know you're about to have some visitors. I passed a fancy wagon headed this way. It was packed plumb full of women an' they looked like they was on their way to a party. That or about to start one."

The men looked up in surprise and some of them sat up. Rufe pulled on his boots and stood excitedly. "If we're havin' company, I want to be ready. Maybe Gabe 'ill play his harmonica so we cin do a little dancin'."

Gabe glared at him. "Sit down, Rufe. There won't be a party tonight. Those women aren't coming in this camp, and you aren't going outside it." He looked around at the surprised men. "And anyone who does needs to take his rig with him, because he won't have a job when he comes back."

Spur chuckled. Several of the men frowned as they leaned back on their bedrolls. Tuff looked surprised. He whispered to Nate, "Why is your brother so unneighborly? Shoot, I'd like to talk to some women for a change."

Sam laughed. "It ain't the talkin' Gabe is worried about. I've never seen one of those wagons up close but I've heard talk of 'em. I might sneak out later just to see for my own self."

Nate looked over at his friend and frowned. "No you're not," he whispered. "Gabe won't put up with that. He'd have to fire you like he promised, and then how would you get back home? Yore ma would be cryin' an' a carryin' on, an' yore pa would whup you. *After* Gabe whupped you."

Sam eased back on the rock he was leaning against and scowled. Nate was right and he knew it. Still, they hadn't had any time off since this drive started. *I thought we would at least be able to stop in one town.*

He looked over at Gabe. *Gabe would whup me. He sure is grouchy a lot. I wonder why he doesn't want those girls to come in. We could at least talk to them.*

Spur offered Posey a cup of coffee but the muleskinner shook his head. "Naw. I need to get back to my mules. I'm a travelin' with a couple of tin horns. I saw yore fire an' thought I'd stop in.

"Ya fellers familiar with this route? I can point ya where to cross the Yellowstone if ya ain't."

Rock stepped forward and offered his hand. "Rock Beckler. These are my cows. I'm familiar with this route but that's mighty neighborly of you. We'll cross at the Ford. That seems to be the best spot."

Posey nodded. "That's the place. Well, I'll get on back to my camp." He stopped to listen and women's voices could be heard in the distance. "Looks like ya are goin' to have yore hands full here in just a little bit. See ya boys on down the road." He was chuckling as he walked away.

Gabe looked over at Rock. "You want to come with me or do you want me to handle this?"

Rock's green eyes were twinkling. "I think I'll come with you. I'd hate for you to tip their wagon over if they won't turn it around." He looked around at the men. "Gabe's right about this. Those women aren't coming in here and you aren't sneaking out. You'll get your time to party when we reach Stevensville. Until then, we'll keep our shoulders bunched and our noses clean."

He looked over at Gabe with a grin. "Well, Mr. Friendly. Let's go show those ladies what kind of welcome they are going to get here."

Angel chuckled as he looked at the two men. "Señors, would you like me to come with you? I think perhaps a friendly vaquero—"

Both men interrupted with a resounding "No!" and the riders all began laughing. Angel tried to look sad but his dark eyes were sparkling.

He looked around at the men and nodded wisely. "Señor Gabe, now that he is married to my sister, he knows how difficult she can be. He is afraid of her, and because of that, we cannot talk to these friendly ladies."

Gabe snorted. "Angel, you are an asset on the trail, but you are trouble when it comes to women. Come on, Rock. Let's get this over with."

=== CHAPTER 61 ===

JUST SOME FRIENDLY WOMEN

SOUND CARRIED CLEARLY IN THE STILL NIGHT AND the men were quiet as they listened. Gabe's voice was loud when he spoke.

"Howdy, Ladies. You stop that wagon right there and turn it around. There isn't going to be any party at this campfire tonight."

"Oh, come on. I'm sure your riders would love some female company."

"I'm sure they would too, but it's not going to happen."

"We promise just to talk. We'll be *real* friendly. Your boys will be happy to see us come." Several women giggled.

Gabe's voice was angry when he responded.

"I said to turn the wagon around and I meant it. Now wheel that wagon around and head on back to where you are camping. You aren't far from Butte City, and you can have all the fun you want there. Our boys have over two hundred miles yet to cover before we get these cows home."

A woman started to argue and Rock's voice cut in. It was quiet but it was hard.

311

"Ladies, turn the wagon around or we'll do it for you. These are my cows and my crew. Now we asked nicely but we mean business.

"Your lead horse is a little jumpy. If I crease his back with a bullet, he is going to run. And who knows where you'll end up? I guarantee you though that your fancy wagon won't hold up over all these rocks. Now it would be a darn shame for such friendly women as yourselves to have to walk all the way to Butte City."

Several women's voices could be heard arguing and then one voice came through clearly.

"Turn it around, Meg. These men aren't going to change their minds. I don't want my wagon destroyed, and I believe these cowboys will do as they say they will.

"Perhaps we will see you in Butte City?"

"Not in that city or any other place, ma'am. Both of us are married and we are afraid of our wives." The humor could be heard in Rock's voice but the wagon was turned around. The sound of women's voices retreated into the night.

Gabe looked over at Rock as they walked back toward the fire and he chuckled. "I don't think I am the only 'sudden' fellow on this drive. I think you have a lot of violence in you that you keep hidden. Mine just hangs around closer to the top."

Rock laughed. "Maybe, but the part about being afraid of our wives was true for both of us."

Both men were grinning as they walked back to the fire. Rock looked around at the men resting there.

"The party was canceled, boys. Get some sleep. We have some hard days in front of us."

Rufe threw his boot on the ground and muttered as he lay back on his blanket. "A wagon full of women an' we couldn't even talk to 'em. It jist ain't right."

Gabe grinned at him. "Rufe, you and I both know those women weren't coming here for a little conversation. I just saved you some money and probably a good case of the lues. Now shut up and go to sleep."

Tuff leaned over to Sam and whispered. "What is 'the lues?'"

Sam thought a moment. "I ain't real sure. I'll ask Spur tomorrow. He seems to know a lot about women an' all that goes along with 'em."

Nate agreed. "Angel does too. I'll ask him and we'll see if they say the same thing."

The three friends mumbled their goodnights and then lay back on their blankets. Tuff was quiet a moment before he commented softly. "I sure am glad you fellows came along on this drive. I think I am going to miss seeing you when we get back to Stevensville."

Sam and Nate didn't answer but Tuff was right. They were going to miss him too.

=========================== CHAPTER 62 ===========================

THE WISDOM OF SPUR

NATE OFFERED TO WRANGLE THE HORSES THE NEXT day and Spur agreed. He settled into drag beside Sam, and the young man looked over at him.

"Spur, we have been talkin', Nate, Tuff, an' me. There are some things we want to ask you."

Spur almost choked. *I've been had by a pack of boys* he thought as he watched Nate head out with the remuda of horses.

He looked over at Sam. His big mustache came in handy when he wanted to hide his smile.

"Shoot. What are you wanting to know?"

"Last night, when Gabe said he saved Rufe from a case of the lues… what was he talkin' about?"

Spur's tanned face slowly turned red as he faced forward on his horse. He pushed back his hat to scratch his head, and then looked over at the earnest young man beside him.

"I ain't so sure I'm the one to be talkin' to you about this. Maybe Nate should ask Gabe."

"Well, Nate is goin' to ask Angel. We know it has something to do with those ladies. We figure you an' Angel know more about women than just about anybody else on this drive." He frowned and added, "Besides, Gabe would probably say they would talk to Merina, an' Nate don't want to ask Merina about women."

Spur laughed out loud as he shook his head.

"Sam, any fellow who tells you he has women all figured out is a fool or a liar, and that is the gospel truth." He chewed on his mustache for a moment and then looked over at the young man beside him.

"See those girls in that wagon—they sell favors. They might act all friendly-like but that's their job. They get paid to please a man. 'Course it ain't just one man. It's any man who needs pleasin'. An' sometimes, one of those fellers is carryin' a sickness. He passes it on to her, an' she shares it with the next feller she pleases.

"Sometimes that sickness is called the lues. An' I can tell you that you sure don't want to get it."

Sam studied Spur's profile for a moment and then he scratched his head. "They get it from kissin'? I've kissed a few girls an' I ain't got no sickness."

Spur's neck slowly turned red and he looked at the young man beside him.

"Ain't yore folks talked to you about the birds an' the bees? I think this here conversation should be with yore ma or yore pa."

"I asked Pa an' he said to ask Ma. Ma said that when folks get married, they get intimate, but she didn't tell me what intimate was. Her face turned all red an' I ran outside. That was about five years ago an' I ain't asked about it since."

Spur drug his hand across his chin and then nodded. "Your ma was right, Sam. You know in the pasture when the bull breeds a cow? Well, he breeds every cow he can find. Now some men, they're the same way. Your pa's not like that though.

"See, there's a difference in folks. Some of them get intimate just to breed an' some do it for love. Your folks are the second kind, an' that's a good way to be. If you act like your pa an' not like an old bull out in the pasture, you'll never have to worry about catchin' a disease from bein' intimate.

"Now those girls in that wagon an' the ones that work the line… well, they sell their favors to those men who act like bulls. Some of the girls do it out of desperation, but others do it 'cause the money is good. It ain't no way to make a livin' though."

Sam was quiet as he listened. He finally asked Spur, "You ever been in one of those houses?"

Spur pulled his horse to a stop and studied the young man beside him.

"Sam, I'm gonna tell you something that I don't tell many men." Sam's eyes grew wide as he slowly nodded.

"My ma was one of those women who sold favors. I don't even know who my pa is. I lived as a kid in a house where all the women did what my mother did, an' it sure wasn't a place I'd wish on any kid.

"Now I have a lot of girls on the line who I count as my friends an' I do what I can to help them if they need somethin'. But I don't frequent whore houses 'cause I know how it is in there." He studied Sam's face closely as he added softly, "I sure don't want to bring a little kid into this world who will have the same kind of life I did as a little tyke." Spur looked off in the distance and a small smile crossed his face. It was serious again as he stared at Sam. He added softly, "They might not have an old nun rescue them like I did.

"See, Sister Eddie took me in an' she changed my life. She bossed me around an' smacked me some like my mother should have. An' she sure didn't let me run wild. I didn't like it or her much at first, but Sister Eddie was the best thing that could have happened to me."

He squeezed Sam's shoulder and nodded toward Tuff who was on the other side of the herd. "You share that story with your buddies, an' you remember it when you think you want to act like a bull.

"Now let's push these stragglers up. Gabe will be back here cussin' me if I act like a slacker." He winked at Sam and swung his rope at the cow in front of him.

"Get up there, old girl. You hang back here too far and we'll have to leave you for wolf bait."

=== CHAPTER 63 ===

FISHING ON THE YELLOWSTONE

THEY CAMPED SEVERAL MILES BACK FROM Yellowstone Ford. Tuff thought they should camp right in front of it but Gabe shook his head.

"There are rules you follow on drives, and one is to never camp on top of a crossing area. There might be someone else who needs to cross. Of course, a second rule is to never pass the herd in front of you, but we don't have to worry about that here."

He pointed toward the river. "Why don't you and your two friends go down and see if you can catch us some fish for supper. If you go out in the water, take off your boots. That current is fast and your bare feet will grip better than boots will.

Tuff raced to find his buddies and Gabe called after him, "Take your ropes. I don't want one of you to fall and be pulled downstream for a couple of miles before we can fish you out."

Spur watched the three young men climb down the riverbank and work on their poles. He looked over at Gabe and grinned.

"I think it is about time you and Stub have a talk about girls with your brothers."

Gabe looked surprised and then frowned. Stub turned red and stomped off. Rock chuckled. He put up his hands and backed away. "Not me. My kids aren't big enough to ask questions. I'm bowing out of this."

Angel began to laugh as he looked at Gabe. "I think, señor, maybe you are waiting for someone to share a little information with your brother. I think if you wait too long, the wrong person might teach him."

Spur nodded in agreement. "Sam caught me today and peppered me with questions. It seems the three of them have been discussing things since Gabe there mentioned the lues."

Gabe's face showed his surprise a second time and then it turned red. He glared at Spur. "I was hoping to have Merina help me with that talk."

Spur laughed and nodded his head toward the river. "Yep, that's exactly what Nate told Sam. But don't worry, I talked a little with Sam. I'm sure he'll share with the other two." He looked over at Angel, "And Nate is going to talk to you next."

His eyes were bright and his mustache twitched as he tried not to laugh. "Apparently, they think Angel and I know more about women than the rest of you sorry cowpunchers."

Gabe snorted as he stared at Spur. "I'm not sure I even want to know how that conversation went."

Spur shrugged. "Ya get what ya pay for. I never said I was good with kids, and I for sure have never talked to one about the birds and the bees. It seemed to satisfy Sam though."

Laughter spilled out of him as he added, "Ya might want to follow up with them though." He grabbed his knife. "I think I'll do a little fishin' with Angel. This might be entertaining."

Soon the two ornery cowboys were headed for the river. Gabe walked over to where Stub was whittling on a stick.

"You think we need to have a talk with the boys?"

Stub paused and then shook his head. "Nope. I'm guessin' Spur related it somehow to cattle, and they probably have the picture." He threw down the stick and stuck his knife in the ground as he looked up at Gabe.

"I wouldn't know what to say. My folks never talked to me. I'm no hand when it comes to that stuff."

Gabe nodded absently as he watched the three boys. They were all gathered around Spur and Angel. Angel said something that made everyone laugh, and then they all settled down to fish.

"Maybe we should just let them come to us if they have questions."

Gabe grinned at his quiet friend. "Let's talk about crossing that river. Cattle we understand."

CHAPTER 64

YELLOWSTONE FORD

THE MEN HAD THE HERD AT YELLOWSTONE FORD BY 6:00 a.m. The sky was cloudy and overcast. Gabe was hoping not to cross in rain. However, the cloudy sky would keep the sun from reflecting off the water. Sometimes that spooked the cattle, and if it did, they would have a hard time getting them to go in.

He had ridden Buck back and forth through the river several times the evening before. The current was fast but the river was low. The water was barely a foot deep, maybe less. The bottom ranged from small round rocks to patches of crushed rock. Buck picked his way across carefully. His shoes cut into the rocks and he had no trouble.

Gabe frowned. *Those cows will slide some. I think I had better put some boys on each bank to rope anything that goes down. I'm not sure they will be able to get back up in that current.*

He called to the men. "Sam, Angel, and Miguel—I want you on the riverbanks ready to rope anything that goes down. And all of you—cross that river a couple of times so your horses aren't surprised by the current. The water is shallow but that current is fast."

Mija and Mona, the two lead cows, were ready to cross. They stopped at the edge and tasted the water. Then they stepped in and marched across to the north side of the river like two little soldiers. The rest of the cows followed. Nothing went down until the last group was pushed in. Two of the weakest cows slipped. One recovered but the second one went down. She was thrashing and throwing her head around as the current bounced her along the bottom of the riverbed.

Angel swung his long rope and began to drag her to the riverbank. Once she reached the shallows, he relaxed the rope and flicked it off.

The cow was mad. She bellowed and charged his horse. Angel raced it up the riverbank calling to her as his horse ran.

"Come and chase me, you sorry excuse of a vaca. For many days, you act so weak. Now you want to fight?" He was still yelling at her when they raced out of sight.

Before long, they were back. The cow was now running in front of him and Angel pushed her toward the herd. He shouted as he rode, "I should ride you, you old bag of huesos. May your bones be tired tonight. Now go and cause trouble no more."

The men watched him and laughed. Angel added a whole new dimension to the drive.

Once the cattle were across, the men hooked ropes onto the chuckwagon. The mules pulled strongly but the wagon bounced sideways as the current pushed the heavy wagon.

Cookie stood up and yelled at the cowboys. "Keep them durn ropes tight. I don't want to tip this here wagon over!" He whipped the mules and they charged through the water, pulling the chuckwagon up on the north riverbank. Cookie slowly sat down and wiped a shaky hand across his face.

"Durn rivers. I'm jist 'bout fed up with crossin' rivers. When I get this here drive done, I'm a gonna park my sorry hindside on solid ground an' stay there." He looked behind him at the swiftly running river and shook his head. It was nearly a quarter of a mile wide.

"Look at all them tomb markers linin' those riverbanks. This warn't a bad crossin' but I'd hate to see it in June with all the run-off from the snow. Then it would be fast *an'* deep." He shook his head again. "Sure am glad Rock planned this here drive later in the summer. 'Course now it's 'most fall. Hope we make it back home 'fore the weather breaks up here."

Gabe rode through the cattle. He called Rock and then pointed at three cows. "I don't think they are going to make it much further. We might want to sell them for beef in Butte City. You should be able to get the price you paid for them." He studied the herd and frowned. "They all three have calves inside but I'm not sure what else to do."

Rock studied the cows and then nodded. "I was hoping to make it home with all of them but I knew that was unrealistic. We've done well so far." He waved his arm as he hollered at the men. "Keep them moving. We are a little over thirty miles from Bozeman Pass. We're eating up the miles, Boys."

As they drove the cattle away from the river, the two lead cows pushed their way to the front and the herd was once again headed west.

====== CHAPTER 65 ======

BOZEMAN PASS

THE TEXAS COWBOYS STARED AT THE MOUNTAINS IN front of them. Tobe looked from Rock to Gabe.

"You sure we can git those cows across there? I never pushed no cows over a mountain before."

Rock nodded absently. "That pass has been used by buffalo for years. In fact, it's been used as a door through the mountains for thousands of years. The buffalo and other game still use it and the Indians as well. It's nature's gateway through the Continental Divide and I'm thankful it's here. Besides, it's not as bad as you might think.

"Let's let the cattle rest tonight, and we'll start through first thing in the morning. That way they will be fresh. The stretch from here to Butte City will be our hardest. After that, we'll wind between the mountains, and the going will be a little easier." He looked around at the men.

"You Texans might want to dig out your coats. That pass will be cold. In fact, we usually run into some snow."

Spur looked over at the men and chuckled as he pulled on his mustache. "Fort Ellis is just three miles east of Bozeman and that's where I deliver my horses. My job is just about over. I think I'll get me a bath and a shave in Bozeman." He nodded toward the cattle.

"I can take those three cows in for you once I deliver the horses if they are still limping. I'm guessing the post commander would pay for some fresh beef. I can ask him when we finish up our horse business." Spur looked over at the riders who were close and added, "Too bad some of you sorry cowpunchers can't come with me."

Neither Rock nor Gabe heard his last comment but the other riders immediately began to plan how they might convince Gabe to let them have a night off.

Gabe finally caught some of the scheming and turned around. "No one is going anywhere. Now get some rest and make sure the horse you pick for tomorrow is a wiry one. We will be doing some climbing and a smaller horse might handle it better."

The sun was shining when they pushed the cattle up the pass. Everyone had their coats tied behind their saddles, but Sam was thinking about tossing his in the chuckwagon.

Nate shook his head. "First of all, Cookie drives way out in front. That means if you need it before we get through here, you'll have to leave the herd."

Just then, it started to snow. At first the flakes were small. Soon they changed to large ones, and the snow started to come down thicker. The wind picked up as well.

Rock rode back along the cattle and yelled at the men over the wind. "Keep pushing them. As soon as we drop down, this should end. Keep them bunched. We don't want any to wander off the trail."

The next several hours were cold and brutal. Sam was glad he didn't get rid of his coat. He shivered as he pulled the wool collar up higher. A cow was trying to turn into the brush and he cut her off.

"Keep movin', girls. The sooner you get over the top of this pass, the sooner we will all be warm again."

Finally, they were over the top and moving down the other side. The pass dropped them into a long valley. Once again, the sun was shining.

Gabe was amazed. "This high country is something else. Sure is pretty though."

Rock nodded. "Lots of pretty country around here. It's rough but the cattle do well."

Once they were down in the valley, Gabe sent Nate and Tuff out to help Spur sort the horses. They were a little less than ten miles away from Bozeman. By the time they arrived with the slower-moving cattle, Spur would have his delivery done.

Rock rode over to Gabe. "We'll camp just outside of Bozeman." He pointed down the long valley in front of them. "

"Riders call this the 'Valley of the Flowers.' They get a little more moisture here than the area we just traveled through. The ground is fertile too so I imagine lots of this will be broken up someday for crops." He was quiet a moment and then added, "I know crops are important but the cattleman in me hates to see good grass torn up." He looked over at Gabe. His face was a little sad. "I hope I'm gone by the time our little valley is all torn up. It's a cattleman's paradise. I fell in love with it the first time I rode through it back in '71."

He pointed toward the town. "This town is named after a fellow by the name of John Bozeman, the same fellow some emigrants decided to name the Bozeman Trail after.

"Not sure what to think of Bozeman. He abandoned his wife and three little girls back east somewhere when he came out here. Never did bring them out. I just don't know how a man could do that.

"He was an adventurer though. His partner and him widened those original trails so they were wide enough for wagons.

"Once gold was discovered, folks started to pour in. Everybody thought they were going to get rich. This was a popular trail for a time even though it was a dangerous one.

"Bozeman worked as a guide for a year. He finally figured out he could make more money off the emigrants by stocking them with supplies—and stay safer too.

"He was a businessman and a wheeler-dealer. Didn't live long though. He was killed three years later in '67."

Rock tapped his reins on his horses neck as he added, "His Bloody Bozeman Trail is much safer now. It's still a drive though."

Gabe was quiet a moment. He nodded down the valley and commented, "Maybe, but this is still going to be my last drive. Being married makes you think a little more about what's to come. There are a lot of ways to die on a cattle drive."

Rock nodded. "That's true but ranching isn't much better." His eyes were twinkling as he added, "You and I will be lucky to live till we're fifty."

"Shoot, you already had a close call with that bull. You'd better stay sharp or you'll make Merina a widow before she's forty."

Gabe was quiet. Rock was right. He thought about the men they had lost on the way up from Texas. He looked back at the long line of cattle and smiled. *At least we haven't lost anyone on this drive.*

"So how close to Bozeman do you want to camp? Maybe we ought to go on by and stop on the other side. We might be able to leave a little faster. I'm not sure how much of a novelty a cattle drive is here, but lookers can sure get in the way."

They made camp that evening in a grassy valley with lots of wildflowers. Rock pointed to the west.

"Our next town will be Gallatin City. It's really more of a settlement than a town. Three rivers join there to form the headwaters of the Missouri. Some folks think rivers always run south, but lots of our rivers up here run north. The Missouri does until she gets farther north. Then she takes off east.

"We'll cross the three rivers at the head of the Missouri—the Jefferson, the Madison, and the Gallatin. Of the three, the Jefferson is the widest and has the most water. We are late in the season though so the levels should be down.

"And those will be our last big rivers to cross. Anything after that will be more like a creek."

Rufe's face looked worried and Rock added with a laugh, "None of those three crossings will compare to the Platte so relax, Rufe. We should be able to walk the cattle across. There are plenty of ferries too so we'll send Cookie across on one of those."

Cookie looked up from preparing supper and beamed at them. "That's good cause I was jist tellin' myself how tired I am a crossin' rivers. I might even make ya boys somethin' a little special to celebrate. We ain't had no bear sign fer a spell an' tonight jist might be the night."

CHAPTER 66

ACROSS THE DIVIDE AGAIN

ROCK WAS RIGHT ABOUT THE THREE RIVERS. THEY crossed with no problem. The cattle were climbing Homestake Pass five days later on September 15.

Gabe shook his head as he looked over the craggy mountains. "We've crossed the backbone of this country twice in less than fifty miles. And we'll cross it again when we leave the Bitter Root Valley. This is a tough territory."

Rock heard him muttering and laughed. "Too many mountains for you, Gabe? Shoot, by the time you get back home, you will be missing these passes."

Gabe laughed with him as he thought about it. *I sure won't miss the rivers though.*

This time they didn't run into any snowfall in the pass. However, it had snowed at some point in time since the trail was white.

The cows slugged slowly up the snowy mountain. When they dropped down on the other side, they could see a mining town in front of them.

Rock grinned and pointed. "There she is, Boys. Butte City. Some folks call her 'The Richest Hill on Earth.' We are just a little over a hundred miles to Missoula now. We about have this drive whipped."

Spur had delivered the horses several days before and he chuckled. "Yep, not much farther for me to travel with you fellows. I'll head west at Deer Lodge over to Phillipsburg and cut through the Sapphire Mountains. By the time you boys get to Stevensville, I'll be kicked back on a train ridin' the cars to Cheyenne."

Rock laughed when the rest of the cowboys glared at Spur. "Let's bed these cows down a little farther west." He waved his arm toward the valley in front of them.

"I think we'll spend a day here and rest up. Most of this valley is settled but there is still a little open range." He studied the men and then looked over at Gabe.

"Want to let these cowboys go to town? We've been gone nearly two months."

Gabe frowned at he looked at Rock. "I don't usually let them go in town until a drive is over." He shrugged his shoulders as he added, "You're the boss." He glared at the men.

"There are thirteen of us counting Cookie. Six can go in town now, and the rest can go tomorrow morning. You have four hours.

"That means whoever goes first needs to be back by 9:00 tonight."

He looked over at the three young men. "Sam, Nate, and Tuff—you are going tomorrow with Stub and me."

Rock laughed and nodded, "I'll go tomorrow." He looked around at the rest of the men. "Get out of here. And just so you know—if anyone goes to jail, he is staying there. We won't be in to bail you out."

There was a rush of horses' feet as four men raced toward Butte City. Spur and Angel followed after them slowly.

Cookie just snorted. "I didn't leave nothin' there the last time I was through here. Don't see no need to go again."

CHAPTER 67

BAD NEWS

GABE AND ROCK RELAXED BY THE CAMPFIRE. THE three youngest riders volunteered to take the first three hours of nighthawk so they could be rested up by morning.

Gabe chuckled softly and Rock looked at him in question.

"I was just thinking how excited the boys were to ride into town. I don't usually let anyone go in until we are done." His face twisted into a crooked grin. "I have all these rules and the longer I do this job, the more of them I seem to break."

Both men sat up at the sound of a horse running in the distance. They scrambled to their feet and grabbed their guns.

A young woman in a low-cut dress raced her horse into camp and hauled it to a stop. Her eyes were large with fear and she gasped as she spoke.

"Your boys—are holed up at the Dumas on—Mercury Street. One of them was beaten badly and Spur—took him there." Tears were in her eyes as she added, "He's bad off. Madam—she doesn't think he'll make it."

Both Gabe and Rock were racing for their horses before she finished. Cookie's eyes were hard as he grabbed his shotgun.

"Ya go ahead an' take them there youngsters with ya. I'll handle things here."

The woman looked at Cookie and tried to slow her breathing down. "I can help you ride nightguard if you want. Madam told me to stay out here so no one would know I slipped away."

Cookie stared at her for a moment and then growled a response. He finally pointed toward the herd. "Ya pick the side ya want to ride an' I'll take the other."

He was muttering under his breath as he saddled his horse. "Durn women. Always where they ain't supposed to be."

The woman laughed as she rode away. "My name's Adelia." The cows looked up at the sound of a new voice and then they went back to grazing. Adelia's voice was soft and clear.

Cookie snorted. "That durn woman's voice is even puttin' me to sleep." His old, gnarled hands gripped the shotgun as he listened to the retreating sound of the horses' feet racing toward Butte.

As they passed each other, Cookie nodded his head toward Butte City.

"What happened in there?"

Adelia's eyes flashed with anger. "Four of your boys were in the Copper Bucket when one of the miners started beating a woman. Your men tried to stop them but then more men piled on. They finally got the red-haired one down on the floor and stomped him. About that time, two more of your men rushed through the door. There was some shooting and a couple of men were knifed. Your boys finally made it out."

Tears sparkled in Adelia's eyes as she added, "The red-haired one couldn't stay on his horse so the two Mexican riders rode with him and held him on. Spur knows Madam Grace and he took your boys there." Adelia was quiet a moment. Her voice was bleak when she spoke.

"Black Jack is the miner who stomped your boy. He's a cruel, vicious man. He led a group of miners to the Dumas. He is threatening to tear the Dumas down if Madam Grace doesn't send your riders out. They didn't take any guns with them so if your men shoot, the miners can claim your men shot unarmed men." Adelia was crying by the time she finished. She wiped her face.

Her voice was hard when she continued, "When this is over, I am going to kill Black Jack. He has beaten his last woman."

Cookie listened quietly and then patted her hand. "I don't reckon y'all will have to do that. When ol' Gabe gets his ire up, he's real sudden. I'm a guessin' yore Black Jack ain't a goin' to be with us no more when our cowboys finish with him."

CHAPTER 68

MADAM GRACE

ROCK AND GABE LED THEIR RIDERS INTO BUTTE ON the run. They didn't see a sheriff anywhere, and Rock cursed as he muttered under his breath, "This town is wide open." They slowed their horses as they followed Rock toward the Dumas. The stopped behind the group of miners lining the street in front of the brothel. All of the riders carried their guns and Gabe's voice was misleadingly soft when he spoke.

"Heard you boys tore up some of our men."

The miners turned in surprise. Their raucous calls and laughter grew quiet as they stared at the armed cowboys.

Several of them dropped their hammers and their clubs.

"Now, Boys, we didn't mean no harm. We was just funnin' those fellows."

Gabe's eyes were hard as he dismounted. He studied the faces of the men in front of him. His eyes rested the longest on the large, smirking man in the middle of the crowd. The man was holding a pickaxe. His eyes were cruel and defiant as he stared at the cowboys.

"Which one of you men started this?"

No one spoke but several of the men shifted their eyes toward that same man.

The man snorted. "Started it? Yur boys started it. I was just funnin' with Mae an' that cowboy tried to cut in."

Angel's voice came clearly from inside the house.

"I think, señor, he is not so honest. He was beating that woman and our vaqueros, they tried to stop him."

He added quietly, "Rufe is dead, señor. Black Jack stomped him to death."

Gabe never answered but his pistol moved so quickly that the miners were shocked. He hit Black Jack with the butte of his gun. When the man went down, he proceeded to pistol-whip the man until he no longer moved.

As the miners stared in horror at the bloody mass on the ground in front of them, Gabe flipped his gun and pointed it at the closest man.

"You fellows empty your pockets. Dump everything in them on the ground in front of me."

One man started to protest and Gabe shot him in the leg. His eyes were hard as they moved from the moaning man on the ground to the rest of the miners.

"You boys watched as a good man was beaten and stomped to death. None of us are feeling too forgiving right now, so I suggest you do as I say and do it fast."

The pile of money on the ground was large. Gabe pointed at it and then at the man closest to it.

"Take off your hat and put that money in it. You are going to give it to the woman who was beaten. Some of my men will follow you up the street." His voice was soft as he added, "And I just hope you try to start something else."

Gabe nodded toward the man who had been shot. "Take him with you. We are going to clean up this town some, so keep him out of our way. You can take him to the sawbones now or after we leave." He pointed at Black Jack's still body and added, "And I don't care what you do with him."

"Sam, you and Tuff follow them. You too, Nate. Stay close and if those boys so much as make a twitch in the wrong direction, cut them all down." He looked toward the Dumas.

"Miguel! You and Stub get out here. You ride one on each side of the street. Make sure those miners take you to the right saloon. Once that money is delivered, you give them something to think about tonight."

Gabe shoved his gun into his holster. He stepped over Black Jack's body and strode up to the door of the Dumas. Bart and Stub both had eyes that were swelling shut. Tobe had one arm in a sling but he was still holding his gun. Angel, Miguel, and Spur were uninjured.

Spur's voice was angry. "I say we burn the Copper Bucket down. Those bartenders were in on this deal. Those who didn't help were laughing."

Gabe looked hard at Spur. The man rarely lost his temper. In fact, Gabe couldn't remember a time when Spur wasn't calm even when he was mad. His friend was breathing hard now though.

"We'll see. I'm in favor of it though." Gabe turned to the women gathered on the porch of the Dumas.

"Ladies, thank you for helping out. We appreciate you sending one of your girls out."

The oldest woman put out her hand. "I am Madam Grace. Adelia isn't one of my girls. Her best friend was though. Black Jack beat her to death about a month ago.

"Adelia was working in the Copper Bucket when your friend was stomped. She came over here with your riders, and I sent her out to get you." Her eyes were intense as she stared into Gabe's face.

She added quietly, "She can't stay here. Her life won't be worth a plugged nickel now."

Gabe studied the madam's face. "How about you? Will they come after you or your other girls?"

Madam Grace laughed sarcastically. "Me? I'm one of the biggest hogs at this trough of a town. No, I'll be fine and the rest of the girls were not involved. You take Adelia with you though, you hear?"

Gabe looked back at the group heading down the street. Spur and Miguel were in front, leading the way.

He nodded at Madam Grace and then looked past her into the house. "If we can come in, I'd like to take Rufe with us."

Madam Grace led the way to one of her rooms. Gabe's stomach turned over when he looked at Rufe. The young cowboy didn't have a part on his body that wasn't beaten or bloodied. Gabe's face was drawn in hard lines and his voice was deceptively soft when he spoke to Madam Grace.

"I reckon we will burn the Copper Bucket. If you have any friends there, you might want to have them get anything they value out."

Madam Grace whispered to the girl next to her. The girl nodded, grabbed a cloak, and rushed out the door.

"Just roll him up in that sheet. We won't reuse it." Madam Grace had seen a lot of beatings in her time but the one this young man received was the worst she had ever seen.

"They wanted to make an example of him," she commented bitterly. "Black Jack rides roughshod over this town. Your boys were the first to stand up to him." Madam Grace's voice was brittle. "Most miners are not like Blackjack. He's a cruel, vicious man."

Angel's voice came across the room quietly. "He is no longer vicious, señorita. I think Black Jack lives no more."

Madam Grace thought a moment and then she turned to Gabe. "Have your men drag Black Jack off the street. Leave him beside my steps. If anyone comes looking for him, I will tell them I killed him."

Gabe's eyebrows went up and he slowly shook his head. "No, I reckon I'll take responsibility."

Madam Grace snorted. "Well I guess you don't *know* that someone in this house didn't finish him off. Every girl here has a reason to want him dead." Her eyes sparkled with hard humor as she added, "He was alive when you came in, wasn't he?

"You take your herd and little Adelia, and you get. We have no law here, not so you'd know anyway. No one will miss Black Jack. If they do, it will only be because he owed them money."

She grinned at the frowning Gabe. "Remember, I'm the big she-wolf here. What I say goes."

Gabe almost chuckled as he looked at her. His eyes were bleak again as he watched Angel and Tobe carry the still figure of Rufe to his horse.

He touched his hat. "We thank you, ma'am. You didn't have to do what you did and we are appreciative." His eyes glinted with humor as he added, "If you ever get down to Cheyenne, let me know. I have a wife who is almost as tough as you are."

Madam Grace chuckled and she followed him to the door. She grabbed a vase of flowers off the mantel and shoved it into Gabe's hand. Her eyes were almost tender as she watched Tobe and Angel drape Rufe over his saddle. She looked up at Gabe.

"Every boy should have a few flowers on his grave."

The women of the Dumas watched the cowboys ride away. Madam Grace smiled and commented softly, "If I had met a man like that thirty years ago, I just might have married." Then she clapped her hands.

"Let's get this place cleaned up. We have customers to take care of."

CHAPTER 69

THE BURNING
OF THE COPPER BUCKET

GABE, ANGEL, TOBE, AND ROCK RODE SLOWLY UP Mercury Street toward the Copper Bucket. They led Rufe's horse. The saloon's false front was nearly on the street. There were more saloons on either side. They were far enough away that they could possibly be saved if their owners were prepared.

Gabe shrugged. At the moment, he didn't care if the entire town burned down.

The riders dismounted slowly. Gabe pulled some matches from his saddle bags and shoved the vase of flowers down inside.

He glanced at the neighboring saloons where the bartenders stood quietly in their doorways. He commented casually, "We're here to rake and scrape, so you fellows pull in your horns. We're burning this whole shebang down." His eyes bored into one of the startled bartenders as he added, "You try to stop us and we'll torch your place too."

Both bartenders stared for a moment and then one rushed inside for a water pail. "Get some water on these walls! Those cowboys are going to burn the Bucket down!"

Gabe's crew stepped through the doorway of the Copper Bucket while Rock stayed outside. He moved his rifle from saloon to saloon. Some men were trying to soak the walls down while others were staring at Rock angrily.

"You fellows just mind what you're doing. You get involved here and you'll get the same treatment these fellows are getting."

Seven miners lay on the floor of the Copper Bucket. Sam had his rifle on the bartender, and Bart had the rest of the patrons against a wall. Miguel was smiling as he pushed his gun against the gambler in front of him. Gabe's voice was hard when he spoke.

"You fellows who are still standing—drop your guns and file out of here." He gestured toward the men on the floor. "Take those men with you if you want them to live. We're burning this place to the ground." He stared around the room and then nodded toward Angel.

"Angel there has a knife and he is itching to use it, so go ahead and try something."

Gabe looked at the angry bartender and then at Sam. "Push him outside and then whack him a good one. He stood by and let those boys stomp Rufe. He might have even encouraged them."

The bartender made a grab for his shotgun and Sam shoved the barrel of his rifle into the man's neck. The young man's voice was soft. "Go ahead. I'm young but I've shot my share a coyotes. I don't reckon I'll feel much more if I shoot you."

The bartender stumbled outside and Sam pushed the men standing there to the middle of the street. When the bartender stopped, he smashed his gun over the man's head. The bartender dropped silently and Sam grinned at the group of startled men.

"One of ya want to be next? This is more fun than shootin' turkeys."

Gabe's men pulled the whiskey bottles from behind the bar and threw them on the floor. Then they began smashing tables and chairs. Spur emptied the cash register and threw the money on the floor. He tossed the bartender's shotgun to Nate. Rock lit a handful of matches and tossed them onto the money. When the flames leaped up, he piled the broken chairs on top. Once the chairs caught fire, the cowboys backed out. Except for the shotgun and two newer rifles, the guns they had collected were thrown back inside.

Rock untied the horses that stood at the hitching rail and smacked them. They raced down the street, stirrups flapping.

The quiet cowboys mounted their horses. Gabe paused a moment as he stared at the group of surly men. His voice was soft but angry when he spoke.

"All Rufe wanted was a drink, a bath, and a warm meal. You fellows could have stopped Black Jack from beating that woman but you didn't. When Rufe stepped in, you watched while he was stomped to death.

"Now you have another choice. You can gather your horses and bring this fight on out to us, or you can grab some buckets and try to save your sorry town from burning down." He stared at each of them for a moment.

"Either way is good for us."

He turned his horse and led the men slowly down the street. Rock, Angel, Miguel, and Spur stayed behind.

Spur rode his horse into the group of men, bumping several of them as he pushed his horse forward.

"Go ahead. Start something. I think we should shoot you all down right here."

When none of the men spoke, Angel chuckled softly.

"Let us go, my friends. We can maybe come back tonight, yes?" He pulled out his knife and tested the edge. "My small knife would be pleased to have a little fun." His face was mournful as he added, "She has been so lonely on this drive. She just wants a warm place to rest for a moment."

Miguel said nothing but he hit the gambler over the head with his gun. His smile was cold as he stared at the rest of the men clustered in the street. His voice was soft when he spoke.

"I hope you come to see us. I will be waiting for you."

The three men backed their horses away while Rock kept his gun on them. Then the four raced down the street to catch their friends.

As they rode out of town, they could hear the ammunition from the burning guns beginning to explode.

Gabe said nothing but Spur laughed grimly. "Rufe would have enjoyed his sending-off party. I can almost hear him laughing."

The men smiled a little at that but no one else spoke as they rode back to the herd.

CHAPTER 70

POINT HIS BOOTS EAST

NGEL AND SPUR RODE OUT TO RELIEVE COOKIE. THE rest of the men stared when the young woman rode in with their cook.

Gabe looked around at his men.

"Boys, this is Adelia. She will be riding with us for a time." His eyes were hard as he looked them over. "And like the last drive, you will leave her alone. No courting or trying to get her to walk out with you." His eyes glinted as he added, "Pretend she's your sister.

"Let's break camp and push on up the trail a couple of miles. I doubt those miners will ride out this far but we are going to be prudent. We don't want to lose any cattle this close to home—or any more of you either."

Rock was quiet as they pushed the cattle up the trail. He finally looked over at Gabe.

"I'm sorry, Gabe. If I hadn't let the men to go to town, this wouldn't have happened."

Gabe was silent a moment. He looked across at the man riding beside him before he faced forward again.

"I reckon Rufe wouldn't agree with you. If he hadn't been there, that gal might have died. Rufe was a good man. He would have gone into that fight even knowing how it would turn out for him.

"Sometimes, the bad element just needs to be cleaned up. I'm sorry Rufe died but I'm proud of him."

"Anybody we need to notify?" Rock's face was hard as he stared down the valley.

"Naw. Rufe didn't have any family. The cholera took them all about ten years ago down in Texas." Gabe's voice was soft as he added, "He rode on four drives with me. I didn't know he couldn't swim until this one."

He flicked his horse's reins. "Rufe was a fine man. He could ride anything with hair but he never bragged. Just a fine man." He pointed toward a large tree.

"We'll lay him down under that tree and point his boots to the east. He always enjoyed the sunrise."

They laid Rufe down around 7:00 that evening. They pointed his boots to the east and the men all agreed it was a fine spot. The setting sun shined through the trees behind them and the birds sang happily.

No one offered to sing so Gabe pulled out his harmonica. He played "Shall We Gather at the River?" The harmonica's notes echoed out across the valley. The men were quiet as they filled the hole. Gabe had dropped some of the flowers on Rufe's body. The rest were left in the vase. Angel filled it with water from his canteen. Bart made a cross. When Bart was finished, Tobe carved Rufe's name and the date.

RUFE GENGLER
COWBOY GENTLEMAN
FRIEND TO ALL HE MET
SEPTEMBER 15, 1879

Three days later, they arrived in Deer Lodge Valley.

CHAPTER 71

DEER LODGE VALLEY

THE MEN SAT ON THEIR HORSES AND STARED ACROSS the lush valley of grass as the cattle spread out to eat.

Gabe whistled. "Now that is good graze."

Rock nodded. "Conrad Kohrs owns this grass. The valley is nearly sixty miles long. It ranges from five to ten miles wide. I rented grass from Kohrs for seven days of grazing. We can take it easy across here." He waved his arm across the valley.

"Kohrs runs close to a million acres of grass right around here. He bought out Johnny Grant in '67." Rock chuckled and shook his head.

"Grant liked to have parties and dances with his Metis family and friends. Then outsiders started moving in and it became too cluttered for him.

"He sold out and moved back to Canada. Kohrs bought Grant's ranch and some of his cattle. By that time, Kohrs was already selling beef to a lot of the mining camps. He was a butcher in his younger years, and he knows his beef.

"Once he started in the ranching business though, he really took off.

"Lots of merchants like to gouge the mining camps and towns. Kohrs isn't like that. He sells for fair prices and his beef business keeps growing.

"Now he's invested in mining as well. Ranching is still his first love though." Rock shook his head.

"You talk about big. Kohrs ships eight to ten thousand head of beef each year to Chicago, and that is on top of what he sells to the mining communities. Word is that with the ranches he owns and the range he runs cattle on, he is operating on over ten million acres of grass."

Gabe stared at Rock and let out a low whistle. "We have the Waggoner and King Ranches down in Texas, but neither of them tops a million acres. How many hands would you need to handle that much grass?"

Rock shook his head. "I don't know and I never will. I'm happy with what I have." His eyes glinted as he added, "That's not to say I wouldn't try to buy more grass if it opened up next to me though.

"Running a crew is a lot of work." He nodded back down the trail. "You're lucky. You've got some good hands. I just started to hire riders full-time last year when I added my second ranch. Stub is my foreman and he does a heck of a job. We have a good crew but it took some time to round them all up." He looked sideways at Gabe and added, "I could even use a few more if you want to leave a couple of your boys here."

Gabe laughed. "Well, I won't encourage them. If any of them want to stay in this country though, I'll push them your way."

Rock nodded his head back to where Spur was riding beside Angel. The two men were laughing.

"I like old Spur. He's been a lot of help on this drive. He'll probably head out tomorrow. We are almost straight across from Phillipsburg and Skalkaho Pass is east of there."

He pointed up at a bluff overlooking the valley.

"I'm going to ride up on that chalk bluff and look around. I worked in this area for a time, and it's kind of like coming home to me. You let the cattle spread out and we'll break for supper."

CHAPTER 72

For a Pair of Boots

ROCK PAUSED HIS HORSE ON THE TOP OF THE BLUFF and looked down at the herd of black cattle below. The cowhands looked small as they kept the cattle grazing north between the mountain ranges. He could barely see the tiny figure of Cookie working on supper. Adelia was helping him. A smile filled Rock's face and he relaxed in his saddle.

"Well, Red, we are almost home. Another eleven or twelve days and we will be in the Bitter Root Valley. And just look at those black cows. Old Darby surely would have enjoyed seeing them graze on his grass." His smile became bigger as he added, "Clare will like that too."

"I can't wait to get home. A pretty wife, a bunch of loud kids, and a soft bed."

Red snorted and Rock laughed. He looped one long leg over Red's neck and rested his hands on the saddle horn.

The valley they were crossing was covered in grass. A single eagle was winging its way across the sky far above. The sun was dropping below the mountains. Their long shadows cast dark fingers over the valley, reaching almost to the mountains on the other side. The sun felt warm on his back, and Rock smiled as the colors of the sky slowly changed.

"This has been a pretty drive, Red. The weather has been mostly fair, the cattle are traveling well, and no trouble with outlaws or trails that we couldn't handle. I'm mighty sorry we lost Rufe but overall, it has been a fine couple of months. And now we are almost home."

He swung Red around as he dropped his leg back down into his stirrup. He felt the thud of the bullet as it hit his horse before he heard the echo of the shot. Red reared as he screamed in pain. The horse went over backwards and the saddle horn slammed deep into Rock's chest.

Red struggled to get back on his feet and every movement crushed Rock even more. It took all of his strength to speak to his horse. "Easy, old fellow. Just stay down now." He tried to roll onto his side but his body wouldn't move. Frantically, he grabbed for his gun but his sprawled arm remained where it was. Red was breathing heavily and Rock tried to talk to him as he gasped for air.

He heard a rider coming up slowly behind him. An old man walked his mount around the injured horse and stared at man on the ground beneath it. He laughed.

"Meant to spook yur hoss an' have 'im throw ya but yur hoss swinged 'round.

"I need me a new pair a boots. Shore didn't intend to shoot a horse so fine as that. Reckon he done my killin' fer me." The old man leaned over Red as he reached for Rock's saddlebags. The horse screamed as it tried to grab the man with its open mouth.

The old man jumped back with an evil laugh. "Well, I ain't a gonna get ta nothin' till yur hoss is dead. Jist as well shoot 'im so's I cin git on down the road."

A whisper of sound made the old man look up. He tried to swing his rifle around but he wasn't quick enough. Two arrows twanged as they entered his body and slammed him back on the ground. A brave dropped down beside Rock while the rest of the Indians circled the old man.

"My brother," Little Bear said softly.

Rock was struggling to breathe and he gasped, "Put—put Red down. Don't—let—him suffer."

Little Bear waved to a brave behind him and the man dropped down beside the dying horse. The brave sang softly to Red and stroked his neck as he reached for his knife. The horse slowly stopped struggling and became still.

The old man was trying to move and the braves tied a rawhide rope around his neck. They drug him to the side of the bluff. All was quiet once again.

Blood leaked from the corner of Rock's mouth as he looked up at Little Bear. "Letters—inside my vest. Make sure—Clare."

Rock's breath was labored as he tried to talk. "Can't move. Can't move my arms." He stopped speaking and looked behind his friend. His voice was clear and his face was full of surprise. "Suzanna?"

The sound of hoofbeats filled the air as three men raced their horses up the hill. Gabe and Angel slowed when they saw the warriors. They moved forward at a walk. Stub continued to run his horse. He dropped to the ground and rushed to Rock's side.

Rock grimaced with pain. Then he gasped, "Your place—it's yours. I give it—"

Stub's eyes were watering and he shook his head. His heart was tight as he stared at the blood seeping from Rock's crushed chest. "Don't talk, Rock. Let me look at you."

Rock tried to shake his head. His eyes were a deep green and were filled with pain. "No good. Take—me—take me back to Clare. Tell Clare—tell them—I love them." Slowly, Rock's body relaxed and his last breath sighed out of him.

CHAPTER 73

TAKE WHITE EAGLE HOME

STUB ROCKED BACK ON HIS HEELS. HE STARED AT HIS friend for a moment. Then he stood. His hand was trembling as he gripped his rifle. He started toward the side of the hill. The braves were quiet but the old man had started to scream.

Little Bear grabbed Stub's arm and shook his head. "No. Tall Horse must do this. Old Pony took his sister two moons ago. We follow him here."

Stub paused and slowly nodded. He stared at Little Bear. His voice was brittle when he spoke. "You make sure there is enough of Pony left to hang. You bring him back to us when you are done."

Little Bear's eyes glinted. He stared intently at Stub and then nodded toward Rock. "You take White Eagle home to his family."

Spur had ridden up and he stepped forward. "I can do that. I know my way through these mountains. Besides, my horses are delivered." He gripped Stub's shoulders and stared down at him.

"Let me take Rock home. You finish this drive. That is what Rock would want you to do."

Stub stared at Spur for a moment and then slowly nodded. He pulled himself erect and stood quietly as Little Bear dropped down beside Rock.

357

Little Bear rocked back on his haunches and sang a death song in the language of the Crow as he lifted his arms in the air.

"Great Father, we send our brother to you, to his home in the sky. Let him ride on the backs of many fine horses. Let his cattle be plentiful and may his days be filled with sunshine. We send him to you, a brave man with many friends. Let him fly with the eagles and let us always remember White Eagle, our brother." He continued for nearly five minutes singing about Rock and all they had shared. When he finished, he rose to his feet. He stood with his hands and face raised toward the sky. He slowly lowered his arms and talked softly as he faced the four different directions, pushing his hands outward.

Little Bear's face was stoic when he finished and the men were quiet.

Stub wiped a trembling hand over his face. Two of the braves wrapped Rock in a blanket. Little Bear was stripping the branches from some young trees. Stub stumbled as he turned and moved to help him. A travois was quickly assembled and Rock was lifted onto it gently.

Angel pulled his saddle off his horse and handed Little Bear the reins. The braves quickly attached the travois. Spur mounted and Little Bear handed him the reins to Angel's horse.

"Travel swiftly. Take our brother home to his family."

Spur paused a moment and looked around at the men. "I'll see you fellows in a couple of weeks." As he turned his horse to move down the hill, Little Bear reached out his hand. It held a packet of letters. The bottom sheet was splotched with blood.

"For White Eagle's woman. My brother wanted her to have them."

Spur took the packet of letters. He stared at them a moment. He tried to wipe the blood off the back one and then shoved them inside his vest. He gripped Little Bear's hand. "You have been a fine brother to our friend," he said softly. He raised his hand to the somber group and moved the two horses down the side of the bluff.

Angel took his rope off his saddle and began to form a noose. He spoke softly in Spanish as he wound the rope and made the knots.

Gabe's face was hard as he watched his friend and listened to the words that Angel spoke.

"Tomorrow, you will hang a man. You will be strong and you will not break. Old Pony will die slowly, and he will think upon his life. He will have time to talk to our Maker." Angel's hands paused a moment and then he continued, "But I do not think he will. I think Pony is an evil hombre who will spend his next life with Diablo."

Stub dug in his saddle bags for a paper and a short pencil. He wrote briefly before he folded the wrinkled paper and shoved it into his saddle bag.

Angel grabbed his saddle and mounted Pony's horse. He held the extra saddle in front of him. The men rode slowly back to the herd. Gabe stopped to talk to Cookie and the man nodded. The cook quickly grabbed a pan and began to mix some batter.

They made camp close to a small creek, under a thicket of trees. Angel climbed the largest tree and tied the noose he had made over a long branch. As the men came in for supper, they stared at the noose and then looked around at the quiet faces of their friends. They had heard the single shot and they did not see Rock. Still, no one asked any questions. When they were done eating, Stub stood and cleared his throat.

"Fellers, Rock was killed by a bushwhacker by the name of Pony Dixon. Pony was court martialed during the War for killing his own men, but he escaped before he could be hung." He looked out at the angry faces and added, "Pony rode both sides of that war. He used it as an excuse to kill freely. He was an evil man who killed as he pleased and mostly for his own pleasure. He stole the boots and the horse from every man he killed. Pony missed his shot at Rock and hit Red instead. Red went over backwards and Rock was crushed."

His eyes were hard as he continued. "Little Bear will be bringing Pony back here sometime tomorrow. We'll hang him and then we'll finish this drive.

"Spur left already to take Rock home. He knows his way through the mountains. He will make better time than any of us could." He studied the faces of the men in front of him and then continued.

"I know Rock was a friend to every man on this drive. He made it a point to get to know each of you. He was a—a finer friend I have never had." Stub's voice caught in his throat and he looked away for a moment before he continued.

"For Rock and for Clare, we'll take these cows on home." He paused and looked over toward Gabe.

"Gabe is in charge the rest of the way. I'll pay out those of you headed back south at Stevensville. Tuff and I will take the cattle on up to the ranch."

Gabe listened quietly and then shook his head. "No, I reckon we'll all take these cows up to Rock's ranch. I think every man here would like to do that for Rock." He looked around at his riders. "You fellows good with that?"

The men nodded silently and Gabe pointed toward the herd. "Figure out who has night watch. Cookie is making bear sign so grab some of that when it's done."

He nodded toward the tree and added grimly, "I am guessing we will hang Pony in the morning. If you don't want to be part of that, head out early to the herd." He turned away and cursed under his breath, slapping his hat against his leg.

CHAPTER 74

THE HANGING OF GHOST KILLER

COOKIE HANDED GABE A CUP OF COFFEE AND THE tall man walked to the edge of the campfire. He slid down and leaned back against a rock as he stared out into the evening.

Angel followed and squatted beside him. He was quiet for a moment and then commented softly, "I think perhaps we should send the young men ahead of the herd before the sun comes up. I think Little Bear will be here at daylight."

Gabe didn't answer. He finally looked over at his friend. "You ever heard of Pony before today?"

Angel nodded slowly. "Sí. He was in the Indian Territory for a time. He killed a man and then tortured the man's family, one at a time, before he killed them. There he was called el espectro asesino—Ghost Killer. He always escaped and left no witnesses. No one knew what he looked like.

"The Ghost Killer—he killed for enjoyment and always took the man's boots—even if they didn't fit him. It was a very strange thing. He took their horses too. Sometimes he killed them. It is said he preferred horse meat over beef.

"Pony was an evil man. I think it is good that Little Bear caught him."

Gabe stared at his friend. "I've heard of the Ghost Killer. He was killed by a tough posse down in The Strip."

"No, señor. He traded horses with a man he took prisoner and that posse, they hung an innocent man. Pony claimed to have caught the Ghost Killer. He cut the man's tongue out so he could not speak, and then he helped to hang him. One of the men who was there told the story to Miguel. That man, he knew the vaquero who was hung was innocent and he was afraid. He told no one until he told Miguel. He also told Miguel the Ghost Killer was tracking him. Somehow the Ghost Killer knew this man recognized him. Then Miguel's friend disappeared."

Gabe cursed quietly as he stood. "Eleven days. In eleven days we'll reach Rock's valley. We lose him this close to home...and to a bushwhacker for a pair of boots." He threw out his coffee grounds and shook his head.

"Clare was worried about this drive. She made several comments the day we rode out to look at the cattle. Three little ones to raise alone and now a ranch to run too. And all because of a lousy bushwhacker."

Angel listened quietly and then squeezed Gabe's shoulder. "I will wake the young men early and send the three of them ahead with the horses. I think there will not be much left of Pony to hang when Rock's brothers bring him back to us."

Gabe nodded and Angel walked quietly back to the campfire. He pointed at the three young men. "Sam, Nate, and Tuff. The three of you need to head out early. Gabe wants the horses across the creek ahead of the cattle. Move them up the valley about five miles and wait for us. The graze is good here so we will move slower tomorrow. Have Cookie pack you some grub in case we don't catch you by dinner." All three young men stared at him and then slowly nodded.

"When you say early, you mean before daylight?" Nate looked from Angel to where Gabe was standing.

"Sí. You will take the last watch. You will gather the horses when your relief comes. I will take watch before you and I will wake you. Make sure each man here has a fresh horse before you leave since you will be gone when Cookie starts the day." He winked at them and added, "Such young and strong vaqueros as yourselves don't need as much sleep as some of these old men." He waved his hand around the fire as he grinned.

Sam grinned back at him. He grabbed their bedrolls from the wagon and the three young men were soon asleep.

Talk was quiet that night, and the men who were not on night guard were soon asleep as well.

The sun was not yet up when the three young men rode back into the camp. They ate breakfast quickly. Sam grabbed the pack of food that Cookie handed him. He could smell the bear sign, and he grinned at the old man.

"Thanks, Cookie. I think today is going to be a long one. We'll enjoy these." Cookie grunted at him and turned back to finish preparing the early meal.

Nate led five saddled horses, and he tied them to a tree. The wooden stakes and rope that formed the horse corral were pulled down and quickly tossed into the chuckwagon. The young men were out of camp before daylight, moving the horse herd up the valley.

The sun was just rising when Cookie banged on his triangle. "Git over here and eat, ya lazy good-fer-nothin' bunch a hayseeds. Eat whilst it's hot or I'll toss it out!"

The men ate quickly and then milled around while they waited for Gabe's order to move out.

As the sun rose over the mountains, a quiet line of braves appeared. A bloodied old man stumbled behind them. When he fell, he was drug.

Little Bear handed the end of the leather rope to Stub. He looked around at the quiet group. "It is good this man will live no more." The braves turned away.

Stub jerked the rope and Pony fell to the ground. A piece of rawhide had been tied over his mouth and Stub pulled it off. Pony spit something out and Bart gagged. The other men stared in horror as Pony struggled to his feet. His clothes were gone. His body showed where he had been beaten and cut. Blood ran down both of his legs.

Stub grabbed Pony by one arm and drug him over to the tree. Two riders bound his hands behind him and they threw him up on a saddle. Angel tightened the noose around his neck, and Stub held the reins as he looked up at the old man.

"You killed your last man, Pony. Rock was not only a husband and a father, but he was my best friend. Your life ain't the equal to his, but we're goin' to take yours anyhow. Your time here on earth ends today along with all of your robbin' and killin'." His face was tight as he stared up at the man. "Now is your last chance to get right with the Maker."

Pony raised his head and stared at the quiet group of cowboys. He leered at them through his toothless mouth. "I ain't a gonna be gone forever. I'll come back an' git all a ya. The next wolf ya see—it'll be me." He threw back his head and howled. Then he gave an eerie laugh.

Gabe smacked Pony's horse with his rope. The startled animal lunged forward, and the Ghost Killer died that quiet morning. Stub pounded his note onto the tree, and the quiet group of men circled the cattle. They rode up the valley without looking back. Pony Dixon swung alone, a bloody specter in the morning sun. The paper attached to the tree he swung from read,

PONY DIXON, GHOST KILLER
HE BACKSHOT HIS LAST MAN

The men all silently agreed on one thing. There wasn't much of Pony left to hang.

CHAPTER 75

THE LONG RIDE HOME

SPUR COVERED THE NEARLY ONE-HUNDRED-MILE ride to Stevensville in less than two days. The high mountain pass he crossed was treacherous in the daylight, and he crossed it in the dark. Skalkaho Pass took him through the Sapphire Mountains and dropped him down about twenty-three miles south of Stevensville.

He rode north into Stevensville on a worn down horse with a second horse pulling a travois. The blanket-wrapped figure it carried drew curious looks as the haggard man rode up the street.

Spur's eyes were red from exhaustion, and his face was dark with stubble. He stopped at the livery and almost fell off his horse. The old hostler looked at him and then at the two worn out horses. He took the reins.

"Let me help ya there, Stranger. I'll git ya a couple a fresh hosses. Mebbie I cin ride with ya a bit an' help ya take yur friend home. Cin ya tell me where yur goin'?"

Spur stared at the old man and slowly nodded. "Fresh horses would be appreciated. I'm headed up to Rock Beckler's ranch. I've been there once but I came in from the northeast, over the mountains. Can you tell me what road to follow up there?"

Ike's hands went still and he stared from Spur to the still form on the travois.

"Is that Rock?" he whispered. When Spur slowly nodded, Ike rushed into action.

"Oh Lordy. Ya want to go on over to the eatin' house an' grab yourself a bite? I'm a guessin' ya didn't stop an' fix no food on the way. I'll hitch up a wagon an' we'll take that boy home."

He grabbed a cowboy who was riding by. "Ya go git Father Ravalli down to the Mission. We's a gonna need him here today. Now git!"

A smiling older woman was hurrying out of the dry goods store. She rushed toward Ike and then came to a stop in the middle of the street as she took in the scene in front of her. Her smile faded and her face went white as she covered her mouth.

Ike rushed toward her and grabbed her arm. "Now Maggie Mae, ya jist come on over here an' sit a bit whilst I hitch this wagon. I sent a feller after Father Ravalli an' then—an' then...Well then, we'll head up to see Clare."

Maggie began to sob and almost collapsed in the street. Ike grabbed one arm and Spur took the other as they helped her to the bench outside the livery. Ike patted her arm for a moment before he rushed inside to hitch his team. He stopped from time to time to rub his hand roughly across his face.

"I hope that padre is around. I jist don't know how to tell Clare." The young man who helped him at the livery was staring from Ike to the sobbing Maggie. Ike grabbed him and shoved him toward the door.

"Git down to the eatin' house an' git that feller a pack a food. He most likely ain't ate or slept in three days, an' we don't need 'im a goin' down on us." As the young man rushed out the door, Ike hollered, "An' put it on my bill!" He moved Spur's rig to a fresh horse and tied it to the back of the wagon.

Spur had set down beside Maggie. He had his arm around her, and he patted her back awkwardly while her body shook with silent sobs.

When the Ike led the team from the barn, Spur untied Rock from the travois. Ike helped him lift Rock's body into the back of the wagon and Spur jumped in to carry Rock forward. The two men gently maneuvered their friend until he was settled on the wagon bed. Spur dropped down beside Rock. He looked up dully as a young man thrust a package into his hands.

"Ike Clampant said to get you some food. And here's a canteen."

Spur took the package. "Thanks. I sure appreciate that." He took a long drink from the canteen and then stared at the blanket-wrapped body beside him. He cursed silently and then called to the young man.

"You rub those horses down, especially their legs. Give them some hay and grain but just a little at a time. Water them too. Put each one in a stall by himself. I'll be down in a few days to pick them up." He waited for the young man to respond and then leaned back against the front of the wagon.

Father Ravalli pulled his mule to a stop. He looked from the wagon to Ike's tight face and then hurried over to Maggie. He knelt in front of her. She sobbed and the priest talked quietly. She finally nodded and the priest led her to the wagon where Ike helped her onto the seat.

"I'll just follow along. That way no one will have to bring me back." Father Ravalli reached out his hand to Spur.

"And tell me your name, young man. It looks like you made a hard trip and a fast one to get Rock here in a timely manner."

Spur climbed over the side of the wagon and dropped to the ground before he took the priest's hand. "George Spurlach but folks call me Spur. My boss down in Cheyenne had me deliver some horses to Fort Ellis. Rock was killed just east of Phillipsburg in Deer Lodge Valley." He paused and looked at the priest quietly as he added, "I know the area so I offered to bring him home."

Father Ravalli nodded. "Thank you for that." He pointed at the wagon. "Why don't you rest a bit. This is going to be a two-hour ride with lots of emotion at the end of it. Ike has a horse saddled for you to ride when you're ready. Just go ahead and eat your sandwich. Then you sleep a bit while we take this wagon up to Rock's ranch."

Spur nodded dully and climbed back into the wagon.

Ike wheeled his team around to head south out of town, and Father Ravalli turned to ride beside them. Ike hollered back, "Ya jist take ya a little rest now, Spur. There ain't no way to hurry this here trip up the mountain now. Ya jist as well sleep a bit. Ya look plumb tuckered out."

Spur nodded again and laid his head against the side of the wagon. He was soon asleep with the half-eaten sandwich in his hand, his head bouncing with every bump the wagon hit.

Father Ravalli rode his mule beside Ike and pointed at the sleeping man in the back of the wagon. "Did he bring Rock across Skalkaho Pass in the dark? I don't like that trail in the daylight."

Ike nodded grimly. "Shore did an' mighty fast too. That trip would be a hard two-day ride on flat land. Both a those hosses are a goin' to be foot-sore fer some time, an' that is fer shore.

"It takes a tough man to do what Spur done, an' fer shore one who knows this country." Ike flipped his lines over the back of a lagging mule and added, "An' he don't even work fer Rock. He done it fer a man he only knowed a short time."

CHAPTER 76

A Sad Homecoming

CLARE SAW IKE'S WAGON COMING UP THE LANE AND she smiled. The smile froze on her lips when she recognized Spur and Father Ravalli both riding beside the wagon. One hand went to her heart. She gripped the side of the doorway with the other hand to keep from falling down. "Not Rock. Please don't let it be Rock!" she whispered.

The three little ones were already running out to meet the wagon. Ike pulled the mules to a stop and rushed around the wagon to help Maggie down.

Maggie's eyes were red and her hands were shaking as she hugged each of the children. Clare stayed in the doorway of the house. She clenched her wadded-up apron.

When Maggie looked up at her, Clare began to shake her head. "No. No. I don't want to listen to what you have to say. It's not true," she whispered.

She walked slowly toward the wagon, her eyes focused on the blanket-wrapped form in the back. She looked up at Spur.

"Open the blanket. I must prepare him." Her voice broke as she touched the blanket.

Spur slid off his horse. He took Clare's shoulders in his hands. His heart felt heavy in his chest as he looked into her eyes. "No, Clare. Rock died two days ago and Little Bear already took care of that. You just tell me where you want to lay Rock down, and I will get a spot ready for him."

Clare collapsed on the ground sobbing and Maggie ran to her. Ike helped his wife lift Clare up, and they almost carried the sobbing woman back to the house.

All three children stared from Clare's departing back to Spur and then to Father Ravalli. Annie climbed up in the wagon and bent over to tug on the blanket.

Spur quickly lifted her out of the wagon. He hugged her as she stared into his face. He held out his hand to Nora and looked helplessly at Father Ravalli.

The priest smiled at the kids and handed Spur some apples. "Why don't the four of you go eat those apples in the barn while I talk to your mother and your grandparents?"

Spur led the children to the barn. Annie wiggled down and raced ahead. Zeke turned around and stared as Father Ravalli hurried into the house. He looked up at Spur.

"My momma is sad. Why is my momma sad?"

Spur sat down in the doorway of the barn and looked at the little faces around him. He did not want to be the one to tell these children their father was dead.

"How about we eat these apples while the grown-ups talk. When they are ready for us to come inside, they will call us."

Zeke stared at Spur a moment. "Aren't you a grown-up?"

Spur grinned at him. "Well, sometimes I am and sometimes I'm not. Today I don't want to be a grown-up. I want to be a kid."

Annie rubbed his face. "You're awful dirty, Spur. And your whiskers are all pokey. I think you need to take a bath *and* you forgot to shave."

Spur rubbed his face and nodded as he grinned at the kids. "Why I think you're right. I sure did forget to shave. Maybe I will shave when I go down to your creek to take a bath."

Annie stuck out her lip. "I want to take a bath in the creek but Mama says I can't. She says I need to take one in the house since I'm a girl. And she wants me to wear dresses. I think dresses are stupid. They tangle around my legs when I run. I like britches like I have on now," she complained as she pulled on her pant leg.

Spur tried not to laugh as he listened. His dark eyes were twinkling and he chuckled. "I reckon that is all true, but that doesn't mean you can't swim in the creek. Do you know how to swim?"

Zeke shook his head. "No, but Papa promised he would teach us when he got back from the trail drive." He pointed at a heavy rope in the corner of the barn. "Papa said he would hang that out over a big tree down in the creek. Then we could swing on it and drop in the water."

Spur looked at the rope and his throat tightened up. He stared at it a while longer to hide his emotions. When he looked at the kids, he forced a grin. "Well maybe we should just go do that right now. I've got a little free time. Since I am a kid today, I can swim too."

Annie jumped up excitedly but Zeke frowned. "I don't think we should do that. Father Ravalli said we should go to the barn."

Spur stood up and brushed off his britches. "He sure did say that. He told us to go to the barn and eat our apples. Are you done with your apples?"

All of the kids nodded slowly as they watched Spur. "Well then, toss those cores out where the chickens can find them. You kids grab onto that rope and lead me down to that big tree you are talking about."

CHAPTER 77

LET'S BUILD THAT SWING

THE THREE CHILDREN TRIED TO LIFT THE HEAVY ROPE, but the coils slid from their hands and flopped as it unwound. Finally, Spur grabbed the rope and each child hung onto a piece of it. Annie soon dropped her coil and ran ahead.

"Follow me! I know where we are going." Zeke dropped his as well. Only Nora continued on with Spur.

"You are sure good help, Nora. I bet you help your mama every day, don't you?"

Nora looked up at Spur and smiled. Her smile faded as she looked back toward the wagon. She tripped once and then looked up at Spur with wide eyes. "Is that a dead man? When my daddy died, they wrapped him up in a blanket. His blanket wasn't that pretty though."

Spur looked down at the little girl. His tongue felt like it was stuck to the top of his mouth. Before he had to answer, Annie yelled back at them.

"Hurry up! The tree is right over here!"

Spur looked up at the big tree with the long branch extending over the creek and he laughed. "I reckon your pa was right. This is a perfect place for a rope swing."

He pulled off his boots, belt, and gun. He stacked them by a rock and slowly waded out into the water. It became gradually deeper. By the time Spur was in the middle of the creek, he could no longer touch the bottom. He looked up at the tree and gauged his distance. When he was satisfied, he swam back to the creekbank.

"Yes siree, that is the perfect place. Now you kids stay on this bank. I am going to crawl up in that tree. You hang onto the other end of that rope and carry it toward me when I get in position."

Spur shimmied up the tree and then crawled out on the big branch. It swayed a little under his weight but it didn't crack. He pulled the rope up to the height he wanted and then tied a sailor's knot.

"See this knot, kids? It's a special knot sailors use. It's called a hitch knot. It allows the rope to slide over the tree branch when you swing on it."

When he finished, he slid off the limb and down the rope. He dropped in the water with a huge splash.

The children's eyes were large as they watched him. He pushed his hair back with his hand and grinned at them. "Now who wants to go first? I will catch you when you drop so there is no need to be afraid."

Annie kicked off her boots and shimmied up the tree. She got partway out on the branch and then stopped. Zeke climbed up behind her.

"Keep going, Annie. Even if you fall, you will fall in the water and it won't hurt."

Annie stared from the rope to Spur and then behind her at Zeke. Finally, she began to crawl again. She slid down the rope partway and Spur grabbed the end of it.

"Hang on, Annie! I am going to swing you!" He swung her gently at first and then tugged the rope hard. "Now jump and I will catch you."

Annie let go and closed her eyes. She screamed as she fell and then Spur's strong arms caught her. He lifted her out of the water and paddled over to the edge. When he got closer, he set her down. "Paddle like a dog, Annie. Move your arms and your legs." Annie's limbs were going all directions but she finally made it to the shore. Her eyes were shining. "That was fun! I am going to do it again. Come on, Nora. You can do it too."

Annie started up the tree followed cautiously by Nora. Just as they got to the top, Zeke dropped down and Spur caught him. Annie crawled quickly over the limb.

"Don't drop until I get back under the limb, Annie. I have to get Zeke to shore first." As soon as he made it back to the middle of the creek, Annie dropped with a squeal.

Nora sat on the limb and stared down at Spur. Zeke and Annie were both in the tree waiting on her.

"Jump, Nora! Spur will catch you."

Spur smiled up at the little girl. "I tell you what, Nora. You just slide down that rope and when you get to the end, I will catch you before you drop into the water."

Nora hesitated and then gingerly lowered herself on the rope. When she was almost to the end, Spur grabbed her and swished her through the water. "Now wasn't that fun, Nora?" Nora laughed and Spur helped her to dog paddle back to the shore.

Before long, Spur called, "The party's over. Let's all get out now." The kids pleaded for more jumping but he shook his head. "You kids plumb wore me out. I'm a single fellow and I'm not used to playing like this. We'll come down tomorrow though and do it again. Maybe Grandpa Ike will come with us."

He looked at each of them seriously. "You never come down here without an adult though. Only big people can catch you when you drop off. And each time we come, I am going to have you paddle a little farther. Deal?"

They all nodded and climbed out of the water. Spur sat down. He took off his socks and pulled his boots on over his wet feet.

Zeke looked at him seriously. "I don't think Mama would like it much if she saw you do that. She would tell you to just go barefooted back to the house like the rest of us are going to do."

Spur laughed and nodded. "I reckon that is a good idea but your feet are tougher than mine are. I have to have my boots on or I would be hollering from pain all the way to the house." He looked at them seriously. "Now you don't want me to be doing that, do you?" He began to hop from one foot to the other as he yelped, "Oooh, Ouch! Those rocks hurt! Owie. Youch!"

The kids were all laughing and Nora took his hand as she smiled up at him. "You're funny, Spur. I'm glad you're a kid like us."

Spur grinned down at her. Even though he had no kids and had no desire to ever have any, his heart squeezed a bit as he looked at her little face. He swung her up and tucked her under his arm. "Who wants to race me back to the house? I think Nora and I will win!" Annie and Zeke raced ahead of him as they ran for the house. The kids were all laughing while Spur tried to catch Annie and Zeke.

================= CHAPTER 78 =================

A KIND PRIEST

THEY SLOWED DOWN AS THEY DREW CLOSER TO THE house and then stopped when Father Ravalli came outside. He smiled as he looked from face to face.

"Did Spur take you swimming? Well, maybe I should go too. It is a fine day for a swim."

Nora slid down and all three children began talking about the rope swing and jumping in the water. Father Ravalli smiled as he listened. When their story was over, he nodded toward a grassy spot with some shade from the large cottonwood tree that hung over it.

"Let's go sit under that tree and talk for a little bit." The kids followed him happily. Spur slowed down and edged to the side. He was getting ready to disappear when Father Ravalli caught him.

"You too, Spur. Come over here and sit down."

Father Ravalli looked around the little group and smiled at each one before he began. "You know, each of us is only here for a short time. Our real home is up there." He pointed up at the blue sky. "Up there in Heaven with God. And it will be so wonderful there. We will never want to come back down to this life." His voice was soft as he talked, and the children stared at him as they listened.

"Even Jesus had to die. He died so we can all go to Heaven. His mommy was sad too even though she knew that was what He needed to do." He paused and smiled at the children. "And today, we feel the same way. Even though we know Jesus will come and take our hand when it is time to go home with Him, we are sad when we think of leaving those we love behind." He made a cross on each of the children's heads and added, "That is what your papa did. He went up to Heaven to be with Jesus."

Annie stared at the priest and her bottom lip began to tremble. "I don't want my papa to leave. I want him to stay here with me."

Father Ravalli smiled at the little girl. "Yes, death is a hard thing. Do you remember when your favorite kitty died last month? Your daddy helped you bury it out by the corral. Do you remember what he told you that day?" He paused and waited for Annie to answer him.

Annie nodded. "He said cats can't go to Heaven. Only people can. But when we get there, we can ask for anything we want. Papa said when I get to Heaven, if I want Pretty Kitty to come to be with me, she can come. And I am going to ask for her too."

Father Ravalli smiled at her and then looked around at the other little faces. "What animal do you think your Papa would want in Heaven with him?"

They all answered at the same time, "Red."

Zeke looked at the priest seriously. "Red is Papa's horse and is for sure his favorite animal. I think he would want Red in Heaven with him."

Father Ravalli's eyes were soft as he looked at the little ones in front of him. "I think you are right. I think God knew your Papa would want his favorite horse. I think Red is up there right now with your Papa. If you listen during the rainstorms, you will hear them racing across the sky. Red will run so fast his hooves will make sparks and we will see them as lightning."

Nora stared at the priest for a moment. Then she asked, "Is our papa up in Heaven now?"

Father Ravalli leaned over and kissed the top of Nora's head. "I think your papa is on his way if he isn't there already. Your papa was a good man and a wonderful papa."

Zeke listened silently. He pointed toward the wagon. "I think that is our papa. I don't think he's in Heaven. I think he is wrapped up in that blanket."

Father Ravalli looked over at the wagon and then back at the three children. He touched his chest as he spoke softly, "As people, we have a soul and the soul is what runs free to Heaven. Our bodies stay here but our souls look for Jesus. Today we will bury your papa's body but his soul will remain alive. It will never die."

Annie started to sob and Spur picked her up. She grabbed him around the neck as she cried. "I want my papa. I don't want him to go to Heaven. My first mama is in Heaven, and I never get to see her."

Zeke began to cry too. "I loved my papa. I prayed for Uncle Rock to be my papa. I don't want him to go either."

Spur leaned over and picked up the little boy. Then he smiled at Nora. "Come here, Nora. Let me hug you too."

He patted all of them awkwardly. "You know, your papa was my friend. Did you know that I bought a horse from him one time? Annie here was just a little bitty girl. I stopped in here on my way back home to Cheyenne. Your papa had a little stud horse he was selling and I bought him. I thought my boss might want to buy him for breeding. By the time I got back to Cheyenne though, I liked that horse so much that I kept him."

He smiled at the three sad little faces. "And do you know what I named that horse?" Three little faces watched him and then shook their heads. Spur smiled at each one of them.

"I named him Rockafeller after your papa. He is tough, friendly, and stubborn. He works hard and he gives all he has to give." He smiled at the three kids as he added, "And he's *my* favorite animal."

Annie lifted her head. "Did you bring him with you?"

Spur nodded seriously. "I sure did. He's down in Stevensville resting up. He had a hard time of it these last two days, and his feet are powerful sore. When he gets to feeling better, I will bring him up so you can meet him."

All of the children were studying Spur's face when Maggie called from the house. "Who wants a treat? I have some warm cookies and cold milk just begging to be eaten."

All three kids raced for the house. Annie stopped and looked back at Spur. "Come on, Spur. You said you were a kid today. You get to eat cookies too."

Spur chuckled softly as he nodded. "I'll be right in. I want to talk to Father Ravalli a bit first."

Once the kids were inside, Spur looked over at the priest. His smile faded and his face twisted in pain. "How does God decide who to take? He could have taken me. I would have barely been missed. Why would he take a man like Rock? Those kids need their Pa...and what about Clare? It just doesn't seem right."

Father Ravalli shook his head and put his hand on Spur's shoulder as they walked toward the house. "We don't think like the Good Lord does, so some things we will never understand fully. We just have to trust in His will and have faith."

He added softly, "Ask God to show you His way, Spur. You must pray for guidance to follow the steps He has lined out for you." He smiled at the tall man beside him.

"Now come. Let's join those children and have a cookie ourselves."

====== CHAPTER 79 ======

Clare's Story

SPUR STOOD IN THE DOORWAY OF THE HOUSE. STRONG emotions made him uncomfortable, and he was edging back out the door when Ike looked up. Ike walked outside and nodded with his head for the younger man to follow him.

"Clare told me where she wanted to lay Rock down. Come on. I'll git us some shovels an' we'll git this job done."

Spur followed the old man to the barn. "How about a box? Do we need to build something?"

Ike shook his head. "Naw. When we buried the last two fellers what died here, we had a few extra boards cut. Rock jist had us make an extry coffin. We stashed it in the top a the barn." He frowned and cursed under his breath as he added, "Shore didn't think we'd need it this soon, an' fer shore never thought it would be fer Rock."

Spur lowered the coffin from the rafters and Ike guided it down to the ground. Spur wiped it off with a saddle blanket, and they carried it out to the wagon. Gently, they lifted Rock's body into it.

Ike stared at the still form a moment and then asked, "Ya never said what happened. Was he shot?"

Spur shook his head. "A bushwhacker shot his horse and Red went over backwards. He crushed Rock. I didn't get a good look, but Rock's horse appeared to be gutshot. Little Bear was tracking the man. He said, according to the killer, he was aiming for Rock but I don't believe it.

"No way would a man like Pony Dixon miss a shot like that. I think he just wanted to graze that horse so it would throw Rock. Rock must have turned Red back just as Pony shot. That bullet caught Red in the side." Spur was quiet a moment and then added, "Rock was worried about Red suffering. He asked Little Bear to put him down."

Spur looked over Ike's head. When he spoke, his face twisted in pain. "Rock asked Little Bear to take some letters out of his vest for Clare and the kids as he was dying. Rock couldn't move his arms. That fall with the horse on top of him must have broken his back."

He patted his vest. "I have those letters here." Spur was silent a moment before he added, "I'm not sure when he wrote them. It's almost like Rock had a premonition he wasn't coming home."

Ike was silent as he listened to Spur. Then he asked softly, "Did Little Bear git ol' Pony?"

Spur nodded. "Little Bear's braves drug him off. Pony had taken Tall Horse's sister several months before, and they had been trailing him. Little Bear said they'd bring back what was left of him for Stub to hang. I reckon that's just what happened."

Ike's old eyes were hard and anger glinted from them as he spoke.

"Let's leave Pony's name out a this here deal. Ol' Pony an' Clare's pa went 'way back. She don't need no more memories muddying up this here day."

Spur stared at Ike for a moment and then slowly nodded. "I'll make sure Stub knows that." He looked out over the corrals for a moment before he added, "I don't know how much longer I can be gone but I'll try to stay until Stub gets back." He frowned as he looked toward the house. "I thought about riding out to meet the herd.

"How many hands does Rock have? I haven't seen any of them around today."

"He has six plus the cook. 'Course Stub an' Tuff is with the herd. The rest is smack in the middle a roundup, so they won't be back till late tonight or tomorrow. They should be 'most done.

"The cook went with 'em. He'll cook fer all the hands. The other ranches 'ill make it right with Rock when he gets back." Ike frowned when he realized what he'd said. "Durn it. I never thought I'd outlive Rock."

Spur was quiet as he listened. He looked toward the house again and then asked, "Think Clare will stay here or sell out?"

Ike shook his head. "She said she's stayin'. She don't want to uproot the kids an' I reckon that's right. She's been a doin' the bookwork since they married a year ago, so she has her finger on the pulse a this here ranch. She don't know much 'bout runnin' a ranch though. She's a gonna have to hire a foreman."

Spur looked at Ike in surprise. "What about Stub? Rock said he was foreman."

"Rock done left 'im some land a his own. Clare told me they'd talked about it. Rock wanted Stub to git a start. They was gonna wait a bit but Rock had a will. They give Stub the place he's a living on plus five hundred acres in the event a Rock's death. Clare don't think Stub will want to stay on as foreman since he'll have his own place to look after.

"It's a nice little place too. 'Course he cain't run many cows on five hundred acres but it'll start 'im. He has a few hay meadows an' the buildin's be solid. Ol' Boswell is the closest neighbor an' he's thinkin' on slowin' down. He might even be sellin' his place. 'Course, I'm not sure how much Clare 'ill want to grow this here place or even if she will.

"Rock jist added the ranch Stub lives on last year, an' that was nigh on fifteen thousand acres. Shoot, Stub might even be offered Boswell's place."

Spur shook his head and cursed under his breath. "Tough decisions for a new widow to make, especially with little ones to worry about." He looked back at the house again. "How old is Clare?"

Ike scratched his head and thought a moment. "I reckon she'd be 'bout twenty-one. She was sixteen when she married the first time an' Johnny died a year ago last spring.

"I don't think she ever loved that boy, but he offered to marry 'er an' give 'er son a name."

Ike's eyes were soft as he added, "Rock be the one she always loved though. She married 'im last year."

Spur stared at Ike in surprise, and the old man's bright eyes drilled into the younger man.

"An' don't ya be thinkin' a Clare in a bad way neither. Her ol' pappy were a bad man, an' the men he run with was too—includin' Pony Dixon.

"Clare's a fine woman. She was jist gettin' things goin' the right way when her pappy an' one a his friends broke into 'er house six years ago." He cursed and spit on the ground. "Nine months later, little Zeke come along. He was born nigh about the same time as little Annie.

"Her pappy disappeared fer a time. Then he showed back up last year out to Fort Owen. Shot his own son tryin' to git to Clare.

"It were Rock an' Clare's weddin' day, an' Rock didn't have no gun. Otherwise, he'd a killed Pappy that day. Instead, we hung that worthless turd. That's when Rock an' Clare adopted little Nora. She be Clare's niece."

Ike spit again. "Too bad Pony warn't with 'im that day. We could a hung 'im too. We heard he was down south in the Indian Territory. Some folks thought he had family there."

He looked hard at Spur and added quietly, "What I done told ya don't need to be said again. Little Zeke thinks Johnny were his pappy an' we's a goin' to hold to that." He kicked at a rock and then looked up at Spur. "I jist wanted ya to know that. If'n Clare falls 'part, you'll know some a the reason why."

Spur muttered a curse and shook his head. "That's a heap for one person to carry around let alone this too."

Ike nodded his head. "An' ya keep that in mind when ya talk to 'er. I jist don't know what she's a gonna do when the shock starts to come off. Now let's get this hole dug so we cin bury Rock."

Ike stared at the ground a moment. He threw down his shovel with a curse. "Ya jist go ahead an' dig this here hole. I'm a goin' to clean out the barn."

= CHAPTER 80 =

JUMPING ON THE CLOUDS

SPUR WAS JUST CLIMBING OUT OF THE HOLE HE HAD dug when Annie wandered up. She stared down into the grave for a moment and then looked up at Spur with sad eyes.

"Is that where you are going to put my papa?"

Spur dropped down on the ground beside her. He nodded slowly. "That is where your papa's body will go, but he will always be in your heart." He thumped his chest. "Right here."

Annie's lip began to quiver. "I think my papa will be lonesome in that hole. I think I should draw him a picture."

Spur studied the little girl's face a moment before he replied softly, "I reckon your papa would like that a lot. Do you want to get some paper or would you like to just draw in the dirt?"

Annie's eyes brightened. "I want to draw a picture in the dirt. Then it will be with him forever."

Spur grabbed a small stick. He dropped down into the hole and lifted his hands up for Annie. She squatted in the hole and drew for a while. Then she stood and smiled up at Spur. "There. Now he won't ever forget us."

Annie had drawn five stick figures. The man was the largest and was much bigger than everyone else. A smiling woman stood beside him. Three stick children of different sizes were in front. An odd-shaped something was beside them.

Spur pointed at the picture and nodded. "I see your mama and your papa, Nora, you, and Zeke. Who is that?"

Annie stared up at Spur. She snorted. "That's Gomer. He's our donkey. I think Papa would like to have a picture of Gomer to look at too."

Spur chuckled. He lifted Annie out of the hole and jumped up beside her. He pointed up at the sky.

"Let's go lay down and watch the clouds. I want to tell you a story."

They both dropped down on the grass and Spur pointed up at the sky. He was just getting ready to talk when Zeke and Nora appeared. Annie sat up and patted the ground beside her.

"Lay down here. Spur is going to tell us a story!"

Zeke and Nora lay back on the ground and Spur began.

"When I was a little boy, I had a special friend named Sister Eddie. She told me all kinds of stories. She baked me cookies and when I was sad, we would lay on the ground and watch the clouds. She told me the clouds were God's playground. She said He moved them all the time so the kids in Heaven always had something new to play with. Sometimes, they are soft and puffy like today. They look like the little blobs of cotton we see on the cottonwood trees. Other times, they pile up on top of each other like stacks of wood. And then sometimes, they are all green and black. We know then a storm is coming.

"Sister Eddie told me the kids in Heaven play on those clouds. They jump on them and hop from cloud to cloud. See in Heaven, you can jump and fly so it doesn't matter how far apart they are." He turned his head to look at the three little faces listening closely as they watched the sky. "Doesn't that sound fun?"

All three little ones nodded quietly.

"Now your papa, he loved to ride Red. You know he will be up there riding every day, watching over you. He will hear everything you say. When you laugh, he will laugh too. Your papa will always be with you because you can carry him in your heart, just like I do Sister Eddie. And when I get sad, I talk to her."

Nora sat up and looked at Spur. "Does she talk too?"

Spur put a piece of grass in his mouth and was quiet a moment before he answered. He looked over at them and nodded. "Sometimes she does. I can hear her voice as clear as it was when I was a little tyke." He grinned at them and added, "And sometimes, she shakes her finger at me. I know then I had better straighten up."

Annie sat up and looked from Spur to the clouds.

"Do you think when we go to Heaven we will be able to play on the clouds?"

"I sure do. Sometimes, I close my eyes and pretend I am jumping now. Shall we do that?"

Three little sets of eyes pinched tight and Spur grinned. "Now run as fast as you can and jump! Higher...higher...higher... Now land and fall flat on your back. Feel it bounce under you?"

Annie began to laugh and soon all three of them were talking and laughing. They pointed at the clouds excitedly. Before long, they were all running around and jumping as they pretended they were jumping on the clouds.

Spur rolled over on his elbow and grinned as he watched them. The running and jumping became more animated and noisier.

Clare came to the door and called, "Children! Come to the house. You need to eat something." She paused and then added, "You too, Spur. All of you can wash at the tank before you come in."

Spur stood and grabbed Nora. "I'll race you!" They all raced down the hill to the horse tank. Ike walked out of the barn with a smile on his face. "Now that there's a noisy crowd. Must be time to eat as happy as those faces be."

Zeke looked up. His eyes were bright and happy. "Spur told us a story about jumping on the clouds and we are practicing." He turned to race toward the house, dodging and jumping as he ran.

Clare watched them from the doorway. Her face was pale but she smiled as she watched the children. They burst through the door, all talking at once.

"Did you know the kids in Heaven jump on clouds, Mama? Doesn't that sound like fun? Spur told us all about it. And Papa is up there riding Red. And he sees us." Zeke's brown eyes were excited as the talked.

Tears filled Clare's eyes but she smiled. "Yes, I'm sure he is riding Red. Now you sit down here and let's eat supper. Father Ravalli needs to get back to Stevensville before dark."

=== CHAPTER 81 ===

LET'S LAY THAT BOY DOWN

SUPPER WAS NOISY WITH ALL THE KIDS TALKING. THE adults were quiet but even they smiled from time to time. When everyone was done eating, Father Ravalli stood. He looked around at the little family and smiled.

"It is time for us to lay your father down. Let's walk up that hill. Now who can sing? I know I can't sing very loud. How about you, Spur? Can you sing?"

Spur looked startled as he stared at the smiling priest. He slowly nodded. "I know a few songs. What do you have in mind?"

"I think "How Great Thou Art" would be a nice song. Maybe a verse or two of that."

Spur nodded and they all followed Father Ravalli to the little cemetery on the top of the hill.

The spot Clare had chosen was next to Suzanna's grave. Everyone gathered around and Father Ravalli began. When he was finished, Ike and Spur lowered the coffin into the ground. Father Ravalli raised his hands in a blessing. "In the name of the Father, and of the Son, and of the Holy Spirt. Rest in peace, Rock. May the angels carry you to Paradise." He nodded at Spur.

"Let's hear that song."

Spur held his hat against his heart. His bass voice was rich and full as he sang the words to the old song. His voice echoed over the ranch and carried off through the valleys.

Clare's hands shook as Spur sang, and silent tears ran down her face. Annie stared at Clare. Her lips began to quiver while Zeke grabbed his mother's hand. Maggie leaned against Ike. He hugged her as they both struggled not to cry. Nora stood silently and stared at the grave.

When Spur finished, he picked up both little girls. They hugged his neck.

Father Ravalli smiled as he patted Clare's arm. He formed a cross over each of the children and shook Ike's hand.

"I hope all of you will be able to come to Mass on Sunday. Praying helps to heal the heart."

He squeezed Maggie's hands and then put his hand on Spur's shoulder. "Thank you, Spur. Thank you for all you have done for this little family."

Ike had the priest's mule tied to a tree, and he handed the reins to the smiling man. Father Ravalli waved to all of them. He winked at the children.

"Now don't fall off any clouds!" He left quietly and the little group moved slowly down the hill.

Clare paused and looked back at Spur. "You are welcome to stay in the bunkhouse. I am expecting the hands home tonight or tomorrow."

Her eyes were moist with tears as she added, "Thank you for bringing Rock home—and for everything else you did today."

Spur nodded. His steps slowed until the family was ahead of him. He ducked behind a tree before he turned toward the corral. A palomino appaloosa walked up to the fence and he petted her.

"Kind of a gloomy place around here today, old girl. I think I'll head down to Stevensville tomorrow and pick up my horses. Wish their feet were ready to travel. I'd just head on south. I'm not much for high emotion."

He grinned wryly at the horse. "I'm a runner and I always have been. I guess maybe that makes me a coward. If it does, then that's the way it is." He looked over his shoulder at the house and shook his head. "I'd better find something to do around here. Otherwise, I won't make it until Gabe gets here with that herd."

Spur could hear the children talking and laughing inside the house and he chuckled. "Kids are always fun though. Glad I could make them smile a little today." He petted the horse again before he turned away.

He grabbed his saddle bags and bedroll out of the barn. He dropped them in the bunkhouse, paused a moment, and then turned toward the creek.

"I just as well shave and rinse off before I head for bed."

CHAPTER 82

A QUICK TRIP TO TOWN

SPUR KNOCKED ON THE DOOR OF THE HOUSE WHEN he heard stirring. Clare opened it with a look of surprise. "Spur? Is everything all right?"

Spur nodded over his shoulder. "I am headed down to Stevensville to pick up my horses. Anything you need me to get while I'm there?"

Clare frowned slightly and then shook her head. A small smile flitted across her face. "I guess that means you are coming back."

Spur looked down at his boots and then lifted his head to grin at her. "Well, I can tell you the thought of leaving did cross my mind. My horse's feet are bruised though. I need to let them heal before I go anywhere. I thought I'd bring both horses up here so I can take care of them myself."

Clare studied his face and then laughed. "Well, even a runner has to stay put from time to time.

"Why don't you pick up a tin of cocoa? Annie loves chocolate pie and I thought I might make her one." She started to turn back into the house and then stopped.

"Anything special you like to eat, Spur? Do you think you'll be back for dinner?"

Spur chuckled. "Well, I like chocolate pie. If you are going to make pies, I'll make sure I'm back in time for dinner." He tipped his hat and sauntered back to his horses. He was whistling "Old Paint" as he rode down the trail.

"Nine more days before that herd gets to Stevensville. I think I should ride up the valley and make sure we have a clear trail all the way. We might have to move the herd around some crops, and I'd like to know where in advance."

Spur arrived in Stevensville around 8:00 a.m. He rode the palomino appaloosa and led Ike's horse. He returned Ike's horse to the livery and paid his bill there. Ike wasn't around but both horses were happy to see Spur. Their feet were still tender but he thought they could make it to the ranch if they took it slow. He rubbed down both horses as he talked to his.

"Good to see you, Rockafeller. I'm taking you with me up to Beckler's ranch. I'm hoping your feet will be healed in three or four days." He paused and then shook his head. "I reckon we will stay until the herd gets back. I can work with Rock's horses some while I'm waiting." Rockafeller nickered softly and rubbed its head on Spur.

"You ready to go home too, old fellow? I think both of us would like to head on south. Well, it won't be much longer. The boys should have that herd here in nine days, ten at the most. Then we can turn things over to Stub and ride on out of here."

Spur loaded the cocoa and some apples in a burlap bag. He dropped some hard candy in before he tied the bag behind his saddle. He had saved several apples back. He broke them in half giving part to each horse. "It's hard to beat the taste of a tart apple. Well, apple pie would but that's rare. Pie is something I just don't get much of."

He was headed back up the mountain by 9:00 a.m. His stomach was growling so bad that he finally stopped and pulled an apple out to eat himself. He walked both horses all the way, and it was nearly 11:30 when he arrived at the ranch. All three children rushed out to meet him.

"Are these your horses, Spur? Which one is named after our papa?" Zeke's eyes were bright as he studied the two horses.

Annie pointed at the large sorrel stud. "That one. He's the prettiest."

Spur laughed and nodded. "You are sure right, Annie. This is Rockafeller. Sometimes I call him Rock and sometimes I call him Feller. He's a fine horse though.

"How about you kids help me lead these horses into the barn. I want to look their feet over and make sure they don't have any cuts in their frogs or in their soles. They made a hard old trip over the mountain."

He looked at the kids. "Do you know what the frog of a horse's foot is?"

Annie nodded her head but Nora and Zeke didn't know. Spur lifted up one of Rockafeller's feet.

"See that raised part in the center? That's the frog of his foot. Outside of that is the sole." He tapped the horseshoe and added, "I think I will pull their shoes off tomorrow and reshoe them."

Both horses had some swelling in their frogs. Rockafeller also had a cut below one hock. Spur rubbed some salve from his saddlebag into it. He forked both horses some hay. Then he grabbed the gunnysack of supplies and they left the barn quietly.

"I think you kids shouldn't play in the barn for a few days. Let those horses get some rest and get used to your place. I don't want those horses getting excited and hurting themselves."

All three kids nodded. They were quiet for a time. Finally, Zeke asked, "Think we can go swimming again this afternoon? We got all our work done this morning, and Mama said it would be all right. She said we had to ask you though."

Spur grinned at them. "I think it would be a fine day for a swim. 'Course starting tomorrow, I am going to have to go to work. Your mother might kick me out if I laze around much longer. I don't think she tolerates slackers."

Annie frowned at him. "Well, we like it when you play with us. Maybe you should just stay a kid and not go back to being a grownup."

Spur laughed out loud and the kids laughed with him.

CHAPTER 83

One Person Is Still Smiling

SPUR SET THE GUNNY SACK DOWN ON THE GROUND and dug in it for a moment. He held up three pieces of hard candy. "Who needs a little snack before we eat?"

The three kids glanced toward the house and then grabbed the candy. They quickly shoved the candy into their mouths, mumbling thank yous around the dribbling syrup.

Clare watched from the window as the three little ones surrounded Spur. He laughed and joked easily with them as he walked.

"Thank Heavens one person here is still smiling. Spur has been wonderful with the children. That is quite amazing since he has none of his own." Clare frowned at the sticky syrup running down their chins as the kids raced into the house.

Spur grinned. "Now don't drip that syrup in here. I don't want your mother to whup up on me. I think maybe she can smack pretty hard."

The three children raced back outside and Spur set the bag on the table. "I picked up a few apples too just in case you like to make apple pie."

Clare smiled softly. "Rock loved pie." Her voice caught as she looked at Spur. "I can't believe he is gone."

Spur reached inside his vest and pulled out the letters. "These are for you and your little ones. Rock wanted you to have them."

Clare touched the letters and the stain of blood. Her hand trembled and she shook her head.

"I don't want to read them. You hang onto them. You can read them to the children if you want, but I can't read them yet." She touched the stain on the top letter and looked up at Spur as she whispered, "Is that Rock's blood? How did he die?"

Spur's face twisted in pain. "Clare, if I could do anything to make this easier for you, I would. Shoot, I'd take Rock's place if I could. Just know his last thoughts and words were of you and the kids. He said to tell you he loved you. That he loved all of you."

Clare's lips trembled as she looked up at Spur. She walked to the window and then finally looked again at the man standing in her kitchen.

"I was worried about this drive. I had a terrible feeling in my heart." She looked away and continued softly. "I worry all the time and Rock was—he was my strength. He barely worried about anything. When he was around, I just knew everything would be alright.

"Now I don't know if anything will ever be right again." She took a deep breath and forced herself to smile.

"I will have dinner ready in an hour. Come on up and eat with us."

Spur nodded and turned toward the door. He paused and then looked back.

"I can stick around until Stub gets here with the herd. Anything you want done while I'm here?"

Clare was quiet a moment. She finally looked up. "Rock was going to work with the horses when he came home. I don't even know what he meant by that." Her breath caught in her chest and her hands shook as she sat down.

"How am I going to run this ranch, Spur? I know so little about anything that goes on. I do the bookwork, but I know nothing of running a ranch."

Spur walked back toward Clare. He took her hands as he talked. "You have Stub. He knows this ranch like the back of his hand. You keep him on as foreman. He can walk you through the daily work of running a ranch."

Clare shook her head. "He is going to have his own place. He needs to put his time in there."

"He wouldn't have that place if it weren't for you and Rock. You let him help. He will want to and you need him." He squeezed her hands before he turned away.

"I'll start working with the horses tomorrow. I think I know what Rock would like done." He touched the brim of his hat and slipped out the door. He took a ragged breath as he stood on the steps. A small donkey pushed past him and rushed into the house. Spur turned to watch it in surprise.

Clare smiled as the donkey rubbed against her. "Hello, Gomer. Did you smell those apples? Well you go ahead and take one." She held the donkey's rough head and whispered, "Oh, Gomer. What are we going to do?"

Spur's throat tightened as he walked toward the barn.

=== CHAPTER 84 ===

SOME HARD DAYS

EVERY MORNING, SPUR WORKED WITH THE HORSES and every afternoon, he took the kids swimming. They all cried for their father from time to time, but their little hearts seemed to be healing.

Clare was another story. She was sad at first. Then she became angry.

Spur didn't know what to do, so he avoided the house as much as possible.

Ike and Maggie had gone home on the fourth day. They were coming back out on Friday. Maggie had even mentioned taking the children home with them.

Spur thought a moment. "Why, today *is* Friday. I'll be gone most of the morning so those loud kids can bother their grandparents." He chuckled as he thought of some of the stories they had told him. "Kids can sure be funny."

Rock had started his hands building fence before he left. They had completed the section he told them to build. However, they weren't sure what to do next. They gathered around Spur and one asked, "Think we should build more fence?"

Spur gazed across the pasture. The grass was starting to dry on the stem.

He looked around at the men. "Do you put up hay here? I know we like to have a little hay set aside down in the Wyoming Territory."

Wiley, one of the older hands, nodded his head. "Rock mentioned he wanted to do that this fall."

"Did he say where?"

"Not exactly but I can show you where we were when he was talking."

"Let's ride out that way and look it over. You can start on that after dinner.

"Stub should be here with the cattle in four days. Once we figure out where you are going to cut, I am going to ride up the valley toward Missoula. I want to see what that trail looks like. I hope it's fenced so we don't have to watch a lot of farms.

"Let me tell Clare where we're going and we'll head out."

Spur walked slowly toward the house. Clare was making bread and her kneading looked more like she was beating the bread. He watched her a moment and just about sneaked away. Finally, he tapped on the doorjamb and poked his head inside.

"I'm going to ride out with your hands and look over a hay pasture. I think we'll start them cutting hay this afternoon. After dinner, I'm going to ride toward Missoula. I want to look that stretch of road over since the cows will follow it down here. I'm hoping we'll have fence all the way."

He thought a moment and then added, "Maggie and Ike should be here by then if you'd like to ride along."

Excitement flared in Clare's eyes for a moment but she shook her head. "I don't think so. I have too much work to do here. Besides the children need to be—"

Spur interrupted her. "And Maggie will be here this afternoon. Why don't you come with me? I know you like to ride, and you won't have many more fall days as nice as this one."

Clare paused as she studied his face and Spur grinned.

"I'll even saddle that palomino appaloosa out there. She's an easy-riding horse and has a pleasant disposition."

"Okay, but only if Maggie is here by the time you leave." She smiled at him as she added, "And come up to the house for dinner. I made apple pies this morning."

Spur scratched his head. "An apple pie for a horseback ride? That works for me!" He grinned at her and sauntered toward the barn.

He saddled one of the Appaloosa studs, and the men were quickly headed toward the hay meadow.

CHAPTER 85

TELL ME ABOUT THE DRIVE

THE MEAL WAS DELICIOUS BUT SPUR WAS EDGY. I *probably shouldn't have asked Clare to go with me. I don't care so much what people think of me, but I don't want anyone to think bad of Clare.*

Maggie looked over at him with a smile. "Clare tells me the two of you are riding north to look over the route the cattle will follow. That is a wonderful idea. It is also a perfect excuse for me to take these little ones home with me." When Clare started to protest, Maggie shook her head.

"Now don't argue with me, Clare. I want to take my grandchildren. You can pick them up after Mass on Sunday. Maybe Spur will drive you down."

Spur could feel the panic rising in his throat. He shoved in the last bite of pie and stood. "I'll go saddle those horses."

He rushed out of the house, pulling on his bandana. He felt like he was choking. Once he got the bandana loose, he could breathe again.

"It's time for me to head south. I can feel these walls closing in on me. It's time to run." Then he began to laugh. "You act all sure of yourself, Spur, but underneath you're a big coward.

"Well, even a coward can take the boss lady for a ride to show her where her cows will be trailing," he growled to himself.

He had the horses saddled and was in the barn brushing Rockafeller when he heard the kids screaming in excitement.

He walked to the barn door with a smile on his face.

"We are going to Auntie Maggie's and Grandpa Ike's, Spur! Won't that be fun? And then you and Mama will bring us home after church."

He strolled toward the buggy with a smile on his face. "Well I reckon that will be just fine. You have fun now and don't eat too much candy." He scratched his head and frowned. "I guess that means I will have to go swimming by myself."

Annie stared at him for a moment and then stated seriously, "We will only be gone two days, Spur. I think you will be okay."

Spur choked and started to laugh. When Annie threw her arms around his neck and kissed his cheek, he blushed. He backed away from the wagon and waved as Ike pulled away. He glanced over at Clare.

"I have the horses saddled. Whenever you're ready, I'll be in the barn." He walked toward the barn slapping the currycomb against his leg.

Clare was out of the house quickly and hurried toward the barn. Spur gave her a leg up. Instead of heading down the trail though, he turned his horse north. When Clare looked at him in surprise, he grinned.

"I've been doing a little exploring, and I found another route down. You can't take a buggy over it because it's a game trail, but I thought you might enjoy some different scenery."

They visited easily for the first half hour and then Clare became quiet. When she spoke again, her voice was soft.

"Tell me about the drive, Spur. Tell me some of the funny things that happened, things that will make my heart happy."

Spur nodded slowly. He told her about the fence that they had cut by Buffalo and how Stub had driven Booker's chuckwagon over the posts. He told her about Angel diving in the Platte River for Rufe's boot and coming up with four of them. Then he told her about the painted wagon and the ladies who wanted to make camp with them.

"Rock and Gabe sent them away. Those ladies said they hoped to see the two of them in Butte, but Rock said they'd never see either of them again. He told them Gabe and he were both married, and they were afraid of their wives."

Spur was laughing and Clare smiled.

"I miss him so much. I find myself watching through the window for him. At night, I miss his arms around me." She laughed softly. "I even miss his dirty socks."

Spur listened as Clare spoke. He finally grinned at her. "Now I can help you with the dirty socks. And if they come back fixed, that would be even better."

CHAPTER 86

SPUR'S HUMOR

CLARE STARED AT SPUR A MOMENT BEFORE SHE laughed again.

"You always see the humor in life, Spur. Don't you ever get sad?"

Spur rode quietly for a moment. "I reckon all of us get sad from time to time, but I don't like to pine on things I can't fix.

"I didn't have much of a mother. I never even knew my pa but I had Sister Eddie. She was the mother I never had, and she kept me on the straight and narrow. Even now, she shakes her finger at me sometimes.

"I reckon I could resent my mother, but why? It won't do any good. Besides, she did me a favor by turning me over to Sister Eddie." He chuckled as he looked over at Clare. "'Course, most of my women friends are in whorehouses from New Orleans to Texas, and on farther north." He winked at her and added, "They are friendly though and a man does like a friendly woman."

Clare stared at him and then slowly blushed. "I declare, Spur."

"Now don't you go high and mighty on me, Clare. Rock told me how your best friends in Helena were the girls on the line. I reckon we both haul around junk we should dump somewhere. Besides, you know and I know those girls can all use a friend from time to time."

411

"You don't really care what people think of you, do you, Spur?"

Spur scratched his head. "Not so much. I don't like it when folks talk bad about my friends though. I'm not big on gossip."

He pointed below them where St. Mary's Mission showed.

"There you are, Miss Clare. See, we are almost to the Mission and it took us less than an hour.

He looked over at her. "Did Rock talk to you at all about those last thirty miles between here and Missoula? I was wondering if he had agreements with any of the farmers. That herd will take two or three days to get from Missoula to here."

Clare slowly shook her head. "Not that I know of. I certainly didn't send any of them payments of any kind. If he had agreements, they were all verbal."

"Well, I guess we'll just stop in and talk to folks then."

By 3:00 that afternoon, they had spoken to five different farmers. The trail ran close to the St. Mary's River and most of the farms beside it were fenced. There was grass along the river though so grazing would be adequate.

Spur looked over at Clare. "We are about halfway to Missoula. Do you want to keep riding north? It's nearly fifteen more miles. That's probably another two hours with all the stopping. It will put us late getting back."

Clare hesitated and then pointed ahead. "Let's go on. You will have to come back tomorrow if we don't ride the full way. Besides, it is a nice afternoon."

It was nearly 5:00 p.m. when they reached the top of the valley. There were only two farmsteads they would have to watch. The rest had fences.

"That shouldn't be too bad. I'll head north on Monday and see if I can meet the herd. You want to come down to Stevensville to watch them trail into town? I can arrange a ride with Ike if you want."

Clare thought a moment. "I'm not sure. I will see how the weekend goes."

Spur nodded. "So what route do you want to take up the mountain? The one we came down or your normal one?"

"Let's take the new one. I think it will be pretty with the sun setting."

"Good, because I have someplace else I want to show you."

When they were about halfway up the mountain, Spur turned to the left and wound his way through some trees. When he stopped, they were on the edge of a high vista. Clare recognized some of the farms below as ones they had ridden by. The St. Mary's River looked like a sparkling ribbon as it wound its way across the valley floor.

Clare was quiet as she studied the view in front of her. Finally, she looked over at Spur and smiled. "Thank you for sharing this trail with me, Spur. I rarely take the time to really look at the beauty around me." She looked around and smiled again. "It is so peaceful here. Beautiful too."

Spur nodded. "Sure is. But you know, I have seen beauty in every place I've lived. Different kinds but beauty just the same."

He turned his horse. "We'd better go. I don't know this trail well enough to travel it after dark."

Clare was quiet the rest of the way home but her silence didn't bother Spur. He knew she had enjoyed herself and that was good enough for him.

She smiled as he lifted her down. "Thank you for a lovely afternoon, Spur. I haven't ridden since our trip to Cheyenne and I enjoyed it."

Spur could see the tears sparkling in her eyes and he looked away. He was smiling when he looked back.

"You are welcome, Miss Clare. Maybe we'll do that again before I leave." He turned the horses and led them toward the barn as he whistled. He started to sing and then remembered there were tired men in the bunkhouse. He chuckled. "I guess I am too used to being alone. I was ready to belt out 'Ol' Paint.' Good thing I caught myself."

CHAPTER 87

AN HONEST MAN

SPUR HAD THE HORSES HITCHED AND THE TEAM pulled up to the house by 7:30 a.m. on Sunday morning.

Clare hurried out of the house. She tugged on her dress to bring it down further over her growing stomach.

Spur grinned as he lifted her up. "I think you'd better let that dress out some. That little old baby in there is goin' to keep growin', and your stomach is too."

Clare sputtered a moment and then glared at him. "I declare, Spur. You have no muzzle on your mouth at all."

Spur was surprised as he looked over at the blushing woman beside him. "It's the truth, isn't it? What is there to be embarrassed about? Women have kids all the time and every time, it's the same. Their stomachs grow, they put on a little weight, their faces fill out, and they get this sparkle around their eyes. They get real pretty. Nothing to be embarrassed about I guess."

Clare stared at the man beside her. Finally, she laughed out loud. "I am guessing you and Rock became friends on this drive."

Spur chuckled as he nodded. "We were already friends but I surely did get to know him better. You get to know all the fellows on a drive because you live with them, you eat with them, you work with them, and you sleep with them. You find out who the quiet ones are and who the funny ones are.

"That Angel. He's quite the character. He talks about his knife like it is a woman. Even though it's huge, he calls it his small knife.

"Now Gabe, I've known him quite a few years, and he's just as sudden as he was when we were young. When he gets pushed, he just blows up. Oh, not at everyone, but for sure when someone hurts those he cares about.

"When Rufe got beaten and stomped, Gabe pistol-whipped the fellow who did it. Then we burned down the saloon. We—"

Spur's face turned red. "Sorry, Clare. You probably didn't want to hear all that."

Clare's face was pale when she looked at Spur. "Did the young man die?"

Spur nodded. "That's when we decided to burn down the saloon. That bartender encouraged the men who were doing the stomping, and no one stepped in to stop it.

"The fellow who stomped Rufe was beating up on a girl and that's just not right. Rufe stepped in to stop him. The rest of the boys were helping. A whole passel of men turned on Rufe. Tobe, Miguel, and Bart tried to get him out, and the whole place took them down. Angel and I heard the ruckus, and we rushed in. We got the boys out but Rufe didn't make it. We buried him in Deer Lodge Valley. We buried him with his boots on, facing the east. It was a real pretty place."

Clare was quiet a moment and then she looked intently at Spur.

"Spur, if I asked you to stay, would you do it?"

"I don't think so, Clare. I have a job I like. And I don't want to be tied down."

He looked over at Clare and studied her face before he continued. "Now if we were in love and you asked me to stay, I might. I'm a runner though, so I don't even know if I would then. I'm not big on commitments. They come with promises, and promises get broken."

Clare laughed dryly. "Wow. You are even more jaded than I am." She studied his profile and then asked, "Have you ever been in love, Spur?"

Spur was quiet for a time. "I think maybe once. I ran so I'm not sure. It seems if it was the real thing, you wouldn't want to run. I guess I don't know."

He added softly, "I was never around any married folks who liked each other that much until I took my job with Rowdy. For the first time in my life, I realized my best friends were all married and married happily."

Spur chuckled. "Well, not Angel but he will be. Angel is a fine man. He will be a good husband someday and a daddy too. Now his brother, Miguel…I'm not so sure about him."

Clare shifted in her seat. "I enjoyed Merina. I wish she was closer. I would love to have a woman friend my own age." She looked over at Spur and commented softly, "Merina is who you were in love with, isn't she?"

Spur almost dropped the buggy traces. As he stared at her, Clare began to laugh.

"You think you can laugh and disguise your feelings, but I see right through you, George Spurlach."

A grin slowly spread across Spur's face. "Well, that was a long time ago. By the time I saw her again, she was in love with Gabe. Gabe and I have been friends since we were both fourteen, and I didn't want an old spark to be a problem. It's not and I'm pleased. They are a fine couple and good friends." His grin became bigger and he bumped Clare.

"I think you have just about analyzed me clean through. How about we talk about you for a while?"

Clare's face became pale. "I don't think so. I'm not proud of my past."

Spur looked straight ahead. He was quiet for a moment before he looked over at Clare. He spoke to her sincerely.

"I don't reckon anyone should be ashamed of things that happened to them, things they couldn't control. You are a strong woman, Clare. You overcame the demons from your past. You built a life you can be proud of, one that makes things better for your children and the people around you.

"What you did for little Rollie about made my heart split wide open. Most folks just clucked their tongues and moved on. You *did* something because of what you went through as a child.

"Your past made you what you are, Clare. Don't be ashamed of it."

Clare stared at Spur and then large tears formed in her eyes. As they slid down her cheeks, Spur put his arm around her.

"Don't be sad, Clare," he whispered. "Rock would want you to be happy. Be happy for your children and for the memories he gave you."

He hugged her and then carefully took his arm away.

CHAPTER 88

I PREFER INTERESTING

MASS WAS NOISY. THERE WERE LOTS OF FAMILIES there, and Father Ravalli made them all feel welcome. The Indian children were quieter but even they were restless after an hour.

Spur decided he liked Father Ravalli. *The man is kind but has a great sense of humor. He's wise too.*

Finally, they were all back in the wagon and headed home. The kids were crawling back and forth from the seat to the wagon bed. Every time, they kicked Spur. He noticed Clare was holding her stomach.

"Now you kids need to slow it down. I think Ike gave you too many cookies, and I don't intend to take any wild kids swimming this afternoon."

The wagon became instantly quiet and Spur winked at Clare.

"How about you, little Mama? You want to come swimming with us?"

Clare laughed when the children began to beg.

"I tell you what. You all lay down in the wagon bed and take a nap. If you are quiet on the way home, I'll pack a picnic lunch and we will eat down by the creek." As the noise in the back of the wagon escalated to a crescendo, Clare added firmly, "But only if you are quiet on the way home."

It wasn't long before the wagon bed was quiet.

Spur looked over at Clare curiously. "So how does it work when women go swimming? What do you wear? I mean, I would just as soon go in my union suit if I can't strip clear down. I never did swim with a woman. I've always wondered what women wore in the water."

Clare stared at Spur and her eyes sparked. "I declare, Spur. You have no muzzle whatsoever!"

Spur frowned and then he shrugged. "I guess I don't see a problem with what I asked. I mean we were having a conversation about swimming."

"I will never go swimming with you, so I guess you will never know."

Spur studied Clare's face and a slow grin creased his. "I reckon I know what women *don't* wear now." He winked at her and began to whistle "Ol' Paint."

Clare sputtered beside him but he paid no attention.

Soon, he was singing instead of whistling and the words became louder with each verse. When he was finished, he rode with a smile on his face.

"You are a strange man, Spur."

Spur looked over at Clare and winked as his eyes twinkled. "I prefer interesting. Think I'm an interesting man?"

She studied his profile and then looked ahead of the wagon. "I don't know. What I do know is you make me laugh."

"Well, that's good enough for me. What shall I sing next? I have quite a repertoire but they aren't all appropriate for a lady."

Clare was quiet and then asked softly. "Would you sing "How Great Thou Art?" That was so beautiful when you sang it at Rock's funeral."

Spur nodded and began. He sang softly through the verses, and then belted out parts of the chorus. His voice went from soft to loud as he sang with emotion.

When he was done, he looked straight ahead for a time. When he heard Clare sob, he put his arm around her. He said nothing. He just held her until her sobs subsided. When she was quiet again, he removed his arm. He was quiet until Clare spoke.

"You are a kind man, Spur. You have a big heart."

"And I'm a runner."

"Well yes, there is that."

=== CHAPTER 89 ===

MEETING THE HERD

SPUR WAS UP EARLY MONDAY MORNING. HE TOOK THE back way down the mountain and cantered the Appaloosa stud he was riding when he reached the valley floor. Fall had reached the Bitter Root Valley and Spur buttoned his vest.

He had ridden about ten miles when he heard the cattle. He rode toward the herd slowly with a smile on his face.

Cookie glared at him and Spur grinned. "Good to see you too, Cookie. How's your helper working out?"

The cook grunted and then his ornery old eyes sparkled as he snorted. "She has all these big plans 'bout what these boys need. Shoot, they've had dessert ever' durn day. She's a spoilin' 'em, that's what's a goin' on."

Spur chuckled and tipped his hat to Adelia. Her pretty face was excited. The hand-me-down clothes from the cowboys hung loose on her and made her look even smaller than she was.

She elbowed Cookie and laughed. "We are getting along fine. He acts all cranky but he's a big softy. He loves these men as much as I do."

Spur was laughing as he rode toward Gabe. The trail boss was in front of the herd where he had been most of the drive.

Gabe's face was strained and Spur looked quickly down the line of riders. Everyone was there except Nate and the horse herd. Then he looked back at the chuckwagon and began to chuckle.

"So how is Adelia working out as the cook's helper? Dang. Another hard rule and you broke it yourself."

Gabe's face slowly broke into a grin. "I'm kind of easy to read, aren't I?"

"Sure are." Spur chuckled as he shook Gabe's hand.

Gabe's grin faded as he looked down the valley. "How's Clare?"

"She's doing better. She cried a lot and then she got mad. Now she is just sad. She smiles more often though, and I have even gotten her to laugh a little. She might meet the herd in Stevensville."

"When are you heading out?"

"Tomorrow. I'll head home with you fellows unless you are staying longer."

"No, we are headed south first thing in the morning. We saw some pretty country but I'm ready to go home."

"Was Tall Eagle going to head west to the Nez Perce? I know he was going to visit some family when we left the Crow reservation."

"Yep. He caught up with us and then cut out two days ago."

"Think this will be your last drive?"

"I know it will be. I'm done crossing rivers. I thought we were going to lose Rufe in the Platte." Gabe was quiet for a bit. "I have been thinking about him this morning. I just will never understand the pure meanness in some people."

Spur nodded and then his eyes crinkled at the corners. "Some folks would say the same about pistol-whipping someone to death."

Gabe stared at Spur a moment and then his own eyes twinkled. "But I guess we will never know if it was me who killed him."

Spur laughed out loud. He slapped Gabe's shoulder. "I have missed you, my friend.

"I think I'll wander on back and say hello to the rest of the boys."

As he rode toward the rear of the herd, he called back to Gabe, "Clare and I rode this route last Friday. You only have two places coming up where there isn't fence."

Spur rode beside the herd and talked to every man. He was happy to see each one of them and that surprised him some. *I have always had lots of friends. I've just never had many I spent extended time with.*

He rode beside Angel for a time. The smiling vaquero looked like he had just walked out of church instead of riding at the end of a ten-week cattle drive.

Spur jerked his thumb toward the chuckwagon where the young woman rode. "So what is Adelia going to do? Stay in the Montana Territory or go south with you boys?"

"I don't know but señor Stub, he thinks he is much in love."

Spur looked at Angel in surprise.

"Stub? I don't think he has ever had a girl, has he?"

Angel chuckled. "No, señor, and he doesn't have this one either. She is keeping her distance from all the men. But that didn't stop Stub from dreaming. Ah, amour. It is much in the air here, yes?"

Spur looked at Angel carefully and then shrugged. "Maybe. I wouldn't know."

"How early do you think Gabe will want to leave in the morning? I am guessing the young men will want to go out this evening since the drive is over."

"And you will go with them, yes?"

"No, I was thinking you and Miguel should go. You are both younger than me."

Angel's dark eyes twinkled. "Perhaps we should all go. It might take both of us to get them back to the rancho because Miguel will be no help."

Spur laughed as he rode away.

"Tobe, Bart. How are you fellows? Ready to move to Montana?"

Bart looked at Tobe and then shrugged. "We have been talking. We are done with drives but we wouldn't mind working up here for a time. Didn't know if they'd be hiring before winter though. Think Mrs. Beckler needs any more hands?"

Spur's surprise showed on his face. "I wouldn't know. They look a little shorthanded to me, but I'm not familiar with the stocking rates up here. Ask Stub. He's her foreman.

"Luck with whatever you decide."

He waved across the herd at Stub and then hollered, "Your men are looking forward to having you back. The fellow who has been hanging around here for the last ten days doesn't seem to know his head from his hind leg!"

Stub chuckled and waved. Spur smiled. *I like that quiet cowboy. He's a hard worker and he doesn't waste any words.*

His grin was big when he reached the back of the herd. Sam and Tuff were riding drag.

"Well, Fellows. How was your first drive? Think you want to do this again?"

Both instantly nodded. Tuff's eyes were bright.

"We were just talking about how much fun we had. I don't know which was more fun—when we fought those fellows by Buffalo or when we burned out the Copper Bucket in Butte."

"Well, you want to be a little leery of Gabe when he gets a mad on. He can be real sudden. And I sure wouldn't recommend you fellows try any of that stuff when you get home." He looked behind the herd for Nate.

"How far back is Nate?"

"Gabe told him to graze the horses awhile and then head south about 10:00 this morning since this trail is so narrow. We left at 6:00 so he shouldn't be too far behind us."

"I think I'll ride north and look for him. When I find him, I'll send him up to ride with you fellows. I'll bring the horses in."

426

CHAPTER 90

BAD COMPANY

THE FARTHER SPUR RODE, THE MORE CONCERNED HE became. Finally, he saw the horse herd. Two rough-looking men had their horses crowded close to Nate. A third had his horse off to the side. Spur's face tightened down and he slipped the thong off his gun.

"Howdy, Boys. Out for a ride or are you looking for trouble?"

The biggest of the three laughed. "No, we were just discussing with this young man where he should take our horses."

Spur kept his hand casually close to his gun. It wasn't drawn but he was ready.

"You have a bill of sale, do you?"

"Sure we do. Now, boy, you turn those horses around and take them back to Missoula. We've argued with you long enough. Or we can leave you afoot right here."

Spur's voice was hard and his gun was pointed at the man who was talking. "You boys drop your guns.

"Nate, you spur that horse and run him into the shyster in front of you. I'll take the other two."

The young cowboy slammed his spurs into the side of his startled horse and Spur started shooting. He emptied the first saddle and had his gun pointed toward the third man. The one Nate had slammed his horse into cursed and grabbed for his rifle. Spur calmly shot him and then looked again at the third man.

"What's it going to be? You want to take your chances with a jury in Missoula or do you think you can pull your gun faster than I can shoot."

The man raised his hands. When his arms bumped his hat, Spur swore under his breath. The man's beardless face showed just a trace of peach fuzz. *He's just a darn kid.*

The young man looked down the barrel of the gun pointed at him and the angry man holding it. He took a deep breath.

"Mister, what I'd really like is to just ride out of here. I wasn't in favor of this deal, and I'd like to go on back to the Idaho Territory where I'm from."

Spur studied the young cowboy in front of him.

"How old are you?"

"Fifteen next week, Mister."

Spur stared at him and then looked over to where Nate waited with his rifle pointed.

"Nate, you help him get those men across their saddles." He took a stub pencil and a paper from his saddlebag. He thought a moment and then scribbled a note.

"Boy, you give this note to the sheriff in Missoula. Then you hightail it back home. And next time, you do a better job of picking your friends." He shoved the note into the boy's hand.

As the young man headed north leading the two horses with bodies slung over them, Spur called after him, "And I'd better not see you in this valley until you are older and smarter!"

The young man didn't slow down or answer. Only when he was within a quarter of a mile of Missoula did he read the note.

Sheriff, this boy is bringing two outlaws in. They tried to steal our horses. If you need to talk to me, I'll be at the Beckler Ranch southeast of Stevensville.

George Spurlach

And so you know, the boy is innocent.

The young man stared at the note and then looked behind him. The horses were nearly out of sight and a chill went through him. "I almost pulled my gun. I was scared though and I didn't. He would have killed me. I can't believe he let me go and sent this note too."

The young man's hands were shaking when he dismounted in front of the sheriff's office. No one was there so he tied the horses in front, laid the note on the sheriff's desk, and rode slowly out of town. When he was north of town a mile, he put the spurs to his horse and headed for the Nez Perce Reservation.

=== CHAPTER 91 ===

A FINE WAY TO FINISH

RELIEF SHOWED ON NATE'S PALE FACE AS HE RODE toward Spur.

"You don't know how happy I am to see you, Spur. Those fellows were riding in front of me. They pulled off to the side like they were going to let me by, and then they jumped me."

Spur's hard hand gripped Nate's shoulder and he gave a low laugh.

"Nate," he drawled, "I think you did mighty fine. I believe I'd hire a young man like you if I had my own place.

"Now let's get these horses pointed the right way, so you can catch up to the herd. I think your buddies would like it if you rode these last few miles with them."

Spur could see folks standing along the road. Most watched quietly as the black cattle trailed by. Some of them called to the riders. Others waved. Spur's smile grew large when he saw Clare and the kids. They were in a wagon with Ike and Maggie. All three little ones jumped out and ran toward the cattle when they saw Stub.

"Stub! We missed you! Where's Tuff?"

"Are these our cows?"

"Did you see any bad guys? Can I ride with you?"

Stub chuckled as he herded the kids back to the wagon. "Now stay back. These old girls aren't used to all your noise yet." He looked toward the wagon.

"Clare." For just a moment, his hand shook as he tipped his hat. He nodded toward Maggie and Ike before he turned back to the herd.

The three young men on drag waved to everyone. They had their hats off and were laughing. Clare's three children were talking excitedly by the side of the road. A few cows swerved away from them but they were tired. Most just plodded by.

The horses were right behind the cattle and Spur waved to those who called. He rode his horse over to Clare and watched as the horses moved by. He pointed at the stallion up front.

"Old Watie, he is Gabe's horse. He was a mustang and Tall Eagle caught him. He's a heck of a horse. Shoot, they don't even need me. Watie just tells those other horses where to go."

He looked over at Clare and smiled. "Your cattle, Clare. A new era in the cattle business here in the Bitter Root Valley.

"I'm glad you came and brought the kids."

The three little ones were running after the herd. When they saw Spur, they all rushed toward him. "Can we have a ride, Spur? Please?"

Spur laughed as he looked down at them. "I reckon that would be fine.

"Nate! Sam! Tuff! Come back here. You each grab one of these kids. They can ride with you a bit."

The three young men swung the children up behind them, and the happy crew went on through town.

Spur smiled as he watched. "A fine way to end a long drive," he commented softly. "Just a fine way to finish."

CHAPTER 92

WHERE DO YOU BELONG, SEÑOR?

IT WAS MIDAFTERNOON BEFORE ALL OF THE CATTLE were penned and the horses were sorted. Gabe's crew wanted their personal horses close to the barn, so they could catch them easily in the morning. The ones that belonged to the ranch were put out in a pasture.

Spur checked Rockafeller's feet. "I don't know old boy. Your feet look better but I'm not sure you are up for another long haul. Maybe I should just leave you here. This is where you belong anyway." The horse nickered softly and pushed his nose into Spur's arm. Spur draped his arm over the horse's neck and stared out the barn door.

"I am going to miss this place and those three little ones for sure." He looked toward the house and shook his head. "I never have liked saying goodbye."

Angel popped his head in the open door. "Are our fine caballos ready for a long journey, señor?"

Spur looked over at Angel and for a moment his face showed his emotions. Then he hid them with a smile.

"Your tough little mustang is, but my horse's feet are still tender." He took his hat off and shoved his hand through his hair. "I was just

433

thinking maybe I should leave him here. I bought him from Rock as a colt. This is where he belongs."

Angel was quiet for a moment. He asked softly, "And you, señor? Where do you belong?"

Spur slapped his hat against his leg. When he looked up, his face showed the emotions crowding through him.

"I honestly don't know. These past two weeks have been hard, but now I don't want to leave.

"Those kids miss their pa. Clare has started to heal. I think it's going to be a long haul though.

"I just don't know which would be better for all of them—whether me leaving would help them all heal, or if my leaving will leave another hole in their hearts."

He pulled three envelopes from his vest. In the upper left corner, "Heaven" was written. Each had a different child's name on the outside. Spur's face twisted with pain as he looked at them.

"Clare refused to take Rock's letters when I got here. She told me to read them to the kids. I haven't done that yet. I thought I might do it today. Ike gave me some envelopes. I thought I'd let them think their pa sent them a letter from Heaven."

Angel listened quietly. "Did the señora read the letter from señor Rock?"

"No. I showed it to her right after I got here.

"It had a blood stain on it. I tried to wipe it off when Little Bear gave it to me, but it was already drying. It smeared and then dried that way.

"Clare stared at it and asked me if it was Rock's blood. I don't remember what I said but she knew. Then she wanted to know how he died.

"I didn't think it was my place to tell her. Stub is her foreman and he was with Rock when he died. I figured I should leave that up to him.

"That's when she refused the letters. She told me to read them to the kids."

Angel was quiet as he studied his friend.

"I think your heart is talking to you, señor. Many times you have not listened to it. Today you listen, and now you are afraid.

"Amour is many things. It can be beautiful but it does not always flow both ways.

"I think the señora is still much in love with señor Rock. If you are willing to wait until her heart heals, maybe she will find a place for you, maybe not. But if you go away, I think she will lock her heart away and become very cold.

"The señora pretends to be brave, but inside, she is afraid. I think she has had a hard life, and her heart has been broken many times. Perhaps by men, perhaps by her family, I am not sure. She struggles to be strong." Angel paused and then added quietly, "I think you give her that strength.

"Can you be her friend and maybe no more? Can you stay and maybe watch her give her heart to someone else?

"It is a difficult decision, perhaps one we should make over many beers tonight." Angel's eyes sparkled and he added, "Or we could just ask your horse. I think maybe he has already decided he is not ready to leave."

Spur stared at Angel for a moment and then looked at Rockafeller. The horse nickered softly and Spur chuckled.

"You are a wise one, Angel. And stop calling me señor. You are my friend. You can call me amigo or Spur." He looked over at Angel's head toward the other riders. Gabe was talking to the young men and they laughed at what he said.

"Gabe said this was his last drive. I think he means it this time."

Angel nodded slowly. "Señor Gabe did not want to do this one so much." His eyes sparkled and he winked at Spur.

"Amour has been good for my brother. My sister is difficult but they make each other happy. He is ready to go home. He is contented on his little rancho." Angel's grin was large as he added, "But he does not know my sister purchased another rancho while he was gone."

Spur stared at the small man beside him in surprise and Angel nodded.

"Sí, Margaret Endicott was ready to sell. Merina told the señora she would buy her rancho. My sister bought it with some of the money we received from señor Cole.

"Gabe was much distracted with all his plans for this drive, so Merina did not tell him.

"She was to sign papers the Monday after we left." His dark eyes danced. "Now we are partners, my brother and me."

Spur began to laugh. "Ol' Gabe just doesn't know what kind of a family he tied onto when he married Merina. Yes, they are good for each other.

"What about Miguel?"

"Miguel is not so interested in cattle even though the rancho is part his. I think he likes his gun too much...and his whiskey...and the ladies. He is talking of going back to Texas. I do not think that is so wise, but Miguel, he does not listen to anyone."

Spur nodded. He had heard stories of some of Miguel's escapades. He too had heard Miguel was going back to Texas. No one seemed to know what he was going to do there though.

"Well, let's go. Stub promised all the riders a steak tonight. He is up at the house putting the numbers together with Clare.

"I want to rinse off in the creek before I take a real bath in town. And then, I just might drink too many beers and let you haul me home tonight too." Spur's grin was large as he slapped Angel on the back.

=========== CHAPTER 93 ===========

THE CONTRACT

JUST AS ANGEL AND SPUR STEPPED OUT OF THE BARN, Stub appeared in the doorway of the house. His face was red and he was angry.

"Spur! Get up here. Clare wants to talk to you." Stub strode out the door and down to the corral. He smashed the top corral pole with his fist before he crawled through. He stared at the horses for a moment before he stomped across the pasture and out of sight.

Spur's eyes narrowed down and he walked slowly toward the house. He stepped into the doorway.

"You want to see me?"

Clare's mouth was drawn in a hard line. "Please sit down, Spur."

Spur stared at her for a moment and then shook his head. "I don't think so. Whatever you have to say to me, you can say while I'm standing—in case it makes me as mad as you just made Stub."

Clare's eyes flashed and she pushed some papers across the table.

"I want to hire you on a ten-year contract. We both know you don't like commitments so I drew up some papers. I think you will find them financially beneficial to you."

Spur's dark brows pulled down in a scowl. "You could have talked to me about this before you made out a contract." His scowl became more of a glare. "This is a heck of a thing to spring on me the night before I am to leave."

Clare drew a shaky breath before she looked up at him.

"Spur, I have a ranch to run and I can't do it by myself."

"You have Stub."

"I just released him. He has his own place to focus on."

"Hell's Bells, Clare! You need him now more than ever! The men respect him and he is the only one who knows how Rock handled things around here.

"Why would you want me to stay? I know nothing about how you do things up here. Besides, horses are my business."

Clare's voice was almost a whisper. "My children need a father. They like you. You play with them and talk to them." Her face was pale and she pushed the papers toward him again. "This is a temporary marriage contract. I want you to give me ten years. By then, the children will be fifteen and sixteen years old. After ten years, you can leave.

"You told me you were a runner. Well, this makes you stay. I don't ever plan to love another man, and you run at the thought of love. This is a perfect contract for both of us."

Spur strode across the room and grabbed the papers. He scanned them quickly and then stared at her in shock.

"You are buying a husband! Clare, you don't have to do this. You are barely twenty-one years old. You are beautiful and you own a profitable ranch. I could come up with ten men in twenty-four hours who would marry you without a contract!"

Clare's chin jutted out even as her face became paler. Her whisper was barely audible. "But my children chose *you*. I am doing this for them."

The two stared at each other for nearly a minute before Spur threw the papers back onto the table.

"I am going to get bloody drunk tonight and then I'll make a decision. If I agree to do this, I'll have my own set of demands—and I won't wait till morning to discuss them civilly."

"How dare you threaten to barge into my home when you are drunk! You will wake the children."

"Not if you answer the door when I beat on it. Let me remind you… if I sign this contract, this house is half mine, and I don't plan to sleep in the bunkhouse!"

Spur was shouting by the time he finished talking. He kicked the chair and glared at Clare again. As he studied her pale face, his voice was quieter.

"This is a terrible idea, Clare. You can't buy love and you can't stop it either. You are trying to put an iron cage around your heart so you won't be hurt again. That's not how it works." He picked the papers up and then tossed them back toward her.

"Forget this idea and hire Stub back."

Clare's face was determined as she looked up at him. "I plan to contract a father for my children. If you won't do it, I will find someone else."

Spur stared at her and his face turned red. "I'm going to tie a drunk on like I have never seen and I'll see you at midnight. We'll see just how bad you want to buy a husband then."

"A father. I said nothing about a husband. This is a contract for a father."

Spur stared at her and then pointed at the wind-up clock on her mantel.

"Midnight and you had better answer that door." He spun around and slammed his fist into the door jamb as he stomped out. Everything in the kitchen shook and Clare jumped.

Once he had slammed the door, Clare lay her head over on the table and sobbed. "Rock, I am so angry with you. You should never have left me. You have been dead for over two weeks, and I don't even know how you died."

Gabe's men were facing away from the house when Spur appeared. While they didn't hear what Clare said to him, Spur's voice had been loud. Every man there heard what he said to Clare.

Angel's face was bland as he looked over at Gabe.

"I think I will ride into town with my amigo. I will make sure he gets back here safely."

Sam stepped up. "How about us? We get a night out."

Gabe nodded slowly. "Stub promised all of us a steak. Let's rinse off in the creek and then head to town. If Stub doesn't show up, I'll buy the steaks and pay you out at supper." He looked at Tobe.

"Tobe, you want to make sure these three youngsters make it back home? Or are you going to come home early and have a quiet night with me? I sure don't want to carouse until the wee hours." He looked over at his grinning brother-in-law and added, "I know I can't count on Miguel to keep anyone out of trouble.

"I was hoping Angel and Spur would be the voice of reason tonight, but that is not going to happen."

Tobe chuckled as he nodded. "I'll be responsible for the crew but I'm leaving now. I want a bath before I eat, and it ain't gonna be in a creek." His grin was ornery as he added, "Maybe you can ride down with Spur and Angel. Might be a good idea to wind Spur down a tad before he hits the saloon."

Gabe nodded. He handed Tobe some money.

"Here is $50. That is enough for $10 each in case Stub doesn't show up. I'll see you for supper."

====== CHAPTER 94 ======

DON'T MIND CLARE

THE MEN ALL TURNED TO LOOK AS A WAGON RATTLED up the lane. An older couple had Adelia between them. Three little heads were bouncing around in the back of the wagon.

The old man's grin was big. "Lookie who we found with Cookie! Adelia here is the daughter a one a my Maggie's oldest friends, Molly Benson. Maggie saw 'er come through town with the herd an' tracked 'er down. She looks jist like 'er mama.

"Adelia is goin' to be stayin' with us fer a time till she gets on 'er feet. We thought we'd bring 'er out an' introduce 'er to Clare. We had to bring these little hooligans home anyway." He looked behind him at the children. "Now out, all a ya. Go play.

"Clare 'round?"

The men were quiet as they all looked toward the house.

Gabe nodded. "She is. She's—she's—I think she might be a little upset. Might be good for her to have some women around for a time."

Ike helped the women down. As Maggie hurried Adelia toward the house, he studied Gabe's face.

"Clare offer Spur a job?"

Gabe's face turned red under his tan. "Not sure. You'll have to talk to her."

Ike's old face softened for a moment as he looked around at the group of cowboys.

"Ya boys did a fine thing. It were Rock's dream to bring black cattle to this here valley, an' he done it with yur help. I know he's a lookin' down on all a ya. He cain't thank ya in person, so I'll do it fer 'im." He nodded toward the house. "Rock an' Clare is 'most like our own kids an' we love 'em to pieces."

He put out his hand to Gabe. "Ike Clampant. Ya fellers pullin' out in the mornin'?"

Gabe nodded as he shook Ike's hand. "Gabe Hawkins. I was trail boss. We are headed to Stevensville to clean up. It's been a long drive and some of the boys are ready for a night out." He paused and added quietly, "It was our pleasure to know Rock and ride for him. He was a fine man."

Ike nodded as he blinked his eyes. He cleared his throat and looked around at the rest of the riders. He asked, "Who be all a ya other fellers?"

The men all introduced themselves and then Tobe led his crew down the trail.

Ike looked toward the house and then back at Gabe.

"Don't mind Clare. Women grieve different from men. Sometimes they say an' do things that jist don't make no sense. Clare'll be all right once she works though the scare a doin' all this alone."

Gabe nodded slowly. He looked toward the barn as Spur and Angel appeared.

Spur glared at Ike. "Ike, you'd better talk some sense into her." He spurred his horse and raced down the trail.

Angel smiled at the old man. "Señor, my name is Angel. My friend, he is angry so I must ride with him." He touched his hat and pushed his horse to a gallop to catch up with Spur.

Ike watched them go and said nothing. When Stub followed on his horse with his mouth set in a hard line and his eyes glinting with anger, Ike swore.

"I been afraid all Hades would break lose 'fore this here deal were finished. Mebbie my Maggie cin talk some sense into Clare."

"Gabe, ya fellers have a safe trip back down to Cheyenne. I'm a gonna see if I cin calm this here place down some. I think we might take those kids right back home with us. Give Clare a little time to rest."

CHAPTER 95

SPUR'S ANSWER

SPUR DIDN'T TALK ALL THE WAY TO STEVENSVILLE. HE barely grunted in response to Angel's conversation. In fact, he didn't say a word until he had belted down his fifth shot.

His eyes were clear when he looked at Angel. "I'm goin' to stay but I have some of my own demands to add to that contract.

"Barkeep! Ya have any paper back there?"

The bartender handed Spur several sheets of paper and the cowboy began to write. The more he wrote, the less angry he was. It took him three more whiskeys to finish what he was writing. By the time he was done, the sheet was full and Spur's smile was large.

"We'll see how Miss Clare likes this list. When she reads it, she'll refuse and this deal will be over."

Angel glanced at the sheet and then read several of the numbered expectations again. He shook his head.

"I think, my amigo, you should never write when you have been drinking."

Spur grinned at him and chased two beers with whiskey. He missed the steak supper and Angel helped him on his horse at 11:00 p.m.

Spur sang loudly all the way back to the ranch. His repertoire of songs was long and not all of them were appropriate. Still, he belted out each and every one.

He slid off his horse when they arrived at the ranch. He pulled the list from his pocket and staggered toward the house. He raised his hand to beat on the door and almost fell inside when a cool and collected Clare answered the door.

"Now I have a list of my own demands. An' ya can sit down an' lissen to 'em."

Clare stared at Spur a moment and then walked around to the other side of the table. "I guess I will stand to listen like you did." Her eyes were bright and her chin was set firmly.

Spur glared at her for a moment. Then he cleared his throat and began. His voice was loud and his hand gestures were dramatic. He stared at her after he read each demand.

1. Marryin is forever. It don't end after ten years.
2. I ain't sleepin in the bunkhouse. This here marriage ain't a sham to me even if ya think it is. An I'll be havin my husbandly rights after the baby comes.
3. There won't be no money paid. I ain't the kind a feller that does this sort a thing fer money.
4. We're hirin Stub an Tuff back.
5. We'll be married down to the Mission by Father Ravalli. Course I'll probably have to go to confession some before we consummate this here marriage cause of impure thoughts.
6. I won't cut off my mustache an don't ya be askin me to.

7. Those kids will be my kids to so don't ya be callin em yores.
8. I can call ya Darlin if I want an I can kiss ya of a mornin.
9. I get to be there fer the birthin of all yore babies.
10. Next summer, we're a goin swimmin alone an I get to see what ya wear in the water.

Spur staggered back a bit as he tried to stand tall. He grinned at Clare loosely. "Now, Miss Clare, soon to be Mrs. Spurlach—whatcha think a that?"

Clare glared at him. Some of his requests were laughable and others made her blush.

"And if I don't agree?"

"Well then, ya can find some other lonesome cowboy an' try that contract on him. 'Course he might not be so easy to look at as me, an' he might not make ya laugh so much."

Spur winked loosely. He tried again to stand tall and grabbed a chair to keep from falling down. He grinned at her. "Them durn chairs jist keep jumpin' 'round."

He let go of the chair carefully and slowly pulled himself upright. He put his hat over his heart and bowed low.

"Will ya marry me, Miss Clare, an' give me the life a hell that all my friends seem to enjoy? Will ya cook fer me an' mend my socks an' cuddle with me a little when the nights are cold? An' will ya try hard to laugh ever' day so this here marriage won't be so glum?"

Clare didn't know whether to be angry or to laugh.

She sighed. "Spur, go to bed. I agree. We can sign the contract in the morning."

Spur shook his head. "Nope. I reckon ya can sign it now."

Clare stared at him for a moment and then quickly signed her name at the bottom of the sheet beside his.

Spur reached for the contract. After the third try, he finally picked it up. "I reckon I'll hang onto this, jist in case I need to remind ya now an' then of what ya agreed to." He grinned at her again and tripped as he tried to turn around.

"'Night, Darlin'."

"Spur, you are a mess. Take hold of my arm. I'll get Angel to help you to the bunkhouse."

She opened the door and almost screamed. Angel was sitting on her steps.

"I am sorry, señora. I did not mean to frighten you, but I knew my amigo could not walk to the bunkhouse by himself. I will take him.

"Come, señor Spur. Now we will sleep."

Clare stood in the doorway. She watched as Angel helped his friend down the steps and across the ranch yard. Spur grinned at the small vaquero beside him.

"Mebbie ya fellers should swing through the Mission on yore way out tomorrow. I'm gonna need a best man, an' you an' ol' Gabe are the best ones a feller could have."

Spur twisted around and hollered, "Be ready in the mornin', Darlin'. No point in wastin' 'round. If we're gonna get hitched, let's do it quick 'fore ya offer yore deal to some other lonesome cowboy."

Gabe stepped out of the bunkhouse when he heard Spur hollering. He started laughing and grabbed Spur's other arm.

He looked toward the house as he called, "Clare, I reckon we can put off leaving until later in the morning so we can attend this wedding. We'll be ready to ride down with you and your groom by 8:00 a.m."

Clare paused and then waved. She turned back into the house and closed the door. She leaned against it as she stared into the dark room.

"What have I done?" she whispered. "What if we hate each other? Dear Lord, please let this work out agreeably for both of us."

Spur was still talking when they led him into the bunkhouse. "How'd I get my spurs all tangled up with this little gal? I was plumb happy runnin' all over the country, chasin' horses an' flirtin' with the ladies. I didn't even flirt with Clare. How'd this happen?"

He stopped talking when his buddies dropped him onto his bunk. Then one eye popped back open.

"I think I'm a gonna like this here setup. Too bad ya fellers won't be 'round to see how it all plays out.

"Who knew I'd marry such a fine woman an' a purty one too." Spur's voice became softer as he smiled up at the ceiling.

"Sister Eddie, I know yore a smilin'. You'd like my little darlin'."

Made in the USA
Monee, IL
31 May 2024

59122195R00267